Alongside genealogical research, the author decided to write a story, based on fact, of a discovered friendship recorded in the diaries of Branwell Brontë, brother of the famous sisters, with his great-great-grandfather, John Titterington. A master's degree to sharpen his writing skills, plus appearances as a television background actor served as preparation for the visualisation of his story.

Acknowledgements

My wife Noreen for her tireless support and constant encouragement to write this book.

Alan Cookson and Bob Titterington – friends and fellow Titterington family genealogists.

Gillian Holt – Descendant of Abigail Titterington, Brontë and family historian, ceramicist and first reader of this novel.

Juliet Barker – Brontë historian, biographer and author, whose excellent books, *'The Brontës'* I recommend for further reading.

Jane Sellers – former Director of The Brontë Parsonage Museum.

Anthea Bickley – former Senior Keeper History Bradford Art Gallery Museums.

Christine Hopper – former Asst. Keeper Fine Arts Cartwright Hall Bradford.

Malcolm Bull – Historian and online producer of *'Calderdale Companion.'*

Jean Tattersfield – a friend, for being the first to draw my attention to Daphne Du Maurier's *'Infernal World of Branwell Brontë'* with its Titterington family references.

Cover illustration: Sketch by P. Branwell Brontë (January 1848) by kind permission of Leeds University Library (Brotherton Collection) and Haworth Parsonage Museum

Alan Titterington

St. John In The Wilderness

AUSTIN MACAULEY
PUBLISHERS LTD.

A CIP catalogue record for this title is available from the British Library.

ISBN 9781786121943 (Paperback)
ISBN 9781786121950 (Hardback)
ISBN 9781786121967 (E-Book)

www.austinmacauley.com

First Published (2016)
Austin Macauley Publishers Ltd.
25 Canada Square
Canary Wharf
London
E14 5LQ

Contents

Echoing still from silent mills, and drifting on the breeze,
We hear it in the woodland glades, and when winter's fingers
freeze,
In meandering brook, or on hilltop farm, in moorland,
township or vale,
It pervades the air and excites the soul! It's the voice of
Calderdale!

Anthem for Calderdale

Preface

I started out in childhood believing the surname Titterington was exclusive to my immediate family. My father had two married sisters, as do I, and whilst my grandfather also had two sisters, there was a brother, Harry Holdsworth Titterington. He emigrated to South Africa as a young man, married and lived in Vryburg, an Afrikaans-speaking mining area, with only a daughter, Maureen (b. c1910), but the family was never heard of again after the mid-20th century.

So I had no Titterington cousins, near or distant and our name stood proudly, yet quite isolated, in the Halifax telephone directory.

As a choir boy I remember singing in the magnificent Halifax Parish Church (now a Minster, since 2011) and eagerly reaching for the oldest register in the sacristy library; it commenced tantalisingly; *"...in the thirtieth year of the reign of our good King Henry VIII – 1539"* and there they were, an entire column in the alphabetical listings for 'T' – Tetrynton (Myles, born 'before 1544'), Titterrington / Titteryngton /Tetrenton /Tytringtone...births, marriages *and* deaths. My phonetically transcribed forebears!

Little did I realise then that by 1700 there were none recorded whatsoever in the entire town. The many different phonetic spellings, often of the same person, related to merely two or three close families. A high predominance of girls, a subsequent re-appearance of a Halifax-born Titterington *(Nicholas, 1551)* christening his daughter *(Ruth, 1579)* in Skellingthorpe, Lincoln and probably the great plague of 1665… all conspired to take the name into apparent oblivion! (Halifax had a population of only 3,000 in 1665 and 500 of these perished in the Great Plague). An earlier visit of bubonic plague to the area had also probably contributed to the decline in 1604.

I believe that this early arrival of the name into Halifax (an obvious staying-over/settling point halfway between Tytherington and York) and similarly the later Lincoln connection probably came about through family pilgrimages to either of these two great mediaeval cathedral cities. William de Tyveryngton is listed as a Freeman of York in 1318 and may similarly have settled there after an earlier pilgrimage from the original Tytherington homestead, near Macclesfield in Cheshire.

As a small boy, playing in my grandparents' attic, I was fascinated by two dilapidated, unframed paintings of a man and a woman, which leaned against the water tank.

And quite remarkably – *their eyes eerily followed me as I crossed the room!* My older sister, Mary, and I loved to visit the musty attic and imagine what life must have been like for this elegant, yet rather sad-looking couple, captured in a moment from the pre-photographic distant past. Best of all was the black dog sitting faithfully by his master's lap with baleful eyes and wearing a collar clearly bearing the inscription '*J.Titterington*' – the dog's owner, presumably,

14

and perhaps the artist's way of identifying the subject of his painting.

After my grandparents' deaths, the paintings were stored, unceremoniously and unseen, high in the beams of my parents' unattached garage roof – damp and cold in winter, unbelievably hot and humid in summer, they languished, yet nevertheless survived there into my adulthood.

At twenty-three years of age and after my marriage and return from three years working in Ireland, my wife, Noreen, and I moved into our first home in Hipperholme, near Halifax, and I undertook the costly exercise of having the portraits repaired, cleaned and framed.

Almost as large as our first house was small, I was nevertheless determined to hang them as a memory from my childhood.

They looked magnificent with new brass picture lights and just about filled the fireside alcoves in our lounge! The newly-brightened, freshly-varnished oil colours brought an as-new vibrancy to the couple with detail unseen before. The dog was especially clear now with a new glint in his eyes...*and on his wet nose!*

But who were these people? How could I gaze at them each and every day and not know? Not be able to answer the rather obvious (and recurrent) questions from guests?

Without realising it, the first seeds of genealogical interest had been sown and I could almost hear the couple begging me to discover who they were, and introduce them to a different century, the now shiny-cleaned eyes drilling into me even more forcefully, pleading for recognition!

And who painted their portraits?

At the central core of this story is my attribution of the paintings to the hand of Branwell Brontë, brother of the more famous Brontë sisters and a known acquaintance of John Titterington, whose friendship he recorded in his diaries...

Chapter One

43, Stonegate, York

The assembled congregation of over 2,000 chosen NHS workers chatted excitedly in their pre-Christmas feeling of euphoria. A hush came over them as diminutive twelve year-old Matthew Rhodes stepped out frighteningly high above the chancel of York Minster to commence the ritual first verse of "*Once in Royal David's City*," opening the annual NHS Northern Christmas Carol Concert on the 14th of December 1994.

Chosen from over 50,000 employees – doctors, nurses, paramedics and a whole legion of the nation's lifeblood of medical resourcefulness and provision of care in anybody's darkest hours, the NHS carers and administrators stood transfixed as Matthew's perfectly enunciated words and exquisite boy-soprano tones chilled the congregation to its very core.

All thoughts of Christmas shopping, parties and what presents to buy were immediately banished as the congregation's collective minds stretched right back to their vividly-stored images and experiences of Christmases past…their first attempts at singing carols at infants' school; listening to the older children's amusing distortion of the words and joining in the joy and laughter of '*While shepherd's washed their socks by night*' and the almost unbelievable feelings of joy and expectation which surrounded the annual visit of Father Christmas into your home…*into your bedroom,* to fill Mother's crisply ironed pillowslip with that perfect gift you had asked Santa for but daren't anticipate too strongly for fear of disappointment. Had I been good enough? Tidied my bedroom often enough? Washed up enough times or taken Fido for his requisite number of walks? The final judgement was about to be made by an invisible yet totally believable bearded entity based somewhere near the North Pole and there was little anyone could do about changing it now.

Matthew completed his first verse and everyone joined in with the rest of the carol – many singing with gusto for that one time every year when they visited church at all – and what a church to do it in! The thirteenth century magic of masons, woodcarvers and glaziers had wrought their craft over two hundred and fifty years to complete their magnificent work, between 1215 and 1472 and York Minster stands testament to their skills. It will surely stand for many centuries to come with the continuing additional ministrations and craftsmanship of present and future generations of dedicated workers restoring the age-worn fabric of this magnificent monument to its original mediaeval condition.

My own thoughts took me right back to my own boy-soprano days, boldly and strangely without nerves as I look back now, stepping forward at nine and again at ten years of age to give a solo performance of Handel's *"Where'er You Walk"* to a packed Easter Sunday congregations at the magnificent Gilbert Scott-designed grade-one listed All

Soul's Church in Boothtown, Halifax, just around the corner from my childhood home at 3, Woodside View.

I looked high into the centuries-unchanged ceiling-vaults of the nave and then, lowering my gaze slowly, I scanned down to the assembled throng, I imagined a pre-reformation Catholic ceremony honouring one William de Tyveryngton, an ancestor, being created a Freeman of the City of York in 1318.

Three of the nine lesson-readers had completed their daunting task of climbing into the pulpit after being ceremoniously led by the mace-bearing sacristan to deliver the traditional biblical Christmas passages to the multitude present and the many thousands more listeners to Radio Leeds beyond.

Following the carefully selected three – a store man, a GP receptionist, and a consultant rheumatologist, came my turn as Chairman of the West Yorkshire Metropolitan Ambulance Service NHS Trust (WYMAS).

Familiar with public speaking and climbing confidently up the spiral staircase to the pulpit lectern, I looked out and drew a sharp intake of breath at the sheer size of the assembled congregation stretching out before me; I had not expected to be so overcome and became acutely aware of the architectural magnificence stretching way up above the multitude. The immense height of eight hundred year-old mediaeval gothic stone masonry dwarfing the two thousand had not been anticipated at the straightforward and deserted afternoon procedural rehearsal. I took another deep breath of air and spoke the first words of St. Luke II into the microphone. "*And it came to pass in those days, that there went out a decree from Caesar Augustus...*" Immediately, the amplified sound system brought my voice eerily back to me as the sound reverberated from a host of speakers, echoing high into the cavernous vaulted ceiling. A vivid awareness of the centuries of similar occasions marking wars, famine, celebrations and family sadnesses overwhelmed my senses and yet I persevered and successfully delivered the sixth lesson. I descended the spiral pulpit stairs and was returned reverently, as I had been brought, to my 'throne' seat in the choir stalls by the solemnly dressed mace-bearing sacristan to join my fellow readers.

I had no doubt that William de Tyveryngton had been similarly overawed in this self-same place.

Listening to the final words and music, I also remembered reading that at the celebration banquet for the ordination of the first Archbishop of York, over a century after building was completed in the mid-fifteenth century, over 1,000 baby eagles had been consumed! Had the dinner been here in the Minster? Quite probably, and what a banquet that must have been, and all in this same place where I had now made my own mark.

The service concluded with a jolly singing of *"We wish you a merry Christmas..."* complete with the customary oft-repeated demand to have figgy-pudding brought forth!

After the service I planned to learn more of my great-great-grandfather and his family's mysterious occupation of 43, Stonegate, York between the years of 1848-50. A creditor's 'pence-in-the-pound' award, reported in the *London Gazette*, had attributed this address to *'John Titterington of Higgin Chamber, Sowerby, Halifax'* – a *'known bankrupt'* who I had learned spent time in the notorious York Castle Debtors' Prison. This was a dreaded short-term abode for prisoners awaiting transportation to

Australia, often to Van Diemen's Land, now Tasmania, occasionally for what might be considered relatively minor offences today. It was John's fate also to endure the same hardships experienced by the notorious highwayman Dick Turpin a century before and prior to his mass-attended very public hanging on the Knavesmire in York.

That he was previously a 'gentleman of substance', recently cut-off by his wealthy family, made such imprisonment all the harder to endure for one so privileged and acutely ill-prepared for the hardships which followed. Most of his immediate family could have easily gained his release by settling with his creditors, must have made it especially hard to bear; his father's public disowning of him had tied the hands of family members; even if they had wanted to help John, they dare not go against his wishes and so he languished in gaol far from his Halifax homelands, but at least with his immediate family nearby in Stonegate. Visiting would have been entirely within the strict privately-owned prison regime's control. The 'turnkey' or head-warder would almost certainly have needed bribing by John in negotiating visiting-rights and even the provision of the essentials for life – such as food itself, would be at his discretion. Mary was the main provider of the means for his survival – and his sanity. Visits with food and her ability to either earn, or secure money by other means to pay for it, whilst bringing up five children under ten years of age marked her out as a true survivor and a dedicated and loyal wife of a very high order.

After the Christmas NHS service, I headed over with my wife, Noreen, to see nearby Stonegate once more where number 43 is now *The Pyramid*, an impressive art gallery owned by The National Trust. A listed building, 43 remains virtually unchanged for well over five centuries and is structurally the same therefore since John and his family's occupancy over 150 years before. The actual stone building, one of the oldest in York, dates back to the fifteenth century and even before then more primitive constructions witnessed the daily sounds of horse-drawn cartfuls of hewn stone arriving daily from the quarries of Tadcaster via barges on the river Ouse and the quayside nearby. The stone was to be added to the thousands of pre- and post-dressed pieces of pure sculpture which were fashioned into the edifice we see today as the magnificent York Minster. Number 43, Stonegate is a mere stone's throw away from the south door, now the tourists' entrance to the Minster. Stonegate's pavings are also fashioned out of huge time-smoothened blocks of stone which some alternatively claim gave credence to its name, rather than it being simply the gateway for the stone which built the Minster.

Six feet directly beneath Stonegate's paved surface lies the Via Praetoria, a Roman road leading similarly from the river to the centurions' Eboracum garrison-base situated where the Minster now stands.

Records of Stonegate date back to 1118 and make reference to the stone brought to build previous churches which were constructed on the same site as York Minster.

Any occupant of number 43 had to be reminded of the mediaeval daily grind and never fail to be awe-inspired by the sight of the Minster's three towers rising above their home as if in promise of a higher, yet-to-come existence in another life. The sounds of the bells and the footfalls of the summoned faithful communicants will always have served as a striking backdrop to their daily existence, measuring time in strictly allotted ecclesiastical proportions. Other occupants of that time were surrounded in Stonegate by the numerous glass makers and painters who serviced not only York minster, but the other amazingly decorated forty-plus churches in the immediate diocese.

Intending to visit a small favourite Italian restaurant for supper before the one-hour drive back to Halifax, Noreen and I buttoned up well from a sudden icy blast. We passed the bustling groups of excited Christmas shoppers and we breathed in the marvellously festive smell of roasting chestnuts from a street vendor's cart as we approached the art gallery. A few flurries of snow blew around Stonegate and a group of about six people chatting excitedly as they entered a brightly-lit number 43. Some kind of a party was clearly in full swing by the sounds of laughter emanating from within as the door opened, and the little shop bell rang as if also to invite us in.

More than suitably dressed from the carol service for a special occasion, we stepped cheekily inside the door and were greeted by a charming girl with: "Lovely to see you both, I'm Alex – please come in and help yourself to drinks."

We entered, took a glass of champagne each from a proffered tray and I whispered to Noreen:

"Well, this is all very nice – we don't appear to need an invitation! The Lord Mayor is over there, and, oh hell! Have you seen the price of this painting? Two grand for something that looks like it took all of five minutes for a demented chimpanzee to fling paint aimlessly onto a canvas. Not surprising they're happy to give anybody a glass of cheap fizz that looks even remotely gullible or wealthy enough to bounce for anything like that!"

"Shh!" said Noreen. "Try to look like a serious collector. Look, the mayor's coming over to talk to us. Behave!"

"Good evening, we haven't met before, but wasn't that you reading the lesson just now at the marvellous NHS carol concert?" the mayor intoned, looking every bit the modern leader of an ancient borough with his rather striking handlebar moustache and his gold chains sitting perfectly on his portly belly. I smiled to myself and thought he would have made the perfect literary Mayor of Casterbridge or some such, or could easily have appeared as a children's television cartoon *'Mr Mayor'* or even a volunteer fireman in Trumpton! *Pugh, Pugh, Barney McGrew, Cuthbert, Dibble...GRUB!* Glancing around, I had suddenly become aware that there were loads of it! Delicious-looking canapés were being passed around by the lovely Alex and her assistants...*and no baby eagles, thank God!*

And no need for an Italian city-priced meal now!

"I'm John Marshall and this is my wife Glenda," the mayor continued as I reciprocated the introductions and acknowledged the lesson-reading observation, with all duly shaking hands. The seemingly long-suffering Lady Mayoress was light in stature by contrast to her over-ebullient, portly, glad-handing husband and was clearly the exact opposite of him in more ways than one. Her chain of office was more delicate, fortunately for her, since anything heavier, like her husband's, would surely have borne witness to gravity and would have dragged her unceremoniously to the floor. I thought she had perhaps learned her place in life on official occasions, but her rather mean eyes suggested to me that she might well take charge of affairs on the domestic front away from all the pomp and ceremony.

John Marshall made peremptory requests for information of what an NHS chairman does and I explained my role and direct appointment by the Secretary of State for Health, Virginia Bottomley. He clearly was not listening and was eager to quickly pass on to describing his own importance to someone he had now decided was a suitably qualified and furthermore worthwhile listener!

I continued stoically with the WYMAS facts: "…covering the emergency and patient-care needs of the constituents of twenty-eight MPs and three MEPs in West and North Yorkshire…over 600 ambulances…the largest service outside London…"

But he wasn't listening, and after several ill-disguised attempts to interrupt, he jumped in and quickly got into his stride: election successes and a career in public service; rising to becoming the something-hundredth mayor of the City of York approaching its 800th anniversary in 2012, *his finest hour*, the final accolade, and probably plucked from an equally unremarkable city council.

I trumped him rather rudely with my own four personal entries in Hansard, but he deserved it anyway. It only slowed him up slightly and he quickly returned to his theme.

As a distraction, I concentrated solely, on the mayor's fat neck upon which was emerging an extremely angry-looking boil, and I became aware of the faint distant sound of children playing, of playful laughter.

On and on he droned. "Won my first election with a record majority of...first mayor in recent times to come from an 'ordinary' background." Whatever that might mean.

And still on and on he went, massaging his ego, not even noticing my glazed-over expression, as I glanced away from the now puss-yielding eruption bursting out above his collar. I nudged Noreen, whispering, "Bit unsuitable for children? No, not his boil! Over there... What's the young girl sitting on the stairs doing here?"

A pretty young girl of about eleven or twelve years of age with striking shoulder-length, ribboned blonde hair was seated on the bottom step of the stairs looking directly toward me, as if in request to a close relative imploring me to invite her to join in with the party. To introduce her, to *show her off*, to ask her to sing a song or recite a newly-learned piece of poetry perhaps to impress all of these smartly dressed jolly party guests.

Her long pretty dress covered her feet, but as she adjusted her posture I noticed she was in fact barefoot and her dress was now in fact a nightie. *Almost as though she had sneaked quietly out of bed and come downstairs to join in the fun!*

But was there a bedroom upstairs? Did anybody live up there? It was certainly possible in a three-storey building, but seemed extremely unlikely with apparently only one single front doorway entrance to such a fine art gallery.

Noreen looked in the direction of my gaze and said, "What are you talking about? I can't see anybody! So I'm driving home...again, as usual!"

"No! It's not the drink. Over there, on the stair. The little girl, with the small boy. Are you blind?" And as I looked back across at the stair again, over the mayor's shoulder, there was a sudden chill in the air. I felt a slight breeze and heard the distinct but distant sound of childish laughter. A dog's bark echoed faintly above the general hubbub, and the stair was empty!

The hairs on the back of my neck stood up!

Had I alone seen the children? Were they an apparition? Ghosts?

Over toward the back of the gallery. I had noticed an artist working at an easel with a clip-on light attached to the top of his board, reminiscent of a night-time street portrait artist at a Mediterranean holiday resort.

Curious, I excused myself from the boring delights of mayoral conversation and ushered Noreen over to where the artist was working.

Alex was working her way round with canapés and seeing us moving across, she interceded with, "I see you have spotted Xavier. He's an up and coming artist from Spain, who we are sponsoring with an exhibition next month. I'll send you an invitation if you like his work. We think his portraiture is amazing. See what you think. I'll introduce you, though, I warn you his English is pretty well non-existent! I'll do my best to translate – I was a holiday rep for a while!

"By the way, if you would like a raffle ticket, the first prize is a pastel portrait of yourself. It only takes him about half-an-hour. He's so quick and so talented; the tickets are £10 each."

She made the introductions and with conversation proving almost impossible as predicted beyond the initial greetings, we moved around behind him to view his work and Alex stayed with us to watch.

Stunned initially into silence on viewing the canvas, both Noreen and I stared in disbelief, then turned to each other said, almost in unison. "It's Lucy!"

Lucy, our fourth child, was a little older at the time, but the resemblance was unmistakable. Without hesitation, we asked Alex to question him about the identity of his subject.

After several minutes of his obviously fluent Spanish and gesticulations, and Alex's brave attempts to understand him, she replied, "It makes no sense to me at all, but he seems to think that there are two children here and he pointed over to the stairs to indicate where he saw this girl sitting with a young boy. He says she is very beautiful and he couldn't wait to capture the expression in her eyes."

"Esos ojos!" exclaimed Xavier, pointing two right fore-fingers toward himself and then toward the stairs – those eyes!

Now wondering if possibly only the artist and I had seen the children, I asked Alex to enquire about the striped top that the girl was wearing in his sketch, and he explained that it was from his imagination since she had disappeared almost as quickly as she had arrived, but he just had to immediately put down on paper his memory of 'those eyes!'

"Esos ojos!"

Alex shrugged her shoulders as much as to say, *"I think he's lost it,"* and excused herself to continue on her rounds with the appetisers.

The children who I, and he alone seemingly, had seen on the stairs, though I couldn't have known it then, were in fact direct relatives – and distant ones at that. The young girl was Grace Titterington, the oldest child of John and Mary Titterington, who together with their entire family had escaped in a hurry from Sowerby near Halifax, to live in enforced exile in this very house, almost 150 years before, in November of 1848; John and Mary, their daughter, eleven-year-old Grace and her four younger siblings, Hannah, Sarah, Rebecca and two year-old, James, together with their faithful black labrador-cross, Blazer, who doubled as both their father's gun dog and as a much-loved family pet, had all come to live in this very house.

Grace's only brother, on the stairs with her that night, was James Holdsworth Titterington, my great-grandfather.

Somehow I was drawn to the unmistakable conclusion that night, that the young girl's eyes had met mine in mutual recognition of a relationship, a drawing together across time, and after my apparent refusal to invite her to join us as a proud family member, to show her off, she had withdrawn reluctantly and sadly, taking her brother and dog with her to play upstairs.

Chapter Two

Into Exile

After the irreparable rift between John and his father there really had been only one choice in the short term; to remove himself and his family away from his increasingly predatory creditors and hope the dust might settle down and give him some breathing space and an opportunity to settle his debts.

An opportunity to escape from the town temporarily had arisen during a conversation at Halifax's market day. Joseph Barker, a buyer from Beverley, who valued John's knowledge of wool and textiles in general, suggested he could do well in the East Riding as an agent. If John ever fancied life in a lively city, he knew of a well-placed fine spacious property to let, right in the heart of the city of York.

Early on Wednesday November 1st 1848, on a bitterly cold winter's morning, Mary got the children up and without bothering to fuel the embers of the overnight fire, gave them a warming breakfast of porridge, bread and tea from the fire's residual heat and prepared to set off for the morning train from Luddenden Foot to Leeds, via Halifax and thence on to a whole new life in York.

John and Mary took their young family and their faithful gun-dog Blazer, together with a hastily packed selection of clothes and personal belongings. They went through the darkness and early morning Sowerby mist, on their horse and carriage, driven by William Foster, down to the station to catch the seven o'clock train to Leeds.

The clock across in Luddenden village was chiming 6.30 as the carriage drew out across the cobblestones of the Higgin Chamber Mill yard and headed along to Brocks, then down to Jerry Fields Road and the steep drop to Luddenden Foot railway station.

Arriving at the station to unload their luggage, John recalled the familiar surroundings where he first met his station-master friend Branwell, and took him, as he so often did at the end of a working day, to relax and unwind with drinks, invariably purchased by himself, at The Anchor and Shuttle. How he regretted the row that night there. The row that landed him in court in Halifax after his drunken brawl and incurred his father's wrath, that fateful time, to land him and his family in their present predicament, disowned and disinherited.

His father had had enough and it really was the straw that broke the camel's back, that and the news of Fanny proving the one step too far, together with his subsequent financial improprieties putting the final nail in his coffin.

Mary glanced at John and guessed his thoughts mirrored hers. *"Well, at least that's one public house I'll not miss hearing about for a while,"* she thought to herself, not wishing to open his wound further at such a sensitive time.

Guessing her thoughts accurately, however, John said, "I've told you already, I'm through with all that, Mary. I'll be a different person away from my father's controlling influence and bullying and when I've sorted out my debts, we will have a whole new life to look forward to and share together. And we will still have our lovely home to come back to, if it doesn't work out and we choose not to stay."

That he did not now have any ownership at Higgin Chamber, including the family house, had not really sunk in yet, but his brother at least had promised he would leave his house untouched until he could sort his personal finances out. He had also made it clear to him that no financial help was to be offered from him or indeed any family member, on pain of death from Eli!

"I'm sure we're going to love York with its bustle and lively streets and markets. So different from the quiet life at Sowerby. The children will settle in well, with many more friends living close by, in Stonegate, which, as we shall see, is right in the centre of the city."

Eleven year-old Grace was the most sensitive to this familiar exchange and the rather strained mood that morning and yet took time to reassure her sisters, Hannah, just ten years-old and Sarah, who was five, that all was well and that they were all embarking on an exciting journey, *an adventure!* Her sister Rebecca, who was four, and little James, the two year-old infant of the family, were too young to question the strange happenings, but as long as the family was all together, with Blazer along, too, then they were more than happy to share in the excitement of a morning very different from any they had experienced

32

before. The three older sisters, as always, ploughed the first furrows and guided them both with unerring care and tenderness.

William unloaded the carriage whilst John lifted the children down and Mary carried James in her arms. Hannah, as always was attentive to Sarah and Rebecca's needs, tidying their smock dresses and wiping Rebecca's runny nose with her newly-ironed handkerchief. "Come on, Becky," said Hannah. "You can fall asleep on the nice warm train, it'll be along in a few minutes. Listen closely and you'll hear it coming."

Little James was less accommodating and disliked being dragged out of a warm bed and out into an unpleasantly cold and misty morning. He hated being carried and wriggled to be put down, but with the train due any minute, his mother was not going to risk placing him in the danger he was only too often simply oblivious to! John always tried not to give his only son special attention, but since the death of his first-born son, Eli, seven years previously, he felt a different kind of attachment to what may now well turn out to be is only legitimate son and heir.

Mary said, "Stay here with your father and hold his hand, James, and watch for the train coming. Listen! Do you hear it in the distance? Our great adventure is about to begin."

William Foster climbed up onto the carriage in readiness to return and John bade him farewell saying, "Take care young man, there'll be some mischief to cope with – mind your back."

John wistfully considered how differently it might have all turned out had his father continued to be drawn to his namesake-grandson. He remembered vividly his father's excitement and pride at his eldest son's announcement that his first grandson was to be named after him. And after his baptism he puffed out his chest and proudly commented, "Young Eli'll turn out to be a force to be reckoned with in these parts. Mark my words, you'll see. Just look at that Tit' chin and sturdy neck!"

There was no denying that little Eli had indeed inherited that same self-determined, resolute Titterington chin, unlike John, whose handsome features more resembled his mother's Ogden side of the family. Eli's sudden and unexpected death from inflammation of the brain (meningitis) at only six-and-a-half months old in February, 1841, had been such a blow to all of the immediate family, but old Eli seemed to be just about the most affected by the loss of his first-born grandson. Young James, on the other hand, resembled his mother's Holdsworth side of the family and had disappointingly, for John, not produced the same pride in his grandfather as he might have, coming after his four sisters and several non-Titterington cousins. Incorporating Holdsworth as his middle name had served only to alienate Eli further, since it would always serve to remind him of his bitter business rival, Mary's father John Holdsworth of Shibden. John and young James had, not unsurprisingly, brought a quite opposite response from John's mother Grace, who delighted in both her first-born son and grandson. She was always there to defend John against the unerring demands and criticisms by her husband, of her somewhat unpredictable and free-spirited son, whom Eli always expected, indeed demanded, so much more from. Ever the successful, practical driving business-force of the Titterington clan, Eli had always found John's rather bohemian ways and wild friends difficult, usually impossible to accommodate, or even be bothered to exchange the time of day with.

John's flair for innovation through new product development and design went largely unnoticed by a father who had made, and continued to make, a fortune from conventional everyday use carpet and shalloon production.

And it was John's attempts to gradually re-structure production at Higgin Chamber toward tapestry and fine jacquard cloths, emulating the successes of John Crossley over in Halifax, which caused Eli to remove the reins from him and land him in the huge debt he now found himself in.

The very public disowning of John, twice, on the front-centre page of *The Halifax Guardian* by Eli had shaken Grace to an unimaginable level. Certainly a totally unsympathetic and insensitive Eli had failed to grasp the impending reality of both his wife's mental and physical collapse. Neither had she avoided the pain and embarrassment of hearing about his unseemly brawl followed by the night in the cells and his subsequent court appearance after the fight with the barmaid in The Anchor and Shuttle public house. Eli's murderous and unremitting public and private attack on his eldest son would indeed alienate his own dutiful wife from him before the year was out. That her dearest boy would be in virtual exile away from his doting mother at the time of her greatest physical collapse was the final cruel blow, from which she never recovered and would die from, before the year was out.

The journey was fairly uneventful via the recently opened Harrogate line and the family was all impressed by the sheer size of York railway station. John had visited the city a couple of times before on wool-buying trips and had also stayed over with friends to join shooting parties.

Grace was quite dumbstruck by the whole occasion and the sheer bustle of the city, as they were driven in their carriage from the station to their new address in Stonegate. Street sellers called out their wares and even street entertainers performed for the attendant crowds, playing music, dancing and juggling. One had a monkey and played a barrel organ and another had a dancing bear on a chain towering above him on its back legs – was it a man in a costume? No! It had claws and huge teeth! The smells and sights of whole animal carcasses being roasted on spits were also unknown to the children who had only ever smelt chestnuts being cooked on rare visits to see their father at Halifax Piece Hall. The younger children were mesmerised as they had only ever seen such creatures as monkeys and a bear illustrated in story books. The Minster came into view from about a mile away, rising high above the ancient buildings which prompted Hannah to exclaim, "I can't believe its size and beauty. Can it really be a church, mother? I wonder if we are going to be able to see it from our new house. I do hope so! Shall we go to Sunday school there, like at home?"

Getting ever closer to the Minster, Grace thought the spires must be growing or bursting up out of the ground and as the streets became narrower and the cobble stones even bumpier. The carriage made one last turn into Stonegate and came to a stop outside number 43, where even Mary was now awestruck by the Minster rising immediately above them, with a splendour and majesty which she knew must have totally enthralled mediaeval pilgrims, visitors and residents alike, for centuries.

36

And Hannah had her wish. The Minster was indeed towering in its Gothic majesty high above the rooftops of the houses immediately opposite in the narrow street.

John stepped toward the door of number 43 and the coachman unloaded the cases onto the pavement beside the door. Hannah, noticing that the upstairs window hung out right over the street, said, "Oooh! Just look at that window bursting right out of the house. I do hope it can be my bedroom and I can look right down on all the people going by doing their shopping, and see the horses and carriages clip-clopping by, right beneath me. And with the big church above me!"

Grace stepped forward after her father invited her to ring the door bell and her firm pull on the metal handle was amply rewarded with a sturdy tinkling sound from deep within, which seemed to welcome them with its friendly tone.

The door opened and a friendly man with side-whiskers and a pocket-watch chain glinting in the sun, stepped out into the street. He surveyed the assembled family and spoke first to John. "You're very welcome to the great city of York, John, and I know you and your fine family are going to be very happy here."

Turning first to Mary, he introduced himself. "I'm Joseph Barker, Mrs Titterington, and my, what a fine-looking family you have!" Winking at John, he said, "They clearly take after their mother. Who do we have here, then?"

The two older girls introduced themselves politely, as they had been taught, whilst Sarah and Rebecca, still to acquire the graces, observed and hung back shyly looking

37

out from behind their mother, whilst little James rushed forward to shake hands with Joseph. "Quite the little gentleman, I do declare! And a fine manly handshake to be sure, young man," he lied, convincingly.

Blazer at the same time was rather more interested in a pretty bitch lurking seductively in an alleyway across the street! But more particularly, he was also aware of a menacing bulldog further down the street, who clearly had his own plans for the bitch and planted a fixed stare on him, together with a low menacing growl; *keep off – or else!*

Joseph Barker had been known to John for some years, from visits to the Piece Hall, where he bought cloth to supply to the wider York and East Riding dress and suit-making trade. A resident of Beverley, he had in fact inherited the Stonegate property from a recently deceased elderly bachelor uncle, and knowing of his good friend John's predicament back in Halifax, he had offered number 43 as an escape whilst he sorted his finances out.

He had also realised the potential for securing exclusivity on the new jacquard-woven fine worsted and silk cloths coming out of Higgin Chamber which were increasingly favoured by the wealthy buying market in the East Riding. Whilst John might have lost ownership of the means of production back home, he still retained the intellectual know-how and thereby the means of producing the subtle designs and textures preferred, over the somewhat tired, outdated and increasingly less profitable, sturdy work-a-day stuff-cloths favoured still for production by his father and brothers.

John might have been about to be physically incarcerated for his debts, but his brain was free to operate.

Under the right circumstances, he would yield profitable business again for Joseph, in this rich and fashion-conscious market. There were, in fact, other manufacturers ready and only too willing to switch production over to John's designs and production techniques; a fact that would cause his brother to relent reluctantly and value him in due course. A nominal peppercorn rent had already been agreed upon with John for number 43, until Joseph decided what he was going to do eventually with the property.

A man of some forty-five years of age, Joseph Barker had been married for twenty years, but he and his wife had not been blessed with children, making it even more of a pleasure to be able to help out a friend and his young family, at no cost to himself. In due course he would prove a good friend to the family and already they all felt a warmth from him and a genuine desire to be helpful.

His generosity in John's greatest hour of need would also turn out to be a wise investment, which would ultimately yield him a fine return, both financially and through the acquisition of a new family; and business partners.

Allocation of bedrooms came first with the children roaming excitedly, scampering over all three floors. The top floor was especially exciting as they looked down to the street from a height unimagined before.

Blazer ran around with them, jumping up and enjoying their excitement and joining in with an occasional bark and a constant flurry of leg-lashing tail-wagging.

Mary cautioned them, calling up the stairwell. "Be careful up there on the stairs, children, and do hold onto James's hand please, girls. They're quite steep."

Everybody gathered at the bow-windowed first floor and gazed up in amazement at the Minster – at its elegance, its architectural detail and the attention paid by highly-skilled mediaeval craftsmen to fine detail and stone carving. St. Peter's in Sowerby, St. Mary's in Luddenden, or even St. John in the Wilderness in Cragg Vale, were well known to all of them and quite impressive in their own way, but here was something quite different to behold. Centuries older and tens of times in size, their wonderment could hardly be put into words. John said, "Just imagine those craftsmen working at such a height for weeks, or even years, in the wind, driving rain or even blizzards to complete their tasks. They must indeed have had a strong faith and have believed in the good Lord's protection over them, both then and for their due rewards in the life to come."

All agreed and finally dragged themselves downstairs, away from the view to enjoy a much-needed meal that Mary had been preparing without them even noticing. She'd also managed to feed Blazer and let him out into the back yard for some exercise after being cooped up all day. The children would join him shortly after their meal as the gathering gloom drew in on a cold November afternoon.

Joseph Barker's wife, Elizabeth, though not present for their arrival, had played no small part in their welcome and Mary's task had been greatly eased by Elizabeth's preparation of a pot of stew which hung over the glowing coal fire, gently simmering, and by her provision of a freshly-baked bloomer loaf from the baker's shop further down Stonegate, which all the family would soon come to know as 'Mrs Brown's'. The children would also learn to love and look forward to her 'special-occasion' pies, buns and cream cakes which she lovingly crafted in her bakery behind the shop, for delighted residents and visitors alike. That they could all visit there safely, without even crossing the street, to make such purchases by themselves, as with many of the other diverse array of provisioners nearby, was the ultimate thrill, allowing them also to handle and learn about money for the first time. The sheer joys of surreptitiously picking away hungrily, yet carefully, nibbling at all of the corners of a hot fresh-smelling crusty bloomer, returning home from Mrs. Brown's, was a pleasure that Grace, for one, would never forget in later life.

'Special-occasion treats' would need to be few however, until the family could get their finances onto a more even keel, but they were happy for now and would settle well into their new home-away-from-home.

Joseph's wife had also provided towels and bed linen for them which meant that they could all have an early night and settle comfortably into their new home.

Mary thanked Joseph for his wife's generosity and for his own welcome, and she looked forward to meeting her at the first opportunity to thank her personally. John added, "You're a good friend Joseph, making us all so welcome and as Mary says, please come back as soon as you can for us to meet Elizabeth and for her to meet all the children."

"And Blazer!" added Hannah. "Don't forget Blazer!"

Joseph laughed and said his farewells. He declined to join them in their meal and left with a feeling of immense satisfaction that he had done a good deed for a lovely family, that he now felt very much a part of, and looked forward to returning soon with Elizabeth to show them all off to.

Mary, John and the children tucked in to their stew and crusty bread. Then they excitedly explored a little along Stonegate, going right up to the Minster before returning to unpack their cases and prepare to put the three younger children to bed at the top of the house. The older girls would follow later, creeping quietly up into the same room and Mary and John retired shortly afterward to their own room – the one with the bow window on the floor below.

They prepared for sleep in the comfort of a wonderfully large old four-poster bed which the elderly gentleman relative had owned before and they revelled in the fact that it had curtains on its three exposed sides, which together with its head-board against the wall protected them entirely from cold draughts.

John kissed Mary goodnight, trying hard to ignore his own nagging feeling whilst fully realising that she, too, was uneasy about the whole situation they found themselves in. Finally, in a vain attempt to comfort her, he said, "It'll be fine, dear. Don't worry. We'll get through this, if we all pull together."

Chapter Three

Bad News and the Sponging-House

The worst possible news for all the family had come from Halifax three weeks later on 21st November 1848, with a letter from John's sister, Eliza. Their mother Grace had collapsed and taken to her bed and the doctor feared that she may not make a recovery. Her speech was slurred and paralysis of her left side made walking impossible – in short she was suffering from apoplexy (stroke) and John's presence was requested with some haste.

Telling the children, especially the older two, who were close to their granny, as little as possible, John had set off alone to Halifax forthwith, to visit his mother.

Taking one overnight stay in the rather sad, cold and desolate, yet still furnished Higgin Chamber, John spent most of the time across the Calder valley at High Lees, at his mother's bedside alongside Eliza. His father removed himself from their presence, refusing to even speak, or much less even look at his son. John knew deep inside that his mother's health had been directly influenced by his father's actions over many years, but that the indirect and inescapable cause must be attributable to himself. His poor mother, he thought, had never deserved such suffering and would be better off in the place she was surely heading soon and was now incapable not only of speech, but of even recognising her own family.

Drawing the doctor to one side for an honest appraisal of his mother's condition he was told that it was only a matter of time before she succumbed to the illness and was now at peace and painless, in a final and permanent state of unconsciousness.

Eliza spent most of the time with her mother and John and his two brothers and sisters passed through to pay their respects, staying varying amounts of time; some weeping, some saying a quiet prayer, but all in no doubt that their dear mother was in her final stages of life. Eli spent no time at all with his wife, leaving ministrations to his eight daughters and two daughters-in-law, who together with their husbands left little room anyway to be with her in her final hours. Mary, the third daughter-in-law, was in York, of course, but was fortunate not to have to share the short shrift that her husband was receiving from his nearest and dearest. He was a leper in his own family home with each sibling guarding against alienating Eli for fear of losing their inheritance.

John returned to York the following day saying his unacknowledged last words to his mother.

Kneeling by her bedside and kissing her gently on the forehead, he knew he would not see her alive again and dreaded passing the sad news to little Grace, especially, since she had grown so close to her namesake on many sleepovers across in Midgley, learning dutifully but always

44

with great joviality and a real sense of fun, the arts of cooking, baking and needlework.

Hannah, too, had joined in often, though with less enthusiasm, possibly through more limited ability. But the fun was enjoyed by her, too, and there would be great sadness upon his return to Stonegate recounting the sad events to all the children.

It was with no surprise that they learned of Grace's death a week later by post from Eliza; she had died peacefully, drifting away at midday on Monday the 27th November. That she had died of a broken heart was the inescapable fact he found hard to forgive his father for, but he still knew he had to bear some of the guilt for the collateral damage that he, too, had been responsible for in her final months.

Two days later on Wednesday morning the 29th of November, all of the family set off back to Halifax to attend the funeral, which was held at St. Mary's church in Luddenden village the following day.

An overnight stay afterward on both Wednesday and Thursday night at Higgin Chamber was a welcome return for the children especially. The thought of having their 'real' home always there, waiting for them as though on standby, gave them all great comfort and a strengthened sense of belonging.

Blazer particularly revelled in his return to roaring around the garden and the cobble-stoned mill yard, chasing rabbits, birds and anything else that moved. It was a pleasure now denied to him, cooped up and mainly getting no further than the tight constraints of the Stonegate back yard for most of the time.

The funeral went well enough, but all of the immediate family gave nothing more than perfunctory greetings to John and Mary. The children fared better and at least had some exchanges with cousins who understood little of the immediate history, but they were occasionally pulled away by parents looking as though they were afraid their offspring might be about to catch some incurable contagion.

Other people attending the funeral included some of John's creditors and he had the distinct feeling that the storm clouds were gathering and his day of judgement was fast approaching, as they got close enough to smell the blood of their quarry.

They also learnt, if they hadn't already discovered it, of the location of his family's new exiled residence and ominously, moreover, were prepared to act on the information.

Returning to York, the family again made the most of their railway adventure, though Grace herself was more contemplative and couldn't associate her memory of the stark ornate wooden coffin being lowered into the grave with such happy memories of her granny with her smiling, shiny face and seemingly permanently-worn apron. And always with the smell of fresh baking coming from an oven full of mint and currant pasties, Yorkshire parkin or lemon cheese tarts in the comfort and warmth of the High Lees kitchen.

Was granny really inside that box? The thought of her lying there helpless, being lowered into the ground sent a shiver through her and the sound of the earth being scattered onto the coffin lid as the vicar intoned "...ashes to ashes, dust to dust…" would return to her, in quiet moments, probably for the rest of her life.

Just one week later on Saturday morning, December 9th, Grace was the first to awake early in the top floor bedroom in Stonegate, where she shared a bed with her sister Sarah. Rebecca shared another bed with Hannah and young James had a cot bed over in the corner by the window. Her parents slept on the middle floor below with the large bow window and the children's top floor room had a smaller version of this bow window, making looking down into the street slightly less severe without the same overhang, but at a height even more precarious, and doubly exciting.

As she had come out of a deep slumber Grace realised that even though it was Saturday, there was complete silence coming from the street. By this time the street traders should usually be creating a hubbub setting up, and the footsteps of the early communicants attending morning mass in the Minster would certainly have been heard. They bustled speedily along the street as though their lives depended on it, and perhaps it did in many cases, by the physical state of some of the elderly York citizens she saw wheezing their way along Stonegate trying to get to mass on time.

Tip-toeing quietly over to the window, so as not to waken anybody up, she realised that she could not see out at all, and whilst hastily scraping a hole in the ice, coating the window pane with her fingers, she noticed that her breath seemed to be filling the cleared space whilst she was still scraping away. She shivered, and scratching faster now, looked down and saw an amazing scene below – a man was attempting to walk toward her down Stonegate, toward the Minster, looking to Grace as though he was trying to straddle a small fence with each laboured step, walking in a half-drunken, exaggerated high-stepping fashion, a bit like a crab might walk, she thought. The reason was clear immediately. There had been at least a two-feet fall of snow while they all slept so tightly bundled up in their cosy beds. The first shafts of pale winter sun were just peeping through, and glancing upward, Grace took a sharp intake of breath at the sheer beauty of the Minster. Driving snow had stuck to the towers and moulded it into a wedding cake of three-dimensional iced splendour. Every crenelation, every small detailed stone carving had formed into a fine white-linened and crocheted christening gown. How dear granny would have loved to see her tatted handkerchief and doily-edgings all so prominently displayed high above the rooftops in crispest white cotton, for the approaching sinners to witness and repent beneath.

But the truth was that hardly anybody *was* approaching. Digging snow from the immediate vicinity of their own properties, to get out at all would be a priority this morning and worship must wait until evensong, at least.

Grace descended the stairs and continued with her usual early morning tasks. As she thought of the Minster towers again, she vividly remembered the joyous sewing and needlework lessons spent with dear granny T. The funeral had greatly depressed her and somewhere deep inside, though she wasn't aware of it, an important chapter in her childhood had ended and her life henceforth would proceed without the protection so lovingly afforded to her as a devoted grandchild.

After rekindling the embers of the kitchen fire and putting on the porridge for breakfast, she fed Blazer and was about to let him into the back yard when something quite out of the ordinary happened. Blazer, who seemed to sense it first, with his hackles rising defensively, broke out into the most earth-shattering yelping and barking and awoke not only the entire household with a jolt but possibly half of the city of York, too!

John came bounding downstairs first and called to Blazer to be quiet. He had feared the worst for some time after his creditors had hung around his mother's funeral like vultures. It couldn't be long until they caught up with him and he was only too acutely aware that he could not meet his obligations and settle his debts. He had only made a few contacts with farmers in the surrounding area to buy wool in the following spring and summer and certainly he had convinced them that his contacts back home were more than adequate to gain an excellent market price for their fleeces. The harsh winter of 1848, however, would not yield any income in the short term and it was time itself that he needed more than anything right now. Their savings were sufficient to live on in the meantime, if they were frugal, but there was no money to settle any of their debts.

"Open the door in the name of the Sheriff. Immediately," a gruff voice demanded from the snow-filled street beyond. Mary and the children, still half asleep, huddled together in fear by the fire, for whatever comfort they could get from its heat. Even Blazer had stopped barking finally and seemed also to sense the drama of the situation and that he could do nothing to assist or improve his master's plight.

They had all also seen through the window the two men standing silently outside the back door. They instantly knew their significance was to block all means of escape. The younger children couldn't know this, of course, but the word 'sheriff' lost none of its significance on the older ones

49

as a word to fear, and in any case, the loud banging and shouting held little doubt for them that there was some kind of trouble brewing and that by his actions, it was probably being aimed at their father.

Two of the bailiffs, the sheriff's men, were let into the street side of the house by John. Mary saw little reason to deny the two men in the yard the same courtesy and duly opened the yard door to admit them also.

"Are you John Titterington, late of Higgin Chamber in Sowerby, near Halifax?"

John nodded acquiescently.

"We have a court writ and can do this quietly, if you agree, or we are empowered to use force if necessary to remove you to the sponging-house to allow you time to correct your affairs and pay what's due to your creditors."

John responded immediately. "I shall come quietly and sort this matter out. I have some very influential friends and will thank you to respect that and treat me in a manner suited to my status as a gentleman."

The sheriff's bailiff seemed pleased this was not to be a difficult arrest and concluded, "I can agree to that, sir, and I will not place handcuffs on you. But you must move swiftly between the four of us and make no hurried or false moves as we pass along through the city. Do I make myself clear, sir?"

John weighed up the situation and saw little value in objecting or indeed of asking who specifically was the creditor who was attempting to gain the 'first-mover advantage'. He was aware of the significance of this

50

through the courts and 'first-movers' basically tried to do just that and get their monies first. And the rest, of which there were many in John's case, could typically go hang.

"It's clear enough, sir, I see you hold a writ and have the necessary powers invested in you. I will accompany you peaceably to sort this all out, with neither let nor hindrance to your party carrying out their lawful duties."

This came as a relief to Mary who was well aware of John's fearful temper, which explained the smaller children's reason for huddling into their mother's nightdress. They, too, were aware of the explosive nature of their father if he was displeased, often by the slightest thing.

John donned his hat, coat and scarf and put on his boots, and the odd-looking party of five headed out into the snow with John rather obviously flanked by the four bailiffs in a manner quite clearly demonstrating to anyone watching that he was a 'wrong-un'! He felt the guilt as passers-by stared at him, but he was not known well in the city and the snow was keeping people away from their normal businesses that morning. Similar processions were also well known and often seen in many other towns and cities suffering hard times and would in any case cause little more than a passing interest to citizens typically used to 'enjoying' miscreants pinned mercilessly and pelted with rotten fruit in the stocks, not to mention their 'excitement' at witnessing the occasional public hanging.

Mary and the children looked blankly at each other while she explained to the children it was all a terrible mistake, but that father might be away from home for some time while it was all sorted out.

That said, they all sat down to eat breakfast with little further conversation and with the inevitable questioning being stalled by Mary, who instead used distraction therapy and talked of the excitement of the day ahead and of the materials they would need to gather together to build a snowman in the back yard. Christmas streamer decoration-making was also planned for later and seasonal preparations would take all of their minds off the reality of the situation.

Down Stonegate the sheriff's party went, then turned away from the Minster into Low Petergate and straight on down Colliergate, Fossgate and Walmgate; the ancient buildings all looking so beautiful bedecked in snowy splendour, hardly noticed by John as he watched his footing through the deep snow. One drift in fact had blown to be almost three-feet deep and caused the party to detour slightly whilst still retaining their perfectly coordinated saltire formation.

Finally, they stopped outside a dingy single-storey house. A place of dread that John was about to learn more about – the sponging-house.

Sponging-houses were aptly named following an adage that sponges 'readily give up their contents if squeezed'. The object being just that, to hold a prisoner and squeeze both metaphorically and physically until the first-mover creditor received his money; the bailiff, too, must have his none-too-cheap expenses for 'lodgings' at the sponging-house settled.

Upon entering the building, John was taken to his room – with a freezing-cold outdoor cage beyond, at the back of the building where he could at least go to breathe some air. A simple wooden bed, a bucket and sand on the floor and the additional feature he was about to get rather more familiar with, both here and elsewhere – bars!

With the door closed and firmly locked behind him, he sat on the wooden bed to take stock of his plight. He reminded himself that he had read somewhere of a sponging-house with its cage being described in a novel like 'a beast-receptacle at a zoo' and here indeed, first hand, was the reality of the statement.

The smell of fine food cooking and expensive cigar tobacco smoke soon permeated John's room and the laughter left him in no doubt that the bailiff and his guests were having a fine old time, and all at his ultimate expense.

But he could not afford to pay any of his creditors, first-mover or otherwise, and neither could he pay the bailiff for his questionable and clearly euphemistic 'hospitality'. So he would remain there until money came over from relatives or friends in Halifax, or the consequences would indeed be dire.

Mary, meanwhile, had put the children to making streamers at the kitchen table and set about the task of communicating with home to ask for funds. A task she felt certain would be fruitless, but must nevertheless be pursued. It was a task made infinitely more difficult since Mary was illiterate and would need a neighbour or friend to craft her a few hurriedly composed begging missives, with the utmost urgency to rush to the lunchtime post for delivery the next morning.

How embarrassed she had been at her marriage ceremony to have to sign the wedding register at Halifax Parish Church with a cross, but now was not the time for regrets about her lack of education.

John Adams had become a good, though, only recent friend to the family and was very much an admirer of John's since he had taken him on a shooting trip to the country, with some impressive friends, shortly after their arrival the month before, whilst on a business trip visiting Dales sheep farmers north of the city. They had enjoyed a successful shoot, bringing home several fine plump pheasants for the dinner table and their day had been rounded off with some fine drinking and eating at a Harrogate hostelry.

John was a recently retired lawyer who lived above his law practice a few doors down in Stonegate, and it was to John's that Mary trudged in the deep snow, leaving the children by the fireside cutting out the strips of paper to glue together for streamer-chains.

John Adam's wife, also called Mary, greeted her warmly as they, too, had discovered a warm friendship whilst the men were away on shooting trips. She had already heard word from a neighbour of the commotion down the street that morning and made a tactful withdrawal to the back kitchen, leaving Mary to converse privately with her husband.

John wrote whilst Mary dictated her identical appeal for funds to three of John's wealthier sisters; firstly to Hannah, who had only recently married a widower, a wealthy mill owner's son, John Murgatroyd, and then two further letters went to his sisters Grace and Eliza who had also married well to James Hartley and James Smith.

Another, but almost certainly pointless letter, was dictated to John's father Eli, in the forlorn hope that even he would not see his eldest son committed to the ultimate ignominy and shame of a debtors' gaol, which in his case would be, almost certainly, the notorious York Castle gaol. She held no hope for this one, but omitting to include pleas for herself stressed the children's unfortunate and totally innocent position in the matter.

She also got John to write a fifth and last letter, a very difficult one to compose, to her own father in Shibden, a beautiful valley to the west of Halifax. It was where she was brought up with her brothers in their home attached to their own burgeoning textile production empire, later to blossom into John Holdsworth's world-renowned multi-mill, international moquette manufacturing facility at Shaw Lodge Mills in south-central Halifax. Mary's father had strongly disapproved of her marriage to John and whilst appreciating his early successes in business and sound family background, was only too well aware of his fondness for the ladies, for drink and for keeping 'bad company'. Fathering a son at the age of twenty-one with a thirteen-year old bobbin-girl in his father's mill would have done little, to say the least, to ingratiate himself to a proud and loving father...*in any era!* But would he, a religious man of some considerable means, see his daughter and five young grandchildren suffer needlessly, however predictably the actions of a wayward son-in-law might have turned out to be?

Mary hurriedly departed to post her six letters saying, "Thank you so much, John, for helping me out. I'm sure we can resolve this misunderstanding quickly and return to some sort of normality as soon as possible. Please give my regards to Mary, but I must dash now to post the letters. The children will be anxious."

Over at the sponging-house John was provided with only bread, water and some rather stale-looking cheese during the long day. Before bed, he settled down as well as

55

he could, after a gratefully received cup of hot broth, on his hard wooden bed, keeping all his outer clothing on and huddling under blankets which were little better than old sacking. He fashioned a pillow as best he could with some more of the crumpled stale-smelling coarse sacks.

The bailiff's dinner party on the other side of his door continued with its merriment to well after he had heard midnight strike on a nearby church clock. With little more than his nose and his condensing breath visible by the dim candlelight, he snuggled uncomfortably down, blew out his candle and tried to sleep and blot out the dreadful memory of the worst day of his life.

Insufficiently-funded and cast out by his family, he had little doubt of the fate which awaited him and that he must prepare himself for much worse to follow.

Chapter Four

Settling into Prison Life

John had resigned himself to a long stay in the castle to avoid disappointment, especially at a time approaching Christmas when life away from home would be at its hardest.

Mary tended to his culinary needs, preparing and delivering his food as she always had, and Grace sometimes came through the city alone or with Hannah or some of the other children. Mary had not hidden the truth from the children; it would have been pointless to try anyway.

John had lots of time to contemplate and reprise the events of 1848, and relive the series of catastrophic errors which had placed him where he presently resided. John felt shamed, disinherited and cast off by his family back home. Without his dear mother and Branwell, his good friend, and Christmas fast approaching, here he must lie and do his level best to think of happier times.

And nothing and no one could have been further away from such times than Thomas Scoggins! His very name struck fear, horror and anger in equal proportions, into his very soul.

Standing over six feet and two inches with cauliflower ears, a broken nose, chipped and stained teeth and a surly and fearsome attitude at all times, the ex-bare-knuckle-fighter Thomas Aloysius Scoggins was the long-time and much-feared turnkey at York Castle prison.

Early on John was finding his choice of cell-sharing, for cost reasons and companionship, a wise one and the Rev. Thomas Williams – 'Tom' as he insisted John call him, had been a good choice. He provided good conversation and, as he would discover later, they had many friends in common from both home and in his favourite hunting areas around the Vale of York.

Exercise time in the prison yard, which could not be avoided however much he tried, was a mixture of verbal abuse and physical violence, generally aimed at the serious criminals awaiting deportation but which even the debtors found almost impossible to avoid getting drawn into. The totally irreligious Thomas A. Scoggins had a deep-seated hatred of what he perceived as the privileged classes. John and his reverend cellmate were prime targets for him to goad and do his very best to coax into arguments, hopefully, in John's case anyway, of causing fights with the deportee ne'er-do-wells, who had little or nothing to lose anyway.

A side-bet or two on the outcome was also worthy of his investment, providing lucrative entertainment in an otherwise boring existence.

Outside in the prison exercise yard, the walls were over forty-feet high on three sides away from the main cell block, and sunlight, even in high summer, could never shine on the righteous, even had there been many such present!

Entering John's cell, totally unannounced, Scoggins would always warm to his task of gleefully goading them both on.

"So, Master Titterington, and of course, your holy reverence, enjoying the fine meals you're being brought, are you? Shouldn't really be here, should you? All a big mistake, wasn't it? A miscarriage of justice that will soon be put right? Well, it won't and you're here because you deserve to be. So get used to it!

"Look down your noses at the common criminals, I'll bet, don't you? And me, too, I'll be bound. Cosseted in your fine homes with your stuck-up friends or your spoilt wives and brats. Well, let me tell you, in the real world, yes, the real world, where you've certainly never belonged, either of you, it's a whole lot different and we learn to respect everybody or take the consequences for our actions. Yes, consequences gentlemen!"

This last word was spat out and used at all times with a sarcastic sneer, only ever adopted through robust class-envy and an immovable chip on the shoulder.

Thomas Scoggins was indeed a well-balanced character in this respect, boasting a chip of equal proportion on *both* of his burly shoulders!

But even Scoggins hated the discomfort of the prison yard in slush and near-frost weather and roared the prisoners back to their cells after little more than a quarter-of-an-hour. He could wait for his fun later and would certainly be trying to goad John, amongst others, into a delicious altercation, a fight even, preferably with one of the hard-nut convicts awaiting transportation.

As turnkey, Scoggins had no income as such, but was allowed to let out rooms or provide services such as renting carpets, chairs, a sofa or a tea kettle and favours could generally be bought from him beyond the standard fees paid by prisoners on both admission and discharge.

Additionally, but only for debtors, the prison master or marshal oversaw all such opportunities for income and for the right money allowed 'whistling shops' or areas in the prison where wine, ale or spirits could be brought in and sold, together with allowing skittles or other games to be played.

Inmates on the 'common' or 'poor' side had free accommodation, but had to make charity payments; begging was even allowed within the prison walls, often from early Victorians who showed a penchant for visiting, for their own macabre enjoyment or sometimes to demonstrate forcibly the dire consequences of criminally debauched living to their wide-eyed accompanying offspring.

Accommodation by cell for debtors with some means involved the purchase of a 'chummage ticket', by which John was able to share with a person of similar financial or social status. For a pound a week all of the 'luxuries' plus a single occupancy could have been bought, but John found this beyond his means and in any case preferred to choose companionship – initially at least, he told himself – and this was proving a good choice so far with the pleasant and quite agreeable company of the elderly Rev. Thomas Williams from Beverley. Debtors otherwise were housed three or four to a cell meant for no more than two, with the consequent deprivation of all personal privacy and with slop-buckets in use all night, and most of the day, too, making life even more uncomfortable.

In the bowels of the prison there was no choice for convicts awaiting deportation, or even hanging, and as many as eight were crammed into a cell no more than ten feet square to be let out only for exercise for no more than fifteen minutes in every twenty-four hours. Their cries during the night were pitiful and the tale of the tragic circumstances surrounding eight prisoners awaiting deportation to Van Dieman's Land was the scourge of all the newly incarcerated souls, who invariably were acquainted with it by Scoggins, with his usual relish at their admission assembly.

The admission had been quite the worst, the most intimidating experience for John. Unable to meet his first-mover's payment and approaching under guard from the court house, crossing beneath Clifford's Tower and entering the castle's oppressive and forbidding portals, gave him a dull ache deep in his stomach and even an unexpected flush, as, quite naked, he was physically handled and pushed clumsily from behind, for the first time in his life, into an unnaturally upright position in an attempt to militarise his stance, though no one else stood alongside him in this imaginary parade, for he was 'processed' alone.

As a valued 'commodity' to be traded, in the sponging-house, John had been accorded comparative luxury due to being regarded as saleable goods, but now any semblance of worth was gone; he was indeed largely worthless and discarded for the first time in his life, and his punishment was about to start for real.

The sonorous thump of the twelve-foot-high timber castle doors, suspended on the ancient stone portals, followed by the dull metallic clunking into position of a battery of heavy-duty bolts and the rattle of steel a dozen or more foot-long keys make, on a small wheel-sized ring, was the most deeply depressing collection of sounds. Sounds which would continue to haunt him in their satanic discordance throughout his stay at the castle, often echoing through the corridors in the dead of night, accompanied by the tympani of heavy chains, as prisoners arrived or were dragged along, heavily manacled to each other, to be taken by coach to a port for transportation, or worse, to the gallows, for an early morning dispatch.

The many varieties of human sounds accompanying all of these activities were sometimes indescribable, ranging from dull despondent groans to the high-pitched screams of a snared animal.

Scoggins relished telling newcomers the story of the actual occurrence of the eight Australia-bound prisoners thus:

One almost unbearable and stiflingly hot summer's night, eight prisoners, crammed into the same cell, found the heat increasingly unbearable and cried out for their door to be opened to at least allow some air circulation, finally shouting out fervently, on pain of death, not to stray outside into the corridor. Their cries became inhuman, wounded animal howls almost, like some demented or wild creatures and then gradually they died away in abjectly resigned desperation until silence reigned after many tortured hours.

At the cell opening the following morning all eight perfectly healthy young men were found asphyxiated in grotesquely contorted, variously interlinking poses, with their hair dementedly ripped out from their own and each other's scalps, in blood-soaked, fingernail-shredded handfuls. Their facial expressions were beyond description, as any recognisable form of humanity, mostly resembling the tormented stone carvings of medieval church grotesques or blood-spouting gargoyles from their self-inflicted head wounds.

"Their own dear mothers wouldn't have known 'em," concluded Scoggins with a final leering grin.

Scoggins, from the outset, had it in for John, taking an immediate disliking to a man who in his opinion was looking down on him and who would unquestionably refuse to engage in any form of conversation had they met up on 'equal' terms anywhere else.

He continued to address him at the reception room; "So it's Titterington is it? Another bad news member of that dysfunctional clan from 'alifax, no doubt, like the last reprobate we shipped out to Van Dieman's Land, with as ragged a bunch of thieves and vagabonds as I ever saw. Good luck to 'em, said I, and good luck to the poor Australians who'll have to live with 'em. They'll rob 'em blind. Should have been 'ung, the lot of 'em. Probably perished on the way anyway, or killed each other! Serve 'em right, nasty bunch!"

He referred to John's first cousin Robert Titterington, a son of his father Eli's brother, Thomas. John and Robert had known each other as young men but John, who was nine years older had little influence over his cousin, being contemporary in neither age nor social circumstance and friendship.

His father was not involved in the family textile interests and Robert, like his father was a miller, when it suited him, for he was quite outside any form of parental control from an early age. He settled into a habitual life of crime and running with 'friends' who were similarly inclined towards a life of petty larceny. A life which when allowed to run could only have led to more serious crime followed by imprisonment or worse.

John would see him in his late teens hanging around the Halifax public houses with a tough crowd, looking generally dishevelled and Eli would totally blank him on market days, where he often hung around the Piece Hall amongst a crowd, looking for any opportunity to take advantage of visitors carrying money to purchase goods. William Barber was a known petty thief and companion of Robert's who would distract well-dressed unsuspecting visitors whilst Barber relieved them of their valuables.

"What a disgrace to his father and the family's good name," Eli had once commented, watching him size up his targets to 'ply his trade' one market day. "He'll finish up being transported or hung one day, you'll see if he doesn't," he remarked to anybody who cared to listen, which had never included his brother Thomas, Robert's parentally-failed father, from his early teenage renegade years.

At twenty minutes past midnight on 6th August 1839, nine years before, Robert Crossley and Thomas Cockroft had been attacked and robbed by a gang of highwaymen as their gig was at Lower Brear, near to Stump Cross in Halifax, returning from Doncaster wool market.

Robert Crossley, a son of John Crossley, founder of the carpet empire blossoming over Godley Hill at Dean Clough Mills in Halifax, was driving the gig.

William Barber, Michael Dawson, John Downs, Jonathan Rushworth, Joshua Wilson and Robert Titterington were a notorious gang by that time, having committed several robberies around Halifax and as far away as Burnley.

Not seriously harming their victims, the gang escaped, taking money and pocket watches with them. Thomas Cockroft had leapt into a field under cover of darkness during the assault and had successfully concealed his purse and several promissory notes which the gang did not find.

In the *Halifax Guardian* it was reported, of the gang, that: *"...their outrages upon life and property were making the night hideous, where they were accustomed to perpetrate their deeds of wickedness."*

The next day they were in Keighley, sixteen miles away, remaining there for two days, where they ordered clothes, which they paid for from their stolen six five pound notes of the Halifax Joint Stock Bank and the Huddersfield & Halifax Union Banks. It was later reported in court that Robert Titterington also had a great number of sovereigns in his possession.

In addition, they stole three bills worth £882 12s 6d, 10 sovereigns and 17s in silver.

Nine days after the robbery on the 15th of August, Rushworth, Titterington and Barber brought themselves to the attention of the constabulary; betting with sovereigns, they were apprehended on the Burnley racecourse by three constables, but someone, (probably one of the gang) shouted, "Chartists!" and a large section of sympathisers in the crowd, half in jest and half in earnest, jostled the constables to the ground, pushed down on top of them and allowed the three of them all to get away, and Barber, who had been arrested first, escaped still wearing his handcuffs.

Robert Titterington drew attention to himself going flahulach in a quayside bar and was arrested in Dublin, where he gave his name as Thomas Thomson, but Thomas Cockroft's gold watch was found on him and a silver watch he had pawned was found to be the one which was taken from Robert Crossley and had his name engraved on it. Taken into custody with his fellow gang members, a check back later at the garda barracks revealed them all to be wanted men.

A Halifax constable was despatched to Dublin to bring the men back, but when the Duke of York stagecoach carrying the men stopped at the New Inn in Soyland, nearing Halifax, to change horses, two of the gang, Robert Titterington and Michael Dawson escaped, 'chained together like Siamese twins' it was reported in the press, and they travelled around six miles before being recaptured.

Brought to trial in York eight months later, on the 5th March 1840, all five were found guilty and sentenced to transportation; Dawson, Titterington and Barber for life and Rushworth and Wilson, inasmuch as their conduct had not been so bad as that of the others and they had rather endeavoured to protect Mr Crossley from further violence, were sentenced to transportation for fifteen years.

And so it was that Robert Titterington languished in York Castle prison from early March until his transportation from Portsmouth some nine months later.

More than enough time for him, a trouble maker, to become more than well acquainted with one Thomas Aloysius Scoggins.

Legs and arms manacled and unable to even contemplate repeating a Soyland-style run for it, at any of the three overnight coaching stops, sleeping in freezing stables, or at several other horse changeovers, Robert travelled in irons by coach for four arduous, bone-rattling days before sailing on the *Lady Raffles* alongside 329 other male convicts similarly shackled.

On the coach journeying to Portsmouth were six other convicts who included his horse racing companion-accomplices, William Barber, his fellow 'lifer' who sailed with him on the *Lady Raffles,* and the lesser-sentenced Jonathan Rushworth, who sailed on a different convict ship, the *Duncan.*

Departing from Portsmouth on 2nd December 1840, the *Lady Raffles* took 105 tortuous days of firstly freezing, followed by stifling equatorial temperatures, arriving in Hobart, Van Dieman's Land (Tasmania) on 17th March 1841, minus only three convicts, who had perished and been buried at sea along the Clipper Route; a journey which could have taken anywhere between 90 and 150, via Cape Horn and might have included delays of anything up to three weeks stranded helplessly in The Doldrums, awaiting the strong westerly winds of The Roaring Forties to carry them on to the Antipodes.

Losing so few passengers was rare, when as many as a quarter of all prisoners perished on some sailing ships and where the additional hazards of disease struck convicts shackled in such close proximity unmercifully.

On arrival Robert Titterington was recorded as being:

Gender: Male
Age: 24 years
Hair: Brown
Eyes: Blue
Height: 5ft 11inches
Remarks: Scar on knuckle forefinger left hand
Sentence: Life
Trade: Miller

He was never heard of again.

John and his cell companion the Rev. Tom also had similar hardships of confinement to endure through the degradation of a slop-bucket apiece, but with just two civilised occupants, some semblance of a regime of near-privacy could be, and had been instigated as successfully as was possible under the circumstances.

John was also aware that in time, and with the permission of the prison marshal, debtors were allowed to go outside the prison and could visit coffee houses or even engage in business. The limit to travelling outside prison was one mile, or in York's case, debtors must not pass outside the city walls. Visits to public houses were totally banned. Failure to follow these strict rules, or to return each night on time, resulted in immediate withdrawal of all outside privileges, harsher treatment and a more-than-likely addition to sentence length through adverse reports to the magistrates.

With trust, persuasion and, of course, money, over time debtors could even live totally outside prison and trade within these strict residency rules.

Back in Halifax, at the time of Robert's incarceration in York, his notoriety had, unsurprisingly, given him the soubriquet of *'Dick Turpin'* which one wag had developed into *'Dick Turperington'* – a new name occasionally aimed in jest at any market trader, not necessarily even bearing the family name, who appeared to be overcharging – '…that's daylight robbery! You're a right Turperington!'

Significantly, Turpin, the original notorious highwayman, was also imprisoned in York Castle gaol prior to his very public hanging on the Knavesmire in 1739, aged just thirty-four. The Victorian novelist William Harrison Ainsworth (1805-1882) wrote *'Rookwood'* featuring Dick Turpin as its leading character a hundred years later in 1834, making his name truly *a la mode* and worthy of some robust schadenfreudian humour at the time. That John would get the same treatment back home only a few years after Robert's departure was without doubt and young male Titteringtons would be cautioned for years to come with "…you don't want to finish up like Robert and John Turperington, do you? So pull your socks up and sort yourself out!"

And even into the 21st century the story was still being told in the family, of *'an old aunt'* once talking of a *'relationship'* between the Titteringtons and Dick Turpin. As one joker once said to me, *"Dick Turpin? Ben Turpin more like!"* recalling the unfortunate image of the strabismus-afflicted silent comedy movie star!

John's future curfew-restricted time outside the prison would not come easily as long as the turnkey would not put in a good word for him with the marshal; a word which was far from forthcoming since their disliking was entirely mutual and intense! Money also would not be sufficient with Mary's father keeping a tight rein on her expenditure to '*solely* maintain herself and the children'.

She would need to go without, but the children, who never knew it, had to also live on a strained yet cleverly managed diet which had been previously unrestricted.

Cells were bolted for sixteen hours a day and beds were notoriously hard, giving John ample time to lie awake and recall the many misfortunes and mistakes he had made during the year and look forward to, as well as he could to what 1849 might bring.

Lying and listening to the distant sound of the Minster's bells summoning the faithful to early communion on Sunday 17th December, John was jolted out of a rare but peaceful slumber by a harsh voice.

"Come on, Titterington. Get yourself stirring, you've a visitor – says he goes by the name of Titterington – another member of your rotten brood, poor sod. I'd change it if it was mine and that's a fact" The unmistakable stentorian utterings of Scoggins announcing a visit in his own inimitably brusque fashion.

He? A *male* Titterington? *Who on Earth could it be?* John exited the cell, trying not to further disturb his slumbering friend who was recovering from the abrupt awakening. He headed on down to the meeting room to discover who awaited him.

Chapter Five

Market Day at the Piece Hall – Halifax

Looking back from his prison cell to the morning of Wednesday 12th January 1848, almost a year previously, things had started out well.

Market day at Halifax Piece Hall was always a lively affair where acquaintances old and new got together to share the news, compare market prices, catch up on family happenings and generally engage and participate in community activities. Buyers came from throughout the country as well as from overseas to trade and purchase goods.

Opened in 1779 and Grade-1-listed, Halifax Piece Hall embodied the vital and dominant importance of the trade in handwoven textiles to the pre-industrial economy of the West Riding of Yorkshire.

Built as a cloth hall for trading 'pieces' of cloth (a 30-yard length of handwoven woollen fabric) Halifax Piece Hall was the most ambitious and prestigious of its type when built and remains a unique structure today as one of Britain's most outstanding Georgian buildings.

Bluff, northern, God-fearing manufacturers such as Eli Titterington who occupied room 63, Rustick, on the ground floor near to the main Westgate entrance, ideally placed for buyers, revelled in the building's neo-classical design adapted from the architectural grandeur of Imperial Rome. In anticipation, his father Thomas, a stuff maker (a course woven fabric for everyday clothing) had first arrived from Waddington in Lancashire two years prior to the opening of the Piece Hall and had established his weaving business, purchasing Old Ridings in Midgley near Halifax in 1777, where he lived, farmed and wove his fabrics. Originally, a timber-framed construction of the 15th century, later stone-clad around a mighty centre-beamed structure, Old Ridings stands firmly to this day, giving us a detailed insight into over five centuries of developing rural Yorkshire life.

A bright sunny morning, though a little seasonally chilly, greeted John Titterington as he strolled through the southern entrance to the Piece Hall after climbing up Horton Street from the Halifax railway station at Shaw Syke where he had arrived from his short journey from Luddenden Foot, half a mile below his Higgin Chamber home, via North Dean in Greetland. His pieces of cloth had been loaded by his workmen at Luddenden Foot and were now being transported up to room 63 by one of John's young apprentices, twenty-year old William Foster.

Dapper as always and ruggedly handsome, John cut a fine figure striding briskly over the cobbles diagonally across toward the Westgate entrance and a familiar voice greeted him from behind a food trader's stall. "Not talking to me this morning then, Master John?" John spun round, recognising only too well the rather throaty and always sensual presence of the delightful Fanny Brearley, the market manager, Isaac Brearley's half-Irish voluptuous daughter and assistant.

Just turned twenty-one, Fanny was a delight to most men's eyes – men of any background or situation who dare approach her, but the independently minded Fanny had an eye herself for the good life and a wealthy suitor and in the meantime, until one came along, she was more than happy to receive the attention and gifts of a wealthy, convivial character such as the forty-one-year-old John Titterington – even if he was a married man. And actually it was this latter fact that excited her more since she knew well how to enjoy giving a man that which a demure, genteel well-brought-up wife could never and moreover would never provide.

Fanny Brearley loved wild, uncontrolled sex and had an insatiable appetite for it.

Rattling her bunch of trading room keys, she sidled up to John and said quietly with a knowing wink, whilst tucking her jet-black tresses seductively behind her ears: "I'll be checking over number 29 up on the Colonnade later this morning, if you're still interested in expanding your interests?"

The deliberate double-entendre "expanding your interests" was Fanny's usual euphemistic way of drawing John into an extra-marital romp and he had found, over the past year at least, that he was unable to resist the temptation at some point on most market days. Indeed he imagined there would soon be hardly a room left of the 315 available in the Piece Hall, where Fanny and he had not left their mark! That her orgasmic high-pitched screaming, more akin to a banshee in remotest Ireland, had not been heard as far as the top of Beacon Hill, just behind the Piece Hall, stood testament to the young eighteen-year-old gifted architect Thomas Bradley's design and his incorporation of foot-thick stone walls and iron-clad stout timber doors on each of the dozens of 12 x 7 foot, perfectly crafted, love nests!

Her olive skin, brown eyes and jet-black hair stood her out from the largely indigenous Halifax population, giving full credence to her ethnic Irish origins dating directly back to the scuppered Spanish Armada that pitched up along the west coast of Ireland and its antecedent crews who settled there rather than face the disgrace and humiliation of a return to their native land.

Fanny's low-cut blouse and now heaving bosom, plus a rather heady scent of sweet lavender emanating from her tantalisingly goose-pimpled cleavage made John move away quickly or be tempted to take her right there and then in full view of the assembled throng. Tingling profusely from head to toe and with his 'interests' already aroused, he departed hurriedly across the quadrangle saying: "Ever the professional, Fanny. I'll come by at around 11 o'clock to consider what you have to offer. I do hope I won't be disappointed."

Fanny was of course by now well acquainted with John's home situation, for he'd told her often enough. His wife, Mary, was reluctant to engage in sex at all with five children under the age of ten having been conceived, viewing sex largely as a Godly marital duty intended for procreation, and moreover, an act which most certainly could never have a 'sinful' semblance of enjoyment about it. There would have been a sixth child, a son Eli, their second-born after daughter Grace, co-named in an attempt to ingratiate John's own father, who had died sadly aged just six months, some years before and Mary had been unwilling to repeat the experience, reluctantly bringing a further four children into the world, each one with considerable trepidation and anxiety, with each confinement generally resulting from John requiring his conjugal rights whilst generally under the influence of drink and though whilst never quite resembling rape had nevertheless involved a high degree of mental, sometimes mild physical coercion – plus an absence of any thought for birth control on his behalf. Abstinence and coitus interruptus were unwelcome bedfellows, literally, and had in any case proved largely beyond John's capabilities or desires thus far.

Enough was enough and she had provided him with his much-desired son and heir, her fifth and youngest child, proudly named for her; James Holdsworth Titterington.

Calling out to greet other market traders along the way, John finally arrived at number 63, where his father Eli and brothers James and Thomas were already setting about presenting their samples of cloth and were moving actual sale pieces into storage at the back of the room.

"Late as usual," said his father. "And I saw you wasting your time in idle chatter with that trollop of a market manager's daughter over there. Thank God I have your brothers to rely on or we'd be in a sorry pickle on market days. And that's a fact."

Eli was despised by John, and in return his father thought him a feckless, unreliable, drunken womaniser. That his mother worshipped the ground her charming, handsome son walked on and that he had a gift for innovation in manufacture and design and a charm to woo even the most difficult customers into a purchase, made his involvement in his father's family businesses essential, though far from desirable, for a God-fearing man of the church who despised and personally eschewed all forms of man's usual temptations of the flesh.

John's magnetic charms and affluence had also resulted in the acquisition of a wide circle of wealthy and highly influential friends. Grouse and pheasant shooting on the wider east and north Yorkshire moors and on the more local Midgley Moor, coupled with stately weekends away mixing with a privileged crowd of titled aristocratic friends, wealthy clergymen and bankers had resulted in substantial business successes for the higher end of their goods such as fine worsteds, silks and damasks. John was one of the first in the north of England to embrace jacquard weaving, allowing for mechanical design to appear for the first time outside the laborious rather plain effects of hand-loom weaving. He had installed one of the first steam-powered operations in the area boasting an enormous 12-feet diameter fly-wheel complete with three-storey mill drive shafts which was the envy of many a mill owner. The gifted John had also discovered a talent for design through periodicals and library reference books and his samples were already winning acclaim and orders from far afield – recently from French and Belgian importers of fine fabrics for the fashion trade, some of whom were due to visit that day.

From birth, Eli had attempted to exert a controlling influence on his eldest son whilst John, through fierce independence and a mother's love and support, had developed into a quite different son from his weaker, more easily subjugated brothers. Poetry, reading and a mastery of language skills together with an appreciation of fine music marked John out as a very different son from all of his siblings.

His brother, James, on the other hand, was an obedient, sober-minded, sound-working, reliable son created in his father's image and Eli's loss of him at the early age of thirty-seven, just four years later in 1852 from a ruptured peptic ulcer was a sad blow and meant that all of their father's efforts, and ultimately his largesse, were then channelled into grooming his only other son, Thomas, then twenty-nine, into the wildly successful, hugely wealthy son he was to become.

Indeed the humourless dull-as-ditch-water Thomas, Lord of the Manor of Midgley, was to die aged sixty-five in 1884, leaving a substantial property portfolio and £13,744 in cash alone – approximately £6.5 million in early 21st century currency.

Thomas also had a wilful spite to hate John's free-thinking way of life – and was jealous of his good looks, for Thomas had inherited the mean facial features of his father complete with hang-dog expression and his rather unpleasant manner of speech. Fanny Brearley took delight in impersonating Thomas and was once nearly caught giving an impression, demonstrating his known parsimony and meanness whilst utilising a droopy narrow carrot for his nose! "Two guineas a year Mistwess Bwearley? For a misewable extwa store woom, and what would I need that for?"

"I'd show you, Master Thomas, if you'd let me. I'd blow more than the wax out of your ears and send you away with a right story to tell your mean-faced misewable girlfriend, that po-faced, so genteel, lady Mary Ann!" she cackled.

Mary Ann Gledhill was a long-time fiancée of Thomas, whom he didn't marry for even a further eight years, in 1856, at the age of thirty-six, the delay causing much ribaldry in many quarters, not least from Fanny who, jealous of her education and breeding, did her usual impersonations of Thomas, whilst revelling in the double-barrelled possibilities of his 'pwonunciation' of 'Ma-wy-Ann!' "Oh! Mawy-Ann, what fine bwests you don't have! And you getting mawwied, if he ever pwoposes, to a right Tit!"

Young brother James was the apple of his father's eye. Open always to a father's advice and guidance, he grew in the image of his father, living alongside him at High Lees in Midgley, but lacked his incisiveness and sound business sense and was always in awe of his father's ease in acquiring property and building a fortune, around and far beyond the expanding worsted manufacturing side of their joint businesses.

And so it happened sadly through the only-too-prevalent disease of tuberculosis and ulcers, that four years later brother James was lowered, as the first occupant, into a brand new cabinet grave prominently placed beside the entrance pathway to St. Mary's church in Luddenden, to be joined only by his beloved mother and father in their due time.

And what of father Eli? How to describe this leviathan of a bluff, successful early-Victorian figure? A gentleman by acquisition and assumption rather than birth, Eli was well on his way to amassing a vast property portfolio in his time to ultimately bestow farms, acres of land and property, stretching as far as Haworth, together with his considerable largess of money, on each and every one of his ten remaining children; which quite noticeably only marginally included his by-then disowned son John, but bestowed son Thomas and every one of his eight sisters with vast money, land and property inheritance, at a time when the women's ownership automatically became their husbands' and was only permissible personally in their own right through the Married Women's Property Act of 1870.

But how to describe Eli? Medium height, about five feet nine inches and stocky, with a florid complexion and large stomach and adequately, yet never smartly, clothed. He was sixty-five that day in 1848. Mutton-chop whiskers, moustache and a startlingly white full head of hair singled him out from his fellow man easily. Blunt, even brusque in manner, he never suffered fools gladly and ruled over his family, including his wife Grace, with the proverbial rod of iron. Several beatings as a child had never cowed John, however, who to his cost, though, with come credit ultimately, had developed into an original creative thinker, bon viveur and general man-about-town who had acquired artists, sculptors and writers into his talented circle of friends. His mother doted over him as her first-born son and especially warmed to his independence of character and determination to be his own man.

She was totally unaware that he had fathered a son at the age of just twenty-one with one of his father's weavers' daughters, a bobbin-girl at High Lees. Many others were also unaware that the now twenty year-old William Foster, John's apprentice moving goods up to the Piece Hall that morning was in fact the product of that illicit liaison.

John and Mary's children were his mother's favourites, with her namesake, their first-born daughter, little Grace, having many sleepovers at High Lees. During these visits Grace learned to become an accomplished cook, seamstress and embroiderer, skills which would prove invaluable to the family's survival in their soon-to-be enforced exile in York.

Eli was the sole owner of all family production at High Lees, above Midgley was his home and textile mill and a stone quarry behind the house produced additional income. An ancient dwelling called Struglar's Hall, since demolished, also occupied this same site. Eli and his family were resident in it initially, following the purchase from Gervase Alexander, a well-known Halifax surgeon, in 1806 and all of his children's births were recorded as being at this hall. The production units here were substantial and were run by Eli and his sons Thomas and James.

Across the valley in the village of Sowerby, John headed up the large textile mill at Higgin Chamber in Boulderclough. Twelve windows along its side and three storeys high, the mill would have stood out to anyone viewing across the Calder Valley from a wide distance. The mill is no longer there, having been destroyed by fire on 5th September 1856, but the deep mill dam and its workings are very much in evidence today, standing testament to the lasting qualities and fine construction techniques of the time. The purity of the water in the dam, collected from the hills and aquifers beyond was the essential ingredient for fine wool and worsted manufacture; for washing, combing, spinning and dyeing and the resultant high quality of the fabrics was always in keen demand by a discerning market located both nationally and internationally. The further extension of the dam to incorporate steam production was the single most important element to all of this, marking Halifax out as one of the earliest entrants into the industrial revolution and Higgin Chamber itself was at the apex of industrialisation in the area at that time.

It also marked itself out as a target for Chartists' discontentment pointing the way toward mechanisation and the consequent laying off of labourers both skilled and unskilled.

It was about this time that interest for both buyers and sellers at The Piece Hall was starting to wane and visiting customers, often from overseas, were increasingly being introduced to the production end of the business. And what better place to entertain and show off both your elegant home and an impressive production facility, could there have been than High Lees and Higgin Chamber? Cottage industry was now well behind the major producers and the first dawnings of the powered industrial revolution had already commenced for the Titteringtons.

John stood at the doorway of number 63, surveying the scene. Traders and customers alike milled around, buying food cooked on braziers and an assortment of buttons, trimmings and general accessories and off-cut pieces of cloth from the market stalls of traders not able to afford or even need the luxury of a room.

Beyond and over to the east was the towering Beacon Hill with its iron brazier always on standby to pass on momentous news along a beacon chain stretching the length of the country. News of the scuppering of the Spanish Armada over 250 years before, at the end of the fifteenth century, was just such an occasion, recognising Halifax's significance in the chain before any of its neighbours in being at the forefront of commerce, communication and indeed culture itself, in the form of internationally renowned visiting concert virtuosi such as Franz Liszt, who had performed before an ecstatic audience in the town seven years earlier.

Also up there in Southowram was Law Hill School, where his friend Branwell Brontë's sister, Emily, had taught ten years before and had suffered the strain of working under such appallingly long hours. It was at John's third-born, Hannah Maria's christening, in Cragg Vale that he first met Branwell's three sisters, and Emily had travelled down from the school in December 1838 to join in the celebrations and see her brother act as godfather to his friend's daughter. That John and Mary had also chosen the name Maria to honour Branwell's dear mother and dead older sister in childhood was a joy to all of them.

Glancing beneath the beacon, John got a slight tinge of conscience looking at the steeple of Halifax Parish Church rising above the Piece Hall's east wall, where he married and exchanged vows with Mary on the 31st of May 1836, just twelve years before. Coming from a successful textile producing family who lived and worked in their Shibden Mill estate, in the eponymous valley beyond Beacon Hill, John had fallen head over heels for her one day, seeing her at the Piece Hall helping her father John to set up his room. John Holdsworth's room was around toward the south side of the Piece Hall and John would go over to greet him at some time during the day whilst making sure his clandestine meetings with the voluptuous Fanny escaped his notice – again!

Little had John realised on his wedding day, twelve years before, how his vows would be challenged and exposed as a sham, so readily and so soon, through the weaknesses of the flesh, and it was that thought that caused him to check the time on the steeple clock – five minutes to eleven! Time to make the trip up to the top floor!

His indiscretion in producing his son William when he was just twenty himself with his father's mill bobbin-girl

Mary Foster still haunted him – especially as he was reminded of it each time he had made his court-enforced bastardy payment of two shillings a week to support the child over many years. A forced marriage was considered out of the question by Eli at the time, yet wouldn't have been illegal, even though young Mary was only thirteen years-old at the time of young William's birth.

William had since become the apple of his father's eye and though still unrecognised as a relative to many, John continued to guide and support him – his 21st birthday was due in three months' time on April 12th and John would be with him on market days, and indeed on most other days, too, since he was an apprentice weaver at Higgin Chamber and spent much time with the family; the children believing him to be a distant cousin of their father's from Lancashire – their mother had always known the truth.

Checking below as he walked along the top corridor to be sure he wasn't being watched from room 63, or by his father-in-law, John tried not to look at or remind himself of the Parish Church and slipped inside room 29 without a second glance. It was official business anyway, wasn't it? And he was looking to 'expand his business' – 'with 'more storage', if anyone asked. Only about 200 of the mainly lower rooms of the 315 available were actually in use so the chances of anybody coming along were slim.

Adjusting to the light inside, John had thought he had arrived first, but a throaty gentle cough told him otherwise; Fanny had already entered room 29, and blinking over toward the back corner, John's eyes met with the splendid sight of her side-on silhouette – completely naked to the waist!

"Fanny! You do it to me every time! Never the same tricks twice and always such a joy to behold – and on such a chilly morning. And your attributes standing to attention for me! Come close and let me warm you."

John took her close to his body and enveloped her in his sturdy great-coat. As he touched and caressed her gently, she exhaled another satisfied sigh and settled to returning his ministrations.

Fanny had prepared for the meeting by placing some discarded pieces of old woollen cloth on the floor and John lifted her slender body and carried her over to the pieces and laid her gently down as a mother would lay a new born child into its crib.

With another piece of soft cloth, he deftly covered both of them with a sweep of his arm whilst each kissed and urgently grappled to remove the remaining items of clothing which remained to obstruct their increasingly urgent need of congress.

With the coupling successfully completed there would be little delay from such heightened excitement and John, sensing Fanny had entered the final straight, gave one final effort toward triggering her completion.

"Go for it Fanny! Release the banshee!" he implored, as always, and without a second's hesitation she shuddered, shook and gave out the familiar roar, a half-scream almost, which never failed and John always found so totally irresistible. It produced for himself a climax so intense and so unlike anything he had ever experienced with anyone before, including his own dear wife.

Beethoven himself could not have conducted the final explosions in his 1812 Overture better, and only Thomas Bradley's foot-thick walls and stout door prevented their illicit liaison facing total exposure to the gathered throng in the Piece Hall below that day.

John adjusted his clothes, straightened his hair and stepped out into the sunlight, telling Fanny to wait a few minutes before leaving to avoid drawing anyone's attention to their clandestine visit.

But drawing attention to themselves was to turn out to be the least of their worries – at least on this occasion, for little did either of them realise that nature had already taken its productive course, due to John's less-than-careful use of the wholly mistimed and undesirable practice anyway of withdrawal and consequently Fanny would discover in due course that she had been well and truly impregnated.

Reaching 63, Rustick, in time for his 12 o'clock appointment, John entered and checked he had his samples and paperwork ready for negotiation with his buyer.

Young William had prepared the samples in order of price and by quality and Monsieur Dubois from Brussels would not be disappointed with the journey he had made over three days, which included a rough crossing of the North Sea from Amsterdam to Hull.

But first came Israel Silver, a shipping agent from Liverpool, who the Titteringtons had not met before. New to importing wool, Israel was nevertheless an experienced import agent who had a cargo of fine Indian wool just arrived in Liverpool. He carried a sample of the wool in a brown paper packet and John examined it by teasing it or drawing it out carefully with the fingers of each hand, whilst securing the wool between the bases of his thumbs. This test of attenuation of the fibres was always used by wool manufacturers and the high quality John was looking for was indeed there to justify an anticipated premium price. Worsted manufacture could only result from a fleece of the longest individual fibres which allowed carding or drawing to hold a continuous filament together in the subsequent spinning process; individual fibre lengths of no less than three inches, especially good Indian wool, permitted the finest fibres to be drawn and held together without breaking, clearly marking out the difference between a silky-fine worsted fibre, from the more common bulky but durable, usually domestic grown, shorter-fibred wools used by John's father and brothers to weave general purpose hard-wearing shalloon cloths.

Bustling around in the room were his father, both brothers and his friend, Branwell Brontë, who had dropped by to say hello and to set up the evening's entertainment at a local hostelry – usually either The Old Cock or The Talbot, both within a stone's throw of the market itself.

Eli, whilst holding forth with a buyer of many years' standing was receiving an equal measure of bluster as a piece price was being finally agreed through hard bargaining. "Tha'd take the clothes from my back, Joshua Broadbent, if I'd let thee! But go on then, I'll take it and put my grandchildren out onto t'street!"

"Alright, Mr Silver." John shook his hand "I'll raise a promissory note to cover the deposit and come over to inspect the shipment and make the final payment in Liverpool when we meet tomorrow. Young William will go up to the bank now and return within the hour." Introducing William to Israel Silver as his 'young nephew', he asked them to agree a suitable time and place for the transaction. He bade him 'good day' until they met again and went over to talk with Branwell.

John's brothers came and went during this conversation and generally hovered around talking to each other. They most certainly did not converse with Branwell, so as not to incur the wrath of their father, who despised him for his wild ways and drunkenness which were well known in the town, as was his known fondness for opiates as much as alcohol. His complete messing up of his job as Luddenden Foot station master had particularly angered Eli, who had been instrumental in getting him his employment in the first place at John's request. As a shareholder, he had not been sorry to endorse his dismissal for gross incompetence. John had, however, prevailed on his father not to pursue charges of theft, as a personal favour for a friend, but even this would be held over him he was fairly certain in due course.

And he a parson's son! A reprobate! As well as an intellect far beyond comprehension or even mild understanding by John's brothers or his father. Even if his brothers had wished to displease their father by engaging him, there would have been little point in attempting conversation, for mere platitudes were of no interest to Branwell, who would have simply ignored them and walked away. James had in fact once made that mistake in the library above The Lord Nelson in Luddenden village, with their brother-in-law John Murgatroyd and Branwell had started sketching him and writing in his notebook as though he was invisible or didn't exist at all!

John, on the other hand, was well-read and well-able to converse with Branwell on a wide range of topics and whilst lacking a classical education, he could more than make up for it with a razor-sharp sense of irony and wit by giving bullet-like retorts to any situation which presented itself. Branwell was a firm friend of John's family, and as godfather to John's second daughter, Hannah Maria, he was a regular guest at Higgin Chamber on stopovers into and out of Halifax from Haworth, before and after his employment at both Luddenden Foot and Sowerby Bridge railway stations.

Branwell had overheard and taken a great interest in the conversation about Liverpool and had already imagined a fine trip over with convivial company on his favourite means of transport – the railway! Always keen to embrace conversation of rail travel, he had talked many times with Francis Grundy, an engineer on the railway who had been instrumental, along with John, in gaining him employment as stationmaster. It was they who jointly saved him from disgrace after he was dismissed from the latter of the two posts for incompetence. Perpetual poetry writing and sketching had distracted him from mundane, boring and repetitious duties, but mere incompetence was a whole lot better than the dishonesty associated with the financial discrepancy he might otherwise have stood accused of, had friends of some standing, in particular Eli Titterington, not vouched for him over irregularities in his station accounts.

Branwell took his leave and said his farewell to John, ignoring the rest of the Tit clan (his name for them) and arranged to meet him at The Talbot Inn for a 'club' meeting after the market closed.

Monsieur Claude Dubois, an overseas buyer, was delighted with John's designs and samples, and he ordered in excess of one thousand pounds worth of fine worsted cloth to be delivered into his Brussels warehouse over the next year; the largest single export order received to date by any of the Titteringtons. Two more customers, one from

Paris and another from London ordered more, which when combined together totalled more than the Brussels shipment. All in all it was a day to celebrate for John, who had been justly rewarded for his choice of designs and colours produced for discerning clients operating in such high fashion markets. Halifax was never likely to be a centre for fashion, but with flair and an eye to market demands, a match could be made between solid Yorkshire industry and the fashion-conscious capitals of Europe.

John Titterington possessed both the flair and the keen eye for design and colour necessary, to move the Titterington mills' offerings to another level.

Chapter Six

Haworth – Another Death

The re-living of the drama of 1848 continued to play out in John's mind to occupy his waking, and indeed he spent many of his sleepless nights at York Castle Gaol, tossing and turning, trying to identify the root cause of any of it.

How had things turned so tragically wrong for him in the space of just one year? The fateful trip to Liverpool to buy the cargo of wool in January and the impregnation of Fanny Brearley. His arrest after the fight with the barmaid in The Anchor and Shuttle in Luddenden Foot in August. His friend Branwell Brontë's tragic early death at only thirty-one in September, which had so distressed his children, losing their favourite Uncle Brannie, followed by his own father's so public disowning in October. Then his mother's death in November and the embarrassment of meeting family and friends at her funeral, not to mention the vulture-like all-pervading presence of his creditors gathering there to plan how best to pick over his bones when they had felled him. There were many pointers and all had contributed in some part to his fall from grace, but at the heart of it was, even here in church, his father's ever-malevolent all-consuming presence.

Had he himself been the big disappointment? The cause of his mother's death; or was that down to the years of oppression and bullying by his father?

His disinheritance with its inherent public disgrace in October, at his father's hand, would prove surely to have been the real catalyst, the reason for his dear mother's demise and the one true proverbial nail in his own coffin!

Had he deserved it anyway, pushing his father to the limit?

And had he caused, or at least hastened Branwell's death by over-indulging him by providing the means to purchase alcohol and laudanum with no thought, or even desire, of ever receiving repayment? His friendship and close family relationship allowed him to broaden his mind in so many ways through spending time with such an erudite, fun-loving, trusted and learned companion.

His attendance at the 'reprobate' Bran's funeral in Haworth with Mary and the older two girls might also even have added to his father's anger just the month before he disowned him.

Rev. Tom very much enjoyed hearing of his old university friend, Patrick Brontë, and the tales of his talented offspring. He did his best to assure John that his friend Branwell's death was not of his doing but was that of the Almighty and that sometimes these things were beyond mere man's control.

And even while John was dreaming away his early countless useless hours in gaol, over in Haworth, things were about to get much worse at the parsonage.

Following Branwell's death in September at just thirty-one years of age and a serious cold infection caught by Emily at his funeral, an October letter from Charlotte Brontë recorded that: *"...all of the family had suffered harassing coughs and colds from the dreaded cold easterly winds,"* but then went on, more worriedly as it happened, to say to her friend Ellen Nussey: *"I feel much more uneasy about my sisters than myself, I told you Emily was ill in my last letter and she has not rallied. She is very ill."*

And again on 16th November Charlotte reported that Emily had *"difficulty breathing and had pains in her chest."*

And so as John came to terms with his early days in gaol and as Christmas of 1848 approached, over in Haworth, the final hours of Emily Brontë's short life were approaching.

On the morning of Tuesday 19th December, that very week, Emily rose at seven, dressed slowly, burnt her comb as she dropped it in the fire and walked downstairs.

She had refused all treatment and medicine sent over by the doctor and further said she would have *"no poisoning doctor near me."* By midday she was worse and only then did she finally concede, saying: *"If you will send for a doctor I will see him now."*

Charlotte reported that her dog, Keeper *"lay at the side of her dying-bed."*

The now two-month decline in Emily's health, taking no medication until this her last day, finally took its toll and at 2.00pm, aged just thirty and whilst sitting on a sofa bed at the parsonage, she took her final laboured breath.

Charlotte wrote sadly, yet resolutely to her friend, Mr Williams, her publisher's reader: *"Tuesday night and morning saw the last hours, the last agonies, proudly endured to the end. Yesterday, Emily Jane Brontë died in the arms of those who loved her."*

A servant at the parsonage said: *"Miss Emily died of a broken heart for love of her brother,"* and the local carpenter reported later that at only sixteen inches wide hers was the narrowest coffin he had ever made for an adult.

Emily was never to know the fame she would achieve with her one and only novel *Wuthering Heights,* published just a year before her death. The success of her sister, Charlotte's *Jane Eyre,* had prompted her to publish her own book, written some two years before, and whilst public acclaim was given firstly to *Jane Eyre,* it was Emily's novel that ultimately won the accolades to become regarded as the best of all the sisters' works. Mental and physical cruelty, religious hypocrisy, morality, social class and gender inequality all challenged strict early Victorian ideals at publication and met with mixed reviews when first published. The English poet and painter Dante Gabriel Rossetti referred to *Wuthering Heights* as *"...a fiend of a book – an incredible monster...the action is laid in hell, – only, it seems, places and people have English names there."*

Never having left her home since catching the cold at Branwell's funeral, Emily's own funeral was attended only by family members and servants – and her beloved little dog, Keeper, who sat in a church pew during the funeral service, and who sat and howled in front of Emily's empty room for weeks after her death.

The innovative and sophisticated structure of *Wuthering Heights* puzzled critics and readers alike, and the book received mixed reviews with some condemning it as a portrayal of amoral passion.

Emily and Branwell could well have been writing their own epitaphs in *Wuthering Heights* when Lockwood looks down at the graves of Catherine and Heathcliffe, then overgrown by heather and moss:

"I lingered round them, under that benign sky: watched the moths fluttering among the heath and harebells; listened to the soft wind breathing through the grass; and wondered how anyone could ever imagine unquiet slumbers for the sleepers in that quiet earth."

Chapter Seven

The Talbot Inn

Young William loaded up the remaining pieces and the samples and set off back to Higgin Chamber while John locked up at the Piece Hall. Eli and James had already left to return to High Lees and Thomas had retired to The Old Cock with another of their customers to have supper and finalise a regular deal for several pieces of stuff cloth to be woven and shipped over to Manchester. His evening would be, like himself, cold, clinical and abstemious and would end after supper and possibly just one glass of wine at about nine o'clock with both retiring to their rooms in readiness for an early start for their respective business duties to resume the next morning.

Down the next street toward Woolshops, a quite different scene was unfolding which could be heard almost as far away as The Old Cock itself!

Always favoured throughout the day by market traders and visitors alike due to its proximity to the Piece Hall's north gate, several of the inn's customers were already in high spirits, literally. Rough guffawing accompanied by cronish cackling split the chill air as even more people crammed in to imbibe and make merry and to either drown out the memory of a poor day's trading or celebrate a good one. It would prove impossible as usual to detect which was which!

Passing swiftly past the public bar areas and in toward the more respectable private rooms, John acknowledged a few familiar faces and headed in to the cosy fire-lit room normally reserved by him for a few friends to hold their meetings and enjoy some food away from what quite quickly was going to turn into an unseemly rabble.

One face he recognised was that of a cackling crone called Catherine Rogers, usually referred to as Irish Kate, a well-known ne'er-do-well regularly appearing before the magistrates and always well up to inventing a credible story to extract a drink from any poor unsuspecting soul. John's cousin, Thomas Titterington, from Mytholmroyd, an illegitimate son of his father's sister Abigail, had recently been such a target and 'lost' the enormous sum of £76 to her wiles, but the magistrates whilst trying her for another misdemeanour in the same public house, The Lamb, failed to agree and she escaped punishment for this crime at least. She recognised John and looked hastily the other way to share a vulgar joke with another of her cackling friends.

Thomas's mother, Abigail Titterington, John's aunt, an emancipated lady in male-centred times, was landlady of The White Lion in Mytholmroyd. She was also a timber merchant alongside her son, John's cousin, Thomas. John called for a drink occasionally to her pub meeting up with Branwell on his way down from the turnpike road between Howarth and Halifax, and they both enjoyed her company and revelled in her outspoken independence and invariably quite fulsome and colourful stories, accompanied by a richness of language more akin to a bawdy men's night. Branwell was a favourite of Abigail's and could count on a free drink or two in return for a reading from his notebook. Recognisable passages from what would later be known as his sister Emily's book *'Wuthering Heights'* were always enjoyed and his wager-winning two-handed simultaneous writing of Latin and Greek were legend wherever performed. Most wouldn't even be able to read or write in English, of course, but the different characters would be apparent and his sheer dexterity of penmanship must have been highly impressive to the illiterate.

And to Aunt Abigail who was a beneficiary from the bets on more than one occasion!

Her son, Thomas, had a curious pedigree which father Eli would never discuss, on pain of death, to anyone foolish enough to broach the subject in his presence. That his very existence came about through an incestuous liaison seemed to be borne out by his not being what was generally known as 'the full shilling'. No bastardy awards were ever requested, suggesting a Titterington in-house deal and his non-conformist baptism, whilst not being totally unusual in fairly recent post-Wesleyan times, appeared to be an attempt at obfuscation. Even Abigail's own will later added confusion to his actual relationship to his mother, who referred to him as both her 'son' and 'adopted son' in the same document.

That the father was also a closely related Titterington seemed not to be in doubt. Baptised by Abigail, some would say defiantly, away from prying eyes at Luddenden St. Mary's church, in her own father's name, at Booth Independent chapel.

Cousin Thomas's mental state and physical disability from birth, in conjunction with an overly keen indulgence in alcohol was highlighted in a court case in which he himself had brought before the magistrates to gain recompense for some timber stolen by one John Smith from the store-yard behind the pub. Thomas, as prosecutor in the case against John Smith, failed to appear to support charges on the day of the trial and an immediate search for him was demanded by the magistrate to avoid wasting the court's time.

Discovered (euphemistically) *"...under the spreading branches of the royal oak..."* (i.e. drunk) he was *"...after some delay, hauled into court staggering drunk – his appearance being the signal for laughter, mingled with indignation."*

The Halifax Guardian at the time continued: *"He could not be got into the witness-box, he was so helpless, and the moment Colonel Pollard (the chairman), saw him, he sent the prisoner John Smith about his business and instead ordered the superintendent to lay an information against Titterington for being drunk and he was then fined 5 shillings with the intimation that if he did not pay it instantly he must spend six hours in the stocks. The simpleton continued bowing solemnly to the bench after the manner of a pot Chinese mandarin, and endeavoured to make them understand he 'wasn't drunk; not a bit of it.' The whole affair did not occupy above a minute or two and was excessively ludicrous."*

And as if the use of the word 'simpleton' hadn't been enough, the court heard in conclusion that: *"Titterington is the same greenhorn who a few months ago was robbed of £76 by some disreputable women at the Lamb Inn."*

Thomas was to be found dead, some ten years later in 1859, aged fifty-one, at the foot of the stone steps behind the White Lion. An autopsy, had one been carried out by the coroner's court, would have undoubtedly found that he was drunk at the time.

Words such as *'simpleton'* and *'greenhorn'* and the somewhat odd behaviour doing the 'mandarin'- bowing, indicate something beyond a merely alcohol-fuelled aberration and fuelled the vexed question of who actually sired Thomas. Abigail was later to marry Henry Patchett and again, possibly to avoid attention, they chose to exchange their vows, seven miles away, at the ancient parish church in Elland, where they would not be known and young seven-year-old Thomas's 'irregularities' might go unnoticed at the ceremony.

There is little doubt that Thomas was in fact the product of an illicit act between his mother and his grandfather; Thomas Titterington was both John's cousin *and* uncle.

Passing between the rooms, John bumped into Fanny Brearley who squeezed his bottom surreptitiously and winked at him as she passed through a narrow passageway.

"Any assets to expand upon again tonight, Johnnie?" she teased and John responded with a whisper and a peck on her cheek. "It'll be a damned sight cosier tonight Fanny, if you're up for a visit to room two after our meeting? Should be through by eleven if you can keep sober enough until then? I'll get a drink sent through for you now and ask Mrs Sugden to put it to my account when you want more."

"Never could get enough of me, could you John?" she responded with a glint in her eye and returned to the main bar where she would load yet more purchases, for herself and her friends, onto an already hefty bar bill of John's.

Little did either of them know that birth control would be quite unnecessary that night since Fanny was already ten hours pregnant!

In the private room the fire crackled and roared up. Branwell had already arrived and was busy sketching in his notebook. John could see he was drawing what looked quite clearly to be a naked self-portrait with a hangman's noose around his neck. Was Branwell having one of his morbidity attacks? John noticed a slight shake in his hand as he drew with less confidence than usual. How long had he been here? The drink he had in front of him would certainly be on John's account and was seemingly taking its toll already. Was it his first? Probably not. John had seen evidence of the DTs before in local public houses, but usually in people much older than Branwell. Back in Howarth they had been referred to euphemistically, or most probably naively by his family as 'fainting fits' – delirium tremens would not be understood and in any case would be an unsuitable topic best avoided altogether in 'polite' society anywhere – and especially at a parsonage!

Mrs Sugden, the landlady, was already chasing a worried Branwell for a hefty bar bill which was giving him concern coupled with an unwillingness to ask John Titterington to pick up the payment yet again.

Talk all day at the market had been of another Patrick – Patrick Reid, the notorious twenty-year-old Irish Mirfield triple-murderer, publicly hanged the Saturday previously before a crowd of over thirty thousand, drawn from as far as York.

"Did you know John, they say that Patrick Reid occupied the self and same cell as Dick Turpin at York Castle gaol prior to his execution?" John remembered now, only too vividly, Branwell asking him that question and here just under a year later, he now languished himself...and in the same cell for all he knew.

Many present that day in Halifax had visited the public hanging and reported that Patrick Reid had admitted his guilt and publicly exonerated one of his fellow suspects, another Irishman, Michael McCabe.

"'oward, t'county 'angman really made Reid suffer," commented a customer at the bar, "...covering 'is 'ead, tying 'is legs and releasing t'bolt didn't despatch 'im; t' rope were too slack and 'e was strangled slowly and kicked and twitched for ages 'til 'e finally croaked."

McCabe, though completely innocent, was still transported to Australia by a less than sympathetic judge, returning in 1880 to live in Huddersfield.

"Serve Reid right," said one of the cackling crones in The Talbot bar, "'anging was too good for 'im!"

And did Branwell have a premonition of his own death at The Talbot that night? In his sketch the hangman's noose was firmly positioned around his own neck for a quick exit – with no slack evident. Just eight months later poor Bran himself would indeed be joining Patrick Reid in the next world. Joining the two that night would be the sculptor Joseph Bentley Leyland and the carver and gilder Joe Drake.

Mrs Mary Sugden, the landlady of The Talbot, came through to check the fire and greeted Branwell cheerily.

Turning to John she said "Master John, how the time flies, yet another market day and you're here again to grace my premises and extend your already large bar bill! How would I manage without such fine custom from you, though I can't say the same for your penniless friends?"

She pulled no punches and gave them all similarly brusque notice that whilst she enjoyed their company, as her husband had before, her patience was wearing thin and her goodwill was not to be trifled with. Whilst John always settled his account in due course, his impecunious friends did not and they needed chasing regularly. Branwell had a particularly large bar debt at this time, which John was not aware of and even he, had he known, would have been loathed to just settle up without question, as he had often done in the past.

Branwell, sitting by the fireside, looked up; "Your father was very sociable again today, John, I couldn't help but notice; not to mention your two po-faced brothers who always look too frightened to say boo! to a goose when your father's around. How he must hate me being around his eldest boy.

"Me! The failed station-master-cum-irreligious drunkard of a parson's son!"

The four of them, together with the recently deceased Dan Sugden, former landlord and husband of Mary, had formed themselves into an imitative version of Sir John Dashwood's debauched and highly irreligious 'Hell-Fire Club'. Records show that they had read up on the subject in the library above the Lord Nelson pub in Luddenden village and their weekly meetings would be philosophically antithetical to the moral principles of masonry and deeply offensive to conventionally-minded, God-fearing citizens such as John's father and at least one of his brothers, Thomas, if not both.

A strong alcoholic mixture was always provided for the occasion and this would be a potent concoction of the landlady's choosing. They knew it as *'Hell-Fire Punch.'* Again, after her husband's tradition, Mrs Sugden would provide an appropriately-named supper of her choosing later on, which, at their request, she gave names such as *'Breast of Venus'*, *'Devil's Loin'* and occasionally, *'Holy Ghost Pie'*. Suitably irreverent and ribald comment, often of a sexual nature, would accompany the food. Members would take turns to present a particular topic to the group which John, as president or chairman, would then throw open to dissolute and ribald discussion and debate.

Ridiculing religion was more of joke, yet was certainly meant to, and would, shock the outside world. Members would sometimes come dressed as characters from the bible and Branwell's intentions are clear here in the next sketch he had now moved on to; with or without such dress he saw them all as heroic characters from a variety of historical backgrounds.

The chairman or president of all Hell-Fire Clubs was in fact the devil himself. And John filled this role admirably, extracting the maximum participation from members; the diminishing of the punchbowl's contents corresponding in direct proportion to the increase in the sheer outrageousness of the group! Mrs Sugden twice came in to remind them to tone it down a bit. There were even complaints about the language from the public bar!

The punchbowl was first to enter the room, held loftily and ceremoniously on high by Mrs Sugden. "Now then my fine specimens of manhood, this'll put hairs in places you never even knew you had places!" And with the punchbowl held aloft, she moved dramatically over to the table, failed to notice an outstretched foot, which she inadvertently tripped over, and only just landed the punchbowl onto the table, with John stepping forward and gripping it as though his life depended on it, coming finally to rest with an deep audible gurgling sound…and only the slightest amount of over-spill!

"God's truth! Woman – what the bloody…in the name of all that's holy…what was that? You damned near flooded the place out. Look where you're going, will you, for God's sake!" John screamed.

"Now, now Master John, no need for all that profanity. There's no harm done, I had it all under control, but I swear I was tripped deliberately there. Who was guilty?"

Seeing a much better subject now come into view, Branwell had immediately stopped drawing the mere outline caricatures of the assembled group of characters and had commenced quickly capturing the attendant drama of the near disaster – the rescue of the expensive heady concoction contained in Mrs Sugden's surprise punchbowl!

Even the deceased Sugden had to witness this one! And Branwell accorded him the privilege, including him in the sketch straight away as a more than active participant.

An animated John holding forth was sketched next, and with a swish of his pen, Branwell planted the devil's tail on him, confirming his status as president of the club, the perpetual devil incarnate of the group.

"SUGDENIENSIS", he wrote next to the backward falling Sugden, Branwell's rather appropriately chosen

culprit for tripping his wife up, since all present were well aware that he had indeed suffered from an unfortunate predisposition toward clumsiness after suffering a stroke; stalwart club member Daniel Holgate Sugden had in fact died a year-and-a-half previously, on 2nd July 1846 and would have enjoyed causing such embarrassment to his over-bearing spouse.

'Dan' Sugden was the most famous of the group, providing the musical input to meetings. His absence was not only a great sadness to his wife, Mary, but to the group as a whole.

No ordinary publican, Dan Sugden was also a musician of some note playing the contra-basso/double-bass and was a prominent organist. Associated also with the Halifax Choral Society, he was the first conductor of the widely attended Halifax Sunday School Jubilee Sings, and gave singing lessons to, and appeared with, such notables as the famous 'Calderdale Nightingale', Mrs Susan Sunderland, concentrating on her rendering of sacred music and introducing her to the Halifax Choral Society. Described as one of the ablest musicians in West Yorkshire, he also ran a music academy in Petticoat Lane in Halifax and taught the extrovert lesbian Anne Lister of Shibden Hall to play the flute.

That he should also seemingly rebel against this strongly religious background on club meeting nights at The Talbot added a special piquancy to such occasions for the participants. That John Titterington fulfilled the controlling role amongst artists, sculptors, writers, poets and musicians speaks volumes of the respect he, a mere textile manufacturer, gained from such a talented, albeit impecunious, bunch!

Joe Drake got his usual nickname incorporated as *"DRACO THE FIREDRAKE"*, appended above his sketch, as Branwell connected the Latin form of Drake or Draco to the gilding connotation of the mythical golden fire-breathing dragon, the firedrake. Joe Drake had a studio for his carving and gilding, situated suitably next to Leyland in the Union Cross Inn yard, barely 100 yards up the road, as many of their commissions were awarded jointly.

"PHIDIAS" was a fifth century-BC sculptor, generally acknowledged as the greatest Greek sculptor of them all, and Branwell properly recognises a high level of skill for which J.B. Leyland, 'JB' to his friends, got little respect or credit. Previously serving time as a bankrupt, when Halifax had its own debtors' prison, the artistically unrecognised Leyland was never paid more than a simple gravestone inscription carver's wages, yet his works that remain today are acclaimed as works of Phidiasian beauty worthy of the great Athenium himself.

Leyland, born in 1811 and aged thirty-seven, first made his name at the age of just twenty-one, modelling a statue of Spartacus 'at great size'. Described at the time as a 'most striking' work of art at the Manchester Exhibition of 1832, it accorded him a rarely given permission the following year to study and draw the Elgin Marbles, on display at the British Museum in London since 1817.

Joseph Bentley Leyland was to die penniless, however, three years later in a debtors' prison again, aged just forty.

Lastly in the group sketch, *'St. Patrick alias Lord Peter'* is yet another self-portrait of Patrick Branwell Brontë himself, with a nod to humour, undoubtedly poking irreligious fun at Roman Catholicism and the then Pope Pius IX (1846-1878), alongside an Angrian-styled Lord

Peter, penned to represent the Catholic-acknowledged and original Pope, Jesus's apostle and disciple, St. Peter; how suitable, and how deliciously irreverent!

Branwell's euphemistic naming of *"St. John in the Wilderness"* in his sketch referred additionally and even more appropriately, along with the reflected humour, to the eponymously named church in Cragg Vale where John's daughter, Hannah, was baptised and Branwell acted as godfather, as well as being a direct reference to the wilderness that John's father was indeed trying to cast him into and furthermore would do, in spades, before the year was out.

Popishly conferring sainthood on the devil himself was also not without its humour!

"That father of yours, John, will see you in Hell alright if you give him half a chance and I'm thinking the wilderness might indeed be preferable my friend!" Branwell added.

The captioning of the sketch is perhaps the most revealing of Branwell's medical condition at the time. The inebriated crossing-out of the miswritten word 'Talbo_' and the addition of 'punch bowl' point to a DT-addled or inebriated brain.

Branwell, rejecting Mrs Sugden's version of events, after she had left the room, interjected. "Well, you certainly saved the day there, John! Tripping over her dead husband's appendage didn't help either, whatever she claimed to have done!" Branwell held up his sketch for his friends to see the joke, eliciting huge guffaws of laughter!

"You captured Sugden alright there Bran – a spitting image of the poor old lad. God rest his soul. He'll be teaching the angels to sing a right tune now and that's for certain!" said Leyland.

"So who's coming on the trip to Liverpool with John and me?" Branwell asked, after explaining the meeting he had overheard at the Piece Hall that morning. He had already told John before Leyland and Joe arrived that he would like to accompany him if he wouldn't mind; a trip on his favourite means of transport, the railway, was too good a chance to miss.

John's acceptance of his companionship, of course, implied his willingness to fund his day out without need to elucidate.

"Well that's perfect, because Joe and I have an invitation to work at the cathedral there and we're to be paid to visit the elders to discuss the commission," said Leyland.

And so it was agreed that a trip would be made by all four of them and John said to Joe and Leyland, "Bran and I will call by the Union Cross in the morning to agree the date we go, but my shipment is due in four days' time, so I need to be there for that."

Mrs Sugden excelled herself that night with supper, producing her always popular *'Breast of Venus'* for the meeting – called just plain belly pork by anybody else, it came with crackling and roasted vegetables and ribald comments could never be avoided by John's friends with obvious and various vulgar connections made between the Venus nipples and John's surname!

"Chew on 'em Tit. We won't tell Mary!"

"Or Fanny Brearley!" came a knowing comment from Leyland, badly disguised in a stage cough from behind his hand, for everyone nevertheless to hear, for she was no secret between this group of close friends.

The evening ended with a rousing and fairly drunken rendition of a few bawdy and irreligious songs and the assembled friends departed, staggering to their various beds around the town. As was usual, John had booked a room for himself and an extra room for Branwell at The Talbot – well away from his own so as not to have the banshee disturbing his sleep!

At least that had been the plan, but in his present condition there would be no arousing the beast that night.

Chapter Eight

The Rev. Thomas Williams

John had made a good choice from the start of his prison life, largely for cost reasons, to pay for a dual cell occupancy and the Reverend Thomas Williams had preceded his preference with the same choice, made for the same reason.

Arriving himself two months before John, he had spent only those few weeks with his former cellmate, a lawyer from Harrogate who had gained his early release through an old colleague paying his debts.

'Tom', as he insisted John call him from the outset, was a genuine man of the people, hugely popular with his parishioners back in Beverley. They would all speak fondly of him and remember his many kindnesses, concerns and empathies at times of family sadness and his joy at sharing fully in their baptismal or marriage celebrations.

At sixty-eight years of age, his gregarious nature, and his bachelor status had allowed him unfettered freedom to develop a thoroughly outgoing personality away from the often introverted constraints of family life sometimes unsuited to a man of the cloth. In this regard he was more akin to a celibate Roman Catholic priest than to clerics of his own persuasion.

With a wealthy family upbringing he had taken easily to a genteel life of privilege and had pleased his parents and his father especially, by gaining a place at Cambridge University where among the many other sons of wealthy parentage, he was afforded an opportunity for indulgence and the chance to pass away a few years pleasantly before returning home to his family's estate in South Wales.

It was here where Tom got a taste for some wild living away from a strict father. He quickly fell in with a crowd of drinkers and gamblers, the latter proving his true weakness which he shielded admirably from his parishioners in Beverley, but which caught him out ultimately through the vindictive actions of an excessively indebted York gambling-house owner applying his first-mover option without the slightest chance of expecting a return. Tom had seen gambling bring down many men over the years, from the rich young aristocrats at Cambridge, to the landed gentry around east Yorkshire, where an entire estate could be lost on the turn of a single card or whilst indulging in some random game of *noir et rouge*.

Never so hypocritical as to specifically preach about the evils of gambling, a casual observer might have never been aware of the supremely well-disguised *bête noir* in Tom's psyche.

John told Tom that he, too, had engaged in gambling many times with wealthy shooting party guests staying over at country houses around York and Harrogate. The *'Games Lists – County of York'* in the Leeds and Hull newspapers attested to gun licences being granted to knights of the realm, politicians, aristocrats and wealthy members of the clergy. John, too, in successive years in the early 1840s was recorded among them, paying £4 0s 10d – about £3,000 today, for an annual gun licence to rub shoulders with the well-heeled in society who were capable of gambling for dizzyingly high stakes.

"I could have lost heavily at gambling, too, Tom, but managed to survive by the skin of my teeth on a few occasions. My downfall was never being in control of my own destiny, with a father who wouldn't share my ambitions and support me to expand and diversify production in the mills. My rather wild side with alcohol and the ladies was the catalyst, alongside which, according to my father anyway, I listed some fairly Bohemian friends, such as one Branwell Brontë!"

Tom's saving grace was the support of several elderly female parishioners to whom he had given devoted service as their parish priest, providing sympathy and succour in their saddest hours and who joyously engaged with him at times of family celebration. Over their lifetimes, he had become like a member of many families and in his hour of need, they would not let him down and provided his lifeblood – a veritable legion of these ladies visiting him daily, supplying him with their home-cooked specialities typical of the fare combined with the companionship he had enjoyed so many times visiting their own homes. They would not make a judgment on his personal mores or on his subsequent fall from grace, it was not their right to do so, and by their very deeds they saw their roles as entirely appropriate to the Christian ethic.

On the very first day John and Tom spent together, a strong friendship was struck up between them and, learning of John's home's proximity to Haworth, Tom asked if he knew a fellow-clergyman friend of long standing – Patrick Brontë, who had been with him at Cambridge.

"Patrick Brontë indeed? I certainly knew him. He became a firm friend at St. John's and we spent many hours discussing religion. I questioned my own beliefs at that time, and it was only through Patrick's persuasion and his deep convictions that I finally came to the Ministry. My own degree from Cambridge paled into insignificance next to the achievements of such a gifted scholar. He also got me to take my studies more seriously and spend less time with the undergraduates, a few of whom were intent on debauchery, hell-raising and not much else."

Having once invited Patrick, not long out of Cambridge, to preach for him in Beverley, they had stayed in touch and visited each other on many occasions, covering for holiday or sickness absences. Tom had enjoyed seeing all of the family growing up over the years and was always made to feel at home at his parsonage, but had lost touch over the last five or so years, finding travel more difficult in later life.

"I visited Patrick in both of his first parishes, at Thornton and Hartshead, where his Evangelical zeal was hard to resist; he has strengthened my faith throughout my life and I owe him much."

Tom had not heard of Branwell's recent death, and he was deeply distressed and shocked to learn the news. He couldn't imagine the sadness that it must have brought to his old friend as well as to his daughters Emily, Charlotte and Anne.

"I know of Patrick's tough upbringing in Ireland, of course, and the strength that he always had and his self-belief and unswerving determination and unshakeable belief in God's will. He will be sorely tried, but not found lacking, I'm certain of that and I must write to him this very day. I had intended to write to him ever since I first came in here, but I never found the courage to confess my shortcomings – I was too ashamed, but now I must write honestly to console my friend. "

The reply from Patrick would sadden him even more, reporting the additional sad loss of Emily during the time of him corresponding from his cell that very month. John, too, only learned of Emily's death through Tom's letter from Howarth.

Tom fondly remembered Patrick's arrival as a sizar at St, John's, Cambridge in 1802 when he was in his second year.

"As one of the best funded universities to assist poor but able young men, St. John's accepted only four assisted-place sizars in his intake and Patrick only had to open his mouth to betray his origins. Through a strong Irish brogue, coming from poor and humble origins and before he asserted himself intellectually, he suffered from the snobbery and elitism of many of his wealthy contemporaries before answering them all by becoming a legend in his time there. Self-taught in the Latin and Greek, essential for anyone entering Cambridge, and seeking ordination, had seemed so easy for him and his academic career flourished. He became one of only seven men in his year to gain a first-class degree and was, moreover, one of only five to maintain an unbroken record of first-class successes in each of the half-year examinations during his entire stay there up to his graduation in 1806.

"No less than four of our tutors at St. John's had also been sizars and the enormity of the task against formidable odds spoke volumes for each one of their talents and inherent intellect. I, wealthy and not excelling in any way myself, was always in awe of Patrick's intellect and supported him throughout, desperately hoping that some of his talent might rub off on me. It didn't, but I always found his company so stimulating."

Tom continued to extol Patrick's virtues. "Can you believe, John, that he acquired the classical skills necessary to enter the finest university in the land coming from a two-roomed, white-washed, thatched peasant cabin at Emdale, in the tiny parish of Drumballyroney in County Down, where he told me he had established his own school at the age of only sixteen? Imagine that! And the meagre fees he gained there he saved for his entry to Cambridge."

"Branwell talked much of his admiration for his father and he, too, of course in turn, alongside his sisters, acquired all of their own literary skills from their gifted father – including the Latin and Greek so easily ingested by Bran," added John, further telling an incredulous Tom of his skill at writing simultaneously with both hands – ample proof, if it was ever needed, of Bran's inheriting his progenitor-polymath old friend's intellectual credentials!

John's own story of university was also found interesting by his ex-Cambridge cellmate:

"We used to read an old family bible as children at my grandfather's house at Old Ridings Halifax. We found an old will dated 1604. 'The second year of the reign of our most sovereign Lord James, by the grace of god King of England, Scotland, France and Ireland...' It was a hurriedly written will made by a Francis Tetherington. We've gotten used to phonetic spelling over the years. Anyway, he was dying of the bubonic plague – 'a fearfull infecion' as it was written, and he needed to place his estate quickly. He died the next day, in fact, and his wife, Janet, the day after. Extraordinarily for the times he stated, 'I give twenty pounds to my son Peter to the end that he may be brought up at school and put to the University of Cambridge if he shall live and become fit for that purpose.'

"I presume this Peter, who was aged nine at the time, survived the plague. He must have or I wouldn't be here. I have no idea if he ever got to Cambridge, but that was some ambition from a father racked with the plague, living in the wilds of Yorkshire!"

During another conversation early in their time together, John told him of his family's temporary residency in Stonegate in the city and of his friendship with the owner of number 43, Joseph Barker, who of course he realised hailed from and still lived in Beverley. Joseph, it transpired, actually resided in Tom's parish and his wife, Elizabeth, who John had not met yet but provided the welcoming meal for his family, was one of Tom's 'angels' who tended to his daily culinary needs with a veritable legion of kindly souls.

"Elizabeth is a wonderful woman! She has the most generous disposition and a heart capable of caring for the worries of the world – I couldn't have managed without her. She's the archangel to all of my wonderful angels!"

John agreed adding, "Well, she certainly made our arrival in York memorable. The house was warm and welcoming with all of the beds beautifully made up, basic provisions bought and a fine meal ready for us just to sit down to. Travelling with five children under ten is very tiring and they were all hungry and becoming tetchy and the younger ones were ready for the aired beds she had so thoughtfully prepared straight after supper. We were not long following the older children!"

Both of them discovered further connections through John's friendships with other fellow high-flying shooting party guests visiting The Vale of York. Both had visited Thorp Green, home of the Rev. Edmund Robinson and his family and were acquainted with Anne and Branwell's employment there as governess and tutor to his and his wife Lydia's children. Tom had learned of Edmund's death from one of his ladies, but was not aware that Lydia had married her cousin only two months ago and was now Lady Scott.

"He was always a poorly man as long as I knew him and that Lydia married again so soon after his death would surprise nobody," offered Tom. "Her reputation, not least the illicit liaison with her son's tutor, was an ill-disguised fact to many."

The story of Branwell's affair with Lydia, which resulted in his dismissal would occupy much of their talk about Thorp Green since both had first-hand knowledge of the circumstances surrounding it, and yet quite differing personal views on what brought it about.

And so the monotony of their enforced residency was to be greatly relieved in the coming weeks and months by such conversations on a wide range of related topics. They had both made a wise choice to share a cell, which was to make life just that little bit easier to accommodate at a difficult stage in both of their lives.

Chapter Nine

Liverpool

John came out of a deep alcohol-induced slumber that morning in his room at The Talbot, following his successful market day and pulled the bed-covers up to protect him from the chill developing around him as the fire in his grate was now almost out.

He became aware, quite forcefully, that he was not alone!

Hidden beneath the bed-sheets he felt, quite literally, the womanly presence of one market manager's daughter – the luscious Fanny Brearley. She was already performing that most alluring of all the party tricks in her repertoire; taking full advantage, completely oblivious to anything else in the world, of what she imagined John had generated exclusively with her in mind. He hadn't, it was nature's own morning provision, but one that John was now taking full advantage of.

His thoughts rushed back to the same experience he'd woken up to twenty years or so before. *"This time I'll be in control of the situation, unlike that fateful morning with Mary Foster! And I'll make sure there's no bastard to provide for either!"* he determined.

Little did he realise that she was, of course, quite fully impregnated from the Piece Hall symphonic performance of less than twenty-four hours ago, as he brought her up onto the pillow and laid her back to engage with her again in full exultant congress.

With over twenty letting rooms surrounding them and without the luxury of the prison-wall sound insulation of a Piece Hall private room, John had to place his hand tightly across Fanny's mouth, as the muffled, but still largely audible banshee cry emanated with total abandon, yet still managed to escape from somewhere deep within her throat, and even down her nose!

Mary Sugden, for one, was already up and about, getting The Talbot ready for the new day's business and serving breakfast. Branwell was somewhere nearby in the corridor; both, indeed any, or all, of the inn's fellow guests that morning could not have missed hearing Fanny, wherever they were, and could only have presumed somebody was being murdered!

John dressed as dawn was breaking and ushered Fanny out through the back corridor. He went down to have breakfast, just as Mary Sugden brought a tray in and fixed a stern eye on him, followed by a knowing wink. "Good morning, Master John. Good night's rest, was it? Eating alone this morning, are we?"

"You mean am I waiting for Bran, I presume, Mrs Sugden?"

"Aye, that, too. Is he up and about yet? Shall I serve you now?"

There was no doubting her biblical emphasis on the word 'serve' to highlight her displeasure at both his adulterous womanising and the fact he would be offering no recompense for his double room occupancy – as usual.

Branwell joined him after a few minutes and they breakfasted together on bacon and eggs, after which John paid Mrs Sudgen – for two rooms and one occupant in each, as she knew he would anyway and which she ignored since his bill was a large one, including the supper and punchbowl for four; plus a cheekily large bar-bill for Fanny and her cronies through in the public bar and for which she had just so vociferously expressed her gratitude.

Mrs Sugden reminded both of them of their back bills – John's was still large, even though he had paid in full this time using some of the money which William had drawn for him for Liverpool.

Branwell's debt was now serious and giving him great cause for worry. He couldn't pay it and was about to receive a formal letter regarding his overdue account from Mrs Sugden for which he would borrow, yet again, to pay.

His health was now also critical and causing concern both back in Howarth and among his friends in Halifax. His delirium tremens were again noticeable at breakfast that morning and he ate practically nothing, pushing his food around his plate.

John headed up to the Union Cross yard to meet up, probably have to drag out of bed, his creative travelling, fellow Hell-Fire Club companions, Joe and 'JB', sleeping their hangovers off in their respective studios above the yard, through the arch at the back.

JB was first to appear after much knocking and calling for attention. Totally dishevelled, Leyland had not the slightest idea what time it was and didn't remember the discussion about visiting Liverpool, but when reminded of the possible commission at the cathedral over there for him and Joe, he was stirred into action and dressed quickly to go for the train.

Branwell had gotten there first and was already in JB's studio, admiring a maquette for a statue he was commissioned to sculpt for York Minster.

"They treat me like a common grave mason inscribing tombstones with their trite memorial messages," JB told Branwell. "Wouldn't understand a decent piece of sculpture if it jumped up and bit them on the arse! But it pays the bills and maybe Liverpool Cathedral have a better fee in mind for my talents – we shall see!

"I can guess what got you going this morning, Titterington! No wonder you're raring to go!"

Joe had remembered the conversation and was actually up and dressed ready for the journey and together they set off to catch the coach down to Sowerby Bridge and from there a train to Liverpool via Manchester.

Slowly recovering variously, they exchanged little enough conversation before Manchester, but after changing trains the group now commenced the second part of their journey on one of the most interesting sections of railway ever constructed.

Branwell not only revelled in rail travel but also became quite an expert in the history of the railways. He could not have embarked on a more appropriate journey to re-tell his most famous stories of the Liverpool-Manchester rail line to his friends that day.

"Most of the regional railway companies are now established of course," he commented. "And the opening of the L&MR or Liverpool and Manchester Railway in 1830, just eighteen years ago, was preceded in October of the previous year by the Rainhill Trials, which had been set up as competition to choose the form of transport which would be employed on the railway.

"Horse-drawn carriages had been favoured initially, but after agreeing that steam would be employed, the L&MR directors arranged a competition to decide who would build its locomotives.

"Entries could weigh no more than six tons and had to travel along a track for a total distance of sixty miles.

"George Stephenson's entry, 'Rocket', as we all know, made the winning performance. The opening ceremony of the L&MR which followed eighteen months later on September 15th of 1830, drew luminaries from government and industry alike, including the Prime Minister, the Duke of Wellington.

"Eight trains set out from Liverpool in the opening procession – George Stephenson led the parade driving 'Northumbrian' followed by his son, Robert, driving 'Phoenix'. 'North Star' came next, driven by his brother, Robert, and then came 'Rocket', driven by his assistant engineer, Joseph Locke."

John interjected, "What a marvellous sight that must have been, Bran, but we all remember the day was marred by a tragic incident?"

"Ah, yes, indeed, John," continued Branwell. "As the more famous 'Rocket' came in to view from the sheds, a crowd pushed forward to get a better view, forcing the Liverpool MP William Huskisson onto the track where he was struck by the locomotive. It was a miracle the Duke of Wellington wasn't also injured since he was standing with the same party of dignitaries.

"George Stephenson continued on to Eccles to seek hospital treatment for the seriously injured Member of Parliament, but he died from his injuries along the way."

Passing from Manchester now and through Salford came a notorious section of track known as Chat Moss. Disputes with landlords owning arable farm land had been accommodated to the detriment of the route which then had to pass over this 7,000 year-old so-called 'bottomless' peat bog, north of the River Irwell, five miles to the west of Manchester.

Branwell continued, as if to add drama to this section of the journey, "Chat Moss threatened the completion of the line – the first public line connecting two cities in the world, until George Stephenson's immense triumph of engineering involving 'floating' the line on a bed of bound heather and branches topped with tar and covered with rubble stone was adopted.

"Daniel Defoe, over a hundred years ago, described 'Chatmos' as 'a great bog or waste'…black and dirty…and frightful to think of, for it will bear neither horse or man, unless in an exceedingly dry season, and then not so as to be passable, or that anyone should travel over them. What nature meant by such a useless production, 'tis hard to imagine, but the land is entirely waste, except for the poor cottagers' fuel, and the quantity used for that is very small."

Detecting some trepidation as the party looked out across the remote black landscape and considered what lay beneath this great weight of steel, Branwell added, "Don't concern yourselves gentlemen. It'll support us today and other travellers for many years to come – it's a remarkable piece of engineering, as is the whole line."

Nearing Liverpool, the group started to get a bit more animated and the conversation spread to planning the day ahead. John would head for the docks to examine the cargo of wool while Joe and JB would seek out George Hilary Brown, Vicar Apostolic of the Lancashire District and Titular Bishop of Bugia and Tlos who was strongly expected to be appointed Bishop of Liverpool in two years' time when the district was to be divided.

The Vicar Apostolic had seen JB's recently installed recumbent sculpture of Dr Stephen Beckwith in York Minster, and whilst being reasonably fit at the age of sixty-four had his mind fixed, beyond his imminent appointment and the corporeal world, to higher thoughts and visions of ecclesiastical majesty, even deity though he wouldn't admit to it, beyond the grave.

JB would get the commission. He felt fairly certain and letters of enquiry in the most glowing terms had been received from Bishop Brown in recent months. Terms of engagement would be discussed today and JB would soon discover if he would be offered a realistic fee for his work and hopefully more than the £250, including materials, he had worked tirelessly for in York. Any gilding required would be included in the overall commission and Joe came along as adviser in this regard and would remain largely silent in the negotiations.

They would both soon learn if the Bishop's criteria for selection had been based on artistic merit or, as they both feared, on the more material considerations of cost. JB had brought his impressive portfolio of sketches of previous commissions and was more than ready to justify his claims to provide skills far beyond that of a jobbing local parish monumental mason.

John would head straight to the newly opened Albert Dock to inspect the cargo of wool from India and Branwell planned to go along with him and explore the famous new docks.

Pulling into Lime Street station, they were in awe of the sheer size of the curved iron roof which was nearing completion. Designed by Richard Turner and William Fairburn and costing £15,000, it was similar to that found at Euston station in London and consisted of an iron-ridged roof supported by iron columns.

Branwell remembered his visit here three years ago with John Brown, his sexton friend from Haworth, and how they had recalled the abhorrent role that Liverpool had played in the 'triangular trade' and its shameful, vast wealth-making consequent involvement in the slave trade. Merchants used to sail from Liverpool to Africa, 'pick up' slaves so brutally captured, and then sail on to the West Indies where they traded them like cattle for molasses and raw cotton before returning to Liverpool. The slaves then produced the continuing flow of raw material in support of Lancashire's emerging wealth through its all-consuming cotton mills whilst at the same time created the emergence of the conduit and basis by which trading on such a scale could even possibly exist, through the establishment of major banking institutions.

It was here that Branwell first suggested, in collaboration with his sister, Emily, after that visit, the possibility that the child Heathcliff, so central to their *Wuthering Heights* who was brought from Liverpool by Mr Earnshaw, could be portrayed as a freed slave; the child being described in the story as *'dark almost as if it came from the devil.'*

Bidding a temporary farewell to JB and Joe, John and Branwell headed off to the Albert Dock after they all arranged to meet up in a couple of hours or so at a conveniently located new dockside pub called The Baltic Fleet, that they had been recommended to.

Opened officially by Queen Victoria's husband, Prince Albert, almost two years earlier in July of 1846, the sheer enormity of the eponymous docks had to be seen to be believed. Taking five years to build on its vast 1.25 million square feet site and designed by Jesse Hartley, its lofty colonnades and statuesque columns are a testament to innovation and sound engineering feats. Previously, the wooden warehouses of the time made fires a huge risk and the Albert Dock was the first enclosed, non-combustible dock warehouse system in the world and the first structure in Britain to be built entirely of cast iron, brick and stone. Sailing ships with a cargo capacity of up to 1,000 tons could be accommodated here.

Built on quicksand at the edge of the River Mersey, the Albert Dock boasts seven acres of enclosed water, uniquely for the time offering direct loading facilities into secure warehouses alongside; a security valued greatly by shippers of valuable cargo such as ivory, tea, spices and precious minerals.

Also about to be opened later that year and in the final stages of construction were the world's first hydraulic warehouse hoists which were taking Branwell's attention at that moment as he questioned a stevedore for more detail.

Meanwhile, John had sought out the dockside office of Israel Silver, who struggled with a pile of papers and ships' manifests in a dimly-lit room which appeared to John to be below water level and surely liable to flooding!

"Good day, John. I trust you had a pleasant journey?" enquired Israel Silver, a man typical of his trade who would drive a hard bargain, but who would be scrupulously honest in all aspects of his dealing. That he was likeable at the same time was never in question since John found it impossible to imagine that anyone could be a friend to this oleaginous, over-preening specimen of manhood!

Eager to conclude the transaction, as quickly as humanly possible, John proceeded to the dockside where the five hundred ton cargo of Merino wool was being off-loaded into a warehouse.

Merino wool is the softest and finest of all of the wool types. It has a bright, white, natural colour with excellent elasticity, and with an individual fibre or staple-length of up to four inches, it lends itself to spinning fine worsted yarns. It is this long staple-length that allows for the satisfactory carding or drawing process which is employed preparatory to spinning: shorter fibres break down during longer attenuations of the fibres and are therefore not suitable for fine worsted spinning.

Arriving alongside the three-masted barque '*Indian Princess*', John reached out to grab a handful of wool which was poking out of one of the bales being craned out of the vessel to be placed into the dockside warehouse.

Noting the fine whiteness and good grease content, John gripped a sliver of the wool between the fingers and palms of both of his hands and drew it gently apart, observing its ability to hold to itself. Still intact after drawing the wool apart for at least three and a half inches, he was satisfied he had the right quality.

At John's request, Israel called to the stevedore in charge of unloading to ascertain a completion time of unloading.

"About two more hours, sir," the stevedore responded and John agreed to return then to complete his inspection – a similar random sampling of several more bales from different parts of the consignment.

"I'll return then, Israel, to complete the purchase at the price we agreed in Halifax. All seems in order and I'm satisfied with the quality so far."

Glancing down into the barque's hold, John wondered how his cousin, Robert, could possibly have survived the journey to Australia down there, shackled for three interminable months along with two hundred other poor souls, passing in and out of the tropics and the southern oceans. And didn't the slavers from these parts subject those poor Africans to even worse conditions? Wrenching them away from their families to be traded like animals and spend a miserable, often short, lifetime's existence thousands of miles away in abject servitude.

The slave trade had been abolished now some forty years since by William Wilberforce, but John still felt the guilt of a nation built on slavery; and none more so than the blood which remained on the hands of the citizens of this great city itself allowing it, like Britain, to become the trading powerhouse of the world.

He too, in his own relatively small way had contributed to the misery through his ancestors taking full value of the trading opportunities which presented themselves through the misery of others.

Moving along the quayside, he quickly located Branwell in deep conversation with an old seafarer, and after asking him directions to the The Baltic Fleet, the pair headed off along Salthouse Quay and Gower Street to find the public house behind the King's Dock in Wapping, only a few hundred yards away from the Albert Dock.

The old seafarer Branwell had engaged in conversation was appropriately called Albert, and after being asked for directions to The Baltic Fleet, he volunteered a little more information of the pub's colourful past.

"Serving seafarers 'since the 1600s' and reputed to be haunted 'by at least six ghosts'," he went on. "There are two tunnels from the cellar beneath the pub; one goes to the docklands and the other to the red light district over in Cornhill, connecting sailors of the square-rigged ships with their two most fundamental needs – beer and the ladies of the night" – at which point he had roared with laughter and spat out the excess tobacco juices from his old clay pipe, just missing Bran's left shoulder in the process. He concluded, "Quite a tidy scheme!

"And on top of that, the tunnel to the docks was also used for victualling ships, with both grog and a ready supply of raw, unsuspecting – usually drunk, naval 'recruits' who were 'volunteered' for service by the notorious crimpers and press-gangers. These same recruits, finding they were not as badly treated as they had thought when they saw what befell their darker-skinned brothers, loaded even more forcibly at the hell-holes of the west African ports with no hope of ever seeing their homes again."

Bidding the old man farewell and synchronously side-stepping a final spirt of foul-smelling tobacco juice which flew harmlessly between them, they proceeded on their way.

Finding the pub easily, Branwell and John settled in to enjoy its hospitality with a tankard of ale apiece – purchased by John, who was about to deeply regret his overly demonstrative public display of wealth, drawing a sovereign from a bulging purse, rather than having it ready in his hand as he approached the bar.

An expensive gold fob watch was also clearly in evidence as he carelessly opened his topcoat whilst fumbling for the sovereign and his total demeanour and manner of dress stood him out as a man of status and wealth.

This was a world apart from Haworth or the tranquillity of the Calder Valley; these were tough surroundings – with a clientele to match and such carelessness would soon meet with the extraction of goods by fair means or foul, invariably the latter, and two scruffily-clad dock workers in a darkened corner of the bar had already spotted the two newcomers as soon as they entered and were now left in no doubt that their fortunes were about to change for the better.

Keeping them both under close observation, their time would come – after a few more drinks. They could wait and when nature took its course, they would be ready round the back of the pub, one to watch the exit door, which they already were seated next to, and the other to do the deed.

The one with the burgeoning purse got up to buy a second drink, they observed. This time, withdrawing his money more carefully, but it was too late – they already knew what he had. They also knew now who would definitely be their exclusive target since the other, rather scholarly-looking stranger wearing less imposing clothing, and no fob watch, had not made the second obligatory purchase and was presumed to be a guest of the other.

John became suddenly aware of faces, many faces, looking down at him, asking of his wellbeing. The sharp pain in the back of his neck told him he must have had some sort of accident. All he could remember was a blinding flash of light followed by nothing and here he was on the ground at the back of the pub. That was it, he'd gone out to relieve himself and could still feel the strong urge to urinate – he hadn't even made it as far as the privy. And with that realisation, he felt instinctively for his purse. It was gone, with all of his funds, as was his gold fob watch and chain – a 21st birthday present from his father and mother, reluctantly given by the former due to the extraneous circumstances surrounding the ill-timed coincidence of the birth of his bastard son William Foster a few weeks before.

Sovereigns, coins, notes and bills of both the Halifax Joint Stock Bank and the Huddersfield and Halifax Union Banks; all were gone.

A largely lawless Liverpool at that time was known to have a notoriously useless police force. Formed only a dozen years before in 1836, its officers were inefficient, rarely turned up for duty and were invariably drunk when they did. The *Liverpool Mercury* described their *Night Watch* at the time as *"a terror to nobody and an amusement only to mischievously disposed lads..."* whose officers *"...slept in sentry boxes, which were a target for the local youths who frequently, for fun, overturned their sentry boxes and stole their lanterns."*

The daytime *Corporation Constabulary* were little better and were described as: *"Corrupt, accepted bribes and deserted their beats."*

A third force, probably the most efficient of the bunch, was the *Dock Watch*, but the rivalry amongst the three groups regularly led to the *Dock Watch* attacking the *Night Watch* and locking them up overnight in the dockside bridewells.

Such was the confidence in policing that nine years previously, a *'progressive improvement'* had been reported stating that, *"only 639 cases of drunkenness and 1,592 other disciplinary offences were recorded that year against police officers, out of a force of 574."* Which, whilst largely unknown in specific detail to Branwell and John, more than adequately ruled out any hopes of redress or assistance from the constabulary in their present predicament.

Branwell, called from the bar to the back yard to assist, had helped John back inside, after allowing him to complete his original journey to the privy to relieve himself. The landlord provided a brandy for John by way of an apology and Joe and JB arrived shortly afterwards to learn of the attack.

The landlord, also more than fully aware of the uselessness of all three forms of the Liverpool constabulary and ever-fearful of the growing notoriety attaching itself to his establishment, made his apologies now to all four of them and, by recompense, offered to send for a doctor and invited them all to have some food.

Staunching the blood from a wound on the back of John's neck and applying a bandage supplied by the landlord, JB proved to be the perfect nurse. "You'll be fine John, a few bruises tomorrow, and your pride hurt – but you'll live to tell the tale. Thank you landlord, but I believe we don't need a doctor."

"Live to tell the tale!" thought John – as if he would even dare to contemplate telling the story to his father! And all on the devil's premises, *"a godless public house of evil intent – What else would you expect?"* He could hear him saying it now. And shuddered at the very thought!

He knew he'd need a better story to tell his father and would have to rely on his companions to desist from sharing the true one next market day – or any day.

His watch was gone – and all of his money, more particularly his father's money, since it was he who kept the purse strings and controlled all of the manufacturing businesses, including Higgin Chamber Mill. It was also going to be just about impossible to convince him of the

133

need to still complete the purchase of the wool shipment, which John alone felt was the way forward to distance production away from the diminishing common shalloon fabrics' business favoured by the rest of the family – albeit on which the family's successes were based thus far.

Monsieur Dubois was in no doubt that John's new jacquard fine worsted cloths would sell well in the high fashion markets of Belgium and France, but only John had the foresight and the design and production skills necessary to realise its full potential and immense opportunities for profitability.

But now, after the food, and feeling much better, he needed to persuade Israel Silver that payment for the shipment would be forthcoming, but not today.

All four walked over to the warehouse where unloading was completed and John satisfied himself that the shipment was good by testing several more random samples from bales within the cargo.

John approached Israel Silver cautiously whilst still teasing out the last sample. "You'll need to trust me Mr Silver if we are to do business again. The generous deposit I gave you in Halifax yesterday will have to suffice until I can send you the remaining funds from my bank tomorrow. Do I have your trust? Shall we shake on it still to seal the deal?"

Drilling into Silver's eyes with this last remark, John was rewarded with his agreement. It was a good deal for both and Silver wasn't about to sour potential future business. He had checked on the veracity of the Titterington businesses and had been encouraged by the family's obvious business skills on display at the Piece

Hall. Without seeming to pry, he had also overheard some of John's conversation with his Belgian customer and was encouraged to believe there was more business, profitable business, to be had overseas.

Neither did he presume to enquire about the bandage on the back of John's neck, his slightly pained movement, or indeed his inability to pay for the shipment as agreed, though he had a pretty good idea what must have occurred; it wasn't unusual for 'gentlemen' to be 'parted from their possessions' in these parts and he felt some of the guilt himself as a fellow Liverpudlian.

"If you would arrange shipment by canal at the cost agreed, to Luddenden Foot, I would be grateful. Good to do business with you, Mr Silver – I bid you good day, sir." And with that, the four headed off to catch the evening train back to Manchester, and from there on to home.

JB and Joe reported finding Bishop Brown easily and were pleased to report that he had a great enthusiasm for JB's work following his visit to York Minster. Furthermore he was well-funded by a private benefactor, who also wished to be remembered similarly and prominently; beyond the grave in his own time.

Branwell pondered the source of the benefactor's wealth, but made no comment to spoil his good friends' JB and Joe's excitement at the prospect of earning a good living for some time to come. The triangular slave trade, however, again came to mind, together with the establishment of the banks and industry in general on its back – and all whilst requiring to facilitate a rich man's passage, *through the eye of a needle*, to enter the kingdom of the almighty; a cynical thought in a cynical world.

And was what happened just now to his friend in the pub any different? Only the 'class' of the criminal was at variance, Branwell decided.

For paid travelling expenses for the day and a hefty deposit of £100, JB was to produce sketches and proposals and return with full costings for the commission within four weeks. Flushed with success and the acknowledgement of his skills and artistic talents, he commented, "There's enough work for a year there and another one beyond that for the bishop's benefactor. Thank you, John, for encouraging me to come along today. I had been putting it off for weeks fearing it would be the usual wild goose chase where I'm undervalued and offered only enough to scrape by on. Joe's part will be substantial, too, as gilding is to be given prominence in the finished pieces. And, unlike York, all materials are to be costed and paid for separately."

After changing trains in Manchester, the four friends journeyed on to home, dropping Branwell and John off at Luddenden Foot station, and taking JB and Joe on to Sowerby Bridge where they took a late coach into Halifax.

After a couple of drinks in The Anchor and Shuttle, John had recovered sufficiently by now to walk up to Higgin Chamber with little discomfort, but he knew full well that the next day would bring bruising to the fore and worse still, his father's wrath.

Mary's concern was obvious as she fussed around John, bathing and re-dressing his neck wound, but he held back the true story and told the prepared one of being taken by surprise and robbed at the back of a warehouse at the dockside whilst going to relieve himself during the business meeting.

The children were fortunately all tucked up in bed and would not have liked hearing, more particularly seeing, how their father had suffered.

John was acutely aware that his story, however well received by Mary, would be as nothing when his father started his grand inquisition into just what exactly happened to make him over £200 worse off.

He went on to Mary, "The different police over there are at each other's throats and all of them are notoriously useless, but I did leave my details on the off-chance that some reprobate felon might be caught. Who knows? Maybe my fob watch might be found on one of them like the way cousin Robert was caught in Dublin with Crossley's engraved fob on him."

"So what of the money then, John? How will you pay for the wool? And what will your father say?" This last question was uttered with some concern for she felt certain that Eli would view it all quite differently and immediately presume the worst.

He certainly was about to do just that when he knew who had accompanied his son on the trip and even though it could perfectly well have happened the way John was now telling it, the addition of a public house, alcohol and the distraction of his three perceived louche companions would lead his father unavoidably to a damning conclusion.

And so it turned out; it took less than an hour at market day the next Wednesday for John's true story to be discovered from Abraham Taylor, a trading next-door-neighbour and business rival of Eli's at the Piece Hall.

No wheedling was remotely necessary with this known gossip. "What can you expect, Eli?" Abraham intoned with his usual relish for tittle-tattle and a healthy dose of schadenfreude. "With those drunken reprobates coming along to help do your business for you!"

It was not the first nail in John's coffin, but it was significant in that fateful year of 1848, coming as it did early in January with the drama which brought him ultimately to his present sorry state, almost a year later, still to unfold throughout that awful year.

"You see, Tom," he said to his reverend cellmate. "I really couldn't ever please my father. He was always the one in charge and everything had to be done his way. I know we're all judged by the company we keep, but these were good friends and I can't regret the times we spent together. I inherited my artistic side from my mother's Ogden forebears who were musicians, artists and writers; so different from the dour, blunt, down-to-earth weavers and businessmen on the Titterington side."

Chapter Ten

A Surprise Visitor

On the morning of Friday December 15th 1848, a young man got off his train at York railway station and proceeded to walk over the river and into the ancient city.

Basically, yet smartly attired, debonair and ruggedly handsome, the twenty-one year-old lissome six-footer turned a few heads as he strode confidently toward the city, carrying his worldly possessions in a sturdy yet battered valise he had borrowed from a neighbour down the street in Luddenden Foot.

Saying farewell to his thirty-four year-old mother, he had set out that morning from home to claim his destiny after a life of feeling denied a proper birthright. Growing up with no siblings and without a father, he had bonded closely with his mother whilst proving himself to be a loving and industrious son. Unlike his near neighbours in Luddenden Foot, he was literate, numerate and comparatively worldly as a consequence, thanks to private tutoring and it was generally assumed, by anyone outside the immediate family, that a successful distant relative had left a trust fund for the purpose taking pity on his bastard relative.

He had supported his mother financially for as long as he could remember, learning the trades of both butchery and textiles, but now at twenty-one years of age, it was his time to strike out for himself. He would never leave his dear unmarried mother destitute and promised to send her whatever funds he could afford in his new life.

His choice of York was an easy one and his dismissal from employment at the textile mill had only expedited the move.

His first views of the Minster towers, which had so impressed pilgrims and visitors alike for centuries, were already clearly visible and were something quite unexpected to a young man visiting for the first time. He had seen illustrations of York and its fine Minster, but he was not prepared for the latter's first-hand sheer size and majesty, even from this distance. Not an overly religious young man, he couldn't wait nevertheless to get up close to experience the awe with which he had heard staunch believers looked up to the heavens through its spires and anticipated a life to come from the streets immediately beneath its grandeur.

Crossing through the city he found himself in a street clearly, and rather suitably named, 'The Shambles' and was taken back to another childhood drawing he had seen of just such a medieval street, maybe even this very same street, with a jolly bustling scene and people wearing wigs and clothing from Elizabethan times; apart from the more modern early-Victorian clothing, here he was taking a step back into history.

Most of all, he remembered the upper storeys almost reaching across to neighbours on the other side of the street. Could they really shake hands with each other, he wondered? They could certainly hang washing lines across so it must be still possible.

Most of the traders were butchers and he had some experience in their trade having worked for the landlord of The Anchor and Shuttle, who ran a butcher's shop behind the pub.

Earning money for his mother and supporting her in difficult times without a father, at fourteen years of age, he disappointed his boss by leaving to work up the hill toward Sowerby village, to learn new skills in the relatively more comfortable, though noisier surroundings of a weaving shed.

The canal had been conveniently placed immediately behind The Anchor and Shuttle to receive waste, especially surplus offal and blood beyond its need, for 'umble pie or black pudding-making. Here in York it was the street itself that flowed red and bloody with the same surplus and the pavements were constructed high above the cobblestones to allow its free passage into the drains. How the rats must love living here, he thought. They must surely be as big as cats, with voracious teeth to match!

Quite frugal in all aspects of his life, he carried enough money from his saved wages to last him a few weeks, but employment would be needed by then and here was at least one place where his past experience could come in handy.

He was acutely aware that he was also needing accommodation and a roof over his head immediately, in this the coldest part of the winter so far. The snows had abated, but cruel frosts had stretched their frozen fingers into organ pipes of icicles suspended all the way along the roof gutterings of The Shambles.

He walked along, or more precisely was jostled along the street by the sheer weight of the crowds of visitors and shoppers dodging between the crown of the cobbles or the pavements themselves to avoid each other and more particularly the fetid torrents of blood and entrails which surged along the gutters.

Stopping to bid the time of day to one of the traders who was swilling a bucket of water into the street to help the ruddy morass along, he admired a cut of beef on display on his shelves and so impressed the butcher with his knowledge of a good fillet that he stayed to engage him further in conversation.

"Travelled far, young man? To visit? I detect a strong accent there I think? And you know a bit about good cuts?"

"Just arrived by train from Halifax and yes, I have worked helping a neighbour out with his butchery as a lad."

"Tha's nobbut a lad still, I'm thinking!" he said, poorly mimicking his West Yorkshire dialect with insufficient emphasis on the hard vowel sounds.

Ignoring the obviously well-intentioned jibe, the young man continued, "You seem to be short-handed at the moment? Out here sluicing whilst nobody is helping to serve in the shop. Look, there's a queue forming, you need to go inside. Maybe I could help you?"

And from a simple meeting and a few casual remarks, Michael Cooper, butcher, of 14, The Shambles, had found the answer to his pressing problem. Here was a very presentable young man who engaged easily in conversation and who had butchery experience. How very different from the city boys he had tried to train and failed, almost before they had become any use whatsoever beyond acting as mere delivery boys to the wealthy clients across and to the wealthier outskirts of the city. Moreover he had warmed to him immediately and felt that it had been his lucky day, an omen even, stepping out and almost colliding with him that morning in the street.

Married, with Rachel, their two year-old daughter and Ruth, their newly-born baby, Michael and his wife, Elizabeth, also lived above the shop and they had both quickly come to the same conclusion: here was an admirably trustworthy young man who they could welcome into their home and who would be just what they were looking for to ease their staffing problem. Elizabeth was finding it increasingly difficult to tend to her new baby's needs and serve in the shop as well. Their sales, with such fierce competition from over thirty butchers all around them in the street, were suffering, at a time when Christmas sales would be affected with dire consequences. If immediate action was not taken, on top of everything else, there were turkeys, ducks and geese-a-plenty to kill and prepare to grace the gentlefolk of York's tables in the coming celebrations!

A spare bedroom was also available which would suit both parties and the young man was shown high up into the attic to his new quarters, which had previously served as their own after their marriage four years before, with Michael's ailing father sleeping below, in the room they now occupied with both of their daughters. Michael's father had died the year before, just short of his fiftieth birthday and his mother, who he did not remember, some twenty or so years before that, in sibling childbirth in Michael's early childhood. With a florid complexion and grossly overweight, his father had typified a master of his trade, working inordinately long hours and eating a totally unbalanced diet. He did well to get to the age he did and exceeded by a good few years the average life spans of his butcher-neighbours packed cheek-by-jowl along The Shambles.

Michael was twenty-nine and already heading in the same direction. Short in stature and overweight, his unkempt red hair highlighted a tendency to look overly flushed and he sweated profusely, even in the winter, as he laboured over his carrying, sawing and chopping of huge slabs of carcass. Elizabeth, too, enjoyed the bounteous produce all around her and had been brought up to waste-not-and-want-not by her own frugal mother who had additionally taught her the high calorific skills of eating, as well as making, sweet and savoury pies and pasties. Both enjoyed life to the full with jolly dispositions and their raucous laughter and repartee could be heard the length of The Shambles. Elizabeth's meat and potato pies were renowned throughout the city and she was already inundated with orders for her seasonal game pies which included extras such as well-hung pheasant and hare to complement the usual base ingredients.

Needing to get back to serving and leaving only one assistant in charge of the shop, they climbed up the stairs.

"We still don't know your second name, William," Elizabeth said, reaching the top floor a little out of breath. With a flourish, William announced proudly, without a second's hesitation, and for the very first time in his life, "It's Titterington – William Titterington!"

Here, away from home, he realised he could be whoever he wanted to be and whilst he bore his unmarried mother's family surname of Foster throughout his life so far, his father had never been ashamed of him. Quite the contrary, and now, William could be who he wanted to be, who he *really was* in any case, William Titterington. How good it sounded. Full family membership, and now with the chance to return some of the favours his father had so proudly, yet of necessity sometimes secretly, bestowed on him throughout his short life.

Across the city in Stonegate, Mary was settling into a life of looking after the needs of five children whilst visiting John on a daily basis with her unerring support and satisfying his food needs. Their savings were now spent and the money now coming from her father for *'the express and exclusive usage of herself and the five grandchildren alone'* was proving vital, but not infinite, unless alternative means of income could be found. Feeding John was already becoming a strain on her finances and could not continue in its present form. The family was already going without to make ends meet.

Little did she realise that just such a means had arrived near her home to offer additional support to the family in such difficult circumstances.

William unpacked his valise and prepared to settle into his new home dizzyingly high above street level and with spear-like stalactite icicles suspended right outside his window. Across the street he could indeed almost reach to the attic window on the opposite side and amused himself by wondering if he would be able to meet, maybe even climb across himself, possibly to engage in a dalliance with a pretty daughter or servant-girl of the occupants. He couldn't do that in Luddenden Foot!

But there was work to do and a new boss to impress and so he immediately presented himself in the shop to don his butcher's garb and take his first instructions for the afternoon shift.

He was shown the slaughterhouse in the yard behind the shop where the live animals and birds were received, butchered and prepared for sale from four o'clock in readiness for opening the shop at eight o'clock.

Michael described the mix of shops in The Shambles, with the larger animal slaughtering, cattle mainly, being positioned at the ends of The Shambles for easier live animal access to the larger slaughterhouses. Positioned more centrally in the street and toward the Minster, Michael's father, and his father before him, had become known for the provision of fowl, mutton and pork, and for the latter he also had the finest smoke-house in the street and was known best of all for his smoked hams and bacon.

The shop front outside displayed chickens suspended from hooks high above street level which were placed there and brought down for sale by a long pole positioned by the door for the purpose. Turkeys, geese, partridge, pheasant and grouse were decoratively arrayed according to size, and pigeons completed the geometrically pleasing ascending and descending outer flanks on both sides like a well-regimented advancing fighting-force. Shoppers were looking for end-of-day bargains and William's first job was to replenish the hooks with prepared birds from the store rooms at the back whilst selling both these birds and the larger joints of meat placed on the wide shelves at street level. First he learned the minimum price expectations that Michael wanted in order to gauge his patter to the clock countdown.

All of which allowed Elizabeth to concentrate on the smaller meat cuts, on the bacon and her own homemade pie sales and the general sausage and mixed offal sales back in the shop. Michael was now freed up exclusively to continue clearing out the slaughterhouse and to removing buckets of waste offal and blood out to be swilled down the street in preparation for Monday's new week opening. In between he helped William when his hands were full with the ever-growing number of customers filing down The Shambles looking for their Sunday joints of meat at the best prices. Lowering prices to match their expectations nearing closing time against the immediate ever-present competition was an art in itself and one that the loquacious William proved to be very adept at, calling prices out, pole in hand, from the street outside. His banter and presence of a ready wit, combined with a bargain, were a winning combination, too good to miss by a discerning audience.

Michael was immediately impressed with William's confidence and easy manner with the customers. From the outset, his easy price negotiation skills, speed of action and a flow of ready banter and personable good humour all came easily to William, and Michael knew immediately he had made a wise choice. And all of this initially without him even knowing what his butchery skills were going to be like on the following Monday morning.

He was not, and never would be, disappointed!

Chapter Eleven

William Foster

And as John headed down to meet his unexpected visitor, with Scoggins's abusive rantings rattling around in his brains, he again questioned; who could be visiting him called Titterington? Certainly not either his brother or father and there really wasn't anybody else, with distant uncles and cousins right out of the question as he was not in contact with any of them.

The meeting room, quite intentionally, was a sorry affair, worse even than the worst cell in the deepest part of the prison. Dungeon-like in the extreme, it served to both humble prisoners and to remind visitors that they were not welcome and so offered no comfort beyond a wooden bench and simple table. It was a ten foot square bleak cell.

Mary hated coming, but would get used to it in time in the months before John was allowed out on day-release, and the girls were shielded from the excesses of prison life by Scoggins at least having the unexpected decency to keep himself scarce and not frighten them half to death on their frequent visits bringing him sustenance.

Opening the visitors' cell door, John entered and in the dim half-light struggling to enter through the smallest of escape-proof windows, he failed initially to recognise his 'Titterington' visitor.

"Well, this is a fine mess you've got yourself in, father," the young man said, applying sarcastic emphasis to the last word and John knew the familiar voice instantly.

"William Foster! How the hell did you come to be here in this God-forsaken hole? And using my name, however appropriate that might be!" John joked, more than delighted to see the son he had always liked to have around, especially recently working alongside him in the mill.

"Couldn't work for your brother Thomas. He managed to find me jobs that were deliberately menial and usually humiliating, and when I objected, he told me I knew what to do if I didn't like it. So I took up his kind invitation and left!" said William, who was very much his own man and did not suffer fools gladly.

He went on, "Time to strike out on my own, I thought, and York seemed as good a place as any to start out, with you and the family already here. I only heard that you were in here last Wednesday at The Anchor when Sarah behind the bar was telling everybody how it served you right and might cool your temper down a bit!

"'A bit of Dick Turpin's medicine won't do that womanising bastard any harm,' she added, knowing I was listening in the snug and giving it a loud delivery with special emphasis on the 'bastard' for my benefit of course – what a bitch!

"So I decided there and then to give Thomas my notice, packed a case, said farewell to my landlady and here I am to support you in any way I can. You've supported me all my life so now it's my turn."

Visibly moved and stuck for words for a moment, John responded, "Well that's very kind and I'm touched by your loyalty, but how will you live? How can you survive here, you can't have much saved? You'll need a job – there's no mill work over here – and what about you calling yourself Titterington? I had no idea who it could be! Certainly never thought it could be you!"

Still now intensely pleased with William's comments and with some considerable pride, John, who knew well how capable he had been at the mill, was about to hear just how resourceful his offspring was further turning out to be.

"I believe you must stay here until your debts are settled and I know from Thomas that neither he nor your father will help you. I can also expect that your sisters, too, will have their hands tied for fear of alienating your father and incurring his wrath, and more particularly also being disinherited like you were so cruelly, through *The Guardian's* front page article. Mary's father, too, I'm guessing, will not support you either. And I'm pretty certain that I'll be the main reason for a large part of that thinking! Not forgetting the nightmare, recently, of course, with the Piece Hall manager's lass!"

He went on, "I've already gained employment. I start work tomorrow, as a butcher's assistant, name of William Titterington! Remember? I helped out, butchering in Luddenden Foot, behind The Anchor with the Slater's before I came up to you? And better than that, I have a room over the shop. It's in The Shambles and couldn't have worked out better. And it all came about from a casual conversation outside the shop within an hour of me arriving yesterday!

"I haven't even had time to see Mary and the children. I trust they are well? It must be hard for them, especially the children? I heard you were living in Stonegate? I'll find it later. I can't wait to see my sisters and little James. Though, I will, of course, not tell them my new name, I'll still be their cousin William Foster…

"Do you mind me using your name?"

John was so impressed and had no intention of objecting to this fine young man's use of a name which as far as he was concerned he was perfectly entitled to use.

"I have no objection to that William, anybody would be proud to acknowledge you as his son and I'm so pleased that I supported your mother and educated you over all the years. You will always be welcome to visit me here and in due time, be a recognised brother to my children when they're a little older."

"I can do better than that, father, and help you to get out of this hell-hole. I have a plan to bring pieces over from other mills in Halifax to sell directly to our contacts and with your help, in return, learn how to buy wool in the area to sell back to the mills in the West Riding. I'll be getting to know the farmers anyway, I guess through Michael Cooper. He's my employer, buying their animals and birds for butchering," said William, with what seemed very mature reciprocal thinking to John.

"That's quite a plan, William, but it will take money to start out with the right purchases. I'll help you to think it through and I can hopefully be, more directly involved, in the fullness of time of course."

William was getting excited fleshing out his plans and he could see that John was warming to the possibilities. "I'll work extra hours at the butcher's and perhaps your buyer-friend, William Barker, over here in Beverley may care to come in with us? I've always got on well with him even though he has no idea I'm your son."

"He's a good friend as well as a business acquaintance, as you know, William, and we are even staying in his recently-deceased relative's house in Stonegate, at no cost. He values the new cloth designs I was working on for the market over here and with your help in due course, if it works out and we get established, I can commission exclusive production of them from one of the Halifax mills – I have a couple in mind," said John.

"A final question before I leave, father, and I know I must never and will never call you that when others around, especially the children, but may I at least call you John if we are to be partners?" he asked humbly, penitently, hopefully.

He was rewarded amply with, "My dearest boy, you may of course, it will be a privilege!"

They hugged for the very first time and commenced a chapter in both of their lives which was to lead on to John's release and a return home with his family to Sowerby.

Returning to his cell, still floating on air – even joking with the dreadful and quite humourless Scoggins as he strode out along the corridor, he looked forward to telling Tom his good news.

After sharing William's plans, he needed to tell Tom the facts surrounding William's birth and especially to explain himself through the undoubted shock he would have of learning that the illegitimate conception was more than ably assisted and contrived by his twelve year-old mother. The facts needed to be robust, yet at the same time truthful, if someone as religious as Tom was not to be outraged, even incensed, at the very idea of such a liaison.

The alienation of his cellmate and friend must be avoided at all costs for the good of their continuing sound relationship.

Paedophilia was an ugly word in any generation.

Chapter Twelve

Mary Foster

That bright summer's morning early in July, 1827, following one of the hottest nights that anyone could remember, Mary awoke in a cold sweat and rose at 5 o'clock in the weaver's cottage down the hill between Midgley and Luddenden Foot. She dressed quickly and slipped out of the back door without disturbing either her mother and father or her three younger sisters.

Her father, William Foster, a weaver up at Eli Titterington's where Mary now worked as a bobbin-girl would follow to commence his morning shift with his daughter at 7 o'clock. Sometimes they walked up together and sometimes Mary walked up with some of the other bobbin-girls. Eleanor Hardcastle, her best friend and workmate, lived in the cottage next door and would usually walk with her, but she would be setting out much later than this at the more usual time of 6.30 am.

She climbed Solomon Hill alone that morning, and passed The Greave on the right, home of the Murgatroyds – her employer's sworn enemy and main competitor in business. Past Turn Lea cottages on the left, she swung around the right hand bend and headed up towards High Lees, and just passing the entrance to Peel Lane she could already hear the masons preparing stone for the wall behind The Greave, where the Murgatroyds were spitefully raising its already considerable height to prevent the Titteringtons looking down on them from straight above and behind them, up at High Lees.

Climbing further up Pin Hill Lane and getting closer now to High Lees, her pace quickened as she pondered the object of her early morning mission, no less than John Titterington, the twenty-year-old son of her boss, for whom she had developed an unquenchable passion over the previous few weeks working alongside him in the mill.

John was a hands-on employer who would tackle any job that needed doing, and the urgent construction of new creels had brought him into close contact with Mary, helping alongside him, passing down his tools and parts as he worked in the creels' bobbin access pits, beneath floor level behind the looms.

Stripped to the waist, in the heat of the day, John's overtly displayed manhood, even his body odour, excited her to distraction and the very thoughts of him being even closer to her, holding her, brought a tingle to her body as she drifted off to sleep each night – and again when she woke – and pretty much throughout the night in her dreams. She was obsessed with him!

But what notice, would he, did he, take of her? And she not even into her teens. None, for she felt like a child in his presence even though her body told her differently; she was a mature woman, mentally, now and she had a woman's physical needs.

The mill yard was deserted as expected and she removed her shoes and entered the servants' door at the back of the house. She headed up the servants' staircase to reach an access door into the main house at the first-floor level.

The house was still. No one would rise for at least another hour and she would have time to attend to her urgent task – even if it resulted in her dismissal. She had thought it all through, prepared herself, and would take the consequences if it came to it. It would be worth it anyway and there were other jobs.

She had seen John at one of the bedroom windows early one morning and knew his room was in an annex over the stable-block, so turning right along a corridor she paused outside the door she guessed would be his. *But what if he shared it with one or both of his young brothers?* James, who was thirteen, or Thomas, who was just nine, might be in there, too. Their many sisters, she guessed correctly, were all sleeping in rooms over to the front of the house, nearer to their parents, in much grander style and with magnificent views right across the valley to Sowerby village in the distance.

The door was slightly off the latch to allow air circulation and she gave it a gentle push, praying it would not creak and give her away. *Would she run if it did?* Yes – the way was clear and in this part of the house, she could say she was looking for Daisy, one of the servant girls she was friendly with.

The door swung open without a sound and she was presented with a view she could not even have dreamed would be quite so exciting! John, and only John, lay in a single bed, gently snoring, in the half-light of the small window, naked, apart from a sheet partially covering the lower part of his body but with his body turned slightly to reveal his buttocks! Mary had to catch her breath. *What a glorious sight!*

Slipping out of her blouse, dress and underclothes and now completely naked herself, she advanced stealthily toward her quarry and slipped in beside him gently placing one hand over his mouth and the other beneath the sheet to grasp, exactly what she had expected and had learned from the older mill-girls to be his 'morning glory!'

Opening his eyes with a startled expression and unable to speak, Mary pushed him gently over onto his back, dispensed with the sheet with her left foot and deftly swung her left leg over his body. She mounted him like a thoroughbred horse, impaling herself on him in one majestic swoop.

Whatever chance John had to object prior to this apparent assault, he now had none whatsoever as he passed the point of no return and surrendered to the total oblivion and sheer frenzy of wild congress.

This was no ordinary girl and she certainly was no virgin. Sexually active and fully developed physically at an early age, her reputation was already well known amongst the lads in the mill and in no way was she considered a child by anyone, including her own parents, even though her first teenage year was still to come.

Leaving John's room as swiftly as she had come – not a word was spoken by either of them, she dressed quickly, descended the stairs and went over to the mill where she was still the first to arrive and nobody was any the wiser –

apart from an exhausted John Titterington who, collapsed and still breathless in his bed, couldn't quite believe what had just happened to him.

He would have to believe it before too long though, for the consequences were about to include one very under-aged and pregnant, young weaver's daughter!

Mary's father first got wind of his daughter's condition some two months later, overhearing his wife and Mary engaged in conversation and guessed what they must be talking about. Shocked by the news and outraged that the boss's son had taken advantage of such a young girl, he headed straight for Eli to demand some sort of satisfaction and to find John to seek retribution!

No amount of explaining by John was going to make any difference and he decided it would be churlish, even unmanly, to tell the true story, and so he would accept the consequences and take what punishment was about to come his way.

Firstly, the possibility of marriage was completely rejected by Eli. "Under no circumstances is my eldest boy going to marry your child," he told William Foster and repeated it even more strongly to Grace with the same emphasis.

And in any case, John had absolutely no wish or desire to marry her anyway, since he didn't really know her at all and had hardly ever even spoken to the girl outside working with her in the mill. Certainly no words at all were exchanged on the morning of the deed itself, but he would hardly be believed if he tried telling anybody that one, so he didn't bother!

'Hardwicke's Marriage Act' of 1753 was well known and prevailed in law at the time and for the next 175 years. It stated that the legal age for marriage was fourteen for men and twelve for women and it remained in force right up until 1929 when the *'Age of Marriage Act'* gave equality and raised the limit to sixteen years of age for both.

"And you know what Hardwicke can do with his act!" said Eli to William Foster at the very suggestion, though he had to concede his son was responsible and must make some form of restitution.

William's response to that was, "In that case you can either pay for your son's mistake or leave him to face the bastardy charges when the child is born."

"And how do I know the child is my lad's anyway? She's got quite a reputation has your child, you know. She's not the sweet little innocent thing you're making her out to be!" demanded Eli, rather more in hope than anything.

Eli did his best, but finally had to concede. With John's acquiescence to the facts, he agreed to make the payments necessary whenever the child arrived, and in return, John was left in no doubt that he would have to make recompense to his aggrieved father as, when, and in whatever manner he wished it.

That this would include suffering excessive and unreasonable unpaid overtime in the mill was not anticipated by John and he rebelled one day by refusing to work an extra night shift.

It had all started off reasonably well with the bastard child, William Foster, a healthy boy named for her father, being born on 12th April 1828.

Baptised a month later on May 11th at St. Mary's in Luddenden, Mary was just thirteen by then and the service was a solemn affair with the shame and stigma of illegitimacy surrounding the attendance of only her parents on the day – plus the infant, of course, and herself along with one totally disapproving clergyman who spat out the child's chosen name; as though the poor child could possibly have had any responsibility in the matter!

It had been decided that the infant, together with his four older 'sisters' would be brought up by Mary's mother and father as their own fifth child and so it was agreed he should be appropriately named William, after his 'father'.

Eli made twenty-eight weekly payments to Mary's father, up until the refusal to work the extra unpaid shift, whereupon Eli, who knew it was coming anyway since he quite deliberately applied unreasonable pressure and said, "Fine by me, lad! Take the consequences and pay for your own bastard child!"

At that time a 'bastardy order' was served by the courts on the putative father to procure an income to support the illegitimate child's birth costs and upbringing, and just over six months after William's birth, the notice below appeared in *The Halifax Guardian*. Eli had swallowed his pride and on what would not turn out to be for the last time, had thrown John unmercifully to the wolves. In the process he shamed his oldest son publicly, to be ridiculed around the greater Halifax area and especially exposed him to the ribaldry of being a 'cradle-snatcher', or worse, on market days at the Piece Hall, wealthy families just didn't do that sort of thing; they took care of their own, including the occasional product of incest.

The twenty-eight weeks of 'hush money' already paid by Eli to his weaver William Foster were not taken into account and John was in no position to enter a dispute about the matter and so was charged from the birth, including the four week lying-in period allowed immediately after the birth when a mother could not earn.

Eli had no problem getting satisfaction from his double payment and duly set William Foster to work far more than its worth by requiring him to work extra shifts – for no payment.

Copy served on John Titterington by James Taylor – 21st October 1828...concerning a male bastard child born 28 weeks ago in the township of Midgley to a single woman and which said child has been and continues to be chargeable to the said township of Midgley, whereof the churchwardens and overseers of the poor have complained.

Upon examination we adjudge and declare that the said child was born a bastard upon the body of the said Mary Foster who is now living and continues to be chargeable to the said township of Midgley and likely to so continue.

And we do further adjudge that John Titterington is the putative father and cannot show any cause to the contrary. We do order to pay to, or cause to be paid unto the churchwardens and overseers of the poor of the said township the sum of five pounds four shillings and shall weekly and every week charge for the expense incident to the birth of the said child and for the month's lying-in of the said Mary Foster.

The male child was begotten on her body by John Titterington and that she had no dealings with any other

161

person whatsoever for the same; and that John Titterington aboversaid is the only true natural father of the bastard child of which she was delivered as aforesaid.

	£	s	d	
Month	2	0	0	*(lying-in)*
Expenses		10	0	
Orders		6	0	
24 weeks	2	8	0	*(at 2 shillings per week)*
	5	4	0	
Per week		2	0	*(thereafter)*

A signature of a cross at the end of the original document states it to be *'her mark'* and next to this, in another's hand, a justice presumably, is written *'Mary Foster'*.

Eli Titterington was in fact both a churchwarden and an overseer of the poor *'...of the said township'* (of Midgley) making this an even greater public shaming. An apparent disowning of his own son, coupled with the fact that Eli in his official capacity as 'overseer' was the actual recipient or enforcer in the matter!

After young William left, all of which was shared with Tom to explain both the reason for his visit and the circumstances surrounding his origins as a Titterington, as announced by Scoggins.

John continued, "I know, it looked bad, Tom – such a young girl, but she was no innocent, and as it turned out, he is a fine boy of whom I'm very proud. As time moved on and I had more money after moving across the valley to establish Higgin Chamber Mill I always supported Mary before she moved away, and always made sure that young William was taken good care of. I educated him by employing my own former tutor for him to visit at his home in Sowerby Bridge.

"William came up to work for me at the first opportunity and the children know him as a nephew of mine – their cousin, who came over from Lancashire to work in the area.

"Not surprisingly, he couldn't work for my brother which is why he got dismissed. I knew Thomas would lose no time getting him out under any pretext and my father would have been behind it all anyway."

Tom had listened carefully to John's story and after turning it all over in his mind he responded: "I certainly know that your father has an in-built hatred for you, John. He does not sound, and clearly cannot be a very nice man. I've also learned that you have a strong Christian ethic and care for your fellow man – I have come to value your counsel and friendship and it is up to another to judge you ultimately and I thank you for telling me such an intimate part of your background. Tell me, whatever happened to Mary?"

"She never married, Tom, as far as I know, and moved away, to Lancashire, I think, leaving William, her only child in the care of her parents. From an early age he worked for the local butcher in Luddenden Foot who also ran a pub called The Anchor and Shuttle – a popular haunt for me, and Branwell, too. I'll tell you of the time I got into more trouble there with him, another time.

"He learned well and tells me now he's found employment helping a butcher in The Shambles. He even has been given accommodation there, too, above the shop, would you believe? And all in the space of a day! I tell you Tom, the lad's resourceful and will go far. Already he has plans to get me out of here!!"

Top: 43, Stonegate, York with its first-floor view of the Minster.
Bottom: Esos ojos!

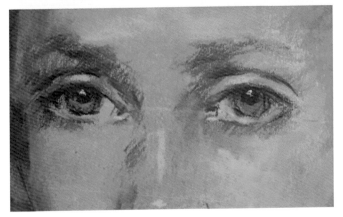

An South View of Manufacturers Hall, Halifax, taken from the West Gate way.

Halifax Piece Hall in 1789 and its majestic 2016 illuminated view (artist's impression).

Top: Higgin Chamber, Sowerby, Halifax with its view towards Sowerby Bridge (below).

Left: The Shambles, York.

Bottom: Oats Royd, the home of John and Hannah Murgatroyd (nee Titterington).

Top: John's waistcoat design overprint and Mary's brooch detail.

Bottom: Branwell's early literary work (aged 13) and comparitive usage of the same kerning and serifs on Blazer's collar.

Luddenden Village, Halifax

Thorp Green Hall (destroyed by fire in 1898)

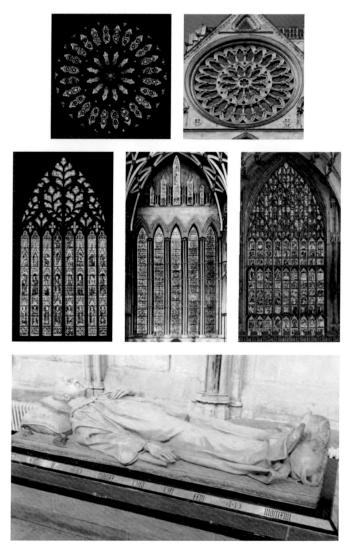

York Minster, Top: Rose Window, internal and external.
Centre from left: West Window, Five Sisters and Great East Window.
Bottom: J.B's tomb of Dr. Stephen Beckwith.

Top: Anne's original and corrected Scarborough gravestones - she was the only Brontë to be buried outside Haworth.

Centre: Banagher, Ireland, home of Arthur Bell Nicholls.

Bottom left: Sir Francis Sharp Powell's statue in Mesnes Park, Wigan, Lancs.

Bottom right, John Bromley's CD "The shearing's not for you" (track 6).

Mary Titterington 1812-1892

John Titterington 1807-1876

Chapter Thirteen

The Anchor and Shuttle

Monday the 7th of August 1848 brought a bright summer's morning to Higgin Chamber, Boulderclough, near Sowerby, as John Titterington arose at around 5.30am, dressed, fed Blazer in the back kitchen and headed across the mill yard to open up and meet the early arrivals for the 6.00am morning shift.

It was the eleventh year of the reign of Queen Victoria and little did he know that he would be forcibly detained at Her Majesty's pleasure before the day was out, and not for the only time that year, in a police cell in Halifax awaiting the magistrates' undoubted *dis*pleasure following a major fracas at The Anchor and Shuttle.

As unofficial president of their Hell-Fire Club, John occasionally arranged for his fellow members to meet up at different hostelries in the wider area for more intellectual discourse with invited guests.

Joseph Bentley Leyland, JB and Joe Drake were staunch original members, as were Branwell and the recently deceased landlord of The Talbot, Dan Sugden. Members met by appointment at a public house of John's choosing and various 'guests' were invited to these soirees. These were often artists, writers and poets and more recently had included exponents of the lucrative 'new art' of photography with its potential for portraiture, much favoured at the time.

Living some distance apart in different industrial towns, members needed to spread themselves around to placate long-suffering landlords, who deserved a break from the ribald evenings spent with these often impecunious customers.

Public houses frequented included the George Hotel in Bradford, the Black Bull in Howarth, the Cross Roads near Keighley, the Lord Nelson in Luddenden and the Union Cross, Talbot and Old Cock in Halifax. Also in the round was The Anchor and Shuttle in Luddenden and it was this latter one, his own 'local' that John had chosen as the venue for that night's meeting.

Apart from the usual crowd John had also been asked by JB to invite William Overend Geller who had recently completed a daguerreotype portrait of him which was to be unveiled and shown to members that night for the first time. Introduced in 1839, the daguerreotype was the first widely used photographic process where a copper plate coated with silver was sensitised to light by exposing it to iodine vapour, exposed in a camera and then developed over heated mercury.

Taking an increasingly not-untypical day away from the mill, as he did with shooting trips on the moors, John had first arranged to meet up with Branwell at his Aunt Abigail Titterington's public house, the White Lion in Mytholmroyd.

A favourite haunt of Branwell's, who dropped down from Haworth's turnpike road on the way through to Luddenden, the White Lion had been used on many occasions by them being fairly equidistant between Howarth and Higgin Chamber from where John now dropped down the hill and caught a train at Luddenden to travel one stop along the line to Mytholmroyd station.

A balmy summer's day saw John arrive first to greet his aunt Abigail, aged fifty-nine and widow of Henry Patchett, polishing brasses in the public bar of the White Lion, a well-used hostelry for locals and travellers on the coaching route through to Lancashire.

"So young John, a nice surprise. How's everything? Mary and the children well? I suppose you'll be meeting up with t'parson's lad as usual? I do enjoy his company and his poetry readings, such an educated young man."

Her son Thomas, John's cousin, was nowhere to be seen and John presumed he must be out and about on his rounds, supplying timber as he usually would be during the day, and working in the bar in the evenings helping his mother. Thomas was difficult to get on with for John and indeed most people, and he was glad he wasn't about. Rather slow-witted and sometimes a little hard of hearing, he also did not take to Branwell either and found that whilst his intellect was outside his understanding, he felt looked down upon and supposed him to be sneering at him. Branwell had once engaged him in conversation when nobody else was around in the bar and actually read to him from his notebook; a wholly unacceptable gesture which Thomas regarded as though being read to as an illiterate child, which of course he was essentially, since any form of education had been ruled out by his perfectly literate mother. He had sworn at Branwell and limped away with his rather awkward gait due to a deformity in his legs and no words had ever passed between the two of them since.

Thomas was nevertheless a tireless worker both in the bar and in the timber yard behind the pub. On his delivery journeys he was fastidious with quantities, strong as an ox and punctual to a degree. He had the additional quality of never getting his money wrong, either in the bar or at his customers, and this unexpected ability was a real bonus to his mother who had made sure he was sound in this most vital area of their businesses.

His weakness was alcohol and his *'excessively ludicrous'…'nodding mandarin'…'staggering drunk'* performance (as prosecutor) in court over the stolen timber and his so-publicly reported description by the magistrate as a *'simpleton'* and *'greenhorn'* in the Irish Kate *'…disreputable women,'* £76 personal robbery case, left little doubt about the origins of his general demeanour.

"So John, I hear you've landed t'market manager's lass i'n't family way? Is it true?"

Somewhat taken aback but never surprised by his aunt's blunt speaking, which in any case was what drew

John to liking her in the first place, he blushed and stammered out hesitantly, "How the hell did you know that, Abi? I thought nobody knew that. And Fanny doesn't even look pregnant. I thought we could hide that for a little while longer, but she's at the end of her sixth month."

"Stories like that get around, John, and I knew your old auntie could easily get it out of you! It's hard to hide a name like Titterington under the breath in bar-room gossip and Thomas and I have had our fair share of that over the years!"

"So now it's out, but my father doesn't know yet, does he? Not to mention poor Mary and the children. It's a complete nightmare, but I'm glad to talk about it with you. It's quite a relief I can tell you. How long have you known?"

"Only the other night in the bar, I heard she was in the family way and your name came up as the prime suspect. Your father will surely disown you, just as he has me – still won't speak to me after all these years; as if it was my fault – and it certainly wasn't!

"And your poor wife – how understanding was she about your other lad? But she married you nevertheless."

John considered the question of his father first and shuddered. It had been coming, of course, since Fanny came to him and told him a few months before, but he was surprised that the news could get out as far as Mytholmroyd and yet not have reached his father from Abraham Taylor next door at the Piece Hall. Fanny really didn't look pregnant, it was true, and John had gone to some considerable expense, as always with Fanny, to keep her from telling anyone.

"Mary concerns me most. I can't really get a worse relationship with my father, after Liverpool in January. You'll have heard, I'm sure, about me being robbed there. I know I'm blamed for that!

"It's my weakness Abi, I know, but what do you advise? Poor Mary really doesn't deserve this and I still love her and the children dearly."

Phlegmatic and down-to-earth as ever, Abigail, who knew the pain of deceit more than any, came straight to her conclusion. "Confess all, John, and as soon as you can. Be straight with it, it's best, and good luck to you! I think Mary will stand by you with five young bairns to bring up, though of course she'll be very hurt and may never trust you again, but your father may well cut you off. He's talked of it before, I know. Are you prepared to strike out on your own? You may well have to."

John's debts were piling up, not only buying Fanny's silence, but in bar bills in several public houses, on top of which his plans to upgrade weaving at the mill were going to be, indeed were already proving, very expensive and he couldn't hide the bills for much longer.

'Utilising' funds from the Huddersfield Union Banking Co., of which he was a director, to cover his debts, would need to be addressed soon before deficiencies were discovered, as they surely would be before long if he delayed any longer.

And his father knew nothing of any of his expansion plans, neither at the mill, nor within Fanny's belly!

"Anyway, John, whatever you choose, you can always rely on me for a friendly shoulder to cry on. Come around whenever you need," said Abigail.

Thanking his aunt and giving her a big hug, he felt comforted and moved on to having her pour out his first drink, a whisky with warm water and sugar, and sat back to await Bran's arrival.

The last time John had seen Bran he seemed much better. The early summer had been warm and very dry and his cough from earlier in the year was much better, as were his shakes. He was much stronger in the better weather, but any early onset of autumn, which often happened by late August in the valley, would not be good for his health.

His drinking also would still be increasing, he felt fairly certain, and opium had also started to enter more seriously into his life – often to John's cost.

The bar-room door opened gently and Branwell stepped inside, tired looking from his journey over from Howarth, mopping his brow.

He plonked himself down onto a bar stool and gasped. "Doesn't get any nearer, JT. And on such a warm day! Pour me a drink, Abi, and I'll be able to speak more presently!"

"I'll stand it for you, too, Bran if you read me some more from your notebook," said Abigail and turning to

179

John added, "fair frightened me to death he did last time reading about some black half-devil child – and a dark night he left me with to ponder over later, I hardly slept a wink all night tossing and turning!

"Find it for me again, Bran. Let John see what I mean."

And with that Branwell opened his notebook, quickly found the right page among all his writings and sketches which even appeared to include columns of figures, pretty well certainly even his railway jottings that got him into so much trouble before, and started to read:

"*Opening his great coat he said...see here, wife! ...you must take it as a gift of God; though it's dark almost as if it came from the devil. We peeped at a dirty, ragged, black-haired child; big enough to both walk and talk: ...yet, when it was set on its feet, it only stared round, and repeated over and over again some gibberish, that nobody could understand. I was frightened, and Mrs Earnshaw was ready to fling it out of doors: she did fly up, asking how he could fashion to bring that gypsy brat into the house, when they had their own bairns to feed and fend for? ...he had found it good as dumb, in the streets of Liverpool; where he picked it up and enquired for its owner. None forthcoming he brought it home with him...Cathy spat at it realising that she had been brought no gift and...the children entirely refused to have it in bed with them, or even in their room. I put it on the landing of the stairs, hoping it might be gone on the morrow.*"

He concluded, "This was Heathcliff's first introduction to the family."

"Oh! Master Branwell it still chills me – 'it', repeatedly, and then such an aristocratic name for your black devil-child, how does it go on? Did they fling 'it' out of doors?"

"You must read the new book for yourself, Abi, it's called *'Wuthering Heights'* and it's by my sister Emily, calling herself Ellis Bell, to hide such a brutal story from sensitive ears!

"Charlotte and Anne have written, too, and also use pseudonyms – Currer and Acton Bell in their case, all three using the capital letters of their own Christian names, a rather neat ACE trio, and the name coincidentally is the middle name of our curate in Howarth, though it was actually drawn from my own first and last three letters – BranwELL. Charlotte's book 'Jane Eyre', written of course as being by Currer Bell, is already in its third edition since the second sold out in January. Anne, as Acton Bell, has success as well – her 'Tenant of Wildfell Hall' published only at the end of June is causing quite a stir already and there is talk of all of the 'Bells' being the same writer. Their publisher is encouraging this, too, by suggesting it to be true in order to sell all of the books in America!

"I can only tell you this now because we all swore ourselves to secrecy with such sensitive subjects. One critic, suspicious of its authorship, has even said of 'The Tenant of Wildfell Hall, 'that'…'it was disgraceful if written by a woman!' So you can see why we devised male-sounding Christian names.

"Only last month have Charlotte and Anne revealed their gender with a first visit to their publisher, Smith and Elder, down in London. Emily has chosen to stay in the background and not reveal herself for the moment, but her book, launched in December, is already causing quite a stir. You may have read about it? Father got quite a surprise when Charlotte told him – he knew absolutely nothing about any of the publications! We all hoped he would not be scandalised after reading the books but he's actually quite proud of our achievements!

"The truth is out now anyway so 'exposure' is not feared anymore and the full, accidental, though the protective, exquisitely apposite, cryptic anagram of mine, 'WARN BELL!' was never needed in the end to prepare any of the ACE trio from some of the sexist outrage which follows to this day.

"Perhaps even more remarkably is the fact that our older sister, Maria, who died so needlessly and tragically in childhood, after the typhoid outbreak at her school for clergy daughters in Cowan Bridge, may well have had a literary talent beyond the reach of all of us. Father told us she proof-read one of his long poems for the printer in Howarth – at only ten years of age! I remember her well, even though I was only six at the time. She would surely have become quite a talent herself."

They had the pub completely to themselves and after a few more drinks, bought by John as usual, Abigail heard the cart arriving in the timber yard at the back and went through to talk with Thomas.

Quickly returning to the bar she said, "It's just after one o'clock, so Thomas is going to have a bite to eat now. I'll give you some broth with cheese and pickle if you like and I've baked this morning, so you'll have a nice crusty bloomer and fresh butter to go with it. And no doubt another glass of ale apiece to wash it all down won't go amiss?"

John and Branwell both responded gratefully to the anticipated invitation to eat, as on previous visits at this time, and Abigail went on. "Thomas has a delivery after lunch up near Luddenden village if you're interested in a ride out with him. I know you might both enjoy continuing your 'day out' with a change of scenery and the Lord Nelson would seem the perfect choice for your needs."

Aunt Abigail delivered the *'day out'* with a wink and emphasis more normally reserved for naughty boys, knowing full well they intended to spend the entire day getting more and more inebriated!

She was a landlady who both knew and appreciated men of a certain kind.

"Perfect, Abi. We'll take you up on that if it's alright with Thomas and we'll give him a lift off at the other end."

Abigail served them both at the bar counter and withdrew to eat with her son at the back. They had not expected Thomas to want to join them and were glad of that.

After lunch, John and Bran climbed aboard the now timber-laden cart in the timber yard and the three of them headed out with no conversation desired or indeed possible above the churning wheels and the clip-clop of the hooves.

Which gave John ample time to work out his planned conversation with Bran about Fanny. He was quite confident of a supportive response from Bran, since he had in turn confided all with him about his illegitimate child in Broughton-in-Furness as well as detailing his illicit affair with Lydia at Thorp Green.

Most of all, John needed to confide in a good friend, to talk about it and get it off his chest.

He also knew that Bran was unaware of the rumour; exactly like Abi, he would quite certainly have had no qualms and would have already raised the subject himself had he known.

Thomas headed onward, slightly stooped as he sat hunched over the reins with his awkward leg tucked away beneath the cart's seat.

Now thirty-six years of age, he had produced an illegitimate daughter, Mary Ann, born to Sarah Slater a servant-girl who had moved away to a position in Rochdale shortly after the child's birth.

Thomas himself of course already bore the lifetime shame of being the progeny of both his mother and her own father, his grandfather Thomas Titterington.

Thomas and his mother had endured more than enough public shaming and gossip themselves which had then continued with Sarah initiating a bastardy order of 28th September 1833 against him in which it was affirmed in court that:

'...the bastard was begotten on her body in the township of Heptonstall about five weeks ago' and that 'Thomas Titterington of Midgley, joiner, is the putative father and after being summoned cannot show any cause to the contrary.'

He was ordered to pay a sum of £2 19s 6d to cover lying-in and expenses and one shilling and sixpence a week maintenance thereafter.

As they rode along Burnley Road, John mulled it all over in his mind; his cousin's daughter Mary Ann would be fifteen by now, but could not have known then that Sarah would return from Rochdale in four years' time to actually marry Thomas, almost twenty years after the illegitimate birth of their daughter. Mary Ann would then, by right of course anyway, change her surname from Slater to the biologically apposite, Titterington.

Turning at Luddenden Lane and climbing up the hill from Luddenden Foot on their two-mile journey, Thomas stopped and chocked the heavy cart's wheels outside a newly-built cottage, beyond the elegant two centuries-old Murgatroyd family home, Kershaw House, and the three of them unloaded floor-boarding into the entrance hallway.

It was a hill that Branwell knew well from his days at Luddenden Foot station, climbing after a long day to his lodgings at Turn Lea cottages or perhaps dropping down High Street into Luddenden village to slake his thirst at the Lord Nelson before taking a shortcut up Old Lane to join Solomon Hill and then on to Turn Lea.

Climbing again up the hill, John said, "Drop us at High Street, Thomas, if you will, please. You can turn easily there and we'll walk the rest of the way."

Thomas gave the merest nod of acquiescence.

Bidding Thomas farewell and waving him off, they gave him only the vaguest mutterings of gratitude, since he had hardly been inconvenienced and had made no attempt to thank them for their efforts assisting him with the unloading, and had as usual made no attempt to converse with them at any time during the journey.

At the Nelson they were greeted warmly as usual by landlord, Timothy Wormald. Also in the bar parlour were John's brother-in-law, John Murgatroyd, and their railway-engineer friend, Francis Grundy, whose ambivalent views of Branwell he recorded in his diaries: *"...poor, brilliant, gay, moody, moping, wildly excitable, miserable Brontë"* – an observation made by him in this very bar-room and even on this day it was hard as always to predict which persona he might have brought along with him!

John Murgatroyd had been visiting his wife's grave across the road in St Mary's churchyard. Betty, nee Forster, his first wife, had sadly died ten years before at the age of just twenty-nine and her husband made visits still on special occasions; perhaps it was her birthday John surmised, but would not pry.

John Murgatroyd, two years younger than John, had married John's sister Hannah just two years before on 21st October 1846. Thirty-three years of age at the time, Hannah had waited for 'the right man' to come along and in widower John Murgatroyd, she had found no less than the richest eligible man in the area as her suitor.

Moving away from his home called Victory, over the hill in Warley, he had acquired the substantial Oats Royd estate six years before, to both live and expand his already substantial textile weaving business. He had just completed building the Oats Royd Mill complex the year before. It was the largest textile mill in West Yorkshire and several times the size of John's Higgin Chamber, which itself towered prominently over the Calder Valley at Boulderclough, visible for miles before it was to be destroyed by a fire in 1856.

Hannah Titterington's patience had been rewarded and much to her father Eli's approval and encouragement she had 'married well' and had moved into their fine on-site house where she was now the 'Lady of Oats Royd'

Eli was proud of his daughter and the old Murgatroyd-Titterington feud was now well behind both families through the passage of time and the continuing successes of both of them. There was now more than enough business for both empires to prosper and grow, without any need of the previous bitterness.

Dr Phyllis Bentley, a local writer, in her book *'Inheritance,'* famously serialised by the BBC and starring John Thaw, chronicled the feud, but even her changing of the main characters' names could never disguise the fact that it was the Titterington and Murgatroyd families who were the main protagonists.

John Titterington was a member of the Luddenden Reading Society, which was the village library, conveniently situated in a room above the bar. Landlord Timothy Wormald was also a member of the society as well as being clerk to St. Mary's church over the road. He kept both a tidy God-fearing house in the bar downstairs as well as in the library. He was the originator of the library's house rules which stated:

'...*that if any members come to the said meeting drunk so that he be offensive to the company, and not fit to do his business, he shall forfeit two pence. Swearing on oath, or using any other kind of bad language judged by a majority of the members to be offensive, also calls for a fine of two pence.*' (Equating to £6.00 today).

John Murgatroyd confirmed he had indeed been visiting his first wife's grave by gently admonishing Timothy Wormald, "Churchyard could do with more care, Timothy. Grass is knee-high in parts and not what we've come to expect. That lad you employ needs sharpening up a bit, hanging around talking with a young lass just now, with work to be done. He saw me and still never budged. I wouldn't have him in't mill if you paid me."

"I'll talk to him and see it improves," the landlord offered and John seemed happy with that.

John Murgatroyd then turned his attention to Branwell:

"So Brontë, now I've caught you, are you ever coming to paint those portraits of me and my wife? You've promised since that time you sketched me in your book, in this very bar, and it's now two years since our wedding and I asked you to paint the pair of us as a present for Hannah, to hang in the front parlour. Hannah's seen the pair you were doing for John and Mary and quite fell in love with the idea as part of the furnishings at Oats Royd house. I've not seen your work apart from that sketch you did of me, but Hannah never stops asking so she must have liked what you were doing."

Branwell gave a fairly non-committal response, but in truth, as both he and Grundy were noticing, he was clearly unwell. His hands shook slightly, he coughed occasionally and his pallor was distinctly pale and unhealthy looking.

John Titterington noticed it, too, and asked Timothy to fill him a good glass of warm whisky and honey to 'remedy his cough', which he duly did and almost immediately Branwell took on a different hue, prompting John to pursue this same line of questioning.

"So Bran, while we're on the subject, it's a few years now since you started mine and Mary's portraits, too, and they're still not varnished ready for me to hang them. I remember you said to wait at least a year before varnishing and that the weather had to be right; warm and dry. You're staying over with us yet again, the time is right and I'll thank you to finish them off as you keep promising – you owe me that. I've even asked over in

Halifax and got the right varnish and brush for you to finish off months ago.

"I'm having important shooting party guests next week to the house and I want to show them off! I can see why your landlady at your studio in Bradford got so angry with you now. You've always been 'meaning' to varnish them, but you never do. I'll thank you to finish them off tonight. And in any case my guests are wealthy and vain enough to want you to paint themselves also. You should be grateful that Frank Powell and Joe Armitage will both see what you've accomplished and I know they'll be impressed enough to commission you. You've made remarkable likenesses of us both – and I'm proud of them, and you, as a friend, dammit!"

Which resulted in an awkward silence for quite some time, but after another couple of whiskies yielded the desired response that Branwell would indeed comply and complete the portraits that very night as requested.

Frank Powell, son of a wealthy clergyman was twenty-one at the time and a rising Cambridge University intellect and law student who John had met out shooting; he was later to be sponsored by John and became Sir Francis Sharp Powell, 1st Baronet and Member of Parliament. Sir Joseph and Lady Sarah Armitage were more frequent visitors to Higgin Chamber; he a wealthy Huddersfield industrialist and fellow founder-director of John's in the Huddersfield Union Banking Company, where both were recorded as *'persons of whom the company or partnership exists'*.

John and Branwell were good friends mostly all the time, but the slight unpleasantness reminded John of the time they had met down near the canal several summers before, and argued over a matter so trivial that he couldn't now remember what it was about. They had finished up wrestling each other to the ground and with both possessing fiery tempers, they had almost come to blows, had tight wrestling not deliberately restricted their fists' movements; neither combatant wishing to physically harm the other, such was their friendship.

Though John didn't know it, Branwell, in his station-master's time, had recorded the disagreement in his day-book:

At R.Col last night with
G.Thompson
J.Titterington
R.L.Col
H. Killiner and another.
I quarrelled with J.T. about going but after a wrestle met him on the road and became friends – quarrelled almost on the subject with G.Thompson. Will have no more of it.
August 18th, 1841 P.B.B.

"Say hello to my dear sister and come over to visit us soon. You can see the finished portraits then," John said, bidding John Murgatroyd farewell a short time later. Toward late afternoon the two of them left the Nelson, saying their own farewells to the landlord and Grundy, who looked settled in for the evening. They headed off down to The Anchor and Shuttle in Luddenden Foot for their meeting.

John had ample time on the walk down the hill to bring up the delicate subject of Fanny Brearley and

191

started out by asking Branwell if he remembered the Hell-Fire Club night at The Talbot in January when the punchbowl was nearly scuppered.

"Remember it? How could I forget it? I even sketched the whole scene!" Branwell interjected.

"I also remember seeing Fanny Brearley heading upstairs later to your room, John, when you thought we were all too drunk to notice! JB didn't, and neither did I! She's a voluptuous, wild, young Irish lady who would set any man's heart racing, there's no doubt about that. And I hear she's with child. Rumours travel fast, John, and you're being spoken of as the progenitor; is it true? I didn't like to ask."

"It's true alright Bran, and I still have to tell Mary, but what can I say to her? Me, with a bastard son already, which she so generously forgave and welcomes young William into our home as one of our own. She really doesn't deserve this, but how to tell her? Abi and I spoke of it today. The rumour has reached as far as Mytholmroyd, would you believe? And she advised honesty and to tell the whole truth as soon as possible, before Mary discovered it for herself from some interfering busy-body."

"Abi's correct John, it must be the best way," said Bran. "You will remember I put myself in the same position at Broughton-in-Furness with the servant-girl, which cost us both our jobs. Maybe a more honest approach to my employers would have helped, but I don't think so. It was unforgivable for me to betray their trust and you're in no better position, I'm afraid. Worse in fact, with a wife and five children under ten years of age. It's a mess and you should have been more circumspect. You must come clean, tell all, be penitent and hope for Mary's forgiveness, but it won't come easily, as you must know. She's a lovely lady who I'm very fond of and she will be very hurt. I do hope you're not planning to tell her tonight? I don't want to be there when you do, with both of us worse for wear after a full day's drinking, looking like naughty boys. I take no responsibility for your deed, John, and you must shoulder it yourself."

All of which failed to give John any comfort and they arrived at The Anchor and Shuttle with John's mind in some sort of inebriated turmoil. Another drink would help.

Sarah Slater, the landlord's daughter was behind the bar; a bad start, she being the niece of her namesake who had produced Mary Ann, the now fifteen year-old bastard daughter of cousin Thomas at the White Lion.

She had muttered a few times under her breath previously about that particular illegitimacy and was no friend of John Titterington, who she had seen too often flirting in the lounge bar and wholly disapproved of as a responsible married man. She despised what she perceived as his arrogance and status as a handsome wealthy mill owner and felt beneath him and looked down on.

The Titteringtons had more than a little answering to do in Sarah Slater's book.

John wondered had she, too, heard the rumour? Luddenden Foot was on the well-beaten public-house-strewn coaching route from Halifax to Lancashire and was itself halfway to 'plaiting its legs' into Mytholmroyd!

The evening proceeded with William Overend's daguerreotype talk taking over most of the discussion in a private room at the back arranged by John. Some poems were read and songs, some raucous, were sung until quite a bawdy evening was developing. Bran and John were the first to show signs of inebriation after their afternoon-long drinking session in three public houses, yet Bran, John noticed, was bearing up well and clearly benefitting from his day out.

John, on the other hand, had a habit of becoming tetchy in drink and had a reputation for a fiery temper, well known to break loose on occasions just such as this and the smallest thing was known to kick it off.

A stranger at the bar, passing through to Lancashire on the next morning's coach, staying over at the pub for the night, had been observing proceedings from a bar-stool, talking mainly to Sarah Slater behind the bar. John came up to the bar and reached across him to collect drinks he had called over for and was annoyed that he remained firmly at his seat, deliberately blocking his reach.

"I'll thank you to be more considerate, sir," John said, admonishing the stranger, who then moved somewhat reluctantly and by no means totally, to still force John to push through to reach the drinks.

The stranger spoke. "Considerate is it? With your noisy so-called intellectual rabble hogging the pub all night, singing vulgar songs and not taking a blind bit of notice of the comfort of other customers or this nice young girl behind the bar. Considerate, indeed!"

Biting his tongue and noticing Sarah Slater's pleasure at the rebuke, John responded, "Why not join us 'so-called intellectuals', then? Come over and I'll introduce you. Show us your intellect and maybe you might like a wager to demonstrate it more fully? Put your money where your mouth is, sir!"

John of course had just the wager in mind – Branwell's party piece!

The stranger came over into the private room at the back and after introductions, a wager was agreed that Branwell could write in two different languages, utilising both hands, simultaneously.

Now introduced as Ted Wainwright, the blunt, blustering, over-dressed commercial traveller, not wishing to tell them that he only knew one language, his own, and that his facility with even that one was limited, was shamed nevertheless into a wager for a sovereign that Branwell could not perform such a feat to his entire satisfaction.

John called for paper, a pen, and ink, and the group moved in around Branwell at his table in the centre of the private room as he wrote boldly, at the left-hand side of the page before him...

'Quod in principio sermonis'

Dipping his pen again, he proceeded to write, again in bold letters, across on the right-hand side of the page…

'Στην αρχή, τι η λέξη'

The small group now strengthened by a dozen-or-so customers from the saloon bar pressed in closer. Many would be illiterate, but all were well able to see that he had written two very different types of script.

Only John and JB, who had seen the trick before, knew what was coming next, though on this occasion with a fully attentive audience and money at stake, Bran was giving it extra panache and a full theatrical performance!

John was relieved to notice that Bran's hands, undoubtedly due to the alcohol, were not now shaking, for the climax which was about to follow under such close scrutiny.

Both texts were written with his right hand and he then called for an extra pen, dipped both into the ink pot, covered over both of the written texts completely with a blank piece of paper and taking up the second pen in his left hand proceeded to write both texts, again, simultaneously at a quickened pace, below the blanked-over paper, *using both hands*!

Uncovering the top two original writings, even the illiterate could now see that Branwell had written exactly the same scripts twice.

"I believe you owe him a sovereign, sir," said JB to the now-flustered, reddening, commercial traveller.

"Hold on, sir, what proof do I have that he has complied with the terms of the wager? How do I know what is written, for I know not the script?" the stranger wheedled, but feared the worst, so impressed was he by what he had just observed.

William Geller, who was over on the other side of the room and had not observed the events, was called over to adjudicate and was asked by JB to translate each text individually.

"Firstly, William," said JB. "Can you confirm that you never saw this trick or anything like it before, sir?" He showed him the full paper with the four phrases on.

"I can indeed, JB, and furthermore, I've no idea what, or even why you're asking me," said Geller.

JB continued. "We have a wager and kindly tell us what you see, and translate for us, please, each piece of text separately."

"The first sentence is in Latin and it says, 'IN THE BEGINNING WAS THE WORD'. Which is repeated exactly the same, in Latin, as you can see, beneath."

"And the second, sir?" A hush fell over the now expectant crowd as several more curious observers had come in from the public bar sensing something dramatic was about to happen.

Geller continued without further prompting, now seeing what the next phrase said and now fully aware of a dramatic outcome with money riding on his words.

"The second sentence, sir, also written twice, and this time in Greek, says..." The hush was now palpable. "'IN THE BEGINNING WAS THE WORD'"

The throng erupted. *How could it be possible?*

John, too, was impressed as always, whispering to JB, "It isn't as though he practises it either JB. We've seen it many times and he never uses the same text twice! Such a brain! It's won him a fair few drinks along the way, too!"

Wainwright had no choice but to reluctantly hand over the sovereign to John and withdraw to the public bar where Sarah Slater, who had also pressed into the private room, now grimaced and glowered back at John who had just won the equivalent of several of her weeks' wages in a trice.

John went over to the bar, ordered two whiskies from the surly barmaid and offered one to Wainwright, which he flatly refused. Maggie McColl, an Irish woman of ill-repute, known well to John, seated next to him, said cheekily she'd have it instead and John responded, "You most certainly will not you old hag, I'll not waste money on the likes of you!"

At which point Sarah Slater could contain herself no longer and exploded out loud.

"You pompous, over-bearing, stuck-up ass, John Titterington. Think you're special, don't you, Mr mill-owner? With your next bastard bun in the oven and a wife and five young 'uns to care for up there at 'iggin Chamber. You're all the same, you Titteringtons, scattering your ill-gotten bastards around. Your crippled cousin Thomas with my poor dear maiden aunt Sarah, and even him, poor sod, your own grandfather's bastard, with his own daughter, not to mention your transported highwayman-of-a-cousin. Should have 'ung 'im! You Titteringtons DISGUST me!"

And with that, John reached out, struck her forcefully across the face and dragged her onto the bar counter. He gripped her blouse with both hands and manhandled her with such force, ripping her blouse and undergarment over her head and clean off her back, totally exposing her bare breasts. While at the same time, he knocked several bar stools and glasses in all directions and caused one of the old rickety stools to smash into pieces against the bar.

Sarah reached out desperately, hair dishevelled, mouth bloodied, wildly clutching and hugging a bar towel up to her naked breasts. She grabbed for the nearest glass and flung the contents of the glass of whisky, intended for Wainwright, straight into John's face. The neat contents of the glass stung his eyes, temporarily blinding him and causing him to stop, just long enough for two tough-looking Irish boaties to restrain and hold on to him. Meanwhile, a constable was hastily summoned and John was arrested and taken under escort to the police station in Horton Street in Halifax, to cool off overnight and await punishment from the magistrates in court the following morning.

A shocked hush came temporarily to the drinkers at The Anchor and Shuttle and Sarah's shouted words still echoed around in the customers' heads, "…with your next bastard bun in the oven."

The truth was out and the rumour was confirmed, or announced to the few of John's acquaintances who didn't already know it, as well as to the gob-smacked rest of the locals in the pub, who certainly knew John well, either as their wealthy neighbour or the boss up at the mill. Several of them or their relatives were his employees and included, over in the corner, John's leering Chartist foreman Joe Saltonstall, who so despised his employer's hunting absences with his titled friends, whilst he was expected to pick up the pieces – for no extra payment.

Branwell, now suddenly remarkably sober, bade his embarrassed friends an early good night. He headed alone up across the fields, the mile or so up to Higgin Chamber, where Mary was expecting him to stay over for the night.

Chapter Fourteen

A First Taste of Court

Tired, bedraggled and looking anything but a gentleman, John was led into court in Halifax to face his fate on the morning of August 8th 1848.

Across the magistrates' courtroom stood a defiant, still-seething, Sarah Slater. At seeing John brought hand-cuffed before the court, she clearly struggled not to continue the outburst of the previous night.

She had an angry-looking bruise on the left side of her face with a black eye. On the other side, her cheek was clearly swollen and also badly bruised; an additional already bloodied bandage right across her forehead looked to John like a clear case of over-kill and a histrionic attempt to gain the court's sympathy; plus the maximum punishment for John, hopefully a gaol sentence.

Seeing the toothless, wizened old Irish crone Maggie McColl in court seated next to her, staring aggressively across the courtroom at him, also gave him no comfort either since she was obviously there not only to support Sarah Slater but presumably to be called as a witness.

Court reporters from both *The Halifax Guardian* and *Leeds Mercury,* present on the day, picked up the story which appeared the following weekend:

On Tuesday John Titterington of Sowerby, manufacturer, was summoned for an assault upon Sarah Ann Slater, the daughter of the landlord of The Anchor and Shuttle public house, Luddenden Foot.

The assault she said was purely unprovoked, but it was sworn Mr. Titterington was drunk. A witness was called who was drinking a glass which Mr. Titterington ordered and according to her account she thought Miss Slater threw some spirit and water in Mr. Titterington's face. This she admitted having done, but said that it was all she could do to prevent Titterington breaking the furniture. The bench thought that under the circumstances Titterington ought to pay the expenses which amounted to 15s 6d.

"Drinking a glass I ordered, indeed!" thought John staring back angrily at the Irish crone. *"In her dreams, the old witch!"*

Equivalent to over £500 today, it is not clear what the 'expenses' were intended to cover. A new bar stool? Sarah's clothing? Broken glasses? Not 'hurt pride' in Sarah's case, for sure, and the drink being thrown in his face appears to have helped him avoid the more serious charge of assault, even aggravated assault, which could have included more serious penalties or even imprisonment in the circumstances.

202

His attendance in court as a 'gentleman' will have helped him, albeit in a dishevelled state, in a dispute with a *female* servant in phallocentric times, moreover one who admitted assaulting him whatever the reason, by throwing any sort of liquid in his face, but the fine demonstrated the court's recognition of his perceived wealth and ability to pay, which was sadly untrue in John's increasingly strained financial circumstances.

Given a day to pay his fine into the court, and wondering where he could lay his hands on the money, John walked down to the Piece Hall for market day, unshaven and generally looking anything but the very tidy smartly apparelled gentleman he usually appeared, especially on market days.

He walked carefully from Westgate and turned left to the trading room, keeping inside the balcony shadows, hugging the wall and desperately hoping not to bump into Fanny who would also be looking for more money.

Entering the trading room, he bumped into his father who eyed him suspiciously. He knew immediately that something was wrong and pitched straight in at him. "Where in the name of all that's holy have you been 'til this time? 11.30. And you roll in looking like you've been dragged through a bush backwards! Explain yourself, to me, first, and then be ready to tell Dubois where you were, both last night *and* first thing here this morning. He's here after your blood, too. I'll warn you now, so you'd better be ready to hear his complaints. He's not a bit happy with your latest shipment to him either. Your quality's gone to pot. Spending too much time on't moors with your fancy shooting friends, when you should be minding your business. I shouldn't wonder, my business. Go and tidy yourself up for heaven's sake before anybody sees you – you look like a tramp!"

No mention of court then, or Fanny, so he must not have got the news. Abraham Taylor would have spread the gossip to him had he been around, but John had noticed his trading room door was shut, telling him he must not be around today; probably gone over to Manchester or Leeds market, but somebody else would tell Eli soon enough, his brother Thomas would for sure, but he, too, didn't seem to be around. Brother James was cutting samples at the back of the room with a large pair of shears and he nodded across to John in recognition of his arrival and kept well out of his father's way when he was in this kind of a mood. He would know nothing about John's predicament since nobody ever confided in him and he rarely engaged in conversation with anyone anyway.

Thomas was the danger; wherever he was, he would be likely to be the first to inform on him and plant yet another foot more firmly on the inheritance ladder ahead of his older brother.

John went over to the toilet room and washed himself. He straightened his clothing, checked and combed his hair, gathered his thoughts and returned to No. 63 to face Claude Dubois and apologise for not coming in to eat with him at the Old Cock the night before as he usually did on his twice yearly visits.

"So James, where's our dear brother today, not off suffering from anything trivial, I trust?" opened John sarcastically over at the pattern table.

"Don't know, John – not heard a word, but I dreaded either of you arriving when it got to this time. Father was getting into a right lather expecting you both and it was really busy first thing. Claude Dubois came straight after opening as well and he's not happy about your last jacquard shipment to Brussels – something about a tied warp thread, not sure in how many pieces. Told him you were very busy and must have got held up back at the mill," said James, always willing to help and quite different from their brother who managed to be disagreeable to just about everybody, except his father.

Seeing Fanny in summer clothes in the distance and noticing that she did now indeed look pregnant and could hide it no longer, John determined discretion was the better part of valour and decided to abscond whilst her and his father's attention was temporarily distracted.

"So James, I've arranged anyway to meet Claude over at The Talbot for a bite of lunch. Just bumped into him on the way in," he lied. "I'll get over there now and probably take him back to the mill, there are some new designs I want to show him and he hasn't seen production yet, or the house anyway."

Only the older more traditional manufacturers from the days of exclusive farmhouse or cottage hand weaving still valued the Piece Hall as both a place to trade and socialise; a time-honoured way of life in short. Along with steam mechanisation had come the establishment of mills, usually adjacent to the fine new owners' homes. In these early days of the industrial revolution, younger manufacturers eager to show off their advances and wealth, increasingly brought buyers to their elegant homes and mills.

Fine furnishings, an abundance of larder provisioning and, of course, the servants needed to prepare food and attend to the everyday needs of burgeoning families and their guests. All contributed to a new opulence, almost even to gentrification, much of which John Titterington already relished, of course, and a pair of portraits of 'master and mistress of the house' hanging majestically in the parlour provided a crowning glory only witnessed previously in the stately homes of the aristocracy or even the royals.

Brother-in-law John Murgatroyd, at Oats Royd across the valley was also a man of such ambition who embraced the modern production techniques and fine living.

The end of the days of textile trading at Halifax Piece Hall were fast approaching and hence the temptation of a plethora of empty trading rooms on the upper floors which had landed John in his present predicament.

Moving furtively again, John retraced his steps through the shadows and exited into Westgate, feeling slightly relieved but still worried about how he was going to raise the cash to pay his fine. Dubois owed money and would have brought funds with him to pay for the last shipment, but news of a complaint was not good and might result in unavoidable discounting; but in any case, he needed to meet with him and stall him from another visit to find him.

John headed up Westgate and along Southgate to the Old Cock to see if Dubois was back at his hotel, and when that failed, he went straight back down to The Talbot where he would occasionally go for lunch.

He needed not to bump into Fanny on this particular day, when more than enough had happened already and whatever he could get out of Dubois must not be swallowed up by one of her stories which had taken on a more threatening tone recently.

The bank's money remained a priority however; his 'borrowings' needed to be replaced and whilst he was indeed one of its directors he could only justify his actions for so long and his time to do so was now well passed if the auditors were called. They would in any case be due their annual audit within the next month and replacing the funds was now an urgent priority if John was to avoid serious consequences.

He shuddered at the thought of the shame of it – imprisonment, even, and his first taste of it the night before made that thought a quite intolerable option.

Down at The Talbot, John found Claude Dubois having some food and a drink in the saloon bar.

"Greetings, Claude! I trust you had a pleasant journey over? Summer-time crossings are much nicer and the weather is kind to us at the moment? Sorry I couldn't join you at the Cock last night I had business to attend to at the mill," John opened, with more than a hint of subterfuge.

Dubois wasted no time with further pleasantries, "And that's just where you need to be attending, John, because your last shipment was a disgrace – one full piece had a tight end running right the way through it, for God's sake! Your weaver needs the sack, must have fallen asleep weaving it. My customer had to cut around it all the way through. Your inspection should have seen it, too, and at least you should have warned me to look out for it and have discounted it. Fortunately the customer, a good friend, needed smaller cut-outs for detailed tailoring and paid me in full anyway. Do you have anybody at all responsible in the mill?

"I like you, John, and I should not otherwise have told you that I got full payment anyway, but please be sure to warn me, or, better still, don't let it happen at all. Don't send me imperfect goods in the first place, ever!"

And so, to John's great relief, Claude Dubois paid up the full amount – more than enough to pay the fine, which he could now take over to the court and at least get one problem out of the way, but not nearly enough to clear him at the bank or pay his mounting bar bills. Also on the horizon were his considerable machinery-update expenses to move him even further toward expanding his specialist production which was involving him, unknown to his father, in scrapping old machinery at near worthless prices; the self and same 'old machinery' which had, and still did, make up the bulk of his father and brothers' every-day product manufacturing wealth over in Midgley.

To John's relief, Dubois said he would not be returning to the Piece Hall in the afternoon now that he had concluded his business; a conclusion which also included a trebling of his previous order for John's specialist jacquard cloths. He would be going on to Hull on the afternoon stage to buy products from other suppliers before returning home as usual sailing via Zeebrugge later the next day.

Relieved that Dubois's need for a further visit to the market was resolved, John thanked him for his order, promised to improve quality control and wished him a safe journey.

He paid his fine over at the court before returning to Luddenden Foot on the afternoon Lancashire stagecoach.

With money in his pocket and time enough for a drink, or several – but not at The Anchor, where he would for certain be banned by Sarah's father anyway, probably for life. He walked up to the Lord Nelson, for the second day in a row, to settle in for an afternoon's drinking – the hair of the dog! And he would try to forget recent events and work out what he was going to tell Mary.

"Got a bit lively down at The Anchor last night I heard, John?" Timothy Wormald said, polishing glasses behind the bar. "Doesn't surprise me – rough crowd of boaties they get in down there. Turned into a brawl, I heard?"

John ignored Wormald's fishing for news, ordered his drink and took it over into the corner where he buried his head in the weekly newspaper and pondered whether a reporter might have been in court earlier.

He also remembered the shock of Fanny telling him she suspected she might be pregnant during a conversation about Queen Victoria one market day in the spring. The Queen and Prince Albert had just been delivered of their sixth child, a fourth daughter, Princess Louise, Duchess of Argyll and Fanny commented: "Won't want for anything, she won't, little mite – unlike some poor devils in the land!"

And not the subtlest of hints was picked up by John instantly and confirmed by Fanny.

Fanny, affronted by John's questioning of paternity had resulted on them parting on bad terms and not speaking for weeks and John, ostrich-like, had hoped it would all go away, not be true, a miscarriage perhaps? But it hadn't and his chickens were well on the way to coming home to roost! Already he had been paying her considerable amounts of money for her to buy 'gifts' – trusting in her silence and still obstinately hoping to delay the inevitable.

Up at Higgin Chamber, production faltered, yet again in the mill, as his inattentive foreman Joe Saltonstall, a known Chartist leader and trouble-maker made love to Ellen Hardcastle, a young trainee worsted spinner, up in the wool-sorting room.

Across the mill yard, Mary had completed house-cleaning after Branwell's departure back to Haworth and was baking a strawberry pie for tea with fruit she had picked with the children in the garden, blissfully oblivious and quite ignorant of the storm that was about to break around her and shatter the peace on her husband's return home from the market.

John descended to Luddenden Foot, hurried swiftly past The Anchor, and climbed through the fields toward Sowerby. He arrived home at his usual time of about 6.00pm.

Eli's elegant coach and four had pulled away from the Piece Hall a little before closing time and accompanied by both Thomas and James, at his insistence, the coachman took them through the wide expanse of fields to the west of Halifax and dropped down into the bustling village of Sowerby Bridge, rather than heading on his usual route home along Burnley Road from King Cross.

Causing a few heads to turn, the carriage passed under the new railway viaduct, gathered speed and turned right to negotiate the steep climb up to Sowerby. Hardly a word had been exchanged between the three, yet all knew and dreaded the purpose of the mission.

During a lull Eli had dropped in next door to talk with Abraham Taylor who had arrived at his room after lunch and it hadn't taken long for the Piece Hall gossip to revel in the maximum schadenfreude from his neighbour's discomfort as he regaled him of his oldest son's misdemeanours. "I'm not one to gossip Eli, but..." It was the standard stock-in-trade opening platitude of a busy-body!

Eli had returned totally flustered with his face even more florid than usual and had immediately instructed

211

James to fetch his coachman saying, "That's it! He's gone too far this time. We're going to have this out, once and for all! And you two are coming with me. Get the carriage, James."

Reaching St. Peter's church, the coachman turned right into Pinfold Lane and headed on toward Boulderclough and his destination at Higgin Chamber Mill.

John was washing himself in the back kitchen when he heard the sound of the horses' hooves and the metal-rimmed carriage wheels on the cobblestones of the mill yard. A carriage door slammed shut with force, causing Blazer to erupt into a fierce cacophony of barking. The horses reared up and whinnied, giving the coachman more than a handful to calm them down and rein them in.

Eli burst into the kitchen as though he'd been shot from a cannon. Thomas was immediately behind him and James hung back at the door in fear of what was to follow, for he, unlike Thomas, knew nothing of his brother's misdeeds, but merely knew that his father disliked him with a passion and took every opportunity to goad and bully him. He knew this was different, much more serious, and he'd keep right out of the way, thank you very much!

"You miserable, snivelling wretch. You misbegotten son of a whore. How dare you? HOW BLOODY DARE YOU?" Eli repeated, shaking and sweating now, with Blazer protectively barking uncontrollably, sensing his master was in great danger as Eli bellowed in John's face, barely six inches away from him.

Mary instantly picked up little James, ushered the others out into the yard and corralled them away like a mother hen as quickly as she could to the farthest part of the yard, out into the orchard. Still she could hear every word of Eli's rantings from inside the house. Desperately fearful for John, she tried to cover her ears, but could still hear every single word.

"Another bastard on the way. And with that trollop of a market manager's daughter! You're a disgrace! Brawling in pubs with your arty-farty no-good friends and getting yourself arrested and fined. And now with a court record! I might have known that apology of a parson's son would be there too – drugged up to the eyeballs as usual, I shouldn't wonder!"

He continued, still shouting at full force. "In the name of all that's holy, just what the hell do you expect from me now, lad? I've had enough! You're getting NOWT! I'm not bailing you out again, ever! And I'm putting Thomas in here to mind you at t'mill. You'll not set foot in't mill without his permission.

"I want a full review of the books, Thomas, every penny accounted for, leave no stone unturned. And you'll help him James. AND AS FOR YOU, you miserable whelp, keep yourself out of my sight and I'll decide what I'm doing with you after Thomas reports back to me."

And that was it. Turning swiftly away, Eli returned quickly, just as he had come, back to the carriage and slammed the door once more. Thomas and James followed dutifully behind, stunned and without comment. They got in the other side of the carriage and the coachman pulled out of the yard and turned left to drop down the valley into Luddenden Foot and on up to Midgley.

"Why is Granddad shouting at father?" asked five-year old Sarah, innocently, over in the orchard. "I don't like all that noise and neither does poor Blazer!"

"Be calm, dears," said Mary, doing her best not to show the shock she had felt at that first outburst of Eli's, almost before he'd got through the kitchen door. She went on, trying to talk over the continuing distant rantings. "It's all a big misunderstanding. You'll see and your father will be able to explain everything later. Look how big and juicy the cox's orange pippins we planted are this year. The cooking apples are ready too – let's all pick up more and take them over to Granny T at High Lees tomorrow. We haven't visited her for ages and Grace and Hannah can help her with the baking, she'll like that; Granddad will like that, too, and you can help her make his favourite apple pie. You can all help, I'm sure, with the pastry."

Returning to the house after the coach disappeared at speed out of the yard, even the horses were agitated and glad to get on the move again, Mary and the children attempted to return to some sort of normality. The children were sent to their rooms and Mary sat down at the kitchen table to attempt to understand what had just occurred.

John, clearly flustered, started with a slight quake in his voice. "It's all a big mistake, Mary. The rumour – because that's all it is – is wrong; I'm blamed because the market manager's daughter at the Piece Hall, who's pregnant, has always had a soft spot for me and the gossips have put two and two together and got five! It's not mine and I'll not be the one having any bastardy orders served against me, you'll see," he said, thinking to himself; *"I've paid her enough to keep her mouth shut, but that damned Irish Kate at The Talbot that night will be the one stirring it up with her mischief – there's no love lost between her and the Titteringtons!"*

He went on. "As for last night I was just in the wrong place at the wrong time, stuck in the middle of an argument down at The Anchor about payment between the barmaid and one of the Irish boaties. The whole thing erupted into a brawl – doesn't take much to get the whole rough lot of 'em pitching in! Sarah, a nice young girl, the landlord's daughter behind the bar, was accused of giving the wrong change and I stuck up for her. She's only a teenager and I've seen the Irish pull that old trick so many times before that I stepped in – and got arrested for my troubles, trying to do a good deed. You can't win sometimes!

"Bran did his best to reason with one of the McColls in his best Irish accent, but it was no good and I told him not to worry you and say I'd gone to town to see this Belgian customer who was staying at the Cock. Did he varnish the portraits by the way?" This last anodyne question, sensing a return to normality, was John taking advantage of what he felt was an improving situation with Mary swallowing his lies, not for the first time.

But Mary had been there before and needed more convincing.

"And what happened in court, then? I heard your father say you were fined and given a criminal record?" Mary probed.

"It all got very mixed up and the magistrate, seeing that the young girl had been hurt in the fracas, had great sympathy, as had I indeed. He felt she needed compensating for her troubles. The penniless, feckless Irish were obviously in no position to make recompense, so guess who copped for it? Muggins here! It wasn't much, so I paid up and put it all down to experience," he lied, checking closely for a positive reaction and thanking God that she would never, indeed could never, read any accounts of the court, if there was even a reporter present.

Not for the first time his cash sales receipts had conveniently bi-passed the ledgers and Mary's illiteracy would protect him, yet again, from her learning the truth from *The Halifax Guardian.*

"The portraits look really good, John."

He breathed deeply, feeling he had succeeded, *again!*

"You won't believe how the colours shine through now – even Blazer has a wet nose! Bran was lovely as usual, taking the time to tell stories to the older girls. And all the while knowing of your plight, and not wanting to worry me. He's a really good friend, John, you are very lucky, we are very lucky to have such a friend; I'm worried though, John, he doesn't look well. He had a shake in his hands; couldn't have painted, that's for sure and even this morning he hardly ate any

216

breakfast and went on his way back to Haworth looking sadder than I've ever seen him. Perhaps he was burdened with the thoughts of the lie he told me? But it was more that. He is not well, John, and he has a worrying cough that is definitely more than a mere summer cold."

John considered what she said, thinking exactly the same from his appearance yesterday – especially at the Lord Nelson and went on. "He'll be fine – let's hope so anyway. I'll go over to see him in a few days. A couple of drinks in the Black Bull will do him a power of good and I need to look at more property for father while I'm over there." This last statement being as far from the truth as it was possible to be; those days were well and truly over and if he was not to be cut off completely, without a penny, he needed to redress his financial situation before his brothers got anywhere near his purchase and sales ledgers.

His 'deficiencies' at the bank needed correcting as a matter of some urgency and his indebtedness to hostelries and to his wealthy aristocratic shooting friends in both West and East Yorkshire precluded any hope of an early resolution. His new machinery also remained unpaid and outstanding – a fact that Thomas would soon learn about within minutes of inspecting the purchase ledger.

"Oh, by the way Mary, we're going to be very busy with the new jacquard cloths for Europe. The Belgian gentleman I spoke about has trebled his order and there's much more in the pipeline still to come. Father has decided, with it being quiet for them over there, to send Thomas and James over to help out until I can get on top of things. You may need to feed them, but you won't mind that I'm sure, will you?" he lied even further, hoping that wherever she had disappeared to with the children she hadn't heard his father's concluding requirements; by her acquiescence he saw this to be the case.

Over at High Lees, Eli continued his rantings to anyone who would listen. James was the nearer recipient, with Thomas having gone on home, along with Grace in the back kitchen hearing such dreadful first-hand news of her favourite, their eldest son.

It was a shock that 'Granny T' would not recover from and with much worse still to come would not even live to see the year out.

Chapter Fifteen

Lies and Deceit

Mary welcomed Branwell warmly as always, as did Grace and Hannah, who alone were still up waiting excitedly for Uncle Brannie's visit and rushed forward to hug him and be lifted into the air.

"Is John out in the yard, Bran?" Mary asked, hearing Blazer scratching at the door.

"No, Mary – young William was sent to tell him a Belgian gentleman wished to meet with him. Monsieur Dubois, I think he's called, had arrived early for the market and was staying at the Old Cock and he has gone in to join him for supper and will stay over I expect, for market," Branwell responded, after having time to hurriedly conjure up a believable story climbing up through the fields.

Branwell sat down at the kitchen table and the girls clamoured for his attention, one on each knee; "So, young Grace and god-daughter Hannah, what have you two been up to? Been good for your mother, I trust? I have a task to perform for your father and we can have a bedtime story as I complete it for him. Father has asked that I varnish and complete the paintings of your dear parents and it won't take long after I've had a little supper.

"Perhaps, Mary, you could bring my supper up to the studio so I can work at the same time?" Branwell suggested.

"Oooh yes! And we can have our bedtime drink with you at the same time, can't we, Uncle Brannie?" said Grace.

All of which excited them considerably since they loved Branwell's stories of imaginary places and people; over the two years or more since he started their parents' portraits it had become customary for them to be allowed to sit with him up in his room and have stories told to them – especially the bedtime stories which sent them off to bed after cups of warm milk to dream of faraway places and adventures.

Sometimes on winters' evenings, a fire was lit in the studio and all of the children loved Branwell's stories by firelight when it was too dark to paint, with shadows dancing across the ceiling as he sat young James on his knee and the other four gathered around him on the fireside rug clamouring for further news of their heroes and their deeds! Occasionally they were allowed to look into Uncle Brannie's room when he wasn't there at all and they loved the smell of his oil-paints and could never resist looking under the covers on the paintings to see the progress he had made after a late night painting session.

"...complete the task for him..." he had said and the girls didn't like the sound of that; a finality, an end to the stories of the mystical place called Angria.

After leaving his studio in Bradford, two months after Hannah's christening, and with limited space at home in the parsonage, John had invited Bran to transfer all of his canvasses, easel and paints into a spare upper room at Higgin Chamber; with good daylight, the room overlooked the mill dam and the hills beyond and it doubled perfectly as his bedroom-cum-studio for occasional visits or sleep-overs.

In return, as with Mr and Mrs Kirby in Bradford, he was asked to paint portraits; the difference being that in John and Mary's case his work was not as payment against lodgings, since no charge for his room was ever required; John's invitation made that clear from the outset, which now especially made him feel disappointed and let down by Bran's seeming unwillingness to complete the portraits, making it doubly annoying and the reason for the contretemps in the Nelson earlier.

"Considering the type of varnish to be used is important and here your father has purchased a good clear one for the purpose, which won't show any yellowness."

Branwell commenced his work with the girls hanging on his every word up in the studio room.

"The painting is varnished with a broad brush, first in this direction across the painting and then the same broad strokes in the crossways direction. I'm creating a glass-like covering since oil-paintings, unlike water colours, have no glass to protect them.

"It's also vital to wait at least nine months to a year for the oil paint to dry before varnishing and that the temperature is not too hot and humid, or too cold – a warm summer night with a breeze like tonight is just perfect.

"So you see…" he went on, with the girls in their nightgowns enjoying the summer breeze gently blowing through the open window and the delicious smell of the varnish; a smell quite unlike anything they had smelt before and would never forget if they were ever to smell it again, easily recalling the evening "…the varnish when it dries will be like a pane of glass covering and protecting the surface of the paintings."

"See how Blazer's eyes sparkle!" said Grace. "And look how the fine design shines on father's waistcoat."

The fine scroll design on the waistcoat was a later addition, which John had asked to be overpainted onto the plain grey material Branwell first depicted, after completion of the main work, since it was now one of the designs bought by Monsieur Dubois for the Belgian market.

Which also caused further delay to the necessary drying-time lapse prior to final varnishing; a fact that both John and the complaining Mrs Kirby both failed to fully appreciate.

"Father loves that design," Hannah went on. "And so do I. It's so smart and father designed it himself one night; I watched him sketch it out first and paint it onto squared paper, before going over to the mill where he showed me how the rows of cards were stamped out, with little holes which he later put into one of the looms to make the pattern appear as if by magic! I also love the way you painted 'J. Titterington' on Blazer's collar – look how clear it is now and I can write my own surname now too, Uncle Brannie, just the same!"

And the children practised copying the signature onto some paper Branwell gave them from his notebook, carefully copying and adding the little lines on the top of the capital 'T' which he told them were called serifs.

He went on. "The waistcoat cloth is made by jacquard weaving, girls, and your father told me he was very proud to introduce it into the mill. He was the first in the valley to make such a clever move. Such pretty patterns! But it was very difficult to overpaint as I'd already put in the shadows – see here how the pattern crosses the shadow, but it's too late now to change it, so hopefully nobody will notice!" he confessed modestly.

Putting John's portrait to dry over on another table, Branwell placed Mary's on the same flat surface and again proceeded to draw his wide brush across in two directions.

"Oooh!" exclaimed Grace, as a broad sweep of varnish crossed their mother's brooch. "Tell us again, Uncle Brannie, of the old soldier from the wars! See how his armour shines!"

"Well, say hello again to General Tom Holdsworth, your mother's, and your, ancestor, a Parliamentarian Roundhead general from the English Civil War. See his long beard and gleaming breastplate armour – he was second in command only to Oliver Cromwell himself and sheltered here in Sowerby village from the King's soldiers, over 200 years ago, in 1643 after the Royalists or Cavalier's defeated them at the battle of Adwalton Moor, just thirteen miles to the east of here over near Leeds."

Uncle Brannie's stories were always exciting and often included *'Alexander Percy, the Earl of Northangerland,'* who Grace and Hannah at least had come to recognise as Uncle Brannie himself, so colourful and personal were his descriptions.

"Hiding with Percy, his trusty companion, the wounded and tired soldiers sheltered at Higgin Chamber, hidden in a secret chamber whilst the Royalist soldiers searched, right beneath this very floor! Hardly daring to breathe, they waited in silence with their swords drawn, ready to defend themselves, but the soldiers never found them and they re-joined the Roundhead army to continue the war another day over in Angria."

"Did he die in battle, Uncle Brannie? Did Percy die with him? Did the soldiers catch up with them? Do tell us more. And where is Angria? I would so like to go there one day when I'm grown up," said Hannah, now quite living the moment and almost hearing the sound of the king's soldiers' horses in the yard outside as they galloped away empty-handed.

Mary entered the room with a plate of food just as Branwell was struggling, unusually, with his story-telling, to tell the girls it was bedtime. She couldn't help noticing in the light of the oil-lamp that Branwell looked drawn and tired – and moreover decidedly unwell compared with the last time she had seen him only a few weeks before.

"Enough girls, leave Uncle Brannie now to have some supper and off you go to bed with your cups of milk," said their mother. Reluctantly they headed off to the room they shared with those awful words of their uncle still echoing in their heads. *"...complete the task for him..."* How they dreaded the time coming when the paintings were to be completed. They had grown up together almost, from the first sketched outlines all those years ago, with mother and father sitting patiently by the window in turn, with the dam and the hills beyond, trying to keep still and not move a muscle – impossible for poor Blazer of course, who had no idea why he was being gripped so forcefully and held down on his master's lap for the few occasions he had to be there.

Over in Halifax, John, now completely and depressingly sober, tried to bed down for the night on the hard wooden bed of a police cell and only then, for the first time, realised, just as now, in the same situation in York, just how he valued freedom and so rued its absence and the consequent intense feelings of abject deprivation.

Chapter Sixteen

St. John in the Wilderness

One quiet evening before bedding down for the night, John set out to recount to Rev. Tom his earlier experiences of meeting and getting to know Branwell.

"I first met Branwell in the summer of 1836 at the Lord Nelson public house, one warm July summer's evening. He was nineteen and I was twenty-nine and I had only been married two months, marrying Mary on 31st May of that year at Halifax parish church. His intellect and conversation was what first drew me to like him and enjoy his company. I, too, was educated at home, alongside my brothers, though not in the classics as Bran had been by his father.

"He was a writer of poetry from an early age and went on to have a dozen or so poems published in *The Halifax Guardian*, from his 24th birthday in June 1841, using his pseudonym 'Northangerland' – a reference to his childhood mythological writings with his sisters, centred on the fictitious town of 'Angria', mainly written in collaboration with Charlotte.

"We got to know Bran well through the next two years and he stayed over at Higgin Chamber on many occasions on his way through into Halifax where he enjoyed concerts and recitals there. I remember a concert by Franz Liszt, the virtuoso pianist, was one of them; Halifax, a highly cultured town, has been a centre for some fine performances for many years; another I remember we enjoyed was a notable visit by Johann Strauss and his waltz band.

"We spent many happy times together – usually at public houses, I admit! – The Lord Nelson and The Anchor and Shuttle were nearest and Aunt Abigail's White Lion in Mytholmroyd were our favourites. In town we would meet up at The Talbot, the Union Cross or the Old Cock, usually on market days at the Piece Hall and always with a lively entourage of artists, craftsmen and generally colourful characters – Halifax was always a thriving centre for the arts.

"Back in Luddenden at the Nelson, we visited the upstairs library and joined in with its reading society. Bran would constantly write poetry in his diary or sketch away happily in a corner of the public bar minding his own business. One night he drew a fine sketch of my sister Hannah's husband, John Murgatroyd and I commented that one day he must draw, or perhaps even paint a portrait of Mary for a present.

"You will be shocked, I know, to hear that it was here that we first read about Dashwood's irreligious

Hell-Fire Club and started to emulate it by forming into one ourselves.

"We also enjoyed spending time with the Irish immigrant 'boaties' – who had constructed the canal system and the railways originally and many of whom had chosen to live in the canal basin in a tented village near Luddenden Foot. They were always a lively bunch who I think brought out the Irish side of Bran, through their folk singing and dancing. Always laughing, it seemed, always able to rise above the squalor and disadvantagement of their meagre existence, we had good times in their company and Bran's Irish accent, like that of his sister, Charlotte, came to the fore!

"I should have been attending to my home life more, I know, in the early stages of marriage, but that's how it was and I suppose I was making up for lost time, free of my father's control over at Higgin Chamber for the first time. Setting up the mill was hard, too, with the embryonic stages of Chartism developing among the workers and I needed to free myself from such constraints occasionally, to relax and unwind.

"On occasions, in those early days anyway, we met with our families at church and a popular one to visit was St. John in the Wilderness, in Cragg Vale – so much so that over those early years of our friendship Bran got to first call me his 'saint' – 'St. John' – I think for the times I came to his rescue, buying him a drink or inviting him to stay over at Higgin Chamber. I also encouraged him to paint and set up his studio to paint portraits which he did later, in Bradford, in the home of some friends of my father, the Kirbys, and after that, to paint a portrait of Mary at Higgin Chamber, where I gave him a spare room so that he could leave all his materials and his easel and continue to paint as he wished. He had a bed in there for stop-overs and he often worked undisturbed well into the night, writing and painting. Later on he painted me, too. They're fine works, hanging still at Higgin Chamber, I hope.

"The whole Brontë family came over to Cragg Vale to worship sometimes, enjoying the picturesque countryside on a fine summer's day out and their father would arrange for his curate to take the services back at home. The vicar there was a friend of their father's.

"Mary also became very fond of Bran's charming ways and when our second daughter Hannah was born, we both agreed he would make a good choice to act as godfather.

"On the 27th February of 1838, Hannah was ten months old and already starting to walk! She was quite a mature 'baby' for her Christening, but we had kept delaying the date to suit our family and guests through spring and into summer – then with Bran setting up his portrait studio in Bradford. So we pushed the date on further to December to let him get established. Cragg Vale was chosen as it was favoured by the Brontës, both for geographic proximity and Bran's father's personal, and the family's friendship, with the incumbent Rev. Thomas Crowther and his wife, Phebe, and their large family. They had eleven children, who were all still living at home at that time – ranging from the oldest Mary, who was twenty-two and helped their mother, along with sister Sarah their next eldest, who was just twenty, right down to the youngest, Ellen, who at just three years of age was thrilled to have Grace and of course Hannah, in her gown, to play with, like a dressed-up doll on the day."

Back at the parsonage that morning, the two sisters breakfasted with their father and prepared to travel to Cragg Vale in the dog-cart.

Wednesday December 5th of 1838 saw a clear crisp morning, with the sunlight low between the churchyard trees as Patrick drove out onto the Oxenhope road with his daughters to commence their journey. Well wrapped up against a nippy but gentle breeze, they chatted away about the plans for the day and viewed the distant hills of the Calder Valley with the usual wonderment as the sun rose. They dropped down into Hebden Bridge and turned along the Halifax road towards Mytholmroyd, where they turned right and crossed over the river Calder to head towards Cragg Vale.

Entering the densely wooded valley, now they passed through Hollin Hey Wood, Holderness Wood and finally Hobson Hey Wood before dropping again to the right to reach the church in the trough of the valley lying next to the Cragg Vale Inn in Erringden; a journey of some eleven miles in total from home and upon their arrival, they were greeted by the landlord Richard Hinchliffe, a jolly man in his mid-thirties who had received the family on many occasions and whose rotundness and conviviality amply personified his role as 'mine host'. This was to be the meeting point as usual for church services and refreshments were duly served to the first arrivals who were an hour early for the one o'clock service.

John and Mary had dressed Hannah for her special day, high in the hills along the valley at Higgin Chamber, but as she was now well able to crawl and was not far from walking, this had proved difficult. Her Christening gown was already looking a little the worse for wear from creeping around on the flagged floor and generally poking around into anything she could lay her curious hands, or her mouth on. Older sister Grace was easier to dress and looked a picture in her new dress with ribbons in her hair. The four of them were in high spirits making their way along the valley from Luddenden Foot, passing Aunt Abigail's White Lion pub on the right as they dropped into Mytholmroyd, turned left crossing the Calder and followed the same route as the Brontës had ten minutes before them; the whole journey being less than five miles from their home.

Next to arrive were John's older sister Eliza who was thirty-four and here to be godmother with husband James Smith, travelling the shortest distance of about two miles in their elegant carriage, dropping straight down to Mytholmroyd from High Lees in Midgley, with John's mother and father, Grace and Eli, and John's sister, Hannah, also a godmother, leaving Branwell and Emily to follow on and complete the Brontë party. Dressed immaculately, the small Titterington family group and their coachman exuded the opulence and demeanour expected of one of the wealthiest manufacturers in the area.

Branwell had made an early start from his new portrait studio in Bradford, had met Emily in Halifax after she had walked down from her school in Southowram. Together they had travelled by coach to Sowerby Bridge, and thence by train to Mytholmroyd station and by phaeton from there to meet up with the rest of the guests at the Cragg Vale Inn, with just fifteen minutes spare to stroll the hundred yards or so over to the church.

St. John in the Wilderness church, at this time was in a sorry condition of dilapidation prior to its complete rebuilding one year later. A visitor a few weeks before, called White, was quoted as saying that the church was *"...so indifferently built that its roof has once fallen in and is now supported by props."*

Dangerous enough one might have thought to go somewhere else, but the allegiance of both families was easily explained by the rather angular, slightly stooped but strikingly impressive figure of the Rev. Thomas Crowther, who now greeted them all at the church door.

At forty-four years of age, he had already been the incumbent priest in Cragg Vale for seventeen years and was to remain so until his death over twenty years later. Temporary uses of a variety of buildings in the area for services during the new church's construction, including the Cragg Vale Inn, allowed him to lend his services to fellow clergyman and it was during this time that he visited Haworth the most often.

Stepping forward from the shelter of the entrance porch, he greeted them roundly; "Welcome dear friends," he intoned. "And what a fine crisp, winter's day you have all brought with you to welcome our new daughter into God's loving care! – I trust you all travelled safely? Phebe has prepared lunch for us afterwards and I do hope you can all join me and the family for refreshments later?"

That said and gratefully accepted by all, they proceeded inside to commence the simple service of baptism with no others present. It was to be one of the last services held there before the building had to be closed for demolition due to the ever-present danger from falling masonry.

St. John in the Wilderness church's foundation had been laid on the 15th of March 1813, only twenty-five years previously. Consecrated four years after the foundation-laying, its 'indifferently-built' description was indeed apposite with only twenty years of service being possible since its first official use.

Rev. Crowther preached many times at Haworth, particularly in support of its Sunday School. He was well-known throughout the region as a friend to the cause of child factory workers and was a strong advocate for the limiting of juvenile working hours by supporting the 'Ten Hours Bill' which had been passing through parliament for years before becoming 'The Factory Act' the previous year, in 1847. He commented previously in a sermon "…the children work fifteen or sixteen hours a day, frequently, and sometimes all night. Oh, it is a murderous system and mill-owners are the pest and disgrace of society. Laws, human and divine, are insufficient to restrain them."

Notoriously guilty of exploitation in Cragg Vale and Mytholmroyd were a large group of mill owners, the worst of whom were the Hinchliffe family, who never spoke to him again. It did not deter this man of strong principle and justice, who additionally held the power to command anyone present in the Cragg Vale Inn to attend services – including a few of the disgruntled mill owners!

Child labour at the time was of course cheap and with mechanisation, the need for adult strength in the workplace was greatly reduced. Children's physical size, with consequent danger, could also allow them to be used to access otherwise restricted working areas such as replacing bobbins beneath creels, or worse, between steam-driven piston-pumping cylinders, drive-belts and shafts, which could rip even an adult's arm off in an instant, or cause the many child deaths which were all-too-frequently reported in textile factories of the time.

The Titteringtons were not recorded as being guilty of child exploitation in any of their mills further down the valley, either in Midgley or up in Sowerby, and so were welcomed at St. John in the Wilderness for their kindness and humanity towards all of their employees in difficult and highly competitive times.

"In the name of the Father, the Son and the Holy Ghost, I name this child Hannah Maria," Rev. Thomas musically enthused, as Hannah stiffened her back and wriggled to be put down. And then whilst being overly restrained by her mother and handed over to the priest, she let out the most ear-piercing of screams as his over-generous cupped handful of freezing cold holy water was generously – almost baptistically, sluiced onto her forehead!

"That drove the devil out!" said John under his breath to Mary and together they lifted her back to comfort her and attempted to convince her that nobody intended her any harm.

Little Grace simply couldn't understand what was going on and why did the man frighten her sister so cruelly by playing that awful trick on her?

Charlotte was the most moved of all the guests, before the outburst that is, being the oldest surviving child of the Brontës who was just four at the time of their mother's death and only nine when her also same-named sister Maria died so tragically young at just eleven years of age. It just brought it all back and glancing across at her father, she could see that it had had the same affect, almost certainly more so, on him too.

Patrick was suffering badly from dyspepsia and had consulted a Keighley surgeon a few weeks before. Non-payment of parish tithes in Howarth was directly involving, affecting, and distressing him. Emily and Branwell's seemingly satisfactory situations in Southowram and Bradford pleased him, but other news would not.

Charlotte was about to tell her father that she was leaving her teaching position with Miss Wooler over in Dewsbury; being expected to play nursemaid to her infant nephew and baby niece and shortly her recently widowed mother, on top of all her teaching duties, was expecting too much of her. Caring for an infant and a baby was bad enough, but geriatric care to elderly family members was beyond reason. It would take up even more of her personal time, and she had given her notice and would not be returning to Dewsbury Moor after the Christmas holidays.

Branwell, being born only the year after Charlotte, also remembered those same sad early family losses and was proud to act as godfather and be a part of this dear child's family and especially since she now bore the name which meant so much to him and furthermore was chosen *because* of him.

Branwell added, "Thank you, John for inviting me to be Hannah's godfather. I will endeavour to protect her in any way that I can, whatever her need, if, and when it arises, and as long as I am able – with every bone in my body. I am so grateful that you chose the name Maria for her, as are all of the family."

Complementing the name choice, John's sister Hannah had travelled over from High Lees with her parents to be a godmother at the baptism.

Back at the parsonage afterwards Phebe, Rev. Thomas's wife, ably assisted by her older daughters, Mary and Sarah, had prepared a fine joint of roast beef for their lunch and upon its conclusion, Charlotte, Anne and their father set off on their journey back to the parsonage. Branwell and Emily were invited to stay the night at Higgin Chamber with John and Mary before heading on the next morning back to Bradford and Southowram.

It was through such shared reminiscences that John and Tom were able to retain their sanity and search for some sort of normality by reliving events, whilst all around them of course it was anything but normal. The trick was obfuscation; blot out the unpleasant and fill it with the shared memories of happier times.

Each had made a good choice of companion.

Chapter Seventeen

The Debt Crisis

Thomas, enthusiastically, with James, reluctantly, following as ever in his brother's footsteps, arrived at Higgin Chamber first thing the next morning. They entered the mill and proceeded directly to John's inner sanctum' – his mill office, without as much as a by-your-leave, and went straight about their work before John had even surfaced from his disturbed night's sleep.

The account books were the first port of call and since they were nowhere to be found until John arrived, Thomas proceeded to tackle his first bone of contention; sending word for foreman Joe Saltonstall to come to the office. He readied himself for a battle.

"Want to know what we're doing here, I'm sure. Don't you, Joe Saltonstall?" Thomas said.

"Where's Master John?" asked Joe, clearly unsettled by the change of events and sensing all was not right, even though he knew full well of the outcome in court the previous day, following the row he witnessed at The Anchor and Shuttle. The raucous visit of old Eli and his sons was not heard across at the mill, over the sound of the looms, but his outburst had not been unexpected. It had been reported on widely by a mill-hand who had been unloading wool in the yard outside and who had heard each and every shouted syllable of every word.

"Think we don't know about your Chartist activities, don't you, Saltonstall?" Thomas kicked off the conversation. "Lots of spare time here, hadn't you? Speaking to that mob over in Keighley and with my brother always away with his fancy friends. Well you're done now – you and your Irish Confederate sympathisers in the valley. Lucky I don't have you arrested and taken over to York for trial, with all your other trouble makers and ne'er-do-wells. Never know when you're well off, do you? And in such hard times."

Seeing the shock on Joe Saltonstall's face and knowing that he must be aware of the York assizes currently handing out stiff penalties, including transportation with hard labour sentences in an attempt to stamp out rebellion, Thomas pushed on, whilst James stood silently but firmly by his side in case of a physical reaction, which it became clear was not likely after the threat of possible arrest.

"Ernest Jones mean anything to you? He should, the leader of your rabble in Halifax. We know he's been here with his henchmen, stirring up trouble, and he's about to get what you will, too, if you don't leave peaceably – right now! Go and fly your Frenchie republican tricolour flags and do your pike-drilling in your own time, sir, better still, get yourself over to

Ireland with your friend Feargus O'Connor and take your black banners with you. You'll be more than welcome there, I don't doubt – see if there's any work for you there, with your English name, among the poor famine-starved wretches. We'll hear no more of you here – be gone!"

"Where's Master John? I'll speak with him first," spluttered Saltonstall, without any conviction or much hope since it was clear that the game was up – for both him and probably John, too, by the looks of it. His dalliances with both politics and sex with his unwelcome weekly romps up in the wool-sorting room, had been likely to come to an abrupt end, sooner rather than later. He knew full well that the quality of the mill's output had gone downhill due, in no small part, to his and his master's inattention in recent months.

"You'll speak with nobody, sir – and certainly not with him! I'm in charge here now and he's not available to listen to your miserable pleadings. Be gone without a penny-piece, sir, and be thankful for small mercies. Any repercussions from your rabble-rouser-friend Chartist sympathisers will be met with a visit to your home from the special constables – you can be sure of it!"

Thomas concluded his rant and leaving him very little choice after being caught red-handed, Joe Saltonstall departed sullenly off the mill yard and away down the road, within the hour, much to the joy and huge relief of young Ellen Hardcastle who couldn't resist a wry smile as she watched him slope off dejectedly from an upstairs mill window.

Over in the house, across the mill yard, John was poring over the mill ledgers at the kitchen table. His sales ledger was in good shape with a healthy flow of new business coming from outside the area, from the affluent markets in the south; from London, Paris and beyond. His purchase ledgers were less impressive and not kept up-to-date and consequently his cash-flow, both from poor record keeping and bad debt recovery was spiralling him into a cash crisis; a crisis he had known was coming for some time causing him to 'borrow' excessively and necessarily, from his own bank.

A directorship in The Halifax and Huddersfield Union Banking Company brought special privileges to John, with advantageous opportunities for drawing out at little or even no interest rates on short-term borrowings, if approved by one other director. Huddersfield industrialist Sir Joseph Armitage was both a good friend and fellow director at the bank and John's borrowings had gone through at a 'nod' from him in recent months.

John, attempting to rationalise production to match the new intake of orders for his cloths from overseas, had determined to sell a significant portion of his existing outdated machinery to make room for the new equipment. Moving away from the production of the old, albeit outdated yet profitable 'bread-and-butter' products, left him exposed due to the loss of still reasonably lucrative sales, on top of which the financing of new equipment purchase had become increasingly difficult until the overlap could be matched up by new sales revenue.

His personal finances intermingled with all of this with creditors from a variety of sources, including provisioners, hotels and public houses. Shooting party trips were costly, on top of which his annual gun licence alone (£4 0s 10d or £3,000 today) would have kept many families for a year; regular payments to Fanny Brearley had also increased as she 'turned the screw' to match her own 'growing' circumstances and to ensure her silence.

The sale of old equipment had been held two months before on the 20th of June 1848 and an advertisement in *The Halifax Guardian* on the 17th of June had read:

Auction at Higgin Chamber Mill;

Whole of worsted machinery:-
Sliver boxes
9 heads of drawing 2 spindles each
1 spinning frame of 112 spindles
8 spinning frames of 96 spindles each made by John Farrar
4 twisting frames of 90 spindles each
1 twisting jenny of 170 spindles
1 head of finishing of 6 spindles
1 warping mill
50 pairs combs
Winding engines etc.

In a depressed market with unrest from the Chartist agitators, John's brothers, Thomas in particular, in common with his father, had neither the stomach, the skill, nor the imaginative flair needed for costly innovation. Aware of the dismal auction prices realised at the Higgin Chamber sale and its poor generation of funds for upgraded machinery purchase, Thomas and Eli had already decided that John must be in trouble. The Anchor and Shuttle debacle and now Fanny's pregnancy had played into their hands and provided Eli with just the right reason to step in and clip John's overly-ambitious wings.

John looked up from the kitchen table as William Foster knocked on the yard door, keen to keep him updated on developments across at the mill.

John had seen his brothers arrive from an upstairs window and so wasn't going to be surprised by their actions so far.

William reported: "Joe's gone, off the end of the yard already, meek as a lamb! Knew the game was up. Thomas knew all about him speaking at that rally in Keighley and his threats were heard by anyone around your office. They've moved in there, by the way, and the word is out that you're in big trouble with Eli. He made a lot of noise in here yesterday and everybody knows by now what he said. Must have heard every word across in Luddenden, I shouldn't wonder!"

"It's not what it seems, William. Eli's sent them over to help out and be sure we're on the right track. He takes the same interest in all his businesses – that's how he makes so much money and invests it into the property I find for him," John said, unconvincingly, as far as William was concerned.

"But they've bitten off more than they can chew already, William," he continued. "They'll have nobody to replace Joe, who as you well know, apart from anything else, knows the machinery inside out, almost as well as me! Their own businesses over there run nothing like mine, they're in the dark ages by comparison, and I

242

have all the books, and a handle on all the finances. Neither of them were ever up to banking; they know nothing about running a bank."

And with that, he concealed the books, returning them to the bottom drawer of the kitchen cabinet and strode purposefully across to the mill.

Everything was ticking over nicely and the gentle whirring of the winding frames on the second floor above greeted him as usual as he passed confidently through to his office at the back, making sure anyone seeing him would give reassuring accounts of his demeanour to their fellow-workers on the upper floors.

Entering his office, John spoke first, "How are you making out with the new designs then, Thomas?" he asked his brother, glancing over at his untouched drawing board. "We need cards stamping and putting to the looms this morning if we're going to make the Belgian shipment by the weekend, and have you got anyone in mind to run the mill without Joe? Just saw him leaving. I expect he wasn't going for a stroll? Know anybody else with his loom tuning or machinery skills? You, James, perhaps? Or you, Thomas?"

Thomas looked particularly uncomfortable since he knew only too well that he and James, unlike their brother, had no such skills and jacquard production was totally outside their experience anyway. They were both used to Eli making all the decisions, doing the hiring and firing. Specialist training skills were never needed since there was always an abundance of labour available in the market to supply the solely traditional skills needed.

In short Thomas and James did not like to, and had never had to, get their hands dirty and were well aware that whilst John 'played away' often with his wealthy friends, his hands-on skills at design and machine maintenance set him apart from all other mill owners. It was for this reason that Eli had confidently put him in charge over at Higgin Chamber in the first place whilst Thomas and James were better working alongside their father where he could keep his eyes on them and mould them into his own image.

It was John, too, who helped his father to add to his growing property portfolio. Through his wide and influential list of acquaintances and his banking customers, John knew of properties becoming available, as far away as Haworth, prior to them coming onto the market. He visited them with the owners, negotiated prices and finalised the deals for his father. For this reason alone Eli was particularly reluctant to sever ties with his oldest son, but the possible financial shortcomings at Higgin Chamber Mill were ringing alarm bells and needed sorting out if Eli's investments and his status were not to suffer. The immorality of his son's actions with the Piece Hall manager's daughter and public brawling at The Anchor and Shuttle were too much to bear for his upstanding Christian beliefs and any additional dishonesty or financial impropriety would most assuredly and inevitably lead to his son's complete disownment; worse still, to his disinheritance.

All of which John was acutely aware. He'd been warned enough times, but still somehow he didn't believe it to be possible. Would Eli so distress his wife and dear mother of their eldest son and heir?

The answer came soon enough, as John, realising he could never make up for his mounting losses, needed help to replace the money at the bank before the auditors moved in and discovered his fraudulent actions.

Further sales of equipment in the mill were unlikely since the market for traditional goods continued its decline and he knew only too well of his father's vehement disapproval of the first sale to advance his production ambitions. Any approach to Sir Joseph was out of the question and only his father otherwise had that kind of accessible money. So he determined to throw himself at his mercy and take the consequences.

"I need a small loan, father, to get me through a difficult patch." It was a weak opening to revealing a dire state in John's affairs at a meeting over at High Lees a week after his brothers moved in to 'help' him with the running of Higgin Chamber Mill.

John had decided to take the bull by the horns and tackle Eli on his own territory, making sure to first greet his mother, somewhat over-effusively in Eli's opinion, though nevertheless with his usual affection for her, whilst Eli was finishing his lunch in the High Lees back kitchen. Here he was away from his brothers' attention, having disappeared under pretext of making a bank visit over to Huddersfield.

"Leave us, Grace," said Eli. "This won't take too long," he said ominously. Grace withdrew to the yard recognising only too well the tone of her husband's voice and fearing the worst.

"A 'small' loan, you say? More like a fortune I'm thinking with the money you chuck around on your fancy friends staying too long away from't mill – not to mention that pittance you got from selling off the machinery I'd built up these last thirty years or more, and without a by-your-leave either. You don't own it you know, you appear to have forgotten, you work for me until I say otherwise."

John knew from experience that now was not the time to interrupt his father when he was in full flow. He also knew that his father had been more than happy for him to run his end of the family business without let or hindrance, as long as it was turning over the good profits it had done for many years previously.

Now getting into full stride, Eli raised his voice with each sentence and would soon be at the full shouting force which could, and was often heard throughout the house and wherever poor Grace had disappeared to in the meantime.

The veins on his neck protruded as his pace of delivery increased.

"You got careless – greedy – and took your eye off the ball. I saw it all coming, the falling off of trade, the damned Chartists and you with your womanising, drunkard ways, brawling like a common criminal in a public house, whilst trying to play the gentleman living it up alongside the landed gentry on your fancy shooting trips. What did you expect?

"Getting that market lass pregnant was unforgivable. And you with five young bairns at home and your wife

246

still grieving for little Eli. What in God's own name were you thinking of lad?

"I don't care what you owe, or even to whom you owe it. You'll not get a penny out of me to pay for your debauchery and your brothers are quite capable with my help of running the Chamber. We don't need you."

Shocked by this last statement John decided to come clean and reveal his situation at the bank and the imminent visit of the auditors.

"Well, why does that not surprise me?" Eli finally exploded. "Fraud and embezzlement to boot! The ultimate disgrace for your family and our good name! You deserve to be sent away on a convict ship like your thieving cousin for that. You're worse than him actually, because you stole from a position of trust – at least he made no attempts to hide from being a common criminal – a rogue and a thief. You're worse than a highwayman!"

John took it all, guessing, knowing, that his father would do anything to avoid the disgrace of defaulting at the bank.

"Alright then, so I'll not see the family name dragged through the mud," Eli continued reluctantly. "I'll cover your bank debt, but that's all! I don't even want to hear what else you're owing. You can drown in your own mire for all I care, or you can finish up in a debtors' prison, where you belong. You'll get no more help from me and you can rot in gaol until hell freezes over!"

John's mother had returned to the back kitchen after the shouting subsided, hoping all was now well, though fearing that it would not be. She was just in time to hear the last part of her husband's threat and knew he meant what he said. Clutching at her apron-clad breast, she collapsed into the nearest kitchen chair, took a sharp intake of breath and considered the situation which had been brewing for several years.

She could not have known it then, but her health had just entered a critical stage; one from which she would never recover, entering into apoplexy and dying from the effects of a stroke before the year was out.

John withdrew to lick his wounds and plan his next moves as he rode back to Higgin Chamber.

With the bank off his back, he could now concentrate on his wider debt list. Suppliers, hostelry accounts and bar bills throughout the area, personal borrowings from his rich friends and household provisions – not to mention expensive drapers' and tailors' bills for Mary and himself. Plus Fanny's 'growing' needs, all had to be met in turn; but he had collateral again now – the mill itself. Higgin Chamber was still ostensibly in his name and he could borrow against it.

Chapter Eighteen

The Public Shaming and the Death of a Dear Friend

Losing his good friend Bran was a sad time for John which, even now only those few months later he found painful to recall to Rev. Tom.

"Since that night at The Talbot in Halifax, in early January, just over a year ago now, we all knew he had been unwell for some time, with occasional coughing bouts and the shakes. But the warm summer months seemed to agree with him and news of his illness had reached us only a couple of days before Frances Grundy decided to visit, since he was going over to Keighley on railway business anyway. Little realising the severity of his illness by either of us, Grundy took a note I had scribbled for him wishing him well and a speedy recovery."

In the cosy bar-lounge of the Lord Nelson pub in Luddenden village, John had been enjoying an early evening drink with brother-in-law John Murgatroyd,

Francis Grundy and landlord Timothy Wormald. A welcoming fire, the first since May, crackled in the grate and the oil lamps were already lit. Saturday the 14th October 1848 was an overcast, early chilly autumn day and Grundy was recounting his visit to see Branwell at the end of September just three days before his untimely death on September 24th.

All three had attended Branwell's funeral just two weeks before in Howarth on Thursday the 28th of September, but only now did Grundy have the chance to tell of his visit, departing immediately after the funeral and only having just returned to the Calder valley from engineering site meetings over in Lancashire.

John's wife Mary had just celebrated her thirty-sixth birthday, three days before on October 11th, and John Murgatroyd had enjoyed a fine dinner of pheasant, shot by John, together with a few friends, including his wife, John's sister Hannah over at Higgin Chamber. Mary had intended it as a family party and joint celebration since John and Hannah's second wedding anniversary was also due the following Saturday.

The evening had also allowed John to proudly, though sadly, show off Branwell's finished portraits, which he unveiled for the first time to his guests that night. In John's opinion, the completion of the portraits so near to Branwell's end was a poignant and sad, yet fitting time, to remember him. Glasses were raised by the guests to their host's toast; *'...to a dear recently departed friend.'*

"I still can't quite get over it, Francis," John questioned Grundy. "How could Bran come to that state in such a short time? Remind us again how he was that Thursday night you visited? – September 21st, I believe it was?"

Another round of drinks was called for by Grundy and he settled in to tell of his curious last encounter with Branwell.

"Stopping off to stay the night in Howarth, on my way over to Keighley, I booked a room at the Black Bull. I ordered dinner for two in the private dining room, sent a pot-boy up to the parsonage to invite Bran down to eat with me and went to my room to wash and get ready.

"Waiting in the private room a little later I was surprised to receive a visit from the Rev. Brontë; Bran's father had a most curious tale to tell.

"I felt he was grateful for, and rather touched by my kindness to his son and he spoke of Branwell with more affection than I had ever heard him express, but he also spoke almost hopelessly. He said that when my message came, Bran had been in bed and was almost too weak to leave it for the last few days; nevertheless, he had insisted on coming, and would be there immediately. Much of the rector's stiffness of manner was gone and he warned me to prepare for a dramatic change in his son's appearance and left hurriedly.

"Presently the door opened cautiously and a head appeared. It was a mass of red, unkempt, uncut hair, wildly floating round a great, gaunt forehead; the cheeks yellow and hollow, the mouth fallen, the thin white lips not trembling but shaking, the sunken eyes, once small, now glaring with the light of madness – all told the sad tale but too surely.

"I hid my surprise and greeted him in my gayest manner, as I knew he best liked. I forced a stiff glass of hot brandy on him, but even under its influence, and that of the bright, cheerful surroundings, he looked frightened – frightened of himself and muttered something about leaving a warm bed to come out on a cold night.

"Gradually, however, with another glass of brandy inside him, something of the Brontë of old returned, though he remained grave throughout the evening. He described himself as waiting anxiously for death – indeed, longing for it, and happy, in these his sane moments, to think that it was so near and he declared that his death would be solely due to his disastrous relationship with Mrs Robinson.

"As I took my leave reluctantly from him after dinner, Branwell pulled a carving knife from his sleeve and confessed that, having given up hope of ever seeing me again, he had imagined my message was a call from Satan! Seemingly he had the knife hidden all night and had come to the inn armed to rush into the room and stab its occupant!"

John Murgatroyd flinched at this, and said, "You were damned close to getting yourself seriously injured there, Frances, you and the Reverend Patrick, too. They must have only just missed each other, maybe they even passed on the street."

"Only the sound of my voice and my manner had 'brought him home to himself' as Bran would have described it," Grundy replied. He concluded, "I saw him out at the door before retiring and left him standing bareheaded in the road, with bowed form and dropping tears; a sad last sight and as we know he died just those few days afterwards."

John Titterington continued, "And as we heard from John Brown at the funeral, just after that, and only two days before his death, he was well enough to walk down the lane to the village. As he returned to the parsonage, he was overcome by faintness and shortness of breath and had to be helped home by John's brother, William, and his thirteen-year-old niece, Tabitha. Apparently there was a low step to mount and Branwell caught hold of the door side and he told John it was such hard work for him. It was the last time he was ever out."

The day after, unable to get up from his bed, the Haworth doctor, John Wheelhouse, was summoned and the family were told he was close to death. His father, in an agony of distress for his only son, for whom he had held such high hopes, knelt by his bedside and prayed for the salvation of the soul he had thought lost by his rejection of the comforts of religion and refusal to repent his sins.

Throughout his last night Branwell talked of his misspent life, his wasted youth and his shame, with compunction.

John Titterington said that Brown, also just after the funeral said, "I was left alone with him on that last vigil night and looking back on his excesses, Branwell made no mention of Lydia Robinson. Calm and self-possessed, he seemed unconscious that he had ever loved anyone outside the family and spoke of them all with tenderness and affection.

"Seizing my hand, he cried 'Oh, John, I am dying!' and then, as if speaking to himself, he murmured, 'In all my past life I have done nothing either great or good.'

At about nine o'clock the following morning, Sunday the 24th of September, the Brontë family gathered round Branwell's bed to witness his life drawing to its close. Perfectly conscious to the end and, to the joy of his family, praying softly himself, went on to add the final 'amen' to his father's last prayer.

After a struggle of only twenty minutes, an eternity for his family, Branwell started convulsively, almost to his feet and fell back dead into his father's arms.

He was thirty-one years old.

"Back at the Lord Nelson that night, Tom, thinking and talking about Bran and his last hours, we were all taken aback by the bluster of my brother Thomas entering the bar-lounge with an unaccustomed swagger. The fact that he was even in the Lord Nelson at all was surprising enough, for he was no drinker, but his demeanour was also unusual – and ominous; I was soon to find out the purpose of his visit, guessing correctly that he knew where I would be at that time."

"Seen *The Guardian*, John, have you?" he blurted out for all to hear "No? – Thought not, just bought this one in Halifax this afternoon, hot off the press.

"Front page makes interesting reading this week," he blurted on. "About somebody we all know, somebody not a million miles from where I'm standing. Why don't I read it out loud? You'll all have your own copies, like thousands of others will, soon enough!"

Now with the attention of both John's, the landlord's and several other locals who had arrived since, he proceeded to hold up the paper theatrically high, arms outstretched in the manner of a town cryer and read loudly from his copy of *The Halifax Guardian*, dated Saturday 14th October 1948, as though it were a proclamation.

"'Oh, yeah! Oh, yeah!' He could almost have started out with, accompanied by a cryer's bell, Tom, such was his delight in what he read."

"Front page – centre-top," Thomas announced, introducing his reading by turning the front page to his audience and showing it flamboyantly around.

"It's headed – PUBLIC NOTICE, and goes on – *Notice is hereby given, that all and every, the household goods, chattels, and effects, in and about the dwelling houses and premises lately held and occupied by John Titterington, at Higgin Chambers, in Sowerby, in the parish of Halifax. And also all and singular, the machinery and utensils in and about the mill and premises adjoining or near thereto, also lately held and occupied by the said John Titterington, are the sole and exclusive property of Eli Titterington, of Midgley, in the parish of Halifax, aforesaid, worsted manufacturer, and that the said John Titterington has no right, title, or interest whatsoever in or to the same goods, chattels and effects, and machinery, or any part thereof."*

"So there it is, dear brother, all gone and serves you right! You pushed the old man too far just one time too many, and that's what you'll get – now, and ever – nothing!" he said, hardly able to disguise his satisfaction and with a clear sight of a quite different inheritance from the one he might otherwise have expected through a triumph of sibling rivalry.

The premature death of their only other brother James, aged thirty-seven, just four years later in 1852, left Thomas a clear winner in this particular race, who would go on to become the wealthy Lord of the Manor of Midgley, leaving the equivalent of £6.5 million in his will of 1884, dying at the age of sixty-nine. The eighth-century Domesday Book showed nine berewicks in the Manor of Wakefield belonging to Edward the Confessor, of which Midgley, then Micleie, was one. Thomas, as the owner of the steam-powered, worsted-producing Pepper Hill Mill, succeeded the Earls of Warren to his title.

"I restrained myself, Tom, more out of shock than anything else, though I could have quite gladly torn out his throat! But father had realised correctly that I would try to borrow against the mill to cover debts worse than I had been honest about, and he'd wasted no time cutting out that line of borrowing. With all means of getting funding now blocked, I had other things to worry about and let him go on his way gloating. I saw little point in rising to his bait and, unusually for me, managed to restrain myself. John Murgatroyd was shocked, too. He never liked Thomas either, but I knew that any help I might have expected from him, even if he'd wanted to give it, would be cut off by father applying pressure on my sister. News would spread fast and I was in no doubt that there would already be rejoicing down at The Anchor and Shuttle! I went quickly past it on my way home that night, I can tell you.

"The vindictiveness of my father knew no bounds and he even paid to have the announcement published in the next edition of *The Guardian* on the following Saturday, centre-top front page, as though anyone who cared would not have heard about it from the first.

"That really was rubbing it in and I worried especially for my mother's well-being, but it was time to beat a tactful retreat and start a new life for my family, a new career, away from the valley."

Chapter Nineteen

Fanny Brearley

On that same Saturday night, whilst John was returning home licking his wounds from brother Thomas's epic and so embarrassingly public announcement in the Nelson, a drama of a very different kind, but nevertheless also of his making, was starting to unfold over in Halifax.

Struggling home slightly the worse for wear, from an evening at The Talbot, Fanny Brearley entered her rooms in Swinegate, just to the east of the Piece Hall, near to Halifax parish church. She clutched with both hands and cradled her distended belly as the sudden sharp jabbing pain hit her so unexpectedly in her stomach, she stumbled, cried out involuntarily and duly collapsed onto her bed.

Her rooms, simple, but well-furnished were paid for by John as part of his 'conscience money' provision immediately following his first discovery of Fanny's pregnancy. She had made the most of the situation by continuing in the same vein, requiring an ever-growing list of the feminine luxuries of life, which even when not available in Halifax could be brought in from Manchester or Leeds following visits on their market days. The finest clothes, jewellery, perfumes and a full purse had marked her out as a 'kept' woman and John, in return, had been a frequent visitor up to her mid-pregnancy.

Previously living on the north side of Halifax toward Dean Clough with her father, Fanny was an only child, whose radiantly beautiful Irish mother had died some years before. Her father played no part in her fiercely independent life and she was free to live her life as she wished. As his assistant at the Piece Hall, she was efficient and well organised at gathering rents, and her beauty and charm together with an undoubted 'Blarney Stone' gift of the gab won her a wide circle of friends from traders and visitors alike. Coupled with this was an undoubted coarseness and tendency towards the profane and downright vulgar, which John especially and quite inexplicably found irresistible, coming from his strictly religious early upbringing which exactly mirrored that of his wife.

Fanny's rooms were situated on the top floor of a large house, the main occupant of which was a Mrs Lightowler, a somewhat deaf widow lady of some sixty years of age who had lived on the premises with her book keeper husband until his death the year before. In need of more income to keep the same roof over her head, she had resorted to letting out the top rooms of her home and had been surprised to discover just how much John Titterington was prepared to pay for the letting; so much more so than she expected, that she, not a religious lady herself, was prepared to turn a 'blind-eye' to – as well as her unavoidably deaf ear – to the comings and goings and go about getting on with her own business. Her urban surroundings in this neighbourhood also allowed for people to get on with their own lives in a bustling town and the few gossips who were there would draw little comfort from a deaf elderly widow.

With waters broken and intense pains already, Fanny called out to no avail for what seemed like an eternity. Even if Mrs Lightowler was in she would never hear her. Struggling over to her bedroom window she was able to open it and call down to a passing stranger to summon help from a midwife who lived in the next street and with whom Fanny had already made arrangements for the delivery.

Returning to lie down, she realised that she had locked the outer street door and the midwife would not be able to make entry. *Why had I not left it open?* she questioned, but knew that the pain only hit her at the top of the stairs. The now-retired to bed Mrs Lightowler would never hear anybody at the door. Struggling downstairs in pain and with considerable difficulty, Fanny completed her task. Returning to her bedroom, she was shocked to see that her waters were in fact blood – she was bleeding, internally, and profusely, and needed immediate attention.

Midwife Sarah Wilkinson knocked at the door and with no reply, she swiftly entered anyway and climbed to Fanny's room which she had visited already to discuss the planned delivery.

"What time did you have your first contraction, Fanny? And what time your last?" asked Sarah urgently, shocked by the amount of blood already in the bed and across the stone-flagged floor.

By the shortness of time given in Fanny's reply and her dilation on examination, Sarah realised that her time had come and that coupled with Fanny's screams and now with considerable continuing bleeding she needed help – she needed a doctor – and urgently.

Again calling down into the street to any passer-by, Sarah was relieved to recognise a woman she knew and directed her to summon the nearest doctor who lived only a few streets away in this densely populated area of ancient east Halifax.

Mopping Fanny's brow and comforting her as best she knew how, Sarah tried distracting her, but the pain was all too much. Fanny, now slipping in and out of consciousness and racked with pain, continued the maniacal scream that had both accompanied her conception and was even now pre-empting its conclusion.

Dr Ferguson arrived after about fifteen minutes, much to Sarah's considerable relief since she knew only too well that it could sometimes take hours when she had difficult deliveries up the valleys or on the outskirts of town.

Slipping quite comfortably now into her well-practised secondary role as nurse-midwife-assistant, she stood by for instructions as Dr Ferguson went about his work, examining his patient. "We have the child in breech, and I need to try and turn it – now!" he said, not wishing to alarm his patient but sufficiently for Sarah to appreciate the urgency of his comment.

What both Sarah and the doctor could see perfectly well, but Fanny couldn't, was the now even more considerable continuing loss of blood. Turning the child proved impossible, and worse still, time consuming, in a worsening situation as far as both patient and child were concerned. The fastest possible delivery of the baby was of critical importance and the doctor feared that it was now the umbilical cord that was tangled and holding back delivery.

After the most dreadfully extended period of time in Sarah's entire career, Fanny gave one last scream and push and was delivered of a daughter; no cry emitted from her bloody form and after clearing her face and mouth and scooping his finger around inside her mouth, Dr Ferguson bent urgently to breathe air gently into the hand-cradled lifeless form, whilst Sarah did her best to comfort her own patient.

Too late to save the baby, now their attention was concentrated on the mother whose immeasurable and considerable loss of blood must take its toll, and worse still, the interminable stresses that had prevailed upon her entire being had simply proved too much for her to bear.

At 9.10pm precisely, on that sad October evening, the doctor declared both mother and child dead and together, Sarah and he departed the building and went their separate ways with Dr Ferguson visiting the undertaker on the way to make the final arrangements.

With no other family member present that night, and with Sarah's permission, he named the child after both her and her dear mother – Fanny Sarah.

Two days later, mourned by her father Isaac alone, together with a few close friends and without even John's knowledge, Fanny, aged just twenty-one and her still-born child were laid to rest together in Halifax St. John's parish churchyard.

"I only learned about it after the funeral, Tom, from William, and I still haven't got over the shock and the sadness. I visited her grave as soon as I could and felt, still feel, such a deep sadness at her passing and take full responsibility for my deeds. It was young William who came into the mill office to tell me with an expression that could not be mistaken for anything but bad news. I was grateful it was him, for he knew, better than anyone, how it might feel for me and that I would only have ever brought up the child – my child, with exactly the same care I had shown for him and his mother."

Tom had listened intently to John's story, most of it learned second-hand from both midwife and doctor, whom John told him he had sought out to discover the truth. Tom did his best to ease his conscience, adding, "These things are in the hand of the good Lord, John, and his mysteries will only be revealed to us in His own good time. Take comfort from the happiness she had in her short life that you shared together, and try not to dwell only on her sad departure from it, which was His way and cannot be borne entirely by you. I will pray for both her and the dead child's souls – may they both rest in peace."

Chapter Twenty

William Settles In

Leaving York prison for the first time that day, William felt a lightness in his step and quickened his pace as he crossed the city over towards The Shambles.

"My name is William Titterington!" he repeated to himself with pride; proud that he was accepted by his father as such and that he could start a whole new chapter in his short life feeling he belonged, truly belonged to a family and moreover was in a position to repay his father for all of his kindnesses educating him and providing the money for him and his mother to enjoy a life unattainable by so many of their neighbours in Luddenden Foot.

He mulled over the plans they had discussed; establish himself at The Shambles, meet and get to know the farmers who supplied livestock for butchery who would also supply wool for him to buy and ship over to the Halifax mills, and in return bring back their fine cloths to sell in York and Beverley to the affluent clientèle in the fashion-hungry tailoring market.

The supply of game birds, poultry, rabbits and hares, from farmers to sell in The Shambles, which he had noticed featured in Michael Cooper's offerings could also be in the back of his mind when he got to know Michael better and John's shooting friends over here must have need of placing their excess game from shoots; to Michael or even other Shambles butchers where it didn't clash.

Best of all, such friends of his father would often be the wealthy land owners, the gentry! The meat and wool producing tenant farmers means of survival. Friends of influence who controlled everything in the area through their wealth; the key to both a steady supply of produce and a ready market for fashionable clothing for their families made from fine Halifax cloths.

He had seen, though as a labourer not been introduced to, several of these contacts at the Piece Hall, one of which was William Barker from Beverley whose house John told him they were living in at Stonegate. The reverend gentleman he'd told him about was also from Beverley and would have influential friends, many of whom, John said, still held him in regard and sympathised with his current plight.

But he was getting ahead of himself. With only the clothes he stood up in, he was a long way from achieving any of this and first he had to prove himself as a butcher's boy and abattoir worker, make some money and with John's guidance, earn enough to gain his day-release away from the ever menacing presence of the awful Scoggins at York Castle who had so deliberately and obviously set out to despise William from the moment he gave him his name, his *new* name!

Walking closer and closer to York Minster, William was simply awestruck by its sheer size and its magnificence. He'd seen illustrations of the cathedrals of England, but only ever imagined they'd be just a bit bigger than Halifax parish church, which in itself was always very impressive to him, compared with the small churches in the Calder Valley.

Finally arriving at Stonegate and feeling the Minster towers might crash down on him any minute, he rang the doorbell of number 43 which immediately resulted in the welcoming bark he knew and loved so well.

Mary opened the door and Blazer shot out and jumped on his hind legs right up onto his chest where he placed his front paws and commenced licking his face.

"Whoa! Blazer, hold on there, don't eat me! I'm glad to see you boy, too, but hold back a bit," he said, forcing him by his collar back down to street level.

"William! William Foster, as I live and breathe, you're a rare sight for sore eyes! Girls! Come down and greet a visitor," she shouted, loudly enough to be heard upstairs.

Their mother's obviously urgent tone brought a loud clattering on the stairs as four pairs of feet clambered down with Grace bringing up the rear, carrying James.

"William! Oh, William. How lovely to see you. What a nice surprise," said Grace almost jumping off the ground in imitation of Blazer. "We were only just talking about you, wondering what was happening back at home and suddenly here you are to tell us."

William was ushered in by Mary and sat down at the kitchen table with all five children now variously climbing up on both his knees or getting as close to him as they could with arms around his shoulders.

"When did you arrive? How long are you over for? Where are you staying?" A dozen questions came from all quarters.

William answered cautiously, "I am no longer needed at the mill so I decided to follow you all over here and try to make a new start, a new life for myself. I went to see Uncle John just now and he looks well under the circumstances. That turnkey Scoggins is never going to help, though, I didn't like him one little bit. Nasty piece of work, enjoys making people suffer, I would think.

"I found myself somewhere to stay in The Shambles, almost as soon as I got off the train, by having a chat with one of the butchers there. He's called Michael Cooper and we got on really well together. I told him how I'd had butchering experience at home and he very quickly realised I might be the answer to his prayers. A wife, two children, one of them a newborn, was leaving him short-staffed and with the busy Christmas period coming up he needed a solution. He's tried training a few local lads in the last few months and all them either proved useless or didn't take to the work, or the hours!

"So there I am for a trial until after the New Year, and with an attic room to myself – I'll make it work, I know the work from training with the Slaters at The Anchor and he taught me well."

Hannah responded first. "Oh! And you could have stayed here, mother, couldn't he? But you're here William, that's the main thing and we shall be able to see you often."

"What happened to your job at the mill, William? Or don't I need to ask that with my dear brother-in-law in charge?" questioned Mary, knowing the answer full well as soon as she saw him on the doorstep.

"Well your house is closed up, ready for you to return, but I never did get on with Master Thomas so wasn't surprised. I needed a change anyway and already thought about a few possibilities over here. My uncle has more ideas and between us I think we can make enough money to get him onto day release and then, together, put the agency work he'd planned already into operation. I start at 4.00am in The Shambles and finish by noon, so I'll have lots of time to do my own, our own work and see how it develops." William said, already warming to the sound of the plans during their first enunciation.

"Well, money is needed," she confided, as the girls had now gone back upstairs to play on the top floor, content that their 'cousin' was staying in York. "My father sends enough for us all to live on, but I have to feed John as well and it's nowhere near enough to buy him his day release. I'll help you all I can, William, and good luck in your new job. It sounds like hard work, but

I know your father is very proud of you." This last sentence being said with Mary first glancing over toward the stairs.

That decided, William returned to number 14 and spent the rest of the day acquainting himself with his duties commencing the next morning.

It was resolved that he would start in the abattoir at the back with the vast array of birds, which came either dead already or live in cages during the night. Then he'd move on to small animals, starting with rabbits and hares which were also already despatched and lastly work up to slaughtering live lambs and small pigs.

By ten o'clock, the front of shop hooks would display the birds in size order, starting with pigeons and working along to turkeys and geese via grouse, pheasant, quail, partridge, mallard, guinea fowl, ducks and chickens or whatever else was delivered in, dead or alive, from various farm suppliers and shoots around the wider York area. The larger animals would hang inside the shop from ceiling hooks and William would have Michael's assistance lifting, hanging and slaughtering them prior to cutting them into saleable roasting joints, smaller chops and usable offal to present on trays on the shop's counter. Pig's blood especially was caught in a tin bath for later black pudding making.

Elizabeth Cooper spent her early mornings before baby Ruth awoke preparing the early bird meats to make her famous pies, and since her work was then limited by the childcare requirements for both her and two-year old Rachel, he immediately spotted an opportunity for employment; firstly for baby and childcare, which Grace and Hannah had experience of with James and could do well with, and secondly for pie-making help, probably back at number 43, by Mary, for sale in the shop. Mary made the best game pies when John came back from shooting trips and here was both the money-making opportunity and a ready supply of a wide range of meats to help her with the task. William had also noted there was a large cooking range at number 43, and saw Mary was already taking full advantage of it, filling hungry mouths both there and across the city at the castle gaol.

He decided to observe Michael's planned routine before making suggestions and in a few days the girls and Mary would probably come along to visit and the Coopers could judge for themselves how they got on and decide if his plans, better formulated by then, could work. William thought that they, like he, were a perfect match for the Coopers.

"I have family over here, Michael. I need to tell you about them before I start working for you. It's the reason I came over in the first place and they are in quite a predicament at the moment. My father John is in the debtors' prison over at the castle. I visited him today and his wife, who is not my mother, and her five children, who are all living over in Stonegate, and here to support him.

"I'm very proud of my father. He is a very talented and much-admired man, who is misunderstood by his family – especially his very wealthy father who has disowned and shamed him publicly in *The Halifax Guardian*. I am his illegitimate child, brought up by my mother's parents as their own, but my father has stood by me and gone to some expense to educate me and employed me at his mill. In his absence, his brother Thomas has taken on the running of the mill, as well as his own and I was not likely to last long since there was never any love lost between the two of them.

"And so Michael, I needed to be honest with you, before you found out anyway; I'm here to help the family all I can and get my father out of prison, firstly on day release and then to totally free him by settling his debts. We have a plan, which with hard work, I believe, can succeed. I do hope my honesty hasn't shocked you – and that you don't think I was dishonest in any way. You will see that I can do a first-class job here for you and I am looking forward to the challenge. You won't be disappointed, I'll make sure of that."

Michael considered this, and for a moment William thought he might have shocked him, but he came back quickly with, "Well, William, I liked you when we first talked in the street and what you have told me has only strengthened my opinion that you are a fine young man who your father has every reason to be proud of. I won't stand in judgement on your father's present position. It's not my place, nor will I ask how he got to be there; you can tell me more, if and when you're ready, in your own good time. Your role here is clear. From what you have told me I think you can do well and let's get to work in the morning and see what you're capable of!"

Relieved that the air was cleared, William and Michael commenced a working relationship the next morning that would be the envy of any partnership, in any walk of life, for several months to come.

271

Mary and the children went to bed over at number 43 a little more comfortably that night, feeling not quite so homesick and Mary especially liked the support that she felt certain William would give to John. She looked forward to seeing him and welcoming him into their home; as before in Sowerby – as a close family relative.

Having a man around again gave them all great comfort and even Blazer could sense a renewed optimism and an opportunity perhaps to get out of his cramped city confines and return to his favourite outdoor pursuit – *the shoot!*

Chapter Twenty One

Thorp Green

Situated in the rich agricultural triangle of the Vale of York, between York, Ripon and Harrogate, Thorp Green was a mansion of some size where its occupants the Rev. Edmund Robinson and his wife Lydia and a family of four lived; Lydia the oldest was fourteen when Anne arrived, Elizabeth (thirteen), Mary (twelve) and their only son Edmund junior who was aged ten. Their baby Georgina Jane had died earlier that year aged just eighteen months.

Set in acres of parkland, near to the River Ouse, the Robinsons employed three male and seven female servants as well as Anne Brontë, who came as a governess in 1840 to be joined two years later by brother Branwell, employed as tutor to Edmund junior.

Rev. Robinson, aged forty, was a wealthy clergyman of independent means who, as a chronic invalid, rarely officiated at church services. As Lord of Ouseburn, the nearest village, he owned all of the land around Thorpe

Underwoods and most of his neighbours were wealthy farmers; the nearest settlement of any size was the busy market town of Boroughbridge, smaller than Howarth and lying six miles to the north-west of Thorp Green.

As an indication of the value of the estate it sold twenty-five years later for the enormous sum of £116,750 – over £60 million.

A prestigious appointment for Anne and later for Branwell, who joined her in 1842, following his dismissal from the railways, the Robinsons lived in grand style.

Both John and Tom, it turned out, were aware of all these facts having visited Thorp Green separately – Tom to preach for Edmund on many occasions, had been delighted to see both Anne and Branwell, who he had met of course many times growing up in West Yorkshire, and John as a shooting party visitor, accompanied by several rich and influential friends including the Huddersfield industrialist Sir Joseph Armitage and Francis Sharp Powell, later to become an MP, knight and later, baronet.

"Sir Joseph was a friend of long standing and both he and I were directors of The Halifax and Huddersfield Union Banking Company," added John.

"I was a supporter of Francis over many years. As a gifted ex-pupil of Uppingham and Sedbergh schools, he was a bright young lawyer fresh out of St. John's Cambridge – yours and Patrick's old college, Tom. I knew then that he had political ambitions and a bright future ahead of him. The Sharps had been the owners of

Little Horton in Bradford, since the English Civil War, and Francis was an heir to its baronetcy. You may have known his father – the Rev. Benjamin Powell of Wigan?"

Tom didn't know him, but nodded to John to continue with his story.

"I remember once meeting Bran at The Lord Nelson public house in Luddenden village where there was a library upstairs. It was toward the end of summer 1840 and Bran was, as usual, passing through between Haworth and Halifax.

"Who could forget his striking appearance then as a twenty-three year-old? You will remember Tom, his charm and that shock of red hair brushed forward, with long side-burns and his straight rather prominent nose? Vivacious and witty, he excelled at conversation and was impressively erudite – well able, in short to sweep any young girl off her feet, you will agree?"

Tom nodded and allowed John to continue.

"Timothy Wormald, the landlord who was also clerk to St. Mary's church, directly opposite the Nelson, was a member, like most of my friends, of the Luddenden Reading Society, which operated one very strict rule lest pub regulars overstepped the mark, that 'if any members come to the said meeting drunk so that he be offensive to the company, and not fit to do his business, he shall forfeit two pence. Swearing on oath, or using any other kind of bad language judged by a majority of the members to be offensive, also calls for a fine of two pence!'

"Branwell was twenty-three years old and always clearly intellectual by the very nature of his conversation; he had recently lost his position as a private tutor up in Broughton-in-Furness and went on to describe his ambitions still to be a poet and have his poems published, but in the meantime, as a poor parson's son still needed an income to survive. A friend called Francis Grundy, an engineer on the railway, was with us in the public bar that night and between his contacts and my father's influence – he was an early railway shareholder – we managed to secure him a job as Assistant Station Master at Sowerby Bridge, just one stop down from Luddenden Foot on the Halifax line. He started to work there in October of that year.

"One quick promotion six months later to Station Master at Luddenden Foot, where he stayed for only eleven months before being dismissed, and then later in March of 1842 to Thorp Green where he joined sister Anne. I'll tell you more later about our rather wild times together during his time working on the railways, but for now I'll move on to Thorp Green."

Tom said, "I can't wait for that one. Branwell was always different, even as a child and the combination of factors you describe must make for an interesting story! Continue please, John."

"He arrived at Thorp Green on Anne's recommendation just after his dismissal from the railway – for incompetence, yes! I'll tease you and save that one for later, Tom! There he took over the tutorship of young Edmund junior, leaving Anne free to extend the girls' knowledge and life-skills; skills which were deemed 'more appropriate' and genteel, leading to becoming eligible young ladies ready for a 'suitable' marriage and leaving Branwell, then, free to move his charge onto the classics and wider worldly topics, more suited to an aspiring young 'gentleman' and man-about-town.

"Poetry and painting in water-colours were added to his curriculum by Branwell to round up his education, and the next three years were spent educating what he described as a not overly-bright, rather effeminate pupil, nursing him through the difficult pre-pubescent years as best he could whilst developing his own poetry, writing and artistic skills. He could not have chosen a more idyllic, indeed grand place to live, but as we both know the lady of the house had other ideas for him!

"As a tutor before at Broughton-in-Furness he had made an auspicious boost to his ongoing poetry writing, gaining the respect of the poet David Hartley Coleridge, elder son of his more famous, but later to become drug-damaged father, Samuel Taylor Coleridge, author as you know of 'The Rime of the Ancient Mariner.'

"Unlike his time at Thorp Green, Bran lived outside the family home there, where he taught two boys of a family called Postlethwaite. Living away from his employer gave him the freedom to take long walks in the Lake District which so inspired other poets such as William Wordsworth and Robert Southey, the latter having cared for young Coleridge in his early years, following his father's descent into opium-induced oblivion and a failed marriage.

"Coleridge further encouraged Bran, sending a translation of Horace's 'Odes' to him – so much so that at his invitation Bran, visited him, spending time reading with him and being inspired to further translation through his recognition and encouragement.

"His time with the Postlethwaites came to an abrupt end after an affair that he told me he had with a servant girl in the house. A pregnancy and an early miscarriage resulted in the girl being dismissed, along with Branwell of course, only six months into his employment. He showed me a poem he wrote in his notebook just afterwards, whilst grieving for his lost child – an imagined daughter he never had, in which he expressed his deepest feelings; it was like an autobiography. He called it 'Epistle from a Father on Earth to his Child in her Grave'. As I was to learn later, it was quite unlike anything he had written before and he was visibly moved reading it out loud to us at the Luddenden Reading Society that night. I, too, was quite overcome as Mary and I had lost our own baby Eli only two months before and his sadness brought it all home to me again.

"But I digress, back at Thorp Green, Joseph, Francis and I had been invited to stay over after a day's shooting on the Ouseburn estate. It was the summer of 1843, which had been one of the hottest I could remember. We all dressed and came down for dinner in the Robinsons' rather grand dining hall. The children must have eaten earlier and we were joined by Anne and Branwell. I'm not sure, but I suspect they were only invited to eat with the family on special occasions and then only because they were my friends.

"It became very clear to me over dinner that Lydia, the lady of the house had feelings for Branwell. I can't imagine how her husband never noticed her many

278

glances in his direction and the gentle touch, almost a caress, she gave his hand when she passed the gravy boat to him. Anne had certainly noticed that, too, as we exchanged glances to observe a mutual recognition of her overtly affectionate gesture.

"I was in no doubt that the servants knew exactly what was going on, too, as they moved around us serving dinner. They would see it all the time. The below-stairs humour must have been rich!

"I think her husband was aware of what was going on, too, he had to be, and I presumed that his chronic illness, denying his wife as it must have, her conjugal rights, allowed him to turn a regretful blind eye for the sake of outward family respectability.

"That all three of us noticed what was going on occasioned much ribald humour afterwards whilst shooting the next day, I can tell you! Anyway, after dinner, I pulled Bran on one side to caution him. 'You're on dangerous ground there, my friend, be careful – tell her at least not to make it quite so obvious in front of guests, I see even Anne knows what's going on!' And of course he couldn't, didn't even try to deny it, but I knew then that it could only lead him into trouble."

Unknown to John, at this precise moment in time and in a not dissimilar vein, on the evening shift back at Higgin Chamber, weaving production was faltering, yet again in John's absence, without the supervision of its mill foreman; Joe Saltonstall, a trouble maker, and local Chartist coordinator, had formed an unwelcome relationship with a young bobbin-girl called Ellen Hardcastle, to whom he was euphemistically 'making love,' as he did against her wishes on a regular weekly basis in the upstairs wool sorting room.

Tom continued, as he, too, had also heard the Lydia-tutor rumours, but had not personally witnessed anything untoward having never stayed as a house-guest at Thorp Green, always travelling back to Beverley after morning services. "Matins were followed by a simple lunch, which was never taken with either their tutor or governess, so I never saw them together really.

"It cost him his position though, didn't it, John, in the end?" Tom queried.

"Well that's what everybody either thought, or was led to believe, but the truth from Bran was totally different.

"At breakfast next morning, we were joined by the older children and it was clear that young Edmund, who hung onto every word of his tutor and mentor, had more than a mere academic interest in his subject matter and worshipped the ground he walked on! He hardly took his eyes off him during the whole meal.

"Just prior to the family holiday in Scarborough, where they stayed each year at Wood's lodgings, Branwell had taken Edmund down to the banks of the River Ouse, which ran through the estate half a mile from the house for a nature and sketching lesson.

"An extremely hot day made concentration on lessons difficult for both pupil and tutor and swimming was out of the question due to Edmund's known fear of water. Feeling sleepy after lunch, Branwell left Edmund to sketch by the river, settled down in the shade of a chestnut tree, closed his eyes and drifted away to the sounds of the water lapping up to the river bank and the gentle drone of bees.

"He had noticed recently that young Edmund had started to idolise him somewhat, generally being a model and overly attentive student. Quite unlike his previous poor attempts at study, he had taken to following Branwell around like a lost sheep dog, and though still a poor student academically, he was at least trying hard to learn something, but mainly was obviously simply eager to please him. Bran put it down to the adolescence of an early teenage boy coming to terms with his own sexuality and burgeoning hormones, in a world where his three sisters completely took over all of their mother's attention and became her main priority; his incapacitated father of course being physically incapable of joining him in the fun a boy might enjoy and expect from a father, whilst growing up.

"As the only boy in his own family, Bran had experienced similar feelings of isolation, lacking a mother figure, after his own and then Aunt Branwell's death and he'd just had to get on with it.

"Coming out of his slumbers with an itch, Bran found Edmund tickling him on the nose with a long blade of grass and a friendly exchange of banter ended in a wrestling bout, which they had often engaged in before down by the river bank, such was their strength of their friendship. I sometimes wrestled with Bran myself in Luddenden Foot and he was very strong and quite adept at the art!

"This time it was different and Edmund, mistaking the signals whilst secured in a tight hold with Bran on top of him, reached up, pulled his head down and kissed his tutor fully on the lips, in an act of complete submission!

"Horrified and stunned, Bran pushed the boy back down. He jumped up, not knowing immediately what to say. How to respond? He also could not help but notice the boy's arousal as they hastily prepared to leave the river bank.

"Returning back to the house immediately, Edmund was clearly hurt by Bran's rejection and he in return, though shocked, had tried not to overly rebuke his obviously embarrassed student who had intended no harm in his sorely misplaced and inappropriate display of affection.

"Then just a few days later, before departure for Scarborough for the family's annual holiday – Bran was not to join them and returned home to Howarth; Anne would normally have joined the family in Scarborough, but she had left their employment of her own free will the month before, in June of 1845; Edmund was about to witness something that was to shock him to the core and dramatically affect Bran's immediate future prospects, both personally and professionally.

"Walking by the river bank again, only a few days later, Edmund heard muffled sounds coming from the boathouse. Bemoaning still his tutor's rejection near this place, he crept up carefully, thinking perhaps there were salmon poachers or hunters in the boathouse, but peering carefully through a window he was confronted by the semi-naked figure of the object of his intense desire – his tutor, hips flailing, at that crescendo stage of sexual congress where nothing and no one could disturb him. But who was the object of his passion? Shocked though he was and intensely jealous of whoever it was, he crept around to a second window to try to get a better view of who was underneath his writhing torso. Which servant girl could it be? And he gasped! With a sharp involuntary intake of breath, he observed his own mother, just as she released the most ear-splitting scream – like the cry of a wounded animal, a fox in a trap. He ran – ran, as fast as his legs could carry him, back to the house in a state of utter confusion. Was she injured? What to do? And he, now rejected so cruelly by the two most important people in his life, felt utterly and totally betrayed.

"His father had left already for Scarborough with the girls and young Edmund followed with his mother by stage coach the next day, still confused and with a burning desire to punish Branwell for his actions. His tutor's now undoubted love for his own mother, rather than himself, had cruelly thwarted his juvenile cravings for his tutor's affections through a hurtful rejection, which in his bitterness he was not going to allow to go unpunished, and with his own dear mother!"

"What was his plan now, John? What an extraordinary turn of events," interrupted Tom, fascinated and eager to get to the denouement.

"Immediately on arrival at Wood's and without passing any comment to his mother, or being able to even look at her on the journey, I should think, he must have headed straight to his father to announce that

Branwell had made an inappropriate overt move toward him, of an unnatural and sexual nature!

"Falsely reversing the details of the 'incident' by the river in some detail, he left his father with an anger beyond belief and he immediately set about writing Bran's letter of dismissal, incredulous that someone in his employment could so badly, and so immorally, abuse his trust.

Tom, guessing the nature of his friend's terse response asked, "What did the letter say, John? How did he phrase such a difficult letter?"

"I can almost remember it verbatim, Tom. Bran re-read it to me so many times back at Higgin Chamber, where he came to spend some time to be with friends, away from prying eyes in Haworth, and to get over his loss of Lydia whom he loved so dearly.

"It was also at that time that Bran turned to opium for consolation and though I didn't join him, I spent many hours drinking with him trying to help, but neither I, drink, nor the laudanum could make up for his painful loss.

"Worst of all, his employer's explosive letter of dismissal, received at the parsonage, threatened Branwell with 'public exposure' – going far beyond the widely believed discovery of an illicit love affair with his wife; he clearly hadn't discovered his wife's affair and may have reluctantly condoned it anyway, turning a blind eye in his circumstances, and why indeed would he submit his own wife to 'exposure' anyway at the same time?. And to whom exactly? And for what purpose? And in any case, I know from friends in the area that their marriage continued outwardly as strongly as it could have under the circumstances, right up to his premature death not long afterwards and Lydia's bequests in Edmund's will were in any case entirely what a good and faithful wife might have expected.

"Young Edmund's lie was of course the catalyst! Bran knew only too well that an 'exposure' of this nature would have prevented him from ever tutoring boys again and would moreover have involved serious legal consequences, possible imprisonment, vilification and an inevitable rejection by family and friends alike.

"Bran's torment at losing Lydia, combined with the threat of wrongful and seriously damaging exposure was just too much for him to bear, without resort to both mental and physical sustenance.

"Branwell had some liaisons with Lydia afterwards, one I know of was in September that same year in Harrogate, where he told me Lydia even suggested an elopement. This was rejected by Bran, but he did nevertheless always have high hopes that one day he might marry her, his one true love, but legitimately, when her husband passed away. She supported him always, sending him money when he needed it, too. I remember once a coachman from Thorp Green was directed over to Sowerby from Haworth with funds for him, so as I suspected before, neither was it a secret 'below-stairs' and would also have been hard to hide from her husband, his 'blind eye' perhaps again?

"How sad that his love for her was to remain unrequited and that after her husband's death they were still not able to be together. At least, thank God, he didn't have to suffer the pain of Lydia becoming Lady Scott, since she married her cousin last year, only two months after Bran's death."

The time on Edmund Robinson junior's fob watch showed ten minutes to two o'clock.

It was as dead as he was – recovered drowned in a tragic ferry-capsizing accident crossing the fully-flowing River Ure near Ripley, on Thursday, February 4th 1869, whilst on a fox-hunt.

The hounds had swum across higher up the river at a narrower point and the hunt, eager to catch up, headed down to the nearest ferry crossing at Newby Hall.

Edmund, aged thirty-seven, died a bachelor, alongside three other members of the York and Ainstey Hunt, including its master, Sir Charles Slingsby, aged forty-five, who without an heir was the 10th and therefore last baronet of his three-centuries'-old line.

Edmund, a non-swimmer, who had a known fear of drowning, remained mounted on board as the ferry slowly sank. He had always said that in a river you should stick to your horse, but when his horse began to sink under his upright weight and he felt himself going, a witness at the inquest said of him "...*his horse was exhausted from the previous gallop; his screams were terrible as they went under and perished together in about five fathoms.*"

Their warnings of danger dismissed, the ferrymen, James Warriner, a gardener at Newby Hall and his son Christopher, also perished.

Foolishly and overly eager to continue the chase, they had boarded the ferry, designed for no more than three horses and men. Eleven riders and the ferrymen were on board, together with their horses, one of whom kicked out viciously at another in a panic, sensing the flat-bottomed chain-drawn ferry was over-laden and about to sink; which it duly did, casting all thirteen passengers and eleven horses into the fast-flowing swollen river.

Eight of the eleven horses drowned. Edmund and the five other deceased, including both ferrymen, were solemnly transported to nearby Newby Hall, where a coroner's inquest the next day could only determine it to have been a *'tragic acciden'*.

Edmund was laid to rest in the family vault beneath their pew in Holy Trinity church, Little Ouseburn, where a marble memorial wall-plaque marks his passing.

Chapter Twenty Two

Haworth to York

It was Tuesday, 22nd May 1849 and John was now well settled into his time in York Castle Debtors' Prison, splitting his time in deep contemplation in his shared cell to pass the time away and utilising his temporary day-release time, within York city boundary walls, to further his textile agency business interests with son William's able assistance.

Charlotte's long-time friend from school, Ellen Nussey, walked confidently up to the top of the steep main street back in Howarth, past The Black Bull and turned left at the church to approach the parsonage. Unsure of how she was going to feel seeing Anne, her confidence faltered and she slowed her pace slightly, hesitating to read a gravestone which she scanned, but would not have been able to repeat a single word for the life of her immediately afterwards.

Her mind was on other things and overhead a storm was brewing with distant claps of thunder threatening a downpour coming in off the moors.

Charlotte had written to her to inform her of Anne's worsening condition and told her of the similarities of her illness with that of her sister Emily, in December just five months before. She had suggested that a trip to the coast may produce the desired effect to lift Anne out of the dreadfully debilitating condition she found herself in. The ozone, cliff top or promenade strolls, good company and food and a fresh view of life with amiable companions would be all that was necessary to improve her condition and lift her out of the wasting illness, which was increasingly consuming her body. Ellen had accepted the invitation and looked forward to the trip.

And all of this also only eight months since their only brother, the tormented Branwell, was taken from them so cruelly.

And Anne herself, as the last born of the six children, had spent a lifetime feeling an inner guilt and a responsibility for depriving the entire family of their mother after she felt she was the cause of her death from cancer, just twenty months following her difficult delivery.

Arriving, unusually nervous at the many-times-visited parsonage door and tugging on the bell-pull, Ellen was met by a familiar sound – the friendly welcoming bark of Anne's spaniel, Flossy, easily recognisable, since she had been given a pup of Flossy's by Anne which was identical in every way, including her bark and which she had rather unimaginatively yet appropriately also named Flossy.

Anne's Flossy had been given to her as a gift by the three Robinson girls, her charges at Thorp Green where she was a governess, in June 1843. She had settled later into a happy life at the parsonage where she lived out her days, outliving her mistress Anne herself and dying in 1854, as Charlotte would later report *'...without a pang...no dog ever had a happier life or an easier death.'*

Anne herself had spotted Ellen coming up the path and was first to the door to greet her. Flossy's exuberant greeting knew no bounds and was clearly occasioned by the familiarity of both her memory of Ellen's many previous visits over from Gomersall and the faint yet distinct odour of her own offspring. Unfortunately, on this occasion she had not brought her own Flossy along as she and Charlotte were due to depart taking Anne with them to the coast the next day.

"Let me get inside, before the storm breaks," Ellen said and quickly stepped in as the first heavy drops of an early summer cloudburst started to fall.

Ellen was greeted by Anne with a peck to both cheeks and Charlotte covered Ellen's shock at seeing Anne so changed by reaching out to her with both arms and embracing her warmly.

She was aware immediately that Charlotte had done this quite deliberately to take away the awkwardness of the moment – the sheer shock of seeing Anne in such an emaciated condition. And it worked, with all breaking into huge laughter, causing Patrick to come from his study and join in the greetings. Tabby and Martha also came to the door from the kitchen to greet Ellen since they too regarded her as almost a member of the family after so many years. Dear-departed Emily's faithful dog Keeper was not to be left out either and joined in with a duet of barking and furious tail-wagging!

And between all of the greetings Ellen was able to take another quick glance at Anne and noticed she now had the arms of a child. Her cheeks and eyes were sunken and her body had become so weakened by weight loss that she had difficulty in walking into the sitting room without catching her breath. Her weight must have dropped to less than five or six stones and though not a heavy girl, she had been her usual self the last time Ellen saw her when she carried perhaps as much as seven or eight stones of bodyweight.

Ellen worried that she might not even be up to the rigours of a trip to Scarborough.

She was certainly going to need their help to get there.

After supper the girls sat by the sitting room fire and Patrick returned to his study to work on his Sunday sermon for the following week's service. Anne had eaten little of her cold meat salad, pushing it around the plate and she alone had declined to try even a small portion of an apple pie so lovingly prepared for Ellen's visit by Charlotte.

Outside the storm continued unabated and rain lashed against the parsonage windows.

"Let's see what the weather's like in the morning," said Charlotte. "We can delay another day if necessary if the storms haven't blown over."

This was a great relief to Ellen since Anne would then at least have a chance to get a decent meal inside her for the journey which would undoubtedly be going to prove arduous for one so weakened.

Charlotte passed the time by starting to prepare a shopping list for the seaside.

Anne decided to retire to bed to prepare for the trip and parted saying, "I'm so glad you are coming with us Ellen. We will have a fine time all together and I just know that the sea-air will allow me to regain my strength."

And, as if to emphasise her final point, she struggled manfully to her feet, headed for the door with some difficulty, and passed through almost holding herself with pain.

"Maybe the storm is good news," Charlotte whispered quietly. "Maybe we should delay and after two good early nights' rests and perhaps her favourite meal of Martha's beef broth tomorrow, she will be better prepared for us to set off on Thursday for York?"

Ellen agreed, as did Patrick, who had heard Anne going up to bed early and had come in to the sitting room to ask of their plans.

"It will be better, father, and we can leave her to sleep late in the morning. Let's keep Flossy down here tonight so as not to disturb her?"

All were agreed and Charlotte returned to her shopping list for York. Neither Anne nor Charlotte had a wardrobe appropriate to a fashionable seaside resort like Scarborough so her list needed to include such items.

"Bonnets, combs, black silk stockings, dresses, gloves, and a ribbon for our necks! All need to be on the list, Ellen," said Charlotte, as she scribbled away. The very frivolity of the stockings and the ribbons causing them both to erupt into bursts of laughter!

"How very fortunate, though I should say, for us, rather than for the poor departed Aunt Fanny, that we have Anne's £200 legacy from her to make our trip a truly memorable one!"

Charlotte, who had already told Ellen by letter, was referring to Anne's godmother Fanny Outhwaite's death in February and she additionally pointed out: "It could not be better employed than in an attempt to prolong, if not restore Anne's life. I'm certain Aunt Fanny would have approved wholeheartedly."

The next day Anne did indeed sleep late and though the storm had passed during the night, they all agreed to delay by one day to allow the weather to be more settled since the skies were still heavily overcast.

After a jolly day planning their adventure, Anne did eat her favourite meal with a relish not witnessed for some time and all three took an early night to prepare for their departure the next morning.

After breakfast they bade farewell at noon to Patrick, Tabby and Martha, at the door. The farewells were fairly muted and Anne gave both Flossy and Keeper what was to be their last caress.

Travelling down to Keighley they caught the 1.30pm train to Leeds station where Anne had to have additional assistance across the lines and in and out of the carriages.

"It's not a problem," Ellen added, assisted by two porters in the task. "We just need to get you to the lovely sea-air and to walk along the promenade to get you back on your feet."

Journeying on to York, they arrived in the late afternoon and took the short ride in a carriage from the imposing railway station to Coney Street where they checked in to the George Hotel, a fine long-established coaching inn in the heart of the city.

After the journey, made more tiring for Charlotte and Ellen with the additionally taxing element of coaxing, still carrying Anne for parts of the trip, Charlotte said: "Let's rest a while first in our room, then I know I'm hungry after the journey, so we'll eat and then step out into the city to do some shopping after dinner."

Ellen had checked when they registered, beyond earshot of Anne, that the inn could provide them with a bath-chair during their visit, so that at the appropriate time it could simply appear by the entrance for either

Ellen or Charlotte to remark casually: "Oh, look here's a fine chair to help us on our travels around the shops. I'll just check that it's available for us to use."

Attention to their need was thus avoided and Anne, who was grateful for the thought anyway, had no problem acquiescing to such a kind thought with a minimum of embarrassment. After a quite substantial salmon salad for dinner, which they all enjoyed, including Anne, they set out with her aboard the bathchair. Settling into it as if she was made for it, they now fairly whizzed along and the mood lightened considerably for the shopping spree!

Heading north up Coney Street, they turned right into Stonegate, heading toward the Minster and started looking in shops along the way.

Entering a fine draper's shop they partially completed their list by purchasing bonnets and gloves, essential for a fashionable seaside resort such as Scarborough, but sensing Anne's tiredness already, they refrained from completing their list of other items; black silk stockings and dresses, even and combs and ribbons for their necks would all have to wait until they went shopping again either in York the next morning or when they got to Scarborough.

"Well, hello Charlotte – what a surprise!" a familiar voice said, as she almost bumped into Mary Titterington, outside in the street, as they were leaving the draper's shop.

"Mary, it's lovely to see you again after quite a while. You know Anne, of course, and this is an old school friend of mine, Ellen Nussey."

Mary shook hands with Ellen, but she was shocked to see Anne in a bath-chair and her thoughts flew quickly back to Branwell's and Emily's so-recent deaths within the year. How sad! How tragic, she thought, could she, too, be suffering from the dreaded wasting disease of consumption? It seemed entirely likely and Mary shook hands gently but firmly with her, trying not to overly emphasise her concern but nevertheless expressing surprise that she looked 'under the weather', prompting Anne herself to explain confidently the nature of their visit and the hoped-for recuperative properties of the sea-air in Scarborough.

Mary returned the introductions courteously, introducing Grace and Hannah who accompanied her on the shopping expedition. Mary had just bought ribbons for the girls' hair in a shop further down the street for the weekend's Whit Sunday morning service at the minster.

"Grace was quite small the last time we saw you and of course, you must remember – this is Hannah. The last time you saw her was probably at her baptism in Cragg Vale – dear Uncle Brannie's god-daughter, who he was so proud of, with both his dear mother's and sister's name. You wouldn't remember, girls, but these are two of Uncle Brannie's sisters – Charlotte and Anne."

"Oh! How smart you both look, girls! I love your ribbons!" Charlotte continued, observing the girls excitedly toying with their purchases. "I had heard that you had all moved to York for John to expand the family businesses? How exciting living here in such a fine city! I'd been told that John was based here to be nearer to your wool suppliers as well as to sell the fine Titterington fabrics and damasks to wealthy clients back over here? How is he? Does his business flourish?"

"Business is good, thank you," Mary lied, somewhat uncomfortably. "But you can ask him yourselves tomorrow morning at the house. He's on a shooting trip today up in North Yorkshire, but he'll be back by the morning. You must stop by and have tea with us. John will be so pleased to catch up on your news and to see you both – and you of course Ellen, too, will be welcome. We don't get many visitors from home."

After a further brief exchange of conversation Mary headed off with the girls down Stonegate calling back saying: "Our house is number 43 – just down there on the right. Do you see? The one with the overhanging first floor window – you can't miss it, we get quite a view of the Minster from the upper floors there. If you have time afterwards we can all go over to the Minster. John loves to give tours to visitors and it's so long since we had any!"

Which caused Anne great excitement, even feeling as exhausted as she did, for she had indeed always planned for just such a visit to one of her favourite places.

Mary trotted along holding the girls' hands and thought to herself how perfect it was that John would be over from the gaol in time to change out of his 'prison-garb' into his more respectable clothes to greet their guests.

John could always be relied upon to look the gentleman, from head-to-toe, at the drop of a hat.

But did Charlotte and Anne detect something was amiss? Something not quite right with her story? Did they already know the truth? Certainly they were not surprised and seemed well aware that the family had moved to York, but back home, John's immediate family would almost certainly be using exactly the same cover-up story outside the family to disguise the shame, so it may well be that they were all succeeding brilliantly in the subterfuge.

That is, all but John's unrelenting creditors who still turned the screw!

Charlotte, Ellen and poor Anne who had certainly had enough almost immediately after this first draper's shop visit, set off back to the George Hotel immediately, with their incomplete shopping list, to allow Anne to take the rest she now so evidently was in need of, yet sadly had done little enough to require.

Charlotte remembered the baptism of Hannah Titterington as she walked along, telling Ellen: "We had such a lovely day at St. John in the Wilderness in Cragg Vale. You visited with us once, I remember, for morning service. How thoughtful it was of Mary and John to choose dearest Mama's name Maria for Hannah's second name and how proud dear Branwell was to act as her godfather that day. Mary and John knew it was our first-born sister's name also of course, as you know and isn't she growing up to be a fine young lady? So pretty and so polite."

Mary came towards number 43 and Grace was the first to question her mother's so-obvious lie. "Why did you say Daddy was shooting? And why was Uncle Brannie's sister Anne in a wheel-chair? She isn't an old lady, is she? She doesn't look like one."

The ever-perceptive Hannah needed to know more of her christening in Cragg Vale. "Was Maria really also their mother's name? Is she dead now? And who was the 'first-born' she talked about with my name? Is she dead too? And why is the lady in a chair with wheels? Has she had an accident?"

Getting inside the house, Mary tried to answer these and the many more questions which flowed from her attempts to explain her actions and respond to the girls' keen observations.

Back inside number 43, Sarah and Rebecca's curiosity had now also been raised and their own questions combined with the general cacophony of sound mixed in with the noise of young James and Blazer rolling around on the floor in the corner together, variously laughing and barking and all making Mary's task of obfuscation the easier!

She would however have to prepare to be questioned more closely later by the older girls when their younger siblings had been put to bed and a quieter atmosphere returned.

Back at the hotel in Coney Street, Anne had been taken up to her bed to lie down whilst Charlotte and Ellen relaxed in the lounge into the early evening.

Charlotte worked on some notes for *'Shirley'*, her current novel which was to follow her highly successful *'Jane Eyre'* published almost a year before, again under her assumed male name of 'Currer Bell'. Much of *'Shirley'* was to be set in the Birstall area where Ellen lived still and where she and Ellen had first met at school. She refreshed Charlotte's memories of their childhood together, to lend authenticity to her chosen locations and characters. She particularly needed confirmation of her descriptions of Oakwell Hall which she was using for Fieldhead, the featured Keeldar family's Elizabethan manor house in her post-Napoleonic war novel, centred on the tribulations of the early nineteenth century Luddites. She was also mindful of her sister, sleeping fitfully upstairs and on whom she was loosely basing her character Caroline Helstone.

Anne tried to sleep upstairs in their room and her random thoughts wandered fitfully to what might have been. Twenty-nine years of age and with her own successful novel, *'The Tenant of Wildfell Hall'* launched only the previous June following her, *'Agnes Grey'*, both under her supposed-male pseudonym 'Acton Bell' might be a great comfort to her, but was she, too, about to suffer the same premature fate as her dear sister Emily only those few months before? She, too, dying with her much-acclaimed sole novel *'Wuthering Heights'* so recently completed before her death under her own, widely-assumed male authorship name of 'Ellis Bell'?

And never forgetting their brother, dear Branwell, who had so selflessly supported and inspired all of his sisters from childhood to produce their epic works to then see his own life end so short of a successful personal conclusion. Writer, poet and portrait painter, yet only through his sisters was he able to shine ultimately, his inspirational mentoring of all of them unrecognised in abject anonymity.

Downstairs Charlotte and Ellen were in deep conversation, worrying how they might cope tomorrow and ease poor Anne gently towards the recuperative powers of the Scarborough air.

"She's gotten used to the bath-chair now and we can get one for her when we arrive in Scarborough. At least she accepts it as part of the route to recovery and can now use one without embarrassment or the feeling of being an unnecessary burden to us," said Charlotte.

She added, "I shall book us all first class rail tickets tomorrow, Ellen, as a holiday treat! Keep it as a surprise. Anne will enjoy the extra comfort and privacy and we can all look forward to arriving at the seaside in some style!"

Charlotte and Ellen had eaten chicken sandwiches and drunk hot chocolate by the fire as they talked. Then they went up to their room with some sandwiches on a plate for Anne, but she was now sleeping soundly and they did not disturb her.

At her bedside in the dim light of the oil lamp she had started to write a poem:

'A dreadful darkness closes in...On my bewildered mind...'

Slipping quietly into bed, they extinguished the lamps and relaxed into sleep in preparation for their journey the next day.

Over in Stonegate, Mary put the younger children to bed and set about answering Grace and Hannah's questions as honestly as she could. Yes, she hadn't been 'entirely truthful' about their father being away on a shooting trip, but she had only 'protected the ladies' from the shock of learning he was in prison – particularly Anne, who she explained had more pressing problems of her own as they could plainly see and did not need to know of their father's predicament.

Why add to the difficulties her sister Charlotte and their friend were having taking care of Miss Brontë on an otherwise social occasion going on holiday to Scarborough the next day?

That they probably knew of John's plight anyway, she didn't mention, but Eli had made a recent purchase of a farm called Long Riggin, in Haworth. That this would be newsworthy in Haworth she didn't doubt and a story such as this about his eldest son would be likely to have gossip-value in a close-knit community; a property Eli would later will, in its entirety, to his daughter Maria, who became the wife of the successful local manufacturer, William Foster. The very name Titterington carrying its own four-syllabled distinctive 'ring' to any receptive ear finding itself in close proximity to a gossip! And as known family acquaintances of the Brontës, it would be likely this would be passed back to the parsonage, probably through Tabby or Martha. Schadenfreud was likely to be alive and well even in those days where the wealthy rubbed shoulders alongside other mere mortals!

In any case, as she explained, it was not 'genteel female conversation', especially when accompanied by young daughters and it gave Mary ample opportunity to give Grace and Hannah a valuable lesson intact and decorum, about protecting participants in discourse from unnecessary distress, as an act of kindness to others.

John settled in to another miserable early night over in York Castle Gaol mulling over plans for the next day's business, 'acts of tact and decorum' being largely unknown to one Thomas Aloysius Scoggins and he would enjoy the light relief he had yet to learn about back at home; a welcome distraction of visiting his favourite York Minster with old friends.

Business could wait for once and in any case, William was now well in control of it.

He bade his reverend cellmate a reciprocated 'good night', turned over and attempted to sleep, as ever, on his unyielding and bone-hard apology for a mattress.

Chapter Twenty Three

York Minster

The morning of Friday the first of June 1849 started out with glorious sunshine – a perfect English early summer's morning. Early risers chatted amiably going about their daily chores and traders bustled around setting up their stores for market day. High above the higgledy-piggledy assortment of multi-coloured medieval rooftops, York Minster glistened in the sun's early rays and swallows swooped and dived joyously around its majestic pinnacles.

Mary was up early, as usual, down below at number 43 and was already preparing food for the children and had fed Blazer and let him out into the yard at the back.

Over at the hotel, Charlotte, too, had risen early and was sitting by the window writing. Ellen was dressing and Anne was last to rise, lifting herself wearily from the bed she had shared with Charlotte. Glancing over so as not to appear she was watching, Charlotte couldn't help but notice that she held herself carefully as she rose and prepared to wash and dress; even brushing her hair appeared to cause her some distress, but Ellen was first to break the silence with a cheery: "My! What a beautiful day it is out there. The first day of June and what a treat we have in store for us on this fine day. York Minster first, at your request Anne, which I have never visited and then to my favourite seaside destination – Scarborough! I can't wait."

All of which lifted the mood generally and the three of them completed dressing and went downstairs for breakfast. Anne again had to be assisted on the stairs by Charlotte and by both as she was positioned in her chair at the breakfast table.

"We need to catch the 2.00pm train to Scarborough," said Charlotte. "So we have plenty of time to visit the Minster with Mary and John, do some more shopping and make it over to the station to book our tickets."

After breakfast they readied themselves to check out and pay for their stay, borrowing the bath-chair again and promising to return it and pick up their luggage on the way through from the Minster to the station. Charlotte also arranged for a carriage to await them at 1.00pm at the hotel for transport over to the station.

Over in Stonegate, Mary had figured that John, who normally left the prison at about 7.00am could be expected to arrive at number 43 by 7.30am, more than enough time to change and receive their guests. She had prepared a simple breakfast for John and had already fed the children – and Blazer.

John arrived just after 7.30 as expected, greeted all of the children, throwing James up to catch him, cuddle him and then put him down to give some attention to Blazer who craved attention from him every bit as much as the five children.

"We're having visitors from home John – Bran's sisters Charlotte and Anne are travelling on to Scarborough this afternoon and are staying overnight in Coney Street with a friend. I bumped into them yesterday evening out shopping. Plenty of time for you to change after breakfast, before they get here and I promised we'd go over to the Minster after a cup of tea." Mary spoke excitedly; visitors were rare and she had prepared a madeira cake which was almost ready and smelt delicious.

"How did you explain my plight to them? Where was I supposed to be yesterday?" queried John.

Mary continued. "I didn't like telling a lie and Grace and Hannah picked me up on it, but it seemed appropriate to hide the truth. I told them you were off up north, on the moors, with a shooting party and back late. Anne, as you will see, is clearly quite sick and they have more than enough on their plate; she's in a bath-chair and looks just awful, poor dear. You'll get quite a shock, like I did and it's hard not to show it. They're going on to Scarborough to aid her recovery, but I fear she is not long for this life and looks to me as though she'll follow Bran and Emily before too long. Still, Charlotte and her friend Ellen are putting on a brave face and we must go along with them. They'll be here at 10.00am and I suggested they may like to have a tour of the Minster – I know how much you would enjoy that and I love coming myself when you do it, with all that knowledge you picked up from your tutor. I'll bring James with us after tea and Grace will mind the girls until we get back. Is that alright with you? What plans did you have today?"

Mary was quite correct about his knowledge gained as a young teenager studying the geography and history of the county with his tutor Oliver Smith who came out to High Lees from Sowerby Bridge to tutor him and his brothers for about four years. York Minster was high on his list of interests and the opportunity to study it at close quarters was taken during his very first days in the city; he'd also shown it to William Foster just after his day release.

"William will be over shortly, but I can delay our meeting for an hour or so, it won't be a problem. It will be nice to see Charlotte especially, who I haven't seen since Bran's funeral. I don't like the sound of Anne's health, but I'll try not to notice too much, though I must express a little concern for her being in a chair and we'll wish them all well on their trip for her recuperation. I think I may have met Ellen, Nussey I believe – over at the parsonage with Bran, they go back a long way together."

The three girls arrived on time and John greeted them at the door. "How lovely to see you again, Charlotte, and it was on such a sad occasion last time – I offer you my sincerest condolences also for the death of your sister Emily. Your family has had a hard time recently." And with that comment, he realised he'd put his foot in it by so deliberately trying not to notice Anne's unfortunate predicament whilst clearly stating the obvious; that she, too, was indeed very much a part of the 'hard time'.

"Lovely to see you again, Anne, and you, too, Miss Nussey – we met before I remember, at the parsonage, I believe?"

Anne returned his greeting and Ellen acknowledged their previous meeting when Mary and John had spent a day looking over a large farm property in Haworth called Lower Horking in Horkingstone, which his father had subsequently acquired and had dropped in for tea at Branwell's invitation to meet the family.

After the other children had been introduced and tea was served, John rather tactlessly, yet proudly, started to describe their home. "The view of the Minster is really quite amazing from upstairs, if you'd like to see it?"

Anne quickly declined saying, "I'll see the Minster soon enough, you two go ahead and see the view."

As always, the visitors gasped at the beauty of the rose window in the south transept rising up above the rooftops opposite and nestling majestically beneath the soaring central tower.

"I know Branwell brought Edmund Robinson here about six years ago and Anne, of course, came twice with his sisters; I, too, studied the Minster – though at a distance unfortunately with my own tutor back home. The rose window in the south transept, quite interestingly, was the first window we studied together. It is the oldest part of the Minster and was constructed, together with the south and north transept in the Early

English style between 1220 and 1260 during the reign of King Henry III – the first Plantagenet, the boy king himself who ruled from the age of nine.

"Interestingly, to me anyway, the stained glass wasn't added until the late 15th century, over two hundred years later, to commemorate the War of the Roses and to honour the beginning of the Tudor dynasty, in celebration of the union of the warring houses of Lancaster and York through the marriage of Henry VII and Elizabeth of York, in Westminster Abbey, on the 18th January 1486. 'Tall, slim, dark-haired, handsome and in the prime of his life', he was twenty-nine years of age and Elizabeth, just nineteen, was described as 'one of the beauties of her age, an English rose with blonde hair, blue eyes and fair skin.' The rose window has seventy-three panels and contains over 7,000 individual pieces of stained glass.

"Let's set off soon and we'll enter, beneath the rose window, through the south transept door."

"My, John, you studied well under your tutor," said Ellen. "I can see you have retained a great interest in its history and I'm looking forward to learning more from you inside the Minster."

And with that the three of them went back down to find Mary and the children, even Anne, having one more piece of madeira cake whilst Blazer looked on longingly with wistful eyes for the morsel of cake he was never going to get.

Planning to head down Stonegate toward the Minster, Mary said goodbye to Grace and Hannah, making sure they would mind their younger sisters and carried young James for a while until she could put him down safely to walk.

Arriving at the south transept Minster steps, John offered to carry Anne to the top whilst Charlotte and Ellen lifted the bath-chair up. Mary held James's hand to help him to climb the steps with the exaggerated swinging out of the legs so recognisable in infants learning to master a new skill.

Anne accepted the lift from John gracefully and looking high up to the central tower, now directly above, commented:

"If finite power can do this, what is the...?" As if dumbstruck by the vista and her own emotions, further speech was rendered impossible. John felt fairly certain that her own impending demise and hoped-for salvation were at the forefront of her thoughts and he did not pursue her comment with a question.

At the top of the steps, Anne remained silent as John placed her slender form gently into the bath-chair. He could not believe how light she was, hardly heavier than his youngest daughter with thin arms to match. He maintained close contact with her by taking over the pushing duties from Charlotte as they entered the Minster through the south transept door.

Immediately opposite them as they entered, over in the north transept, they advanced toward the early-Gothic Five Sisters window, with each of the five delicate lancets soaring over fifty-seven feet high and five feet wide.

"Never ceases to amaze anyone, whether you see it for the first or the umpteenth time, does it?" said John. "The oldest window in the Minster, each of the five delicate lancets are five feet wide and soar over fifty-seven feet high. Completed in 1260 and the largest single composition in Grisaille glass anywhere in the world; over 100,000 individual pieces of a grey monochrome glass originally, which was painted later."

"Shortly before you and Bran first came, Anne, Charles Dickens visited the Minster with his cartoonist Hablot Knight Browne, or 'Phiz' as we know him, and around this window he created the traveller's tale in '*Nicholas Nickleby*,' featuring Alice, a beautiful embroiderer and her four sisters being chided and cajoled into nun-hood by a visiting monk. In Dicken's story, Nicholas tells of this traveller's tale after their coach is overturned on a journey to London between Grantham and Newark."

"I taught the girls all about that of course," added Anne. "And Bran embellished it later by adding his own five sisters into a much more interesting version of Dickens' story as only he could! I also visited once with dearest Emily on a two-day excursion in the summer of 1845, just four years ago now, bless her, how the times have changed since."

She continued, "Dickens completed '*Nicholas Nickleby*' back in London and it sold 50,000 copies on its first day of sale in 1838 – one of the first copies was enjoyed by all the Robinsons after its early addition to the Thorp Green library."

From there the group moved toward the east end and the Lady Chapel with its Great East Window. John went on. "Finished in 1408, it is the largest expanse of mediaeval stained glass in the world.

"But before we go over to see it, let's pause here in the north choir aisle to admire the fine work of Branwell's and my very good Halifax friend, 'JB', Joseph Bentley Leyland."

The group paused at the stunning full-sized sculpture of Dr. Stephen Beckwith reclining in his death-pose who had died six years previously in 1843.

"JB told me he was paid only £250 for his work and from that he had to buy all of his materials. It took him almost a year to complete and the Beckwith family proved difficult customers putting JB through hell to arrive at the finished work. They treated him no differently from the mere stone churchyard engravers employed in every parish in the land.

"Agreeing the list of benefactions you see around the effigy took an eternity to agree on with the family and the gilding was carried out by another good friend of ours, Joe Drake who occupied a studio next to JB in the Union Cross Inn yard in Halifax. He, too, had to be paid out of JB's original commission fee. With visits to York and final installation costs, JB struggled as always to make ends meet."

John continued, "Under Dr Beckwith's will he gave the peal of twelve bells we hear in the south-west tower to replace the peal of ten destroyed in the fire of 1840 and the chapter house has been recently restored, between 1843 and 1845 – also under his will."

Charlotte admired the beauty of the craftsmanship and added, whilst gently stroking Dr Beckwith's brow, "How sad it always is to see someone reclining thus, forever cast into the deathly cold marble of eternity. He must have been a much-respected member of the city to be accorded the privilege of lying here among the exalted hierarchy of the church, his bequests will have helped; I never met Branwell's friend, but he spoke of him fondly and admired his largely unrecognised genius."

"Thank you for telling us about the Halifax connection John," added Anne. "I can see you and my brother had a fondness for such a good friend. How sad that the Beckwith family seemed to show such scant respect for his skills."

Swinging right round and moving directly along beneath the central tower and over to the West Window, Anne took up the story here, which was so loved by all of the Robinson girls.

"At this end of the nave, constructed in 1338, is the West Window, and if you look to the top centre you can clearly see the 'Heart of Yorkshire' window. Couples kissing beneath this window. Look, you can see a couple over there now, exchanging an embarrassed peck! Believe they will stay together – forever!"

"I didn't know that one," said John. "But thank you, Anne, I'll include it on my next tour!"

Finally moving back to their entry door in the South Transept, they stopped to admire again the spectacular internal display of a myriad of dazzling colours in the Rose Window, so visible, yet so different when viewed externally from across in the upper rooms of number 43, Stonegate.

"Sometimes known as a 'spiked' or St. Catherine's window before the 17th century, after the saint who was executed on a spiked wheel, I always think it is the most beautiful of all the windows," John went on. "Mary and I are privileged to see it every morning from our upstairs window of course as we rise for another day." He realised immediately the untruthful nature of this last remark and with a sheepish glance over toward Mary, he was glad that James couldn't understand what he said and that the older girls were not even there at all.

Entering through the South Transept door, John saw that William was now approaching them and he hastily introduced him to the visitors. "This is William Foster, my nephew who works with me. He's come for a meeting to discuss a few details. He represents me with the manufacturers back in the West Riding and is also a wool buyer for me here in the East Riding. He is my right hand man and quite invaluable to me!"

William puffed out his chest a little at the praise being given to him, but secretly wished that he could be recognised publicly by the name he now used over in The Shambles, and of which he was so proud.

John continued, "I think perhaps we ought to return you to your hotel, ladies, in time to prepare for your departure to Scarborough. William will escort you to the station if you wish and I will come with you as far as the hotel."

Mary clasped James's hand tightly, preparing to say what she knew would almost certainly be a final farewell to Anne and said, to Charlotte in particular, "You must write and tell me news of your visit and do please send me a report of Anne's increasing strength from the sea-air." This latter request more in hope than through any belief she really felt for an outcome other than the one they all clearly feared was inevitable.

Mary and James stopped off at number 43 along the way, with Charlotte saying, "You will be the first to hear our news, Mary and thank you all for your kind wishes and thoughts." Thus said, Mary held James in her arms and they both waved the girls off down the street. Back at their hotel, after pushing Anne's chair along, John said his farewell and returned to number 43 where he had arranged for William to return for their previously planned business meeting.

John was now quite certain that Anne would be joining Emily and Bran, probably before the summer was out and it was with some sadness that he had remarked finally, "Do have a safe journey, ladies, and enjoy your time in Scarborough. I believe we are in for a fine spell of weather and you will feel much strengthened, Anne, I'm certain, by the bracing sea air. Goodbye and good luck!"

The phaeton taking William and the three ladies to the station arrived after about half-an-hour and William carried Anne from her chair and lifted her into her seat in the carriage and then helped the driver to load all of their luggage before climbing on-board himself for the journey.

Chapter Twenty Four

Anne's Last Journey

William turned away from the carriage and with one final look over his shoulder, he watched as the train pulled out of York station. All three ladies gave him a fond farewell wave as they had become quite drawn to this splendidly handsome and courteous young man.

He waved and the train quickly drew away in a rhythmic belching of smoke and steam, as the pistons drove into action in preparation for the forty-two-mile journey to Scarborough, on a line only opened four years previously and constructed in its entirety in the spectacularly and proudly proclaimed short time, by its constructors, of *'one year and three days'*.

Charlotte had surprised Anne by leading her to a sumptuously fitted out first class carriage and Anne had been lowered by William into a seat which he had noted would surely have been fit for Queen Victoria herself.

"Surely we must be in the wrong carriage," said Anne. "You'd better help me, William, please, if you will, to the next carriage before the guard comes along and checks our tickets."

"No, no," insisted Charlotte. "It's my little surprise and I've treated us all to a special trip to Scarborough on this most beautiful of days."

And without further comment, all three of them settled into a journey of a previously thought unaffordable, or even worse, profligate extravagance.

Crossing the River Ouse immediately over Scarborough's railway bridge, the train headed on to traverse, what some considered as the rather flat and uninteresting Vale of York.

Anne nevertheless quietly reflected on some strong memories having served as governess at Thorp Green, the fine mansion being in the centre of a great estate in this rich agricultural triangle of the Vale of York between York, Ripon and Harrogate.

An inadvertently glimpsed image of her own pale complexion in the carriage window brought her back to the reality of her present predicament, yet she couldn't remove the thought of those happy times looking after the Robinson girls.

Little was said during this part of the journey as they settled in to the sheer luxury and opulence of the seats and admired the general carriage fitments.

Charlotte, realising the poor state of Anne's health, had pushed out the boat in the interests of her personal comfort and if, as she feared, it might be her last trip on the railway, or indeed anywhere, she was going to make it a memorable one and both she and Ellen could revel and share in its unaccustomed luxury at the same time.

After about eleven miles, the train started to slow down as the gradient increased and the views improved dramatically. This was Barton Hill where the Howardian Hills begin to close in and the train then followed the tight curves of the River Derwent.

"Look," said Anne. "Over on the opposite bank of the Derwent – the ruins of Kirkham Abbey."

They were all in the high spirits that only travel – an adventure – could bring. The child in everybody would always be brought out at such times and the sounds and smells of steam rail travel, especially in the pioneering days of such travel, had a particular and unique way of invoking such euphoria.

Another couple of miles brought them to a brief stop to collect passengers at the picturesque east Yorkshire village of Huttons Ambo and from there the line crossed the Derwent over a girder bridge and proceeded to Malton, the halfway-point of their journey, where a flurry of activity heralded on board more excited seaside-bound holiday makers and a cacophony of clucking basket-caged chickens surely sufficient to feed a multitude.

Now in conversational full flow the three chattered animatedly and as excitedly as any children of any generation would, as the intense anticipation associated with the end-point of the journey was aroused – *the seaside!*

Anne could hardly believe the speed of travel – her previous visits, only a few years before with the Robinsons, had taken over a day by stagecoach and involved an overnight horse-change and stopover at a hostelry.

A straight run on then to Rillington Junction followed by Weaverthorpe, Ganton and Seamer stations followed to near the party toward their destination. Anne had taken on a seemingly renewed vigour with the excitement of travel, but the underlying disguised mood of both Charlotte and Ellen nevertheless held a deep foreboding of sad times to come.

Pulling in to Scarborough station, Charlotte and Ellen physically lifted Anne from her seat and proceeded to the carriage door with each of her arms around their shoulders, arms, which Ellen noted again, seemed to have grown even more slender, if that were even possible in the space of just two days. She avoided a worried stare which she felt sure Charlotte was giving her as they stepped down onto the platform, with Charlotte delicately balancing Anne between herself and Ellen, from both above and below.

A porter assisted Anne to a waiting phaeton for hire and once the luggage had been loaded by another overly-eager-to-please first class passengers' porter, they were off rejoicing inwardly at the delicious smell of the ozone, the incessant cries of seagulls swooping and soaring overhead, and the clippety-clop of horseshoes on cobbles.

Charlotte sat back in her carriage seat and thought to herself, *"Whatever it is in the world that could possibly help poor Anne, if it isn't here...it surely isn't anywhere!"*

"Wood's Lodging House, driver please – on St. Nicholas Cliff," said Charlotte, at Anne's prompting, for she had of course stayed there on summer holidays with the Robinsons, in each of the years from 1840 to 1844.

It was whilst Branwell was here also that he was dismissed, almost before he arrived by the Rev. Edmond Robinson, after his student Edmond junior poisoned his chalice in a fit of jealousy by inventing an improper sexual advance by his tutor. Branwell's clandestine adulterous liaisons with his mother proving too much for a jealous adolescent, confused and desperate with desire for his tutor's attentions.

A mere five-minute journey to the lodging house brought them to the view which never failed to take Anne's breath away. Immediately below the cliffs were the South Sands in the South Bay and to the left, up the coast northwards, visitors and residents alike could only gaze in awe and wonderment at the stunning vista of the harbour and the castle on the hillside beyond, whilst drawing in the deepest breaths of salty sea air and relishing the joyous cries of a thousand seagulls proclaiming their welcome.

Back in York, John had returned to the misery of his cell by eight o'clock for lock-down at nine and Mary had washed the children and put them up to bed. She sat by the last embers of the fire pondering the developments of the day. Charlotte had promised to write to keep her in touch with Anne's progress when she was leaving, though Mary didn't feel her optimism held the conviction necessary to expect good news; the inevitability of death would not be avoided.

She mulled over her own good fortunes with family health even though she was denied a normal family life while John was in prison. As always, at quiet times, she remembered the lifeless form of her first-born little Eli after he gave up the unequal struggle to finally draw breath and succumb to the brain fever after such a pitifully short life in her bedroom at Higgin Chamber. How she had worried that perhaps she was to be denied the fulfilment of motherhood, but now praised her good fortune in bringing five fine children into the world. The older two, Grace and Hannah, now blossoming into mature confident young ladies whilst still retaining the aura and innocence of childhood.

Unlike her own father's failure to educate her and her sisters, Mary was making sure that her own illiteracy, like that of her own mother, was not replicated in her own daughters. Signing the wedding register at Halifax Parish Church with her 'mark' – a cross, was a humbling experience and Branwell's sisters' literary successes were already coming to her awareness though she would never be able to appreciate them directly. Both the elder daughters had voraciously absorbed Branwell's early alphabet and number lessons during visits and especially whilst story-telling during portrait painting sessions and her retired-solicitor friend down the street John Adams' offer to continue their lessons had been accepted gratefully. Mary was increasingly relying on Grace especially to read her mail and Charlotte's letter was eagerly, though concernedly anticipated, for Grace to read out to her.

Young William, whilst not being her own son, was also proving a worthy son for John, ably helping to dig him out of his wretched position and John's indiscretion in his youth was now long forgiven as she had learnt to accept him almost as one of her own. William had also benefitted from an education with John providing him with the services of his own tutor at his mother's home in Luddenden Foot, which whilst like his own, did not include the classics yet was a more than adequate basis for sound business, commercial and social intercourse. Certainly all of the children loved 'cousin' William, hated when he had to leave and pestered their mother for him to live with them, but Mary explained that, apart from working with their father, he needed a place of his own and in any case had very early starts in the abattoir behind The Shambles preparing for the butcher's shop to open each morning.

Back in Scarborough the girls were settling in, busying themselves unpacking and discussing plans for Whitsuntide weekend and their few days away.

Anne had taken many walks with the Robinsons over the dizzyingly high, elegant, iron footbridge spanning the gorge along the cliff path which ran from St. Nicholas Cliff via a toll booth on Wood's Lodging's side, where tickets purchased allowed unlimited access to both the bridge and the Spa beyond for a one, two or four-week period: season tickets were also available.

Anne had already secretly sent out a servant, whilst the other two were distracted, to purchase three two shillings and sixpenny tickets in advance, as a surprise to chaperone Charlotte and Ellen along the bridge. Charlotte recorded this expense in her cash book afterwards to include it against Anne's inheritance from her Aunt Fanny Outhwaite in the total holiday accounts.

"I'm looking forward to a fine day on Sunday, let's hope the weather stays good," Anne interjected with an unexpectedly re-invigorated spirit. "I have a surprise planned for you both!"

Charlotte's own surprise at Anne's comment was mirrored by Ellen, who added, "How lovely to see you looking so much better, Anne – the sea-air is doing its work already!"

"Thank you, my asthma, too, is also always eased here.

"Charlotte knows this, but let me tell Ellen about Lydia Robinson's escapade four years ago now, after I had left their employment only four months before, in June of 1845 and with Bran's dismissal coming just one month later," Anne continued, warming to a round of reminiscences.

"The family used to make visits to The Theatre Royal on St. Thomas Street – just along from St. Nicholas Street. It's only about three minutes' walking from here, so it was a popular venue for a night out and sometimes I was invited to accompany the girls.

"Owned and run by the Roxby family, entertainment ranged from Shakespeare plays; Richard II was excellent on my last holiday with them the summer before, as well as musical recitals, right through to what they termed 'fashionable nights' on Saturdays, which could include conjurers, music hall singers and comedians such as Robert Roxby, the manager of both this theatre and The Royal in Manchester, who was quite famous and so funny!

"So, anyway, four years ago, back at Thorp Green after the summer holidays, in October of 1845, without anybody suspecting anything was amiss, Lydia, their eldest, aged only eighteen, eloped from Thorp Green in the dead of night and married Robert Roxby's son Henry, one of his play actors, at Gretna Green. Her mother must have been devastated, they were really quite close and I don't believe her father ever got over it – the cruelly incapacitated reverend gentleman passed away the following year, in May of 1846, aged just fifty. Though Lydia and Robert were received and stayed for a couple of days at Thorp Green just before his death. Lydia wrote to tell me the home-coming had actually all gone very well but still, I'm so glad that I wasn't a party to knowing of any clandestine meetings between them that summer! I got out just in time those few weeks before.

"And we know now of course that the mother went on to remarry last November and is now the wife of Sir Edward Scott – Lady Scott! A so richly undeserved status after corrupting dear Branwell so shamelessly."

All three spent a relaxing evening after dinner and retired early spending an uneventful, peaceful Friday night sleeping well after their journey and succumbing easily to the inevitably soporific effects of the sea air.

After a light breakfast of toast and tea, Anne insisted on going to Travis's Baths nearby along the cliffs where she had visited many times with the Robinsons to bathe in the 'freshly drawn sea water brought up daily by horse and cart'. As they walked slowly together, she said, "I would like to be left alone please, to enjoy the solitude, as I soak in the briny water and remember the happy times I used to have with the girls. We all got such a shock when the first cold rush of sea water took our breaths away. It's always so invigorating and health giving!"

Ellen and Charlotte were reluctant to acquiesce, but Charlotte final acceded to her request saying, "I know we're only a few hundred yards along the cliff path, but the water will weaken you and you must take care returning." Another guest at the lodgings would later that day confide to Charlotte privately after supper, through concern for Anne's welfare, how she had seen her returning alone and stumble and fall exhausted at the garden gate. She had dashed out and assisted her into the house but had already detected that all was not well with Anne and felt sufficiently concerned to tell what she had seen.

After resting in the afternoon, the three headed out again down to the beach and a re-exhilarated Anne hired a donkey cart for an hour but took control away from the boy driving it, fearing he was driving it too fast, imploring him angrily, "You drive him too fast and show little regard for his well-being, you would do well to treat one of God's dumb creatures with a good deal more respect than you are showing." And just at the end of her ride, Ellen came along to help her down and knew full well that Anne's outrage would be justified and that she could never bear cruelty to any animal. Indeed this very topic of animal cruelty had been a theme in Anne's novel *Agnes Grey*. Ellen offered her hand to help her down from the cart and echoed her sentiments, "Bear her advice well young man and be kinder to your charges."

It was after supper in the dining room at Wood's that a Miss Appleby, on holiday from Harrogate, drew Charlotte on one side to tell her of the fall at the garden gate. "I do hope you don't feel I was interfering, Miss Brontë, but I was concerned and couldn't find either of you to tell. Your sister insisted on me not telling you and seemed much recovered quite quickly, but I felt it could only be in her best interests to relate the story to you. Please do not disclose the fact that I went against her wishes."

Charlotte gave her comfort saying, "You did exactly the right thing, Miss Appleby, and I thank you for helping. My sister, as you can see is quite unwell and I will not breach your confidence. Thank you so much again for your concern and assistance."

On Sunday morning the 27th of May, Anne said at breakfast, "I'm looking forward to going to church; Christ Church is only about a four-minute walk to the top of Vernon Place; the Robinsons always worshipped there and I think you will like it as much as I always did."

"I think we should rest a little today and not go to church, perhaps we can take a short walk later,"

Charlotte said and Ellen nodded in agreement, both feeling increasingly concerned now for Anne's health and being prepared to forego their own wishes to attend church so as not to leave her unaccompanied.

Anne did not protest and positioned herself at the window seat to admire the sea view whilst Charlotte settled at a writing desk to compose some letters. The first went to her publisher friend Smith Williams; just as Anne drew a pitifully impeded breath, and to emphasise the concern she was just about to intimate in her letter, she wrote, *"...write to me in this strange place, your letters will come like the visits of a friend."*

A second letter to her father, which whilst expressing due concern for Anne's continuing health problems, also spoke of her donkey-cart trip and her lone visit to the baths to at least project some semblance of hope for him, though she wished later, after posting the letter that she had been more honest with him.

A third letter would not be read by its intended recipient, for she could not read; by the time young Grace Titterington struggled to read out loud its rather more honest contents to her mother at 43, Stonegate, Anne would indeed already be dead.

Back at the lodgings the denouement was approaching fast that Sunday afternoon, but Anne rallied sufficiently in the afternoon to suggest taking a walk along the cliffs – she had her surprise still to spring on her companions!

At the top of the cliffs, after resting on a bench for some time, admiring the cool clear blue of the sea and inhaling the air, they headed over to the box-office of the famous Spa Bridge and Anne produced the tickets to surprise the girls with a trip across saying, "I treated you both in the hope that in time you might learn to love Scarborough as much as I have." After pausing in the middle of the bridge to take in the view as well as feel and breathe in the strengthening wind, Charlotte reciprocated her gesture at the other side by treating them to a three-penny glass of lemonade each and then purchased half a dozen oranges for four pence to enjoy the freshly squeezed juice later back at the lodgings.

Overcome by exhaustion, Anne asked to rest a while on a comfortable seat after crossing to the other side of the Spa Bridge. "You two go on ahead, I'd like to rest here to enjoy the view." Charlotte and Ellen confirmed that Anne would remain there and not move and they headed on to visit Henry Wyatt's 'Gothic Saloon', a notable landmark much-frequented by Scarborough visitors and residents alike. Situated on a rock and concrete platform on the sea-front in the southern part of the bay the saloon had opened in 1839, the year before Anne's first visit to Scarborough and each year orchestras would perform there. Charlotte said, "Anne loves music, as you know, Ellen, and she told me of the many times she visited with the Robinson girls to see concerts here on warm summer days, describing her joy at feeling the cooling sea breezes swirling around blending in majestically with the ethereal sounds of stringed and woodwind instruments."

"We need to get back to Anne shortly, in case she's tempted to return to the lodgings by herself, but let's have two of her favourite, though a little expensive, dandelion coffees, first."

Parting with two shillings for the coffees, which both agreed were indeed delicious they returned to Wood's after collecting Anne from the seat exactly where they had left her; they told her more of the orchestra, though she had of course heard it from where she was sitting, but they avoided telling her of the dandelion coffee treat denied to her, saying they just enjoyed the walk.

Back at the lodgings, Anne tried to persuade them to go to evensong at Christ Church without her, but realising that she had neither a wish nor indeed the strength to go herself, they declined and she settled again to the window seat to watch one more remarkably colourful sunset; her last.

Charlotte was no stranger to death herself having witnessed both brother Branwell and sister Emily's deaths within the previous twelve months. The memory of her older sisters Maria and Elizabeth dying at the ages of only ten and eleven within a month of each other back at the parsonage, when she herself was only nine years old, was indelibly etched in her psyche.

It was now clear to both Ellen and Charlotte that Anne did not have long to live.

After the last rays of light disappeared she returned to the fireplace and with typical unselfishness and genuine concern for others tackled the propriety of making a return to Haworth.

"Not for my own sake, you understand, but because I fear others might suffer more."

'*The others*' clearly signifying Charlotte and Ellen and particularly her dear father and a direct reference to the inconvenience of her death occurring in Scarborough.

The discussion remained unresolved as Charlotte and Ellen, though not saying so, realised that Anne was simply not up to the rigours of a return journey home. The three retired early to bed with Anne being assisted up the stairs, helped to undress and laid into bed by Charlotte on her pre-plumped pillow.

Anne passed a reasonable night, rose and dressed herself before seven o'clock. It was Whit Monday 28th May 1849 and she was ready to go down before either of the other two.

Overcome with faintness at the top of the stairs, smiling, she turned and said to Ellen and Charlotte, "I'm afraid to descend." Immediately Ellen, the stronger of the two, offered to carry her. Anne was delighted with the suggestion which she accepted gratefully and Ellen stepped below her by a couple of stairs preparing to give her a piggyback. Charlotte was less than charmed by her sister's apparent exclusion of her and said so, causing an exchange between them.

"I suggest you go back to the room, Charlotte, so as not to witness us!" chided Ellen.

Ellen looked up at Anne from two steps down and turning to face downstairs said, "I will carry you on my back like a baby, put your arms around my neck and if you get too heavy I will pause to put you down to rest."

More by determination than physical strength, Ellen succeeded in carrying the prostrate Anne downstairs, but just as she reached the bottom Anne's head suddenly fell forward like a leaden weight on top of Ellen's head.

Shocked by the blow and thinking only death itself could have occasioned it, Ellen staggered to an easy chair and, dropping her into it like a sack of coal, fell in front of her on her knees. Despite being clearly shaken and sensing Ellen's alarm, she put out her arms to comfort her and said, "It couldn't be helped, you did your best." Charlotte appeared in the lounge shortly afterwards unaware of the happening and at Anne's facial pleading, Ellen did not regale her of the detail.

Boiled milk for breakfast, specially made for her, was Anne's only sustenance that morning followed by her returning to her window seat in the lounge. At about eleven o'clock she announced, "I feel a change. I wonder if it might still be possible to return home in time…?" She didn't finish the sentence but there was no doubting that "…before I die" would have completed it.

Charlotte successfully avoided answering her and instead sent a servant girl to summon a doctor to come, having already checked that one was close at hand if the time came.

After about fifteen minutes the doctor arrived and checked Anne, now sitting in an easy-chair. Charlotte led him to the door where she asked, "How long do you think she might live, doctor? Do not fear speaking the truth for she isn't afraid to die and I'm prepared for bad news."

The doctor responded, honestly, as requested, "Death is close at hand, I fear – I will return again shortly."

"I thank you for your honesty and your truthfulness, doctor and I feel comforted by your continuing empathy for our plight and your promise to return," said Charlotte resignedly.

The doctor returned three times in the following few hours to check on his patient.

In between visits Anne continued to sit in her easy-chair looking as Ellen was later to describe as, '...*so serene and reliant...*' as she prayed quietly, invoking blessings on Charlotte and Ellen and enjoining Ellen, "Be a sister in my stead – give Charlotte as much of your company as you can."

When Anne became breathless as death approached, Charlotte carried her across to the sofa and laying her down gently, asked, "Is that easier?" To which she responded, without apportioning blame, "It is not you who can give me ease, but soon all will be well through the merits of our redeemer."

On the last of the doctor's visits to his dying patient, he remarked with incredulity, "I am in wonderment at her fixed tranquillity of spirit and settled longing to be gone. In all my experience, I have never seen such a deathbed and it gives evidence of no common mind – even as she lays dying her thoughts are for others."

And, as if in support of this thought, seeing Charlotte barely able to contain her grief, Anne said, "Take courage, Charlotte...take courage."

Conscious to the last, still praying quietly, Anne passed away very calmly and gently at about two o'clock in the afternoon of Whit Monday, 1849 at the age of just twenty-nine.

First published to acclaim eighteen months before, the second edition of her *Agnes Grey* (attributed to her alias Acton Bell) followed a year after her death; her other classic novel, the most shocking of all of the Brontë sisters' works, *"The Tenant of Wildfell Hall"* had been completed by Anne and first published the year before, in 1848.

Her passing was so quiet that no one in the lodgings, except the attendant mourners, was aware of it.

Lunch was announced through a tactfully positioned half-open dining room door, even as Charlotte leaned over to close her dead sister's eyes, sending Charlotte, through this dreary mockery of such a mundane everyday event – an intrusion of daily life, into paroxysms of weeping.

Well away from the sadness in Scarborough, over in York, Mary and the children had spent a happy weekend enjoying the fine late spring weather with a visit to York Minster for morning service followed at home in Stonegate by a roast lunch of succulent spring shoulder of lamb, brought over as a gift by William from the Cooper's. By eating early, John was able to join the family, later returning to prison accompanied along the way by William who strode out proudly with his father before dropping off at his Shambles lodgings and bidding him farewell.

In Howarth, the news which was so dreaded, yet expected, was still awaited by Rev. Patrick Brontë as he tried to busy himself writing poetry and preparing his next week's sermon in his parsonage study. Anne's faithful Flossie, as if sensing something more than her mistress's mere absence was occurring, spent the days sleeping fitfully and wasn't enjoying eating at all. Keeper, as usual, showed no sign of distress at all and gratefully consumed both portions of food put down by Tabby without interruption by Flossie!

Chapter Twenty Five

Laying Anne to rest

Charlotte decided that returning to Haworth with Anne was out of the question, as was bringing father over to Scarborough unnecessarily, to undertake his third funeral service for one of his children within nine months.

"I can think of no better resting place than here in Scarborough, Ellen," Charlotte confided, "such a favourite place of Anne's, she couldn't have chosen better herself and probably had it in the back of her mind when we decided to come here together anyway.

"How resigned she seemed to her own passing and so different from dear Emily who fought so hard to cling on to life."

Charlotte found acceptance of Anne's death easier since she believed that her sister was glad to die.

Charlotte recorded at the time, "Anne, from her childhood seemed preparing for an early death and died without severe struggle trusting in God. Emily I could hardly let go – I wanted to hold her back then and I want her back hourly still. Like Branwell they are both gone and Papa has now me only, the weakest, puniest, least promising of his six children. Consumption has taken the whole five."

Ellen and Charlotte occupied themselves making the funeral arrangements, registering the death as 'consumption six months' and preparing an obituary notice for the local papers. Ironically, in the self and same issue announcing the death in the *Scarborough Gazette* the front page included an advertisement for Scarborough library which proclaimed Charlotte's *Jane Eyre* to be the top of its 'list of popular new novels.'

Charlotte settled down at the lodgings to write two letters; one to Mary Titterington in York as she had promised, which she posted immediately and another to her father, which she deliberately delayed posting for a day making it impossible for him to come over since he would only receive it on the actual day of the funeral, which she had fixed for Wednesday 30th May.

Mary received the letter, took it to be read by John Adams across the street and returned to share the sadness with the older girls. She could not leave the children to attend the funeral and knew neither would she be expected to and would get John to write her condolences in a letter to Howarth in a few day's time.

Next day, the day of the funeral, the service had to be conducted in the small Christ Church right next to Wood's lodgings due to St Mary's Church itself, her chosen burial ground being closed due to extensive rebuilding work at the time.

The small cortège of two carriages left Christ Church with only its principal mourners Charlotte and Ellen following a plumed black horse-drawn hearse, which wound its way slowly and solemnly up the steep narrow streets to St Mary's churchyard, where Charlotte, observing the dilapidation of the church itself was reminded of the similar state of St. John in the Wilderness church at Cragg Vale, contrasting it with the unhappy memories of Branwell, Emily and now Anne against both families all gathering together that day to celebrate little Hannah Maria Titterington's baptism.

Up there, on the headland, beneath the ruins of the castle on the cliff-top, Anne Brontë was laid to rest looking out across the bay which had always given her such pleasure.

Just a few unknown locals and residents from the guesthouse had gathered that day, down at Christ Church, to pay their respects. Both were glad to see their good friend Margaret Wooler seated at the back of the small church. Part-owner of Roe Head School in Mirfield, where Charlotte met Ellen, 'Miss' Wooler, firstly as headmistress, then employer of Charlotte, later a teacher herself, was holidaying in Scarborough in her home in the North Bay, when she read the tragic announcement in the paper. She had known already of Anne's illness and planned recuperation and had invited them all to join her, but Anne had preferred Wood's, together with its fond memories, in the South Bay.

Emily had also been a pupil at Roe Head and after returning to Howarth with homesickness, was replaced by Anne herself who won a good-conduct medal.

Roe Head was a haven for the three girls, by comparison with the privations of the Clergy Daughters' School at Cowan Bridge, suffered by their unfortunate older sisters and Margaret Wooler became a firm, lifelong friend of Charlotte.

Deciding to leave Scarborough and its inappropriate gaiety for a quieter time of contemplation Charlotte and Ellen decided to set forth to spend time in the less fashionable Filey, ten miles further south on the Yorkshire coast.

On the day of their departure from Scarborough, Charlotte received a letter from Martha Brown at the parsonage, which she was glad to read, informing her that all was fine in Haworth and that she should take more time and remain at the seaside.

Charlotte replied to her father informing him that all was well under the circumstances and that she and Ellen would take a little more time at the seaside before returning home, moving on to Filey, where she wrote again to her father telling him of her new address and of the arrangements made in Scarborough.

In the letter she informed him that all expenses for the funeral were paid for out of Anne's bequest from her godmother-aunt, Fanny Outhwaite – quite ironically of course, the self and same money intended for quite the opposite purpose of recuperation.

She informed him that included in the expenses was a headstone for Anne's grave, which would have 'suitable embellishment' and was to read:

Here lie the remains of Anne Brontë, daughter of the Rev'd. P. Brontë, incumbent of Howarth Yorkshire. She died, aged 28, May 28th 1849.

Arriving by means of the year-old recently completed train service to Filey they found lodgings, to the south, away from the town centre in the appropriately named Cliff House, home of land agent's widow Mrs Smith. Her late husband had built the property and with its cliff-top full view of the magnificent bay and clear beach stretching from its Filey Brig headland towards Scarborough in the north and Flamborough Head leading south towards Bridlington, it gave Charlotte consolation viewing the wild rocky coast and very solitary sands which suited her desolate mood at the time.

The 'Royal' Crescent as it was to be known originally, one of the most elegant addresses in the north was under construction at this time and was to largely block the sea view from Cliff House, later to be known to this day as *'The Vinery',* less surprisingly also as the *'Brontë Cafe.'*

Memories came flooding back – as a young child Charlotte had been invited to share a holiday with school friend Ellen's family and never forgot her first taste of the sea, later writing of *"...the glories of the sea, the sound of its restless waves, formed a subject for much contemplation that never wearied the eye, the ear or the mind."*

340

Charlotte would have preferred to stay longer than a week in Filey but Ellen found her grieving melancholy stressful and suggested they would be better in company, "I believe we should move on south to Bridlington, Charlotte, where we can stay with the Hudsons at Easton Farm."

Charlotte was persuaded to move, but they spent less than a week in Bridlington, returning to Howarth after a tiring journey a little before eight o'clock on the evening of the 20th of June to find all well and were greeted by the excitement, even the ecstasy of the dogs who thought that their return would bring others, absent for so long, who couldn't be far behind.

But 'far behind' and indeed never to return, weighed heavily on Charlotte and her evenings, so recently spent with all four of them together in the dining-room after supper as night approached – talking – were now spent in silent solitude.

And worse, later in bed when she did finally sleep, fitfully, she dreamed of all three – but only of them in their suffering and tormented final hours and never of them in happier times.

Confiding in her friend and publisher Williams she determined work would be her best companion and the best cure of all for grief and loneliness, writing, *"...labour must be the cure, not sympathy – labour is the only radical cure for rooted sorrow."*

Later she also confided, *"...my work is my best companion – hereafter I look for no great earthly comfort except what congenial occupation can give."*

She threw herself and initially projected her sadness into finishing her two-thirds completed novel *'Shirley,'* which had remained untouched since before Branwell's final tormented days, now almost a whole year before.

Chapter Twenty Six

A new year – a new beginning – day release

January 1849 brought a chill factor to York never previously experienced in living memory. Rivers, lakes, ponds and even window panes froze solid during that first week of the new year.

Christmas had been mild by comparison though cold too and a pattern of life, very much as William had envisaged, had developed; all around the city there were encouraging signs of better times to come.

At the Shambles a working pattern had developed over the festive season, rushed of necessity to begin with, as Christmas was so near to William's baptism of fire, but now steadier, allowing him to utilise his spare time some afternoons to visit farmers in the area. Initially with Michael Cooper, to both help with arranging supplies of poultry, game and smaller live animals for the shop, whilst at the same time he was able to sow the seeds for wool purchase for the West Riding, principally the Halifax mills, when the shearing season came.

He took John's gun with him on such visits and Blazer, cooped up in a bustling city for the first time in his life, revelled in the near-forgotten freedom and knew as soon as William arrived at number 43 and took up the gun that his time had come and he barked and wagged his tail until the children thought it must surely drop off!

Michael Cooper and William became firm friends through these times away from the shop on the less-busy post-Christmas winter days and Michael, a 'townie' at heart, learned much of country ways from William who had occasionally acted as a ghillie for John up on local Midgley Moor shoots. John had also been able to bond with his son on such occasions and William had demonstrated a keen shooting eye from an early stage in his mid-teens.

Sometimes he would invite his father's retired-lawyer shooting friend John Adams along, calling in for him across the street having fixed for him to join him the day before.

Returning with pheasant, grouse or rabbits, usually more than enough for Mary, the surplus went to the shop for the next day's sales.

Mary too was now much more settled and the children were all well occupied in their various duties.

As William had correctly surmised, Mary had got on immediately with the Coopers and in their turn Elizabeth and Michael had warmed to her, and particularly to

Grace and Hannah, who they saw as very caring and responsible, even quite motherly to their own young daughters and knew that they were in safe hands, whilst Elizabeth would also be freed up to resume her shop duties whilst the children slept.

Grace and Hannah spent the mornings at The Shambles sharing time helping Elizabeth both in the shop and especially looking after the children. They were also the main visitors to gaol in the afternoons, along with their mother, though quite often alone, now supplying their father as well as Rev. Tom occasionally with a welcome array of sustenance comprising pies, pasties and cold meats, which they received as part payment for their duties at the Coopers.

Elizabeth Barker, Joseph's wife, who had prepared number 43 for their arrival so beautifully, also called at the Coopers for discounted provisions for her team of 'angels' who kept Rev. Tom supplied.

Even Scoggins didn't eat as well sometimes, giving him cause for yet further envious taunting…"Doesn't pay to be honest…that's what I say!" he belly-ached.

Mary, at home, had more than her work cut out bringing up Sarah, the oldest, now five, Rebecca four, and the handful that was little two-year-old James, but she nevertheless had found time to make pies for the Coopers in a range of whatever fillings were brought over from the shop. Sarah was a great help making the pastry and she and Rebecca loved cutting out the pastry animal shapes to denote the pies' contents; a rabbit, perhaps a chicken, then best of all painting the pies with an egg wash, which even James was allowed to help with and Hannah would always remark that this was the very brush that Uncle Brannie used to finish the paintings, the night before that dreadful day she would never forget, with that awful row, when their grandfather shouted at father and she had hidden in the orchard and covered her ears.

William sometimes brought in apples from the farmers' store rooms, wrapped in old newspaper, and Mary made fruit tarts which she sold to Mrs Brown, their neighbour further down Stonegate, to sell in her bakery shop. The children especially loved cutting out the pastry apples to stick on the top of these tarts with the egg wash again and a sprinkling of sugar. Mrs Brown had become very fond of the children and as well as paying Mary for her pies usually sent them on their way with a jam tart or a bun apiece!

In the evenings, twice a week, Grace and Hannah would go across the street to have lessons with John Adams. Small blackboards and chalks had been purchased by Mary and the girls skipped across Stonegate, eager to learn, and enjoyed every minute of his thoughtfully structured English and maths sessions. Mary Adams would invariably have a homemade toffee reward for the girls after classes, which they always looked forward to and skipped home again afterwards, happy with what they were learning, to practise together some more. At home the lovely rainbow-coloured chalks would also be enjoyed by James whose artistic talents would spread occasionally onto the kitchen flags, causing Mary to rebuke him and necessitate an extra mopping session for her and the girls!

Joseph Barker and his wife Elizabeth from Beverley, who had made their life so much easier by providing the family with a roof over their head, were both also regular visitors; he visiting customers in the city to sell fabrics, and she, now with an extra reason beyond shopping and provisioning Rev. Tom, since she had grown fond of Mary and the children and sympathised with the difficult situation which was not of their making.

William and Joseph Barker knew each other from his buying trips to the Piece Hall of course, and Joseph had spotted, and been impressed by, the young man's enthusiasm, all-round personable qualities and growing technical knowledge of weaving, from the first moment he saw him. He was not surprised to see him come over to York, to help his 'uncle' in his time of need and admired the way he had organised his life since arriving, making every effort to gain employment, find accommodation and support Mary and the children, with a selfless altruism unknown to him previously in one so young.

He would learn of William's true paternity in due course, but for the moment was more than delighted to hear of the young man's further plans to establish the means by which he planned to make enough money to buy his 'uncle' John his daytime-release; a plan which he immediately recognised would work and moreover would like to share in, if his new 'partners' agreed.

By the second week in January, Joseph Barker, together with William, had visited the Castle several times together to discuss and agree a working partnership with John; a partnership which would allow John the dignity to 'earn' his way out rather than have

347

the humiliation of Joseph paying to have him put on day-release; how could he do that anyway without doing the same for Rev. Tom?

In the meantime Joseph would take William under his wing and introduce him around to his clients in the city, after work in the afternoons of his long working days.

William had also observed a very pretty young girl occupying the upper room of the butcher's shop opposite the Coopers – literally an arm's length away, and embarrassed glances at such close personal proximity had already been coyly exchanged. A proximity so close in fact that when open-window warmer evenings arrived they would finally exchange their first whispered conversations across the tiny divide, discover each others' names and were soon to be seen 'walking out' together on Sunday afternoons.

Rachel Fairburn, the twenty-year-old daughter of butcher James Fairburn and his wife Martha was to play a significant part in William's life.

In late spring William and Joseph together would also visit supplier contacts in the wider area to agree purchasing terms for wool and John would supply land-owner contacts from his wide circle of influential game-shooting friends, rather than from their tenant farmers, where greater influence could be gained. John, on day-release, would provide designs and technical expertise for production in chosen mills, under licence, starting with his brother-in-law John Murgatroyd's Oats Royd Mill and initial samples would be made available for both Joseph and William to show to both draper, tailoring and dress-making clients, as well as to their

348

new wealthy property and land-owning contacts and their wives and families.

The forward-thinking Crossley family's mills at Dean Clough in Halifax would be a suitable target as well. Eli's poor attempts at cheaper carpet production had struggled meanwhile, whereas the Crossley mills continued to expand at a prodigious rate, through superior product innovation and placement, leading up to their stunning tapestry successes at the Great Exhibition of 1851. Resistance of course could be expected at first from the Crossleys since the not-so-distant highway robbery would ring an unpleasant bell at the very mention of that so-memorable, sonorous quadric-syllabic Titterington surname!

John was aware that his father had blocked all means of financial support from the family, on threat of disinheritance, but brother-in-law John Murgatroyd was his own man; the Titterington-Murgatroyd family disputes were not that long past and even if Eli did disinherit his own daughter as a result, he would not care since he was far beyond needing his father-in-law's money anyway and John was a long-time favourite brother of his wife.

John was well aware that his father and brothers would not welcome this competition but felt that they had had their chance and failed to appreciate his wider plan to update machinery and production at Higgin Chamber, whilst they stuck doggedly, yet by necessity, to their unfashionable traditional production methods.

As spring approached Michael Cooper, realised that William's strengths lay in butchery, which together with the wholly alien-to-most start time of around 4.00am allowed him to finish at just after midday. This gave him the freedom, with the longer days, to move out more to visit the farmers and to attend markets such as the Halifax Piece Hall. He was young and fit enough, took to his bed around 9.00pm and revelled in the wider tasks leading up to John's day-release in late March.

All the family's considerable efforts, plus Mary's father's regular money 'for the children' had yielded sufficient funds to buy John his daytime freedom albeit with the restriction of never leaving the city walls or visiting a public house, on pain of instant withdrawal of privileges and an immediate return to lock-up. In this regard, the oldest public house in York, Ye Olde Starre Inn, would prove to be a great temptation for John, with its close proximity, almost next door at number 40, Stonegate, following his lengthy enforced abstinence from alcohol, but it wasn't worth the risk and he'd determined to move on anyway and would not embarrass his family and new partners by a return to his more colourful Anchor or Lord Nelson ways, especially after their considerable efforts to return him to the flock, albeit temporarily, reporting back to Scoggins every night…on time, or else!

A sufficient promised flow of funds and goods – pies included, had allowed the hardly-ever-seen marshall of The Castle, persuaded by his joint but minor-beneficiary-henchman Scoggins, to be certain that John was not likely to abscond, that the agreement was sufficiently lucrative, and posed no risk to the strict enforcement of the court's terms of imprisonment.

Offered the chance to take day-release two weeks earlier, John had reluctantly declined to accept the offer without the same privilege being afforded to Rev. Tom, and William, with Joe's and other angels' additional personal support had delighted his wife Elizabeth by acceding to John's request.

Freedom!...only temporarily...but worthy of a joint celebration, nevertheless, and a few days later sitting down to a late-afternoon roast dinner at number 43, were seventeen diners; all of the Titteringtons, including William, Rev. Tom, the Coopers and their young girls, the Barkers, and the Adams from across the street, who provided extra chairs, cutlery and crockery and even brought a gift of a large cake and fresh cream buns for dessert from Mrs Brown, such was the delight for everyone that Mary, William and the children had all been justly rewarded for their stalwart efforts, irrespective of their father and husband's unfortunate misdemeanours!

In difficult times, debtors' prisons generally were all too much in many people's minds and sympathy rather than stigma was more likely gained, especially where a known and cruelly harsh regime such as the one in York Castle prison was involved.

John, of course, that day, was known to all but the Coopers, who immediately appreciated William's strong bond and loyalty to his instantly-likeable father; a relationship which William had stressed to them must never be referred to in front of the children; John had always insisted that Mary would be the only person ever to share this information with them, when she alone determined the time was right.

Rev. Tom was also known by most present, apart from the Adams, the Coopers and the younger children, who had learned to be very respectful to members of the clergy, and Rev. Tom, who had donned his clerical collar for the first time in a long while, seemed somehow to exude that holiest of auras for their beliefs to remain unshaken: yet still they wondered who on earth he was and why he was here! The Barkers were of course his ex-parishioners in Beverley and Elizabeth's additional efforts with her team of 'saviours' placed both her and them forever in Tom's debt.

An unavoidably necessary, early-afternoon, alcohol-free toast – for John and Rev. Tom anyway, was proposed by John, as they all prepared to eat. Raising high his glass of water he enjoined them; "To all gathered round this table today, I raise a glass...but especially I raise it to my young nephew, William, whom I regard as surely and certainly as I would my own son – please all raise your glasses... to William – well done, my boy!" The children warmed to the idea of William being like their brother and for the very first time William felt like he belonged to a real family. Mary liked the idea as well, but the time would not be right, for some time yet, to reveal the true story to inquisitive children and be able to adequately respond to their many questions.

And so a social and business pattern had developed for all of them with William very much taking a leading role in bringing it all together and moving it all forward like a well-oiled wheel.

John, tied to the inner city, set up an office at the top of the house in a back-bedroom, where he designed and developed new products and cloths to be licensed for commission production and sale by William and Joe, to both the leading mills in the West Riding and to their output to their own customers beyond. His engineering and weaving technology skills could not be equalled from his time spent on the shop-floor from an early age, together with innovative ability, an interest in new production techniques, plus design and colour flair and creativity; a formidable combination in one man as the industrial revolution dawned on a fast-growing industry now serving a world market.

The Crossleys at Dean Clough, the Holdsworths at Shaw Lodge Mills, in Halifax, and John Murgatroyd at Oats Royd in the valley had all moved away from the Piece Hall now and conducted their businesses within their own mills, receiving clients from all over the country and beyond to wonder at the sheer size of their new production facilities and burgeoning multi-storey mill complexes.

Eli, Thomas and James by comparison were in a dwindling shalloon market. Eli's attempts to produce carpets over at High Lees lacked appeal in both colour and design and they were one of the last manufacturers to remain at Halifax Piece Hall, to receive an ever-dwindling straggle of traders and buyers through its draughty portals.

William and Joe had early successes at Dean Clough and Oats Royd, so much so that John's family producers at High Lees and Higgin Chamber and Mary's father at Shaw Lodge Mills couldn't help but notice and be impressed. Their occasional visits to the Piece Hall and the Talbot, keeping in touch with the trade and old friends during trips to the larger mills, had drawn traders' attention to the general demeanour and undoubted confidence of successful business men.

That John's skills were behind their successes, at Dean Clough in particular, was never in doubt.

Mary's father determined to continue to make what he felt were now superfluous payments to support his grandchildren over in York, whilst Thomas Titterington, for similar reasons, guarded the one asset John would desire most, after full release...his ace card – Higgin Chamber House, now his own property in all but name, fully-maintained, heated-through and still fully-furnished, complete with, in his opinion, "...that pompous, over-preening, self-indulgent pair of oil-portraits on the oak-panelled dining room wall, painted by that opium-fuelled, drunkard of a parson's son from over in Howarth."

Both would look to a return on their investment in due course.

Chapter Twenty Seven

The homecoming

Another Christmas came and went in 1849 and the pattern of life continued well and the new year brought yet another bitterly cold winter, even colder than that first Christmas in York the year before.

William had now firmly established himself as a partner to John and Joe, travelling out to surrounding farms buying meat in the late autumn and winter months and wool in the shearing season. His so-early hours at the Coopers continued unabated and his overall services there had become indispensable and far beyond Michael's wildest ideas of a mere employee, so essential had he become to the business. Two or three afternoons a week, now freed up, allowed him a wide roving role alongside either Joe or his father, in York or the West Riding, where he proved himself also to be invaluable, blossoming into entrepreneurship of the highest order, in every regard.

William had also found time to court young Rachel Fairburn, the butcher's daughter from across the street in The Shambles and long summer evenings that year had been spent together walking around the leafy parks and along the riverside. He had already introduced her to Mary and the children, taking her for tea to Stonegate, and John was delighted that he had met such a lovely young girl, who allowed William to take his mind off his increasingly onerous and lengthy working hours.

Rachel, as the youngest of six daughters, with her older siblings all married and moved away, was special to her now ageing parents, James and Martha. The patently visible and obvious talents of William, assisting his competitor across the street, coupled with their immediate liking for such an eminently suitable suitor, augured well for the future of the business and gave them both great encouragement to consider their own futures and a possible retirement.

Joe concentrated on buying and selling the Halifax cloths made now under licence to John's growing range of designs at the Crossleys' Dean Clough and Murgatroyd Oats Royd mills and John accompanied him occasionally to his local contacts to gain an up-to-date feeling for trends in the fashion-conscious city's tailoring and costumier market and now increasingly in the needs for tapestries and carpets. If anyone knew of John's situation on day-release, they weren't showing it and York was a big enough city for people not to care anyway and simply get on with their business in a thriving marketplace.

Grace and Hannah's studies progressed well across the street in Stonegate with John Adams and their duties over at the Coopers were now highly valued looking after 3-year old Rachel and the now-toddling Ruth, freeing up Elizabeth Cooper to attend to her shop duties.

Mary's days were filled with caring for the younger three children, and James especially had now grown into a more-than-a-handful three year-old who was generally 'into everything!' She still managed however to keep up a steady supply of meat pies for the Coopers and fruit pies for Mrs Brown and Sarah and Rebecca, now six and five, had developed into reliable helpers and took turns to occupy their brother, taking him out daily for walks with Blazer.

John spent most mornings up in his office and had meetings with William or Joe after lunch and sometimes went with either of them to customers in the afternoon. An early family supper with all of the family, after the older girls came home, allowed him to return to the Castle in time and sometimes William accompanied him after joining them all for supper.

Joe also had a desk up in John's office, mainly for clerical work – general administration, letter-writing, arranging shipments, invoicing and generally running the buying and purchasing ledgers. He also did much of this work over in his own office at home in Beverley.

The partnership protected John from his creditors and his indebtedness, disguising his true worth from those who would still wish him ill; albeit the very same people who were genuinely owed monies by him, but who might still hold out hope for a payout from his father's legacy in due course – would Eli cut out his

357

eldest son, completely, however publicly he had disowned him for expediency at Higgin Chamber mill?

The terms of John's imprisonment meant that he could not be released until his debts were adequately 'dealt with' and his creditors were satisfied that he had been punished sufficiently; there was always a certain amount of vindictiveness involved, since full repayment was never made, with debtors declaring bankruptcy after release and having their 'goods and possessions' assessed for a 'pence-in-the-pound' pay out.

Over in Halifax, Mary's father and John's brother Thomas had observed the growing successes of the enterprise and, quite independently and secretly, planned their next moves. Thomas, without even his brother James' knowledge, so as not to give even the slightest hint to their father, decided to take the bull by the horns and play his ace card; a visit to York was required and Higgin Chamber house was his bargaining tool.

Deciding to visit John in prison, for extra humiliation, Thomas booked into The George hotel in Coney Street the night before and arrived at the gaol at 6.00am the next morning, knowing his brother was on day-release and would probably be leaving early; he couldn't possibly miss the opportunity to gloat!

Scoggins crept up quietly to Rev. Tom and John's cell and burst in, shouting and flailing his arms around like a mad man, waking them both up with a start; "Wakey, wakey, you 'orrible pair of misbegotten thieves and rogues…you, your reverence!…with your pious women running round after you like you were the Lord himself and butter wouldn't melt in your lying, sanctimonious mouth! And you, Tit'rin'ton, flouncing in and out of here every day like you owned the place...and...would you believe it?...there's another one of your rotten, misbegotten breed here to see you from 'alifax, and a right mean mouth 'e 'as on 'im, this one, I declare – soon sort 'im out when we got our 'ands on 'im, just like we did you and your convict cousin...be 'ere soon enough, shouldn't wonder...you're a devious bunch of bastards, you Tit'rin'tons!"

Who could it be?...John pondered – *and from Halifax? Brother James was the most likely, but what news was he bringing? Must be serious to bring him over.*

"Pity it's not to the gallows," continued Scoggins as he led the way along the corridor, "I've brought a few dozen cocky souls like you along these corridors to dangle, kickin' at the end of a rope before now, Tit'rin'ton – they soon change their tune when it's their turn to meet the almighty! Yer reverend friend can't save 'em then!"

In the half light of the interview cell, John couldn't immediately recognise James, who he had expected, but was completely taken aback by the presence of Thomas, his hated brother, as he stepped forward, a shaft of low late summer's early morning light illuminating his profile in relief, his mouth looking even more mean and sinister than usual.

John re-coiled visibly, "What the hell do you want?...come to gloat have you...finally?"

"Don't be like that, John, what could I do anyway? – with father watching every move we all make. You'd have to be a magician to get anything past him and he'd cut us all off without a penny without a moment's hesitation given half a chance!" He lied of course, and John saw straight through him; *what was he up to*, John wondered, *the devious sod!?*

Thomas continued, "But he's changed…not as bitter any more, misses mother. Maybe he's not well, I'm not sure. Wouldn't talk about it even if he was. Anyway, he's not getting any younger and his memory is going badly…already I'm covering the mills and managing his properties too.

"Anyway, it's only partly the reason why I'm here. Production is fine at the mills, but now James is struggling with his health and I'm split trying to juggle all of the balls at the same time."

"I'm sorry to hear about James, but couldn't give a damn about father…what's James' problem?" John asked, ignoring the 'production is fine' which he knew was a lie and must contain the key to his visit.

"He's not well – coughs, colds…missing too much from work – we've seen it all before, John, only too often…coughs blood…looks worse even than consumption to me and he doesn't look like getting better. He never was all that fit and he's struggling badly…I'm struggling – can't be in two places at the one time." he concluded.

Turning it over quickly in his mind John saw the dilemma; output suffering – he knew that anyway from

Joe and William, and poor James…wouldn't hurt a fly, why did such things always come to the least able to manage – to the least deserving?

He also realised that his father must be more unwell than he was being told. Must be a mental as well as a physical failing? Certainly Thomas would never risk incurring father's anger, more particularly his inheritance, coming over to see him; the old fox must have some form of dementia.

And what was on offer for John, to bring him all this way over to York anyway?

"As I said, production is good, but I think we need to move the businesses forward – explore new markets…abroad…offer new cloths."

A little more informative, John thought, but still lying about present production.

"So what can I do, stuck here in York? I'm on day release now but can't leave the city walls…and can't even go for a drink then!"

Thomas considered his next move carefully and thinking of this last curtailment to his brother's social life, feeling the conversation might be moving in the right direction, attempted to introduce a lighter tone.

"Well that can't be too much fun for you…and takings at the Nelson, for one, are well down, I hear from Timothy Wormald!"

John ignored the barbed attempt at humour, but smiled slightly, opening up the possibility for Thomas to move forward into his proposition.

"I'll do what I can, John, to get you out of here; not sure what it might take, but I need your help back at home...your home – I've kept the house in good order, while you've been away, kept it heated – what do you say?"

Not surprised that the house would be offered back to him – his own house anyway, he thought, but unlikely to remain so when father died, John needed assurances about what was being offered.

"So what's in it for me, brother dear?! Am I to be the hired hand, answering to your every beck and call? I don't think so...I already have a new business over here, which you may know about? And I fully intend to remain here after my release...my house in Stonegate is a fine one and Mary and the children are quite settled. Thank you for sacking young William by the way...for no sensible reason, other than he's my son...he could have helped save you from the pickle I know you're now in, with your failing businesses. Oh, yes, I keep in touch with Halifax...you don't fool me with your 'production is good' – it's not and you need to offer me more than that to come back to wipe your arse!"

Thomas countered, "I know all about your house in Stonegate...Joe Barker's house...you don't own anything over here and you'd be out of this god-forsaken hole by now if your so-called 'business' was anything like as good as you say it is...even your father-in-law keeps your children clothed and fed, I know that too and your poor wife, hardly better than a scullery maid...baking pies, for god's sake!... your 'son'...sorry... your business partner, keeps a roof over his head slaughtering squealing porkers at all hours of the night. Don't tell me you're doing well!...you're a joke, John Titterington...or Turperington as they call you now back home, from being in this hell-hole...did you know that?...you're a joke!"

Thomas was now back to his charming self and in full flow.

"So much of a joke, in fact, Thomas, that our brother-in-law, John Murgatroyd and the Crossleys come to me for design and production help – tell me they're struggling and I'll call you a liar!...face facts man and let's talk serious business."

Stunned into silence now by this last comment, Thomas realised that his brother had recovered some ground and knew the true situation in the Halifax mills.

Pushing home the advantage John kept speaking, not offering his brother any opportunity to interrupt.

"With poor James sounding like he's not long for this life, I'm presuming firstly that my miserable father will leave you just about everything, as his only recognised son, so this is what I propose; get me out of here, give me my home back, my family's rightful home, and give me a proper share, an equal partnership, in Higgin Chamber mill – my business...the one I built up from nothing and you are now doing your best to drive into the ground by the sound of it."

Thomas felt under pressure.

A partnership? It would need to be a trading arrangement only – he didn't want to share ownership of the mill...nor of the house itself...so he decided to bluff his way out of it and do what came naturally to him...to lie!

John too had other plans; like keeping his options open to continue providing consultancy and design services to Oats Royd, Dean Clough and now the Shaw Lodge Mills of Mary's Holdsworth family. So far he had only dealt, indirectly through William, with Mary's brothers, thus avoiding dealing directly with her father.

"This is what I'll agree to, John." Thomas was ready to make his offer, "I'll give you an equal 50-50 partnership in the business immediately, and the right to occupy the house."

"<u>The right to occupy it</u>?! – It's not yours yet! Though it probably soon will be, I admit; I can't change that, but I'll need assurances, some guarantee of the terms of occupancy for the future...for Mary and the children...if I'm gone, say...as for the mill, I need a right to regain at least shared property ownership, even the right to total ownership, beyond profit-sharing...when we're successful?"

"We can talk about that later," he bluffed, "let's shake hands and move it forward," Thomas put out his hand and the two shook hands, with John feeling cheated in some way and Thomas knowing full well that he had been; any of the arrangements would be worthless without written agreement and no witnesses were present to vouch for their verbal understanding that morning – delay and prevarication would be the order of the day for Thomas, once he had John back where he needed him.

And John was free to pursue his own personal business interests elsewhere, without them needing to clash; an amazing opportunity for him to broaden his skills in such fairly disparate businesses, and without conflict to each other.

Mary and the children greeted the news somewhat differently. Their time in York had been an anxious one initially, but the many distractions of a bustling city had served them all well, under the difficult circumstances they found themselves in.

The two older girls had matured immensely working at the Coopers, taking lessons across the street at the Adams' and visiting their father in the Castle; even Scoggins had come to enjoy their visits and his originally intimidating manner had even mellowed into him producing sweets for them occasionally! The girls additional duties helping their mother bring up their three younger siblings, whilst being no different than it would have been at home, contributed together to turning them into two very confident and capable young ladies who were now well equipped for whatever hardships lay ahead of them in their lives back in West Yorkshire.

Mary had never worked so hard in her life. Back home she had been used to two servants taking care of both the house and the kitchen duties, freeing her to concentrate exclusively on bringing up the children. Her illiteracy had been a big problem and she regretted the lack of education, so lavishly, and, typically for the times, provided by her father for only her brothers. Grace and Hannah did their best to pass on John Adams' teachings to her in the evenings and already she was starting to master simple reading and arithmetic with them on their slates. How different from the well-educated Brontës she thought, writing books that people talked about. The memory of her pathetic wedding day offering of a simple cross to the Halifax Parish Church register, was still an acute embarrassment to her and one that she was glad to be expunging, however slowly. Her children would never be humiliated in such a way and she intended to continue the education of all of the children back at home by engaging a tutor as John had done for William.

Saying their goodbyes had been heartbreaking for all of them but father was back to stay now and return visits to York were promised to everyone they now felt so close to.

John had regrettably left Rev. Tom behind, albeit still on day release, and this was the saddest farewell of all. Tom was looking old and tired now and there was a tear in both their eyes on that last day when John said his farewell in Stonegate, along with the few close friends they had all made during their eighteen-month stay. Both promised to write often and a regular flow of communication developed between the two; a lifetime's bond that was to survive unto death itself.

William was to remain at the Coopers and pursue their business interests in York and Rachel Fairburn was now, much to her parents' delight, just about inseparable from the personable young butcher's assistant across the street!

The summer of 1850 was exceptionally hot, and the family arrived home at Higgin Chamber in late July, exhausted after the dusty rail and road journey, to re-commence a life they had variously thought lost forever, probably never to return to.

Chapter Twenty Eight

Two funerals, a wedding, and Eli's grand will reading

Business proceeded well for a few years in all of the factories in the area and the early 1850s showed a resurgence from the slack times of the late '40s with their attendant industrial unrest through the now-exhausted forces of Chartism.

Brother James' sad early death in September of 1852 and Eli's decline into senility, and his death just over a year later at the age of seventy, on January 2nd 1854, left Thomas and John to run the three mills at High Lees and Old Riding in Midgley and Higgin Chamber across the valley in Sowerby.

John pursued his own business interests as before in the Halifax mills whilst moving Higgin Chamber's production to a new level. The machinery purchases which so badly went wrong with his bank borrowings and general indebtedness were now in place and fully functioning and once again John's skills were proving fruitful in improved market conditions.

Bank interests and political campaigning marked John out again as a man of influence, though his excesses on the wider 'country gentlemen's' scene, shooting and weekending with the minor aristocracy were now curtailed, of necessity, with his onerous work schedule.

Over in York, William, taking less of a role now in partnership with Joe and his father, prior to concentrating exclusively on a life away from textiles, had married Rachel in 1853 and moved into the large three-storey Fairburn's home and butcher's shop across the street at The Shambles. Rachel's father was now almost totally retired, coming into the shop more and more rarely and enjoying seeing his business run more profitably than ever before, affording his daughter a sound future and himself and his wife a comfortable retirement.

Michael Cooper had needed to employ an experienced butcher, at some cost, across the street, since William had left a void needing virtually two men to fill it! Worse than that he now provided the competition at such close proximity.

The new Mr. and Mrs. William Foster – for William had decided it was time to revert to his correct name, were married in a small church in York, at a quiet ceremony attended by immediate family and friends, which included the whole Titterington family coming over and the younger girls acting as bridesmaids, with five-year-old James making a reasonable attempt to control his over-exuberance acting as page boy. William was the children's cousin and Mary had decided that the children would never be told otherwise.

Irrespective of the new competition, his ex-boss and now firm friend, Michael Cooper, was delighted to be invited to act as William's best man and little Rachel and Ruth, now seven and five years old, were thrilled to act as flower girls.

To William's great delight his mother, now in her mid-thirties, who he hadn't seen for over ten years, and his step-father, who he'd never even met, had also come over from Lancashire at William's written invitation. The children loved meeting William's mother and 'father' and a wedding reception party was held back at the Shambles afterwards with the Adams' from Stonegate and the Barker's coming over from Beverley to join in the celebrations.

Back home a year later the family were summoned to the Hebden Bridge offices of Eli's solicitors, Sutcliffe's, for the reading of Eli's will.

"It's a waste of time us going, Mary," John said after breakfast the same morning, "but hopefully you, and surely the children, will have been provided for by the old buzzard!"

The two of them rode along in their carriage to the reading, passing through Mytholmroyd, commenting as they passed by the bridge over the river to Cragg Vale about Hannah's Christening, 15 years before, "Hard to believe what's happened since that happy day, Mary, and only Charlotte now of the Brontës left behind to comfort their dear old father.

"We'll have to be nice to Thomas and my sisters and grin and bear it, as the will is read, it isn't going to be easy."

"Not difficult for me John, I've done nothing wrong and neither have the children. If we're cut out altogether it's all your doing, though I admit your father never liked me...blamed me probably for not curbing your excesses – giving you too much rope...which you nearly hung yourself with in the end! As if I could have made any difference anyway!" Mary tutted.

"We're here now anyway, and a fine line up of carriages there is – they've all come to pick over the old man's bones...brace yourself!"

Climbing down they passed the reins to a young boy in attendance and walked over to John Murgatroyd, a trustee and executor of Eli's will who had summoned them over.

"Morning, John, no sign of my dear brother yet?" said John, glancing round looking for Thomas, a co-executor, who he now noticed was coming over the bridge, walking along with the very smartly dressed young Eli Foster, his sister's boy and the third trustee-executor of the will. Naming him for her father had proved a shrewd move, and John whispered to Mary as they moved inside the entrance to the solicitors, "Our own little Eli was supposed to fill that role, Mary, wonder what he's going to get? – looks pretty pleased with himself...knows what's in it of course!"

371

"I don't need reminding of that, John – not today...or any day, in that guise, thank you," she went on as they entered the main office, "it's not all about money, you know."

But it was...it is, damn it! thought John, *of course it is*...and settled down in his seat to prepare for the worst.

All of his sisters were now in the room as well, with the three trustees and executors seated facing them. Seated at a large desk in the centre between them was a distinguished looking elderly gentleman who clearly had to be the lawyer.

Introducing himself as Abraham Sutcliffe, senior partner-at-law and *'personal friend of the deceased,'* he gave his condolences to the family and introduced the trustee-executors to everyone.

He described their three appointments to act as trustee-executors, detailing them as: "Thomas Titterington of Upper High Lees, Midgley, manufacturer, the son; John Murgatroyd of Oats Royd in Midgley, aforesaid worsted manufacturer, the son-in-law and Eli Foster of Denholme in the parish of Bradford, aforesaid worsted manufacturer, the grandson." And stating them further as, "...sworn well and truly to execute and perform the same," finishing with, "...and that the whole of the goods chattels and credits of the said deceased within the Province of York do not amount in value to the sum of Twelve Thousand Pounds."

Twelve thousand pounds! There was an audible gasp at such a figure and even Abraham Sutcliffe had to take a sharp intake of breath; never had he acted for such an estate (valued at over £8 million today in comparative average earnings.)

"This is the final Will and Testament of Eli Titterington, who died on the second of January in the year of our Lord 1854. It is dated the third of February of 1853."

Not so senile then, John reflected – within a year of his death, but as expected of the eldest son, his name was immediately read out causing him to stir in his seat and straighten his position.

"To my elder son John – an annuity of £30, plus:

The rents from a farm called Ing Head in Sowerby, including barn, cottages, buildings, closes, lands, grounds and appurtenances.

The rents from eight cottages or dwelling houses at Broad Lane in Sowerby with outbuildings and gardens.

The rents from Lower Benns Farm, Warley – including messuage or tenement, barn, cottages, buildings, closes, lands, grounds and appurtenances. The property all to be left to my grandson James and his heirs – if no heirs then left to my son Thomas.

I also leave £500, after my son John's death, to go to his children."

His senses were enraged!...*THE BASTARD!*...thought John – *'After my son's death, indeed!'* No chance of touching any money there. And £30 a year! Plus rents, rents and more rents; what the hell could he do with them, except be forever chasing them up from idle, recalcitrant poverty-stricken tenants in the Broad Lane cottages? And, no mention of Mary at all; blamed her to the end for poor little Eli's death...as though it was *her* fault; the helpless little mite fighting for its life, so incurably fevered in his brain and slipping away, with nothing any doctor could do for him. Just six months old, the apple of his grandfather's eye and gone forever; somebody had to bear the blame and he'd clearly decided it was all through the mother's neglect – not calling for the doctor soon enough. So untrue, she couldn't have done more, sitting up cradling him for three whole nights without rest, watching his little frame lose its fight for life.

And the sadness of recording little Eli's age of death with the registrar as 'six <u>and a half</u> months'; how they had all suffered those last two weeks, but none more so than the brain-fevered, pain-racked child itself, screaming incessantly, day and night, until it drew its last blessed breath.

Shifting uncomfortably in his chair, John prepared himself for the reading to continue; as the second and only other surviving son, brother Thomas came next, and he daren't even risk a glance in his direction, being absolutely certain that he would explode if he caught sight of the guaranteed expression on his smug, mean-mouthed, self-satisfied face.

"To my son, Thomas Titterington," after a short pause and an adjustment of his pince-nez, Abraham Sutcliffe continued, "I leave Upper High Lees, High Lees Head and New House in Midgley, Upper Benns, Saltpye in Warley, two cottages at Lower High Lees, the tenement and farm at Higgin Chamber, The Mill or Factory at Higgin Chamber, with dwelling houses, other buildings, water wheels, steam engine, boilers, dams, goits, reservoirs, water privileges and appurtenances for ever, subject to paying my son John his £30 annuity and the £500 legacy as previously described."

...and a partridge in a pear tree, thought John, who was now, as he suspected anyway, not to be the owner of the mill itself; Thomas took that all, lock, stock and barrel, every square inch, every cupful of even the damned dam water!...but John had still hoped against hope to keep ownership of his house and a roof over his family's head, but his brother was now to be his landlord there too...his paymaster of the miserly £30 annuity...and trustee of everything, including overseeing even young seven-year-old James' rights to inherit Lower Benns Farm; and even then, should the poor little lad have no heirs, to keep it for himself anyway! What a diabolical liberty! And totally intended as a punishment and humiliation for him, by a vindictive, controlling father. Oh, how he must have enjoyed composing his will, visualising all of his children, gathered together in this very office, acting out their various roles...dancing to his tune, in some macabre Victorian melodrama!

He also noticed that Saltpye in Warley was included, and gave a wink to John Murgatroyd at its mention. He'd kept that quiet, thought John, selling his fine home with his first wife to the old man, obviously to finance the

375

purchase of Oats Royd house, at the time of his marriage to Hannah.

An excited bustling of taffeta and silk at the back of the room, accompanied by some genteel, nervous-sounding coughing, signalled the turn of the assembled female contingent to hear of their own good fortune; presuming, hoping, that they were all to be included.

Unsurprisingly, firstly was a bequest to Alice Titterington, nee Shepherd, Eli's late brother James' widow, who still occupied the old family home at Old Riding, where Eli was born and brought up. Alice had taken turns to nurse Eli, alongside John's sisters in his final days at High Lees and was rewarded with this fine ancient roof over her head; for life. Mentioned as Oldrydynge as early as 1561, Old Riding, stone-clad around its sturdy original 16th century timbers in the 17th century, was the home of Thomas Titterington, the first of the dynasty into the area in 1777, coming over from the Pendleton area of Lancashire, to take advantage of the lush grazing and soft water in the Calder Valley for woollen weaving and finishing, and especially for conducting business in the newly-opened Halifax centre for cloth trading – its majestic Piece Hall.

"I leave Alice Titterington Old Riding in Warley, the farm, barn, cottages, buildings, closes, lands, grounds, woods and appurtenances. To be in trust for my daughter Grace Hartley, now the widow of James Hartley deceased, for life as long as she remains a widow. After her death or second marriage, in trust for her son William Henry Hartley and his heirs forever, unless he dies without issue aged under twenty-one, then to revert to his mother Grace and her heirs."

It was John's sister Eliza that had sent the tragic news of their mother's severe illness to the family in York, that short time after they had moved into Stonegate. And it was to Eliza that the avuncular senior partner turned next.

"To my daughter Eliza, nee Titterington, wife of James Smith, dwelling houses or tenements with the combing shops and outbuildings situate at or near Coat Hill in Warley and also the cottages and premises situate near to the May Pole Inn in the town of Warley with their respective appurtenances. And from monies held in trust by the trustees, of the £300 owing to me on security of the Halifax Waterworks. I also leave £300 in trust for my grandson Lister Smith, son of my daughter Eliza and on to his heirs."

There was a gasp from behind at the two sums of money...for only the first of the daughters – plus the letting cottages and fine houses in Warley village (the £300 alone equating to almost £200,000 today).

More rustling of skirts and shuffling of finely shod feet...the anticipation was almost palpable!

"To Maria, my daughter, nee Titterington, wife of William Foster, the messuage tenement and farm called Long Riggin otherwise Lower Horking or Horkingstone in Howarth, in the parish of Bradford, together with the barn, cottages, buildings, grounds and appurtenances."

No money this time but a fine big property, which she and her husband would probably move into in time, but for the moment would yield more than a decent rent.

John knew best of all what an excellent dwelling house it was with a large lush acreage…since it was he who negotiated and purchased it on behalf of his father in the first place, having first heard it was for sale during a Hell-Fire club evening in the Black Bull in Howarth, with Branwell, Leyland and a few others; Dan Sugden too was there that night he remembered, not long before he died; the self and same night in fact that John proudly took over the presidency of the club, by popular request of the assembled raucous members.

How his father would have hated knowing that was when and how he acquired Long Riggin!

But it certainly wasn't coming *his* way as a reward for his work finding and buying it! …however, brother-in-law William Foster, namesake and an uncle to his own son, as beneficiary, compensated for his loss and it pleased him in spite of it. His young executor son Eli, from over in Denholme however, was very likely to know all about Long Riggin, and his smile confirmed this, through his obvious pleasure at being in line to inherit it.

Not many of the others present would know Long Riggin, but no accompanying monies for Maria gave the sisters the clue that it must be a substantial property indeed, in its own right.

"To Sally Nicholl…" on he went, disregarding the muttered chattering between Maria and William Foster, "…nee Titterington, my daughter and wife of David Nicholl, a pecuniary legacy of £600…" (£400,000)…more sharp intakes of breath from behind, "…to be paid twelve months after my death with no interest. And..." Still more, they wondered at the back. "...my messuage or tenement and farm situate at or called Burnt Moor in Soyland with the barn, cottages, buildings, closes, lands, grounds and appurtenances belonging thereto."

Soyland? Now there's a place to conjure up a memory or two!...dear, transported cousin Robert Titterington...*Turperington himself!*... escaping, handcuffed to his fellow vagabond from the returning overnight stagecoach at the New Inn in Soyland...maybe running across the very fields of this 'Burnt Moor' he'd never even heard of – you couldn't make it up, it was the stuff of legend.

But the property and £600! A fortune!

Now clearly enjoying the drama and especially the audience's reactions, Abraham Sutcliffe continued, fully intending to make the most of reading the largest will ever drawn up by the practice.

"To my daughter Hannah, nee Titterington, wife of John Murgatroyd..." John's eyes met John Murgatroyd's and he gave him a knowing wink. Saltpye had been a revelation, but what was in store now? God knows they were already wealthy enough!

"...a pecuniary legacy of £100 paid twelve months after my death without interest and the rents from Burnt Moor for life with ownership to her heirs thereafter."

A lesser amount for a richer lady, he thought, but this Burnt Moor fascinated him. Sally just inherited it but Hannah would draw the rents – maybe it was a sizeable property? He would check later.

(John Murgatroyd died, in 1880, at Oats Royd, leaving a personal estate valued at *'under £200,000'* – over £107 million in average earnings today!)

Three sisters still to go!

With no let up and the usual tautological legalese preventing the audience, each time, from hearing what it was they really only needed to hear, it was getting a little boring by now; but not for Grace, Ellen and Rebecca who came next in seniority.

"To my daughter Grace, nee Titterington, widow of James Hartley…" poor James, remembered fondly and taken, sadly, at such a young age. "…a farm called Trees in Sowerby and a pecuniary legacy of £150 payable in twelve months without interest."

Another purchase I made for him, thought John.

Appreciative sounds of approval came from everybody; without exception, everyone was very fond of young Grace, who had had a tough life bringing up a young family on her own. Trees gave her a roof over her head…which unusually, she could retain for life, even if she remarried, which everyone agreed would the best thing to happen for her…plus, a tidy sum to invest and draw interest from.

"To my daughter Ellen, nee Titterington, wife of Nathan Buckle, now resident in Church Street, Todmorden and Walsden; Hoyle Bank Head farm in

Sowerby together with barn, cottages, buildings, closes, lands, grounds and appurtenances thereto belonging."

And yet another of his own purchases for his father, who strangely yet prudently as it turned out, relied on John's judgment and recommendation in many property matters, even though in general terms they never did get on together; the exception so far in the will, apart from Saltpye, being the unknown property at 'Burnt Wood'.

Nathan Buckle was a spirit merchant and the couple lived together with their young daughter Mary, aged six, a 24 year-old half-brother of Nathan's called Thomas, and their widowed mother, Mary Buckle, who was 66.

John thought Hoyle Bank Head would be perfect for a move up the valley, into the countryside, and for Nathan and his half-brother to have both a farm and warehousing for Nathan's spirits' business.

Last of all now was young Rebecca Titterington, aged 26, unmarried, still living at home and Eli's main helper and nurse throughout his dying days up at High Lees.

"To my daughter Rebecca Titterington, I leave the farm called Thorp House in Sowerby, with barn, cottages, buildings, closes, lands, grounds and appurtenances. Rents and profits during her lifetime then to pass to her heirs."

Hmmm...thought John, no reverting to anybody else, not even to dear brother Thomas, in the event of Rebecca having no heirs then, like with his own little James, and no husband to produce heirs yet either.

Vindictive even to his own grandson...just to spite me! Couldn't help it, could he?

And a nice property in Sowerby – another farm, with cottages and a decent acreage, negotiated and purchased on behalf of his father...for no return!

What a disastrous day!...worse...far worse, than he could ever have imagined and now the tenant of his brother in his own home.

"Let's get to hell out of here, Mary! I've had more than enough for one day and if Thomas even looks like coming over to talk to us, I swear I'll have to kill him first! I'm stopping off in Mytholmroyd for a drink with Abigail as well; she'll need some consoling too, when she learns she got nothing from her miserable brother!"

Chapter Twenty Nine

Charlotte

Stepping down from the lunchtime Keighley coach, the
distinguished looking old gentleman, with a distinct
pallor, was slightly stooped but agile enough for a man
of obviously advancing years.

There was the usual bustle in the bleak, windswept,
yet always welcoming parish of Haworth and the old
man's clerical collar was now clearly visible as he
entered the Black Bull at the top of the main street and
registered for his two-night stay.

His old university friend would have welcomed him
to stay at the parsonage as usual, but it was not
convenient on this visit, as other priorities took
precedence; there was a wedding due and closer, family
guests, needed to be accommodated.

John and Mary too travelled to Haworth very early,
leaving just after dawn, that rather dim 29th day of June,
1854, with John still recovering from Eli's hurtful and

distinctly under-whelming bequests at the so-embarrassing will-reading earlier in the year.

Nevertheless, he had a mill to run; a birthright to earn from his brother, whilst continuing to provide technical services and sales advice to the other Halifax mills and especially now to his close friend and brother-in-law, John Murgatroyd at Oats Royd mill. His interests in York were still being handled by William and Joseph and their partnership was thriving with good sales over there from all of their local mills.

Their older girls, Grace and Hannah, now aged seventeen and sixteen, accompanied them in the carriage and the mood was jolly going over the old pack-horse road across Warley Moor, high above Hebden Bridge, to meet an old friend.

They were not to be official guests at the wedding but looked forward to seeing the bride in all her finery and to meeting the bridegroom.

Today was dear Uncle Brannie's only surviving sister's wedding day and the girls especially had looked forward to their day out since their father had said they were to visit a few days before, following his customary weekly letter from Tom in Beverley.

"I can't wait to see what she'll be wearing...she's so pretty," said Grace excitedly, as they pulled their way up the impossibly steep cobbled main street to the Black Bull and climbed down; John handed the reins of their now heavily-breathing two-horse team over to a stable-lad who took the carriage around to the stable-yard at the back of the inn.

Entering the Black Bull, a familiar voice came from the shadows across in the saloon bar, "Looks like John Turperington, with his fine family to me...my, how the girls have grown into fine young ladies..." Stepping across from the shadows, he went on, "...and you, Mary, looking as lovely as ever...pity I can't say the same about your husband ma'am – this sorry specimen of manhood!!"

The two shook hands...and hugged – well over a year sharing a small cell together, in one of the harshest prison regimes in England had changed their lives forever and it was only through a shared sense of humour that they had weathered the first few months prior to day release.

The gambling house owner, Tom's main creditor, had relented and released his grip, allowing Tom to be released just over a month after John.

"You sly fox! And as rude as ever, you old reprobate – you're looking in splendid health! Don't think the good Lord needs to make any preparations for you for a long while yet!"

The girls hugged Rev. Tom too and an animated catch-up session followed over a brace of whiskys, with Mary and the girls drinking the landlord's homemade lemonade.

Up at the Parsonage, Charlotte was concerned about her father; inclement weather and an understandable reluctance to give away his only remaining daughter was giving both of them a serious problem.

He never was to perform the marriage service himself of course, and the bridegroom, his own curate Arthur Nicholls, finally had to choose his own friend Sutcliffe Sowden, from Hebden Bridge, due to Patrick's stand-in curate's premature departure.

Patrick had been left without a curate for two weeks, when the somewhat aggrieved soon-to-be-displaced George de Renzy petulantly left his service, taking an extra two weeks holiday he was not entitled to, leaving not only this, but all weddings and services up in the air.

But would Patrick really not be giving Charlotte away?

She knew he disapproved of her husband-to-be for his lack of money but Arthur's health too was of concern to both of them; his liability to rheumatic pains. Patrick was also fearful of the dangers of pregnancy and childbirth to a woman of delicate health in her late thirties and had conducted more than enough funeral services for women in similar circumstances.

As was customary before *The Married Woman's Property Act* a marriage settlement had been drawn up and signed by Charlotte, Arthur and Patrick and duly witnessed at the parsonage four weeks before.

Charlotte was not able to own money and estate, whether earned or inherited, before or after marriage, without this settlement and everything would revert to her husband and would possibly pass on to Arthur's Irish relatives if Charlotte died first, childless.

Charlotte didn't wish for this to happen and so determined that in such a case her monies would pass to her father. Arthur Nicholls was therefore dependant entirely on a meagre parson's stipend and Charlotte's good will during her lifetime.

The amount settled, which was entirely her own, was £1,678 9s. 9d., *'for her sole and separate use.'* Totally at her disposal, and entirely self-generated, this was the sum of her writings and what was left of some railway investments; a substantial sum, equivalent to £137,500 today, by historic standard of living values.

The day itself had been chosen as soon after de Renzy's departure as possible, and Ellen Nussey and Margaret Wooler had arrived to stay at the Parsonage the day before. Arthur Nicholls, at Charlotte's express wish had kept all of the arrangements as secret as possible so that the parishioners would not know of the wedding.

Patrick had informed Rev. Tom in his regular letter to him. Both kept up regular communication after Tom wrote from York Castle, expressing his sympathy for Branwell's death, renewing a sound friendship from their time together at Cambridge and his visits to Thornton and Hartshead in the early days of their ministry.

Patrick had already decided the night before that he would not give his daughter away. Now aged 77, it was just too much to ask of him and a hurried reference to the Book of Common Prayer yielded the answer that *'a friend'* was also eligible to give a bride away.

Dressed simply and plainly in a white muslin dress with delicate green embroidery and matching short veil, a lace mantle and a white bonnet, trimmed with lace and a pale band of small flowers and leaves, Charlotte was led down the aisle by Margaret Wooler, who gave her away, with Ellen Nussey performing her perennial role as bridesmaid.

Grace and Hannah had positioned themselves next to their parents, on the aisle side of a rear pew so as to get the best view of the bride as she entered the church. They were far too interested in the bride's dress to notice that anything was different but John whispered to Mary, "No sign of her father – wonder if he's unwell? And did you ever see so many clergymen all together in one place? – the groom must have a wide circle of friends in the ministry!"

"Doesn't she look beautiful in white and green?" whispered Hannah to Grace, "…Just like a snowdrop!"

Ellen and Margaret witnessed the register signing in the vestry and the little party slipped out of the side door into Church Lane, then up to the parsonage for the wedding breakfast where Ellen spread flower petals on the stone floor.

John and Mary, together with the girls, returned to the Black Bull for some food whilst Tom went off to the wedding breakfast.

Later, meeting up with Tom at the parsonage gates taking a stroll, they were delighted to see the happy couple coming out of the parsonage to be driven away in a carriage and pair to Keighley station to commence their honeymoon, which Tom told them he had learned was to commence in Wales.

"Oh, look Hannah, how beautiful she looks now in her going-away dress," said Grace, completely taken up with the drama and the romance of the day.

Charlotte's dress, one of several purchased in Halifax, was fawn-coloured silk. Grace said, "I love the large sleeves which go narrow at the cuffs…and her full skirt – such a tight waist…and the velvet trim on her neck just complements it all so beautifully!"

The girls talked about the wedding for days and especially of their joy at the couple both waving to them as their coach passed along the cobbles to commence its steep drop down into Keighley. Mother and father waved too and it was clear that Charlotte recognised their parents and then gave them all an extra wave.

Rev. Tom joined them again now and together they strolled back to the Black Bull where Tom stayed one more night before journeying back to Beverley via Keighley on the next day's coach.

Mary and John and the girls set off back to Higgin Chamber after about an hour of John chatting to Tom at the hotel, reminiscing about the happier times they had spent together in York; even in their cell there had been lighter moments, though few, causing much laughter from both of them. Meanwhile Mary and the girls had walked further down the main street to visit a dress shop, before returning and climbing on board their coach, which the stable-lad had now brought round from the coach house at the back.

"Take care, old friend!" said John as he pulled away after one final handshake and looking back he saw a rather tired-looking old friend, standing, waving and looking a little forlorn; he thought, but didn't speak of it, that he would almost certainly never see his old friend again.

By then it was a glorious early summer evening and the four chatted away animatedly after their long but wholly enjoyable day out on the thirteen mile journey back home via Hebden Bridge, not stopping this time, as they had at Aunt Abigail's in Mytholmroyd after the dreadful will-reading.

Sadly, John was to learn, in a letter from Joseph Barker in Beverley, that Rev. Tom had caught a chill, probably on that very day in Haworth, from which he had not recovered. He had died from pneumonia just two weeks after his return – surrounded and cared for to the end, by Elizabeth and a loving group of his loyal angels.

Suffering from a cold, Charlotte and Arthur arrived in Conway, in north Wales to begin their honeymoon in a *'comfortable inn'* as she described it that night in a bridesmaid's 'thank you' update letter to Ellen.

After exploring the coast from Conway to Bangor and the spectacular Snowdonia valleys, they travelled across Anglesey to catch the packet steamer to Dublin on July 4th.

"My cold is much worse this morning, Arthur, I'd like not to travel far and keep near the hotel while we're in Dublin," Charlotte said, and Arthur kept within the city accordingly, showing off his old student haunts;

especially taking pride in showing her round Trinity College from where he graduated; the sheer size of its library, housing the magnificently illuminated 8th century gospel Book of Kells which would be a talking point for a long time to come.

Meeting Arthur's hotel-manager brother and two of his cousins, who were at University in Dublin, Charlotte was happy to share in her husband's obvious delights of feeling very much 'at home' and they all escorted the couple the eighty miles inland to their home town of Banagher in Co. Offaly, or King's County, so named by Act of the Parliament of Ireland in 1556, after Philip the King of Ireland.

At her husband's fine family home where he was brought up by his uncle, Dr Bell, Charlotte learned first-hand that Arthur was a highly regarded member of the community and far from the humble parson that she, and others, had believed him to be in Haworth.

A kindly Mrs Bell nursed Charlotte back to health and after a week the honeymoon continued to Limerick, along the banks of the Shannon and Lough Derg, before cutting across to Kilkee in Co. Clare, on the west coast, where she recorded being stunned by… *'the magnificent ocean – so bold and grand a coast, I never yet saw.'*

A further fortnight from Kilkee took the couple to the extreme southwest corner of Ireland via Tarbert, on the mouth of the Shannon, to Tralee, Killarney, Glengarriff on Bantry Bay, with its Gulf Stream-bathed climate and its palm trees, ending up in Cork.

The only mishap of the honeymoon was when Charlotte fell, uninjured but shocked, from her horse, on a path through the Gap of Dunloe, and the couple finally arrived back in Haworth in the early evening of Tuesday, 1st August, after almost exactly a month away.

Patrick was unwell on their return, unlike Arthur who had gained twelve pounds enjoying his Irish home-coming and Charlotte recorded *"...the improvement in him has been a main source of happiness to me; and to speak the truth – a subject of wonder too."*

Charlotte soon brought her father back to health and he was preaching again before the month was out; Arthur in any case, to his wife's entire delight, had now more than enthusiastically assumed all of her father's duties, giving Charlotte great hope for him and for their lives together as a family unit.

But their happiness was to be short-lived, for within six months of the marriage Charlotte aggravated a cold she had caught at the end of November, by walking in thin shoes on damp ground. She had also been caught in the rain while walking on the moors above Haworth to see the snow-swollen waterfall on Sladen Beck.

She was in fact pregnant and though the nausea did not prevent her fulfilling her normal duties at first, and unable even to reply to a letter from Ellen, she obliged Arthur to send just a plain brief statement of fact on her behalf.

By the end of January, so concerned about the deterioration in his wife's health, he sent to Bradford for a Dr MacTurk *'...wishing to have better advice than Haworth affords'.*

Dr MacTurk came the next day and advised that be *'...of some duration'* but that there was *'...no immediate danger.'*

Two weeks later she still showed no improvement and replying to an avalanche of letters from Ellen, Arthur replied that she was *".......completely prostrated with weakness and sickness and frequent fever – all may turn out well and I hope it will. If you saw her you would perceive that she can maintain no correspondence at present."*

Three days later, on February 17th, she made her will; overturning the careful arrangements of her marriage settlement she left everything to Arthur, with no provision for her father, whose name appears only as a witness with that of Martha Brown next to Charlotte's shaky signature, thus confirming her complete trust in her husband to take care of her father.

On the very same day she made the will their other servant, of over thirty years, Tabby Aykroyd passed away peacefully aged eighty-four.

Arthur buried her in the churchyard, just beyond the parsonage wall and within sight of the room where his own wife lay dying.

Charlotte wrote, shakily, to a good friend, Amelia*"...my nights are indescribable, sickness with scarce a reprieve – I strain until what I vomit is mixed* *with blood. I have quite discontinued medicine. My husband is so tender, so good, helpful and patient."*

Some days were better and she was able to take some beef-tea, a spoonful of wine and water or a mouthful of light pudding at different times but she grew inexorably weaker and closer to death and by the second week of March could no longer hold a pencil.

A week later Charlotte was no longer fully conscious and slipping into a state of delirium murmured her last words to her husband, "I am not going to die, am I? He will not separate us, we have been so happy."

Patrick wrote now to Ellen informing her that *"...my dear daughter is very ill..."* and that she was *"...apparently on the verge of the grave...the doctors have no hope in her case...we have only to look forward to the solemn event..."*

He asked that she write to Miss Wooler and inform her that he requested her to do so, telling her of the present position.

Early on Sunday morning, 31st March 1855, Charlotte died, just three weeks before her thirty-ninth birthday. Mr Ingham, the Howarth surgeon, certified her death as 'Phthisis', a progressive wasting disease but it seems without doubt that it was the pregnancy and its consequent violent nausea which had worn her down.

The baby, of course, died with her – there would be no more descendants of the Brontës of Howarth.

Only hours after her death a saddened and aggrieved, and unwelcome Ellen Nussey, arrived on the doorstep, catching the first train after reading the letter telling her Patrick's shocking news.

Aggrieved, for she felt that she had not been kept informed, and should have been allowed to come sooner.

Patrick did not come down to greet her but sent her a courteous note inviting her to stay until the funeral.

Martha Brown escorted Ellen upstairs up to the bedchamber to see her friend's body laid out in death and it was Martha who invited her to perform the funeral obsequies later.

Ellen recorded, *"Martha brought me a tray full of evergreens and such flowers as she could procure to place on the lifeless form…impossible at first…was the rushing recollection of the flowers I spread in her honour at her wedding breakfast."*

Wednesday, the 4th April saw the small funeral cortège accompany Charlotte's coffin the few hundred yards from her home to her final resting place. The church and the churchyard were crowded with parishioners paying their last respects to the woman who had, so unexpectedly, made Howarth eternally famous.

Sutcliffe Sowden, who had married them just nine months before, performed the service and committed Charlotte's body to the family vault beneath the church aisle.

Having outlived all of his six children, his wife and his sister-in-law, all but one of whom lay in the same vault, the eighty-four year old Patrick returned to the parsonage with the son-in-law he had so disapproved of but who was now to be his prop in his declining years.

Patrick looked wistfully out across the churchyard as autumn drew in. A cool breeze was already turning into the early stages of a much bleaker and colder winter which was to follow that year, and the last of the dried leaves were whipping around the gravestones in a macabre death spiral.

How many times had he prepared his sermon and walked that short journey to deliver it...and back, to prepare yet another...walked down and delivered it...and back; and all around him were the sounds of children's laughter – he could hear Branwell, as ever, leading the girls with all of their writings in the tiny exercise books he had showed them how to make, role-playing his Angrian scenes, marching up and down in military style, whilst the girls laughter filled the whole house.

In his study he walked over to his bookcase and took down and fondly handled one of the books which now gave him such pride in what had been achieved.

Dear Charlotte's writings he perused first, taking down *Jane Eyre* – a first edition by Currer Bell, with poor little Helen Burns, so closely based on his dear daughter Maria and that dreadful school which cost him his two oldest daughters in a self-and-same typhus epidemic she depicted so graphically in her book. Then *Shirley,* a year later, followed by *Villette* four years after that, written by the then-acclaimed Charlotte Brontë. Patrick ran his fore-finger proudly over the gold tooling of his surname on the binding, placed it down and reached for – *Wuthering Heights,* by Ellis Bell – again a first edition print and accompanying it a later version giving correct authorship to Emily.

Then he reached for yet another of his so well-handled copies – *Agnes Grey* by Acton Bell; dearest Anne, he thought, not with the rest of his family in Howarth but out there, all alone, as the bitterest of winters approached, on the hillside looking out over the North Sea from her resting place beneath Scarborough Castle.

And finally Anne's last book *Tenant of Wildfell Hall* published the year after, in the month that dear Emily died; just six months before her own sad death, away from home.

Chapter Thirty

Fire!

Tuesday the 9th of September 1856 started like any other ordinary day up at Higgin Chamber.

Mary and the older girls, Grace and Hannah, now aged 19 and 18, bustled around in the kitchen whilst 13 year-old Sarah set about making the fire in the sitting room, helped by Rebecca, now aged 12, who was rolling paper and breaking up summer-dried twigs for the kindling.

All were capable and well able to undertake chores after their time in York, which was fortunate because no servants were now employed in the household due to their constrained domestic budget.

Ten year-old James was playing with faithful old Blazer who needed to get out for some exercise, teasing him playfully, swinging his lead around his head over by the door.

It was 7.30am and father was already across in the mill since six, opening up for the early shift and supervising the re-stoking of the boilers to generate the steam in the 22hp wagon boiler which drove the huge 12ft. diameter flywheel, connected to the shafting of all the machinery, attached to belts on all three floors above. The steam-driven looms were already sounding their gentle rhythmic beat whilst the unmistakable crack of the shuttles flying across the cloth could be heard from a distance away.

Father would come across for some breakfast at 8.00am and the girls would have porridge made by then and bread cut for all of them, including mother who had only just arrived down after dressing.

Over in the mill John checked his raw material stores and chased the creelers and bobbin girls to ready two of the looms which were standing idle. They were behind with one of Dubois' Belgian orders and needed to ship out another thirty rolls of cloth to him by the weekend.

John would go in to Dean Clough, in Halifax, after breakfast, for a meeting with the Crossleys at lunchtime, but only when he was sure that all of the production at the mill was well in hand and his mill foreman Henry Saltonstall would assume full control when he left for the day.

Henry had proved a godsend after losing several charge-hands and foremen following the Chartist upheavals of the late 40's and was now fully capable, more importantly willing and keen to impress, to take full charge in John's absence.

John's days of disappearing for extra-long weekends with shooting parties over in east Yorkshire, were now well behind him and shorter trips up to the Midgley moors allowed him to concentrate his attention onto his local duties, more especially to the full functioning of Higgin Chamber mill.

Only now was he recovering to regain his interests in politics, acting on behalf of prospective parliamentary candidates and attending meetings again in Halifax, usually at the Old Cock, to discuss campaigns or select candidates. Francis Sharp Powell, still a shooting friend of John's was such a candidate seeking a seat, and John supported him up to and beyond his selection as the member duly elected ultimately to parliament for the first time, to represent Cambridge, seven years later in 1863.

Francis, an ex-Uppingham public school boy and graduate of St. John's College, Cambridge, was called to the bar at Inner Temple three years earlier in 1853, practised on the Northern Circuit and was a JP for Lancashire and the West Riding of Yorkshire, bringing him often to the area and stop-overs with John and Mary at Higgin Chamber.

It was John's intention to get Francis elected as the member for the Northern Division of the West Riding of Yorkshire, which John succeeded in achieving finally, at the 1872 election, at the age of 64; Francis succeeded John's friend, Dean Clough's Francis Crossley, later to be Sir Francis, who became a distinguished parliamentarian and philanthropist of the period.

400

Marrying Anne Gregson in 1858 both she and Francis became lifelong friends and John, first recorded politically as, *"Overseer for the West Division of Morley in 1867,"* followed this with a further official public listing on January 25th 1872, as *"John Titterington of Sowerby...gentleman consenting to act on the general committee for promoting the election of Sir Francis Sharp Powell Esq. as the Conservative Member of Parliament for the Northern Division of West Yorkshire."*

A far cry from his 'public listings' of former years, being disowned and brawling in a public house!

And hugely demonstrative of his personal strengths and ability to rise above hardship, even infamy, to recover the respectability to move in such exalted circles.

Francis and Anne were themselves childless and a subsequent baronetcy was therefore his first and the last in his line, with no son to succeed him to the title.

His commemorative sculpture in Mesnes Park, in the centre of Wigan in Lancashire, is made of bronze and is green in colour. It shows him sitting at his office chair, deep in thought and his protruding right shoe, ever-gleaming, and in fact never allowed to go green, from constant rubbing, has been buffed by locals and tourists alike for good luck to this day!

And all of this after a father's public disowning, imprisonment and the bankruptcy notices which had followed in the *London Gazette*;

Court of Relief to Insolvent Debtors – Sat. 29th September 1849

On their own petition John Titterington, late of York, commission agent in wool – in the gaol of York.

And then following John's return from York to Higgin Chamber in late 1851, the *London Gazette* announced;

The creditors of John Titterington, formerly of Higgen (sic) Chamber Mill, Sowerby, near Halifax, in the county of York, Worsted Spinner and Manufacturer, and late of No. 43, Stonegate, within the city of York, Commission Agent in Wool, an insolvent debtor, are requested to meet at the office of Messrs. Alexanders and Hemmerton, Halifax, in the county of York, on Monday the 22nd day of December 1851, at twelve o'clock at noon precisely, for the purpose of approving the manner and the place of sale, by public auction, of the real estate of the said John Titterington.

Followed two whole years later, with no 'real estate' to realise, by another *London Gazette* notice:

13th December 1853

Insolvent Debtors' Court – Dividends

A dividend of one shilling and three pence three farthings in the pound is now payable to the creditors of John Titterington, late of the City of York, commission agent in wool, No. 71,684C.

402

Five years after his imprisonment and hardly what the creditors were looking for, yet entirely corresponding to Eli's final express wishes, ring-fencing through his executors, even the relatively small bequests left to John in his will.

After checking all was ready in the mill to leave Henry in charge for the day, John crossed the yard, ate breakfast then saddled up and rode over into Halifax, dropping first down through Sowerby Bridge.

He hadn't seen Thomas for several weeks now and decided he was avoiding him; firstly he knew John was running a tight ship and was well capable of running the mill when he wasn't playing at being a gentleman, off shooting and weekending with his fancy friends, and secondly he was indeed avoiding the vexed and still unresolved question of ownership, shared or otherwise, of either the mill or the house.

More importantly, the few times they did meet up together, visiting the Piece Hall to keep in touch with the wider market, after relinquishing use of their trading room there, Thomas was well aware of clients' overall complete satisfaction with the Higgin Chamber production output.

Profitability too was excellent, and Thomas avoided contact with John and let him get on with it; conveniently avoiding the question of any profit sharing...worse still, ownership, shared or otherwise.

John's design and product-development commissions and consultancy earnings from the Halifax mills was more than sufficient for the family's now-modest needs, but he knew Thomas would yield nothing until he really had to, beyond the pittance he was presently paying John to run the mill; and he'd prevaricated successfully over possible contracts, forever 'being drawn up' by Sutcliffe's in Hebden Bridge, and who continued to handle the winding up Eli's large estate monies along with the affairs of Thomas himself and his fellow executors.

Riding up from Sowerby Bridge towards the hilltop at King's Cross and looking down towards the east, into the valley which cradled Halifax in its natural hollow, John kicked on now and contemplated his next moves. He had sent word over to High Lees that he needed a meeting with his brother to discuss further investment in new machinery and asked him to come over to meet him at the mill at 8.00pm that day. It was a ploy – he'd had enough, his patience was exhausted; even though his commission payments were adequate, he would not remain the hired mill-hand living in grace-and-favour accommodation and intended to finally have it all out with Thomas and claim his fair share of both the mill and the house, with the threat of moving himself and his family out – completely if necessary.

After a successful day moving several projects forward in Halifax he set out back to the mill in the late afternoon, arriving home at about 7.30pm.

Greeting Mary, patting faithful old Blazer on the back as he welcomed him through the kitchen door, John ate some cake that Mary had made, had a drink and sat and warmed himself by the fire on a cooler-than-usual early autumn-like evening. He'd eaten a midday meal later in the afternoon before leaving Dean Clough and told Mary he'd have a light supper later, before retiring for the night.

A cool evening breeze blew some waste yarn playfully around the yard cobbles as Thomas rode in and took his horse into the stable and tied it up.

Entering the kitchen he greeted Mary and John courteously, ate the cake proffered by Mary by the fire, and exchanged rather forced pleasantries with them both; all of the children kept their distance, never entering the kitchen; they knew of his ill-will towards their father and in any case had never liked him – the uncle who never even spoke to them. Even Blazer reserved any tail-wagging, sensing he would, as indeed he had already before received a curt brush-off – once even a kick when nobody was looking, rather than his more normally anticipated obligatory pat on the back.

"So, let's go across to the mill Thomas, I need to show you some projections and discuss how we can move the business forward," said John, who getting bored with false pleasantries and platitudes changed tack and headed out of the kitchen, across the cobbles, with Thomas following him.

The day-shift workers had left now, after their twelve-hour day, and the extra production for Dubois was well underway on just four looms, operated by a skeleton staff on the late overnight shift which would run until 6am the following morning.

In John's mill office, so rudely invaded by Thomas and James that awful day, after the Anchor and Shuttle debacle, John lit the oil-lamp in the half-light and they sat down and John got straight into his well-prepared presentation, turned over and practised to the clip-clop of hooves, on the journey that day into and out of Halifax.

"So, am I to be grateful to you forever, for getting me out of York Castle? Do I ever hear anything other than you're 'sorting things out' with Abe Sutcliffe? – The mythical contract that never materialises! I work here, all the hours God sends, – FOR YOU, my younger brother – for a pittance in commissions, in lieu of a proper partnership agreement; and certainly far less than I'm earning from Mary's family over at Shaw Lodge or from Dean Clough. Even then you make me chase it like some starving dog looking for a treat it never deserved…I've had enough and I'll give you no more time to give me what I deserve…a share of the mill and my own roof over my own family's head."

"Deserve? Deserve?" Thomas was clearly riled, and went on angrily, "How do you reckon that one out? You deserve exactly what father gave you, out of the goodness of his heart – which had precious little goodness left in it, at the end, for you dear brother! After your philandering and womanising…your brawling and thievery…deserve is it? You deserve no more than I've already been too generous giving you…you'd still be rotting in York Castle if it wasn't for me!"

The red mist of the Anchor and Shuttle descended.

A rage, even more violent than that of that fateful night in the Anchor, erupted from deep within him at the realisation that he had been taken for a fool – clearly there never was a contract being drawn up, and his brother's plan of getting him out of prison in the first place was a complete subterfuge.

John lashed out, swinging a fist wildly across his desk, missing Thomas by a whisker, as he anticipated the move and drew away. John bounded around the desk immediately, even more angry now, grabbed him by the throat and proceeded to strangle him, pushing him up against the wall, feet dangling, kicking out helplessly like a marionette, whilst violently shaking him by his scrawny neck.

Unable to respond or free himself from John's vice-like grip he struggled in vain, kicking out helplessly, struggling for air and knocked over the oil-lamp on the desk, smashing it into a thousand pieces on the stone-flagged floor.

The confusion caused by the temporary darkness allowed him to shake loose, but the stream of oil, stretching across the floor, ignited immediately, illuminating the scene. John's anger, knowing no bounds now, continued unabated. He knocked Thomas to the ground, dropping him with a blow so severe the sound of his jaw cracking could have been heard throughout the mill. He then knelt down on him, pinning his shoulders to the ground and proceeded to extract his revenge pounding blow after blow onto his face; his now clearly dislocated jaw spilling several splintered teeth out onto the floor in a bloody mess.

Adding to Thomas's pain was a searing pain in his right shoulder; he smelt singeing hair and flesh, and struggled in vain to free himself from the flames which were now enveloping him and were burning his hair.

John too had to release his grip and get up, as the flames threatened to burn his hands and the dense smoke and fumes were causing him to choke.

Coughing and spluttering he released Thomas from his abject helplessness on the ground and rose up, shielding his eyes and his face from the flames, which had now spread right along the dispersed oil spillage, igniting the desk and the papers on it along the way, and were now lapping up the office walls, threatening a possible escape through the only door.

Opening the door to get out he allowed a back-draught of air to fully ignite the office, as the flames now caught hold of the oil-soaked mill floor beyond and spread rapidly across the ground floor enveloping the machinery as it went.

Thomas was helplessly unconscious, lying in a pool of blood and broken teeth and John, glancing back, in an unexpected surge of a fraternal love he would never have believed possible, returned with his jacket covering his head to grab him by the shoulders and pull him along the office floor, out through the mill's now well-alight ground floor, out into the glorious fresh air of the mill yard, where he extinguished his burning jacket by beating the flames out with an old sack he'd grabbed along the way and his own jacket.

Several mill-hands were now bustling around, shouting instructions, passing buckets of water from the yard pump along a human chain, whilst John shouted to the nearest man, "Is everybody out?"

A confirmation was shouted and the skeleton night-shift workers continued, now with John's assistance to do what they could in an increasingly hopeless situation.

The urgent ringing of the mill bell summoning help and warning of danger could be heard for miles around on the still night.

Mary and the children had joined in now, bringing more buckets from the house, filling them up at the pump and passing them along the line, but after about a further half-hour they conceded that there was nothing further to be achieved, but to let the fire take its course. No lives were threatened now and the house was far enough away, with a wind now in the opposite direction, to be secure as well.

The only life that was actually threatened that night had now been helped to his feet by a respectful worker who gave him a cloth to wash himself and helped him over to the melee now encircling the pump. In the panic nobody even noticed as his bedraggled form slunk and shambled over to the stables, mounted his horse with considerable pain and some difficulty, and rode out, unnoticed, quietly hugging his aching shoulder, into the night.

The fire was visible for miles across the valley as the illuminated mill's three storeys with its twelve windows along its side lit up the night sky for several hours.

Total fire damage reported in the *Halifax Guardian* the following weekend was £4,000 (£2.8 million). Built originally as a corn mill in the early 19th century, the site itself dates back to the mid-17th century and the use of the word 'chamber' suggests an even earlier medieval origin, first being recorded in 1534 as Hegynchawmbre.

The mill was never rebuilt and Thomas sold off what remained from the fire, built cottages on the site and, out of gratitude for saving him from the fire, as he learned later, made arrangements with his solicitors for John's continued occupancy of Higgin Chamber house, which was undamaged by the fire.

A pang of conscience perhaps? Doing what was only fair anyway? John would never know, for they never spoke again.

A letter followed a few weeks later from Sutcliffe's solicitors in Hebden Bridge, advising of a codicil in Thomas' will which stated that Mary and John would have a roof over their heads at Higgin Chamber for the duration of either or both of their lives, in the event of Thomas pre-deceasing either one of them.

A notice in the *Halifax Guardian* of 11th October 1856, three weeks after the fire announced:

17th October 1856 – Auction at Higgin Chamber Mill, Thos. Titterington, due to fire:

Steam engine nearly new, 16hp made by Bates & Co. Sowerby Bridge
Wagon boiler 22hp;
Flywheel 12ft. diameter; shafting etc;
26 pairs ¾ Lasting power looms; piping, pickers, cloth, yarn, mill bell, bobbins etc.

Yes, even the mill bell that had tolled the demise of Higgin Chamber Mill, and almost that of the seriously injured Thomas himself, that fateful night! The condition of this 'fire-stock' is not known but suggests the heart of the mill, the boiler room and main drive function, might have been relatively undamaged.

After John's peaceful death in bed in 1876, aged 67, following a total stroke-induced paralysis, Mary relinquished residency in the big house and moved into Higgin Cottage, a newly-built, more manageable-sized property on the roadside to the front, where she brought up her motherless grandson James Henry Mitchell, the only child of daughter Rebecca, who had died, sadly, of consumption, aged just thirty, when the boy was just five years old and came to live with his grandmother.

Sarah, the third born daughter had not been baptised like Hannah at St. John in the Wilderness, but back in the more usual family church of St. Mary's in Luddenden. The day of her baptism was a great national day of celebration marking the day Queen Victoria's first-born son, the Prince of Wales, later to become Edward VII, was also baptised, at St. George's Chapel in Windsor Castle; unbaptised children of all ages were similarly 'received into the church of Christ by baptism' in large numbers, throughout the country, on that same day. Sadly, just three years after the Higgin Chamber fire, Sarah died aged just 16, yet again of that most dreaded of diseases at the time, phthisis; the progressive contagious wasting disease of consumption, later to be called tuberculosis that had taken firstly Uncle Brannie followed by his sisters Emily and Anne, all within a year of each other, and would take her own dear sister Rebecca.

411

After Mary's death, at the fine age of 80, in 1892, at Higgin Cottage, from pneumonia-induced cardiac failure, the portraits of John and herself passed to daughter Hannah Maria (Whiteley), Branwell's godchild. She and husband Eli Whiteley were childless; living at *'Strathmore'* in Savile Park Terrace, Halifax, she died first in 1916, during the first world war, aged 78, leaving £803 (£47,000), followed by husband Eli, who died in the same house in 1924, aged 85, leaving effects valued at £25,837 (£1.3 million).

From John's meagre inheritance Mary had left just £52 with probate granted to her son-in-law Eli Whiteley.

Among Eli Whiteley's effects were Branwell's portraits of his wife's parents and without children to inherit, he passed them on, appropriately, to the only surviving male Titterington descendant; the son of his wife's only brother, James Holdsworth Titterington – to my grandfather Ernest James Titterington; and through him they passed via my own father, his only son, Geoffrey, into my safe-keeping.

James Holdsworth Titterington, that small boy arriving so excitedly to the bustling streets of York with his family, all those years before, had married Mary Armitage, a niece of Sir Joseph Armitage, John's banking and shooting friend, at a grand wedding at Halifax Parish church, attended also by Sir Francis and Lady Anne Sharp Powell.

Sadly James died from tuberculosis, aged only 31, never to see his son, my grandfather, Ernest James, whom he pre-deceased and who was born later that same month, in April of 1879.

Patrick Brontë co-operated with Elizabeth Gaskell on the biography of Charlotte and was also responsible for the posthumous publication of Charlotte's first novel *The Professor* in 1857. Arthur Bell Nicholls, faithful to the last, stayed in the household until Patrick's death at the age of 84, in 1861 where Patrick unfortunately sullied the Brontë family name somewhat, towards the end, by selling portions of Charlotte's letters, signatures especially, to eager souvenir hunters.

Arthur Bell Nicholls returned to Banagher, Co Offaly, in Ireland, after Patrick's death, to Hill House where he married a cousin, Mary Bell, and left the church. After his death in 1906, at the age of 88, his widow, who was short of money, sold many of her husband's souvenirs of his former wife to the Brontë Society, including Branwell's portrait of his three sisters which had been kept, folded in four, on the top of her wardrobe. It is the 'most viewed' painting in the National Portrait Gallery in London and still shows the crease marks – plus the famous deliberately self-obliterated Branwell himself who stood originally between the sisters.

John and Mary Titterington lie together, in a grave recorded in the church registers, but not now locatable, at St. Peter's Church in Sowerby.

Even in death Mary would not commit him to lie in proximity to his father in the family graveyard over at St. Mary's in Luddenden village, joining him at St. Peter's in February, 1892.

Epilogue

In the summer of 2013, Noreen and I visited Higgin Chamber, having seen the overhead view of the site on Google Earth, which showed that the mill dam still existed as well as giving me, for the first time, a clearer idea of the location of the actual footprint of the mill itself in the void between the later-built roadside houses and the dam itself.

On a lovely summer's day, we tried to imagine the day of the fire and could almost hear the urgent ringing of the mill bell drifting on the warm breeze, summoning buckets of water – the sheer panic of everyone, including Mary and the children trying to extinguish it in relays across the yard as Thomas slunk away to lick his wounds – it all seemed so real as the picture in my mind's eye unfolded before me and my imagination raced.

Music drifted in incongruously from a barn across from the dam…a singer with a rich, deep, melodious tone and, out of curiosity, we crossed towards where the captivating sound was emanating.

A recording studio had been set up in a barn and through a slightly open door we caught sight of the singer and the sound mixing deck, with its headphone-wearing technician in close attention adjusting the sliding control buttons.

During a break from recording we met John Bromley, the singer, and his recording technician Ross McOwen in the yard at the back and learnt that John had been a member of *Kimber's Men,* a folk group, since 2001 who were famed for their take on songs of the sea, especially shanties, many of them Scottish.

Again singing traditional songs, some a cappella, some with simple guitar accompaniment, John told us he was putting together a collection of established favourites – 20 in all, including, *"A Begging I Will Go"* and Archie Fisher's *"The Shipyard Apprentice".* The one he had been singing as we peeped in to the studio was *"The Shearing's Not For You"* – he explained that it was an old Norfolk folk song about a young lad and his girl who tells him she is pregnant...*so he tells her he's off to join the army!* Not completed yet, they returned to the studio and we wished them good luck and walked away around the dam towards the side of the original old house.

Oh the shearing's not for you, my bonnie lassie-O...faded almost completely away behind us on the warm breeze again, as we arrived at what was probably the orchard originally, at the back of the house – the same orchard where the children had hidden, so frightened by their grandfather shouting at their father until they felt sure there would be a fight.

Everything had changed for them that day, in a way they could never forget and life was never to be the same again.

An old woman in a pinafore sat beneath an old apple tree, on a low three-legged stool, shelling peas into a large baking bowl on her lap. She obviously lived in one of the cottages on the side of the road.

Noreen was more interested in identifying some unusual wild flowers over by the roadside, so I headed over towards the woman. As I drew closer, I heard that she was also singing, sweetly and very quietly as she shelled away, popping the pods, bouncing the peas into the unnecessarily large bowl and discarding the pods, "...Oh the shearing's not for you, my bonnie lassie-O...O the shearing's not for you, for your back it wouldna' bow, and your belly's o'er full, my bonnie lassie-O."

"Sad words...sad song..." I said to her, "...and you've heard it before?"

"Oh, yes, young man, I know it well...a familiar song – I've heard it <u>all</u> before!" she said, and turning she fixed her eyes firmly on me...*and gave me a wink!*

'Young man!' – ha!...and a cheeky wink to go with it!...but didn't I know this face?

Noreen was coming back over towards me as I turned, walked towards her and told her about the woman's wink that accompanied her song.

"What woman? What are you talking about? Where? What song?" she said incredulously, and I turned round to show her, to see...*absolutely nothing!* No woman, no stool, no baking bowl or peas...*nothing!"*

"Well, unlike before, I'm still driving home this time anyway! And I know what I saw! And heard!" I said; "I can even sing you the words she was singing…how could I have known those?"

In the distance, I heard the faintest yet unmistakable sound of children playing happily, small children…and a dog barking – a large dog.

And I did know that woman…those eyes…the eyes that had looked down at me, newly brightened and shining, alongside her husband all those years ago…pleading to be recognised…and asking to be introduced to a different century.